THE WOLF AT HER HEELS

Book 2 of The Figs' Mysteries

MILA DOUGLAS

I dedicate this book to those who read in public places, like trains and planes. Nosey old me always cranes her neck to check the title of your book. My writerly dream is that one day I'll find you reading mine.
If that happens, expect an almighty, joyful scream!

Mothers believe they know what's best for their sons—but in matters of love, the heart answers to no one.

Chapter One

Maria, Australia, Present Day

An antiseptic smell from the visitors lounge seeps out into the courtyard where I sit with the stranger. The piquant odour competes with the candy-sweet perfume of the potted plant. I run my fingers over the fragrant white petals. The flower is called...Jasmine.

Merda.

My cruel brain remembers the name of a plant but can't grasp the threads of my story... I search again, but the memory crouches beyond my reach.

"*Italia?*" the stranger prompts me again.

Italia? It's been so long. I'd blocked old memories before losing those I wished to keep. My lip trembles, and although I do not wish to cry, unbidden tears spill down my cheeks.

The stranger leans in and squeezes my hand. "*Non importa.*"

He wants me to talk about my past, but I can't recall

entire events. Not on demand. I tap my forehead, commanding memories to reveal themselves in order, but they scramble around like naughty children.

I grip my plastic mug and swirl the milky liquid. Barely warm, it hardly passes for coffee. I need a muscular drink like *ristretto*. A concentrated shot of caffeine might help me remember. Instead, I'm stuck with feeble pre-sugared dishwater and slush for a brain.

"Let's try again," he says in Italian.

"*Merda! Troppe domande.*" Too many questions.

The stranger touches my arm gently. "*Signora* Maria? Your son, Joe? He wants to know about Italy. Remember? He asked me to translate."

"Joey?" I sit up at the name. "*Joey sta bene?*"

"It's okay, Joe is fine. He'll be here soon." This time, when the man speaks Italian, I breathe in the sounds— almost my native Calabrian, yet more refined. The singsong cadence soothes my frazzled mind.

"*Italia?*" he asks.

The cloud inside my head clears and a memory comes into focus.

Calabria, Italy, 1966

The cobbled road from Scilla led to a cliff-side tunnel—our secret meeting place. I leaned against one of the giant arches and watched weathered fishermen pull brightly coloured boats into shore. These outings over the past year had filled me with delicious anticipation, but also an undercurrent of dread. I fanned the back of my neck to cool and settle my nerves.

A car slowed behind me. "Waiting for a lift, good looking?" Emilio's phony gruffness softened into his usual seductive tone. "My *Bella*."

I spun, nose in the air, feigning displeasure—but he greeted me with a smile-filled kiss blown across long fingers, and my insides turned to jelly.

After checking we weren't being watched, I climbed into his car and slumped low in the passenger seat, as usual.

"Where to today?" I whispered.

"Shhh." He touched the back of my neck, pressing my head to my knees. "Mariella Borelli, stay down 'til we're through the village. Your wild hair will get us noticed. Houses have eyes."

Guilt filled the space where my breasts and legs touched. I was Emilio's toy, ready to spring from a box.

We rounded several bends on the windy, mountainous road. "Nearly clear," he said, running his fingers through my long curls. His touch didn't soothe me. I'd raced from church for yet another secret meeting. A temporary arrangement. Or so Emilio said.

My father often told me there was something amiss when people felt a need to hide. Although I shrugged off those words, they left me with traces of shame.

But not enough to stop me hiding in a man's car like a *puttana*.

Australia, Present Day

I'm frightened. I'm often frightened. And as always, it takes a moment to work out where I am. Who is this stranger?

"Signora Maria?" he asks. "Are you okay? Can you go on?"

"*Sì. Mi contrentrerò.*" But instead of concentrating on Italy, I think of Joey—long grown into a man. Most people are 80% water, but my Joey's 80% lonely. He needs a woman *simpatico*. How can I help him with my mind the way it is?

"Do you remember the rest of your story?"

I shrug. I stopped speaking English when my brain started playing cruel tricks. But I still understand most things others say.

"The rest of your story?" he repeats.

I shake my head. Things go astray since being in this place. Shoes and hairbrushes. Faces and names. They fall into the nooks and crannies of forgetfulness. I hold onto fragments—a few in my head, the most precious in my heart.

Joey wants to know what happened. I close my eyes. If it's important for my son, I'll try. An automatic sprinkler bursts into life; the fine spray caught by the breeze, cools my arms and washes cobwebs from an old memory. Calabria. Sun on my skin. Mist from a fountain kissing my face. A coin in my hand, ready to throw.

A smile lifts the corners of my mouth. "*Tre desideri,*" I say. Three wishes.

For a flash, I see a face from my youth, but his features fade. He disappears along with a half-remembered name.

"*Tre desideri,*" I repeat.

Another smile. Then a moment of painful clarity.

None of the wishes came true.

Not one.

Calabria, 1966

Emilio tapped my shoulder. *"Bella*, we've reached the open road."

My eyes welled up and I couldn't face him. Instead, I wound down the window and allowed hair to whip my face and the wind to dry my tears as I stared over the bergamot groves.

Oblivious to my misery, Emilio slid a hand over my knee, steering the car with the other; chatting with the enthusiasm of one on a high adventure. "No one will recognise us in Catanzaro and we'll be able to return before dark."

I brushed away his hand. "Concentrate on driving."

He smiled and saluted. "For once I agree. The road's as curvy as your leg, but your leg demands my attention." He laughed enough for both of us, not noticing I hadn't joined in.

I didn't want to ruin our outing before it began, but surely there was an easier solution than meeting in far-flung towns. I tilted my clenched jaw toward the car roof. "When do you plan on telling your parents about us?"

"Timing," he said flippantly. "I know their moods. We'll talk when the moment is right."

For the rest of the two-hour drive to Catanzaro, he kept both hands on the wheel, and his eyes on the road. I thought about Mamma and Babbo. I hated going against my parents' wishes. Church every Sunday was non-negotiable for the Borelli family, and lunch with uncle Tonito was almost the third commandment. When my mother's younger brother had asked how hungry I was, I'd said I was meeting a friend, which wasn't exactly a lie. Just the same, I'd avoided eye-contact, but even without looking, I could feel my parents eyeing me with suspicion.

I loved Emilio. My family didn't know how gentle and funny he could be, or the way he made me feel special. No one else would ever love me the way Emilio did. But it was time everyone knew about our relationship.

"Come," he said, prodding my arm and trailing his hand down to my knee. "Gift me your beautiful smile."

I kept my lips sealed and my skirt wrapped tightly around my knees.

Emilio drove along the ocean road until I pointed out an amenity block along the beach before the town of Catan-zaro. "Stop here, please. I need to change."

As I unrolled my sundress and took out the sandals hidden in my bag, I thought about the good times we had. Our chasing games through the olive groves, the silly voices he imitated to make me laugh. I glanced over my shoulder at Emilio leaning against the car, his beautiful face frown-ing. He was worried too. While changing my outfit, I replayed Emilio's promise, and remembered the truth shining in his eyes. Mamma had taught me that people look away when they lie. But Emilio had looked straight at me. He meant what he said.

I shed my heavy church clothes along with the guilt, and sauntered back to the car in a lighter outfit, with a lighter heart.

Emilio's whistle of admiration was loud enough to reach Scilla. "*Mamma Mia*. You look sensational." He flashed his movie-star smile, displaying the whitest of teeth.

"I designed and made this dress last week. Is it too short?"

"Not at all." He looked at me with the eyes of a beast

that had been starved for months. He bit down on his lip. "Let's skip lunch and find somewhere secluded where I can tempt you to take it off." His voice was like melted chocolate over ice-cream and the fight to resist grew more difficult each time he asked. I sighed, imagining him lifting his shirt to display his smooth, tanned body.

"I'm basically a stomach with limbs," I said. "If I don't get food soon, I'll turn into a monster."

"Like the one in the straits of Messina? The one who eats all the men? I can think of worse ways to die."

I shook my head and tried not to laugh as he drove through the town centre. He often teased me about my interest in the old legends. When I first met Emilio, a group of men—young and old—were celebrating in Scilla's main piazza. They were outdoing each other in a performance of a traditional Calabrese dance. Clumsy vino-fuelled leaps and kicks abounded. Emilio stood on the sidelines satisfied to stand back and clap in appreciation. He was the most handsome man there, glossy dark hair and delectable skin. But it wasn't just his looks that drew me that night. The town's old shoemaker became unsteady on his feet, and we both raced to help him to a seat. For the rest of the evening, we sat either side of Signor Gallucci, who regaled us with tales and myths from the ancient Greeks who'd lived in the south of Italy before the Romans. I became enthralled by the legends of Gods and Goddesses, and although Emilio listened, there were many moments where I caught him gazing at me over the shoemaker's shoulder.

"You daydreaming?" Emilio asked.

I was. I hadn't realised he'd already parked the car in central Catanzaro. We walked arm in arm down the main street, and I considered sharing the memory of our first meeting. But I was so hungry I barely paused to check out the delicious butterscotch painted houses with masses of date palms. My stomach rumbled, ordering me to stop outside the first café. I stood under the striped canvas awnings and admired the sidewalk tables and potted jasmine bushes. "This place looks welcoming. Perfect."

Emilio read from the chalkboard menu, "*Calamari fritte. Insalata di polipo.*" He was intentionally mispronouncing every word, but I kept a straight face.

I had to practise being serious, or the situation between us would never improve. There was the danger of losing Emilio through my impatience, but I couldn't keep up the pretence of being happy to wait indefinitely.

"*Risotto allo zafferano.*" When he impersonated the voice of Bugs Bunny in *Lollo Rompicolla*, a movie we'd watched together, I relaxed and chuckled out loud. Just being here with me was risky. It wasn't Emilio's fault his family didn't want him choosing a wife from outside the *Ndrangheta;* the Calabrian mafia.

"I love hearing you laugh." He lifted my hand to his lips and covered it with kisses, leading me to a table away from other diners. The touch of his mouth made my entire body tingle. It took several sensible breaths before I composed myself enough to choose from the menu.

A waiter took our order then I spun a fork on the empty table as we waited. I considered ways to reintroduce the subject of his parents without spoiling the lighter mood.

"Emilio," I said seriously. "You know I want us to marry. If you don't feel the same way, we should stop seeing one another."

"No, Mariella. No." He narrowed his eyes. "Have you met someone else?"

"Not yet," I said, without caring whether this would

hurt him. "I want children. My parents want grandchildren. I cannot and will not wait forever."

Emilio didn't answer and we sat in stony silence. Our waiter hovered nearby, as if sensing a problem. Emilio beckoned him to set the meals in front of us. Once the waiter was gone, he replied, "My parents want grandchildren, too. They want all their sons to marry."

"Then what do they have against me?" I asked.

"It isn't you. They don't know you like I do. They have old-fashioned ways and believe marriage is best kept within the *Ndrangheta* clan."

I forced myself to swallow a mouthful of spicy eggplant pasta, but it added to the burn in my chest.

"My job is important. If I lose it by disobeying the family, I will not be able to support you in the way you deserve. We need money to bring up our children the way they deserve."

I stabbed at my food, no longer ravenous.

"Please, Mariella, a little longer. I will convince them."

"Soon?" My question hung in the hair like a hangman's noose.

"Of course," he said. "It's difficult to catch my father alone. He thinks he makes all the rules, but my mother has strong opinions." Emilio covered his eyes with his hand, and I battled with the niggling feeling that soon would not be soon enough.

He waved to the waiter and paid for the food.

The heaviness in my chest grew. "Where to now?" I asked.

Emilio picked up the shiny 100-lira coin from his change. "Heads, the beach. Tails the town." An obvious change of subject, but Emilio exuded sexuality even when I found him frustrating. Instead of tossing the coin, he inspected it. "Caesar on one side and a woman with a tree on the other."

"Can I look?" He handed it over, and I studied the pressed figures on each side. "1966. Brand new. But the laurel-wreathed head isn't of Caesar. It's too feminine."

Emilio's smile returned and he tossed his head in a deep laugh. He didn't care about being right, he just wanted to tease. "Hail, Caesar. *Veni, Vidi, Vici.*"

"This side," I said, turning to tails, "shows the goddess Minerva; one hand on a spear ready to declare war, the other reaching for an olive branch in case a truce is the wiser choice."

He reached for the coin, circling his thumb in my palm. "Which do you choose, love or war?"

I pulled my hand away. "The choice is yours, but I won't wait forever."

His usual cheeky grin was absent. "Perhaps you'd rather a handsome man walk into your tailoring shop and whisk you away?"

"This is silly talk. We're ruining our day." I squeezed Emilio's biceps. "You're plenty man for me and you know it." I expected him to strike a strongman pose, instead he hung his head. "What's going on, Emilio? You've never been jealous."

He pouted, pausing to ensure I noticed. "You have many opportunities to meet men. I'd prefer you had a female-only clientele."

Emilio was playing me. Trying to paint me as the one in the wrong. "If you're afraid of losing me, then hurry and ask your father."

He flipped the coin so hard it bounced off the table and rolled into the gutter. We both stood to look.

"Tails," Emilio called. "The woman. A woman always wins. We'll walk through the town."

We strolled the cobbled streets without holding hands. A woman was winning, but not me. The entire town of Scilla knew that Emilio's mother called the shots.

He kept walking when I peeked through a shop window, then grunted when I dallied by a fountain. "Why are you stopping?"

"Give me the coin." I held out my hand. "I want to make three wishes."

I tossed it high in the air, watching it somersault before splashing. Water droplets scattered, like minuscule fish escaping a pond, and I pressed my praying hands to my chest as I made my wish.

"What did you ask for?" Emilio's eyes were soft and apologetic.

I shook my head, touched a finger to my lips, then pressed my hand to my heart. It beat with desperation. "I can't tell you," I said. "Otherwise, my wishes won't come true."

Chapter Two

Joe, Present Day

The Figs' Aged Care reception room stinks of sodden clothes, furniture polish, and extra strong peppermint. The mix of odours is perfect for testing dear Katerina's memory theory. I breathe in through my nose and try to make connections between these smells and experiences from my past. When Mum's friend and aged care resident Katerina explained the science behind aroma-based memory retrieval, I was optimistic. Now, not so much. I inhale several more times out of desperation, but come up with *nada*.

If it's failing me, a man with an arguably fully functioning brain almost half the age of Mum's—how will it possibly work on her?

My sigh is a little too loud. Bettina, the front desk receptionist, looks up. I ready myself for her habitual one-hand-clapping wave. But today her hand rests still and her gaze intensifies. "Mr Blake?"

Over a hundred visits to Mum in the past year and

Bettina's never stopped me. She's said 'hi' but never said my name. My stomach does a twenty-storey elevator drop; the way it did when Mum was admitted days after she lost her ability to speak English. "Is my mother all right? Something happened?"

"Ah, no. Don't worry. Nothing like that. I'm just curious, that's all. Minutes ago, a handsome Irish fellow signed himself in to visit her." Bettina flicks her neon hair—a red not seen in nature. "Then you turn up in an expensive Italian get-up looking as if you own the place..." She poses with one hand on her swaying hip. "...or have enough money to buy it."

I glance at my tailored trousers and they glare back. *Told you so. Overdressed. Too much.*

Bettina taps lacquered fingernails on the dividing counter while checking the sign-in sheet. "You here alone?"

A strange question from someone who's never seen me with anyone else. I shake my head -no- rather than say 'I'm always alone'. I decide talking about my suit is the lesser of two evils. I pull the lapel of my jacket. "It wasn't expensive." I end my sentence dismissively, like closing a door, but her curiously arched eyebrows open it again.

"Worked in men's retail for years before I took this job. You can't tell me that suit didn't cost big bucks." She looks at my shiny shoes, tilts her head to check out the haircut, then sidles around the counter and heads straight for me. "I'll look at the label."

Backing myself against the wall does no good. Bettina yanks the collar from my neck, and opens the front, she even checks inside the wrist. "No label. My bet is you had it tailor-made in Italy. Somewhere exclusive where they don't need names or prices. Did you go on a holiday with your mother?"

"No." I leave it at that.

I wore the suit to put Mum in a good mood for the start of the memory project, but I have no intention of telling Bettina Mum actually made it for me. A grown man whose mother used to make his clothes has a creepy lives-in-the-basement vibe.

"Sorry," she says. "Don't know where I left my manners." I open my mouth to say it's okay, but Bettina cuts me off. "I prefer people to say what they're thinking, but even to me my questions sounded nosey."

Her broad smile suggests the suit has transformed me into a more interesting prospect than I am in my usual work clothes. I'm the same average-Joe, except in fancier wrapping.

"I've never been to Italy. Mum said she'd never, ever go back."

"So, there's truth in the hospital gossip?"

I shrug and say nothing. Bettina doesn't need my encouragement.

"One of the wardies from your mum's wing reckons you're trying to find out why she left Italy, except she only speaks Italian and you don't. What a mess! How's this project going to work if you don't understand each other? Sign language?" Bettina makes a heart with her fingers.

My eyes blink way too fast. "You met the interpreter this morning."

"An Irish translator? Speaking Italian? Sounds like a joke." The hair flick again, this time with a wink. "Maybe stop in and tell me the punch-line on your way out."

I laugh and fumble to key the escape code into the security door, but it slides open before I finish. Nurse Izzy is standing on the other side. "Step away from Mr Blake,

Bettina. You've seen a man before." She laughs and herds me into the corridor.

Everything is different today. Bettina stopping me for a chat, and Mum's favourite nurse, Izzy, wearing civilian clothes. Admittedly, her clothes are a more natural choice for an off-duty nurse than mine. I stick out like a sore thumb, or a man wearing a suit when t-shirt and shorts would have done.

"Did I ruin your fun?" she asks with a laugh. "I would have left you with your admirer, but you looked like a deer caught in headlights."

"I doubt she's an admirer. Besides, life's too complicated for new relationships, Mum doesn't have anyone else, so I'm here a lot." I'm feeling flustered. Maybe the suit's too hot, or maybe it's talking to women other than Mum.

Izzy marches down the corridor at a brisk clip. "Better hurry. Dermot and your mum have already started."

We stop at a visitor's nook with three chairs and a view to the courtyard. I sigh seeing Mum outside, looking strong as always. She can walk for miles and her hair is more dark than grey, so I still get a shock that what's inside her head isn't compatible with her still healthy body.

"I'll find Katerina, you wait here for..." Izzy stops and narrows her eyes, looking straight at the suit. "I hope you've put the entire day aside, Joe. Maria will need lots of rest in between the chats, so it won't be your usual hour's visit."

"Course. I'm here all day."

"Oh. Thought you must be attending a funeral or some-thing." She scrunches her smooth forehead. "Love the shirt. Bit bright for a memorial service."

Bright is an understatement. Until dementia, Mum sewed all manner of things. She picked this fabric. Loud. More Mum's personality than mine. When she gave it to me, I asked whether it was blue or green. Mum threw me a conspiratorial look and said, 'Peacock.' The significance didn't escape me. Mum creating showier plumage so her drab son could attract potential mates.

From the moment I saw my reflection this morning, I knew I should have changed, but I was already running late. I chucked normal clothes in the backseat hoping to get a smooth run, but I caught every red light. It seems mothers do know everything. Well, she was right about the clothes, I've had two women comment in one day.

Izzy doesn't blend in today, either. Instead of being pulled back into a ponytail, her wavy brown hair is loose. "You look different out of uniform."

She crosses her arms.

"I mean...not like a nurse...you look normal...like a normal person."

The look she shoots me reminds me of a chocolate bar I bought last week. Salted caramel. I didn't read the label before I took a bite, and while ready for the sweetness, the saltiness was a shock. An unexpected combination, but I liked it.

Izzy clicks her fingers near my ear. "Earth calling Joe."

"Sorry, I was day-dreaming." I shake my head, continuing to stare.

"Something affecting your vision?" she asks.

She's right. I am a deer caught in headlights.

"Joe?" She smooths her skirt. "What are you looking at? If it's the creases in my clothes, they'll drop out. Well, I hope they do, cos I'm going out this afternoon." She scrunches her nose. "The only thing I iron is my hair."

I grin through my confusion. Izzy's hair is more wavy than flat. "Maybe you're using the wrong board?"

She throws her hands in the air. "Go on. Explain."

"Instead of an ironing board, you've maybe picked up an irony board. They can be quite contrary."

"Most words you've said in a year, Joe." The half-smile suggests my attempt at humour worked. She even throws in a chuckle which vibrates in my chest and for a moment my confidence matches my shirt.

"You're almost funny," she adds.

"And sometimes it's deliberate." I cover my mouth so she won't see me smiling at my own joke.

"Back in a minute." Izzy disappears at a speed only nurses and Olympic athletes seem capable of. Leaning my head against the window, I watch Mum and Dermot in what seems a heart-to-heart. He pats her hand gently as she speaks. Wonderful choice as a translator, his kindness and patience takes away some of my guilt.

I'm self-sufficient, ordinary, and perfectly content with my life. Usually, anyway. But there are darned unguarded moments when emotions escape and bounce erratically, until I recapture them and shove them back in their box.

As if arriving to rescue me from my thoughts, Katerina, Mum's friend and saviour, rolls towards me, a ninety-four-year-old knight in shining wheelchair with rapier sharp wit.

"Perfect. We're all here." Katerina's eyes twinkle as she holds out her hand for a kiss. "I can't wait to hear Maria's Italian memories."

She turns and winks at Izzy who follows behind. "And I am so looking forward to how you write up her life story."

"Thanks for encouraging me." Izzy claps her hands like a child. "I would never have enrolled in the memoir writing classes without your support. I'm dying to know what Maria got up to."

"I've thought of a title for your collection." Katerina's

chuckle is younger than her years. "We Didn't Always Drink Cocoa & Knit Scarves."

I whistle my appreciation. "That's really catchy."

Izzy purses her lips. "I'll think about the name." She bends towards Katerina. "Come on, spill the secret formulas you've concocted."

"No secrets. I bought a bulk pack of essential oils. Anything's worth a try." Katerina shrugs. "Maria didn't remember Dermot. Not at all." She looks at them sitting at the table on the other side of the glass then gives me a thumbs up. "They're talking okay, now. We might not need the 'secret concoctions' after all."

Chapter Three

Maria. Present day.

The stranger looks at me intently. "Signora Maria," he says.

He looks familiar, but I'm not sure where from. Was I telling him about Italia? I sigh and shake my head. It's so empty it doesn't even rattle.

Katerina sits beside me. I always remember her.

"Everyone's arrived now, Dermot," she says to the stranger. "Looks as if you've made a good start. Would you rather us leave you out here with Maria?"

I study the stranger. Dermot? Yes, that's his name. He squeezes my arm reassuringly. "We were about to have a break weren't we Maria? Remembering is tiring work."

I look around the courtyard. Where am I? I've never been one for potted plants so it can't be home. Plants, like some people, are best left wild and running free.

Katerina gestures for me to stand. "Come, Maria. You push my wheelchair inside. We'll find your Joey while

Dermot sets up our memory room. Did you remember the surprise?"

English words like surprise and shock are too similar. One is good and one is bad but I get mixed up. A smile stretches across Katerina's deeply-lined skin, bunching her cheeks into rosy-pink apples. Surprise must be the good word.

"*È Mercoledì di nuovo?*" I ask. Is it Wednesday? Joey visits on Wednesdays, but it doesn't feel like a week's gone by. Katerina nods as if she understands, but she doesn't.

I'd like to ask in English, I understand most of the words people speak, but I no longer know how to say them. The doctors say it isn't unusual to revert to the mother tongue. Older, tougher memories bully the younger into submission. Doctors and nurses use the same word whenever they're discussing me. Dementia. They say it so often it's as if *Dementia* is my new name.

I stride alongside Katerina as she wheels past the mauve-blue walls. Our rooms are across from each other in the lilac wing. If ever I'm lost, I look for the colours, and if that doesn't work, Katerina always finds me.

"Why are we heading this way?" I ask in Italian.

Katerina smiles at me with a blank expression and keeps moving.

If my question was about something concrete, I could draw a picture in my sketchbook, but there are many things which can only be felt and many which can only be conveyed through words.

"Izzy and Joe have gone to check out the room. They'll be back in a minute," Katerina points to the empty nook. "We'll wait here."

I love the nook table. With all its windows, it has a view

up to the sky. Expanses of clear blue, like today, remind me of Calabria.

A firm hand grabs my shoulder from behind and I touch my *cornicello* pendant for protection as I spin towards the offender, a curse word on my lips. Joey holds his hands in surrender, but his eyes can't lie. He's not frightened at all, he's excited. "Sorry to scare you. You ready for this, Mum?"

"Ready for what? What are we doing?" I ask in Italian.

He creases his forehead, darting questioning glances at Katerina, reminding me for the thousandth time that even my son doesn't understand the only language my broken mind speaks.

"I'm on leave from work, so I'm coming in every day. Helping with your memoirs. Do you remember?" He dances his fingers lightly across the table, awaiting my response.

Joey's memory must be as bad as mine. He often looks expectantly. Wanting me to talk like we used to, even though there've been many times when his eyes fill with sadness as he remembers my English words have long been stolen.

"You've already seen Dermot, haven't you, Mum? You know, the man who speaks Italian. We're all going to help— Dermot, me, Katerina, and Izzy. Izzy's taken leave from her nursing duties, especially for you."

Joey smiles at the woman next to him. She resembles my nurse. A lot like Izzy, except she isn't wearing her blue Figs' uniform. "Izzy?" I ask.

Katerina grabs my sketch pad from the side pocket of her wheelchair, and opens it to a drawing of Izzy's face.

"*Sì.* Izzy." I slide my fingers over the fabric of her yellow blouse; it's a hue I call butter-cup. People complain they can't wear yellow, but that's because they've chosen the wrong shade.

If I had a dressmaker's dummy and my sewing machine, I'd sew Izzy a shirt in saffron. Saffron's the perfect yellow to compliment her brown hair and peaches and cream complexion.

Joey taps the table again. Someone who didn't know him might think him annoyed, but I recognise the excitement. He's like a kid at Christmas.

"Time to start," Katerina says. "Bettina's organised an empty room for us, and Dermot's setting up the equipment."

Izzy scans the visitor's lounge. "Before we head off, is there a comfortable chair we can borrow? The repurposed residents kitchen has awful plastic seating. Maria will need to relax when we do this."

"What's happening?" I ask Joey, but he and Izzy are too busy lifting the manky fur chaise that usually skulks like a pantomime wolf costume against the far wall.

They carry it down the green corridor and I skip-shuffle beside them.

At the old kitchen door, Katerina wheels herself out of the way to make room for the piece they're dragging inside. She points to an empty place in the kitchen. "Put it over there." While they are bumping into the doorway, she raises a cheeky eyebrow. "This will be fun, Maria. We're trying something new."

New? Everything is new, now. I search my mind for something familiar. The dementia doctor told me to anchor myself on one thing I know to be true. "Your name," he suggested. "Maria."

Except Maria hasn't always been my name.

"Hello, again." Dermot smiles.

I like this man's voice. He's neither Australian nor Italian. Where is he from? *"Di dove sei?"* I ask.

"Ireland," he says. *"Come te, ho trovato la mia strada per l'Australia.*" His smooth university Italian contrasts to my coarser Calabrian dialect. He leans on the kitchen bench and translates Italian to English for the benefit of others. As he speaks, all eyes lock onto me.

Nurse Izzy and Katerina nod expectantly, while Joey clasps his hands under his chin in a semblance of prayer. Is this what Joey really wants? The kid at Christmas is expecting to unwrap sparkly new memories, but I withheld my stories for a reason. I'm not sure soft-hearted Joey will ever be ready for lumps of coal. How will a man whose eyes moisten at every sad news story cope when the drama involves his mother?

"Concentrate, Mum," Joey says. "I want to know why you left Italy. All the things you never told me."

Katerina moves closer and speaks in soft, soothing tones. "We're trying something different. I found a study showing essential oils can help retrieve faded memories." She points to the brown glass bottles Dermot is lining up on the bench.

Brown bottles? Poison? I've trusted people before, and been wrong. My heart pounds. "*Veleno?*" I shout.

When Dermot echoes my words in English, Joey looks horrified. He's staring at my hands. I follow his eyes and realise I'm wringing my hands. I close my mouth and hold them still. Joey would never let anyone hurt me.

"It's okay, Maria," Dermot says in Italian. "You're doing fine. Just tell us what you know. We'll try without the bottles, first."

I trust Dermot. His face is kind and honest like Joey's. Men wear their forties and fifties so well. A little of the boy. Much of the protective man. I would enjoy this whole project more if it did not remind me of spells cast by *stregas*.

Katerina strokes my arm as they wait for me to talk. But

23

as minutes crawl past, the atmosphere is no longer optimistic. Joey looks at the floor and Izzy is trying hard not to sigh. I've disappointed them. They were all hoping I'd do better.

I wave my arms emphatically to make Joey grin. As a boy, Joey often joked about my talking-hand-movements. Said they were those of a grand orchestra conductor bringing in the loud trombones.

I never forget my jokes with Joey. My chest hurts suddenly at the thought of forgetting my son. When I do, he'll be alone. How can a man as beautiful as my Joey not have a woman?

Joey tries to close my eyes, but I push him away and jerk upright, catching my fingernail on the matted fake fur. "*Merda!*"

"What's wrong?" Dermot asks. "*Dimmi.* Tell me."

I jab at the offensive fabric and Dermot creases his face in a smile. He strokes the fabric of the chaise, and pretends to retch. "I agree," he says. "This beast is revolting. A flashback to the fashion apocalypse of the seventies."

I don't understand his joke, but the atmosphere lightens, so I smile, too.

Joe helps me up and covers the offending chaise with a towel. "That's better, Mum. Relax."

I lie down again and Izzy passes me a cushion. "Put this under your knees and you'll be more comfortable."

As I lean back, Katerina drips oil from several bottles into a steaming bowl. "See if this works, my friend.

"Mum?" Joe whispers. "You don't have to do this."

I wave my arms again to show him I'm fine. I don't want to stop the essential oil hooey-phooey because it might help with *my* plans for Joey.

"Try inhaling slowly," Katerina says.

"You okay now, Mum?"

Everyone speaking at once. I press my hands over my ears. *"Puoi stare zitto, per favore?"*

"Can we all be quiet, please," Dermot says. "Maria is stressed."

Once the room is silent, I close my eyes.

"Sei pronto, Maria?" Dermot asks.

"Sì." I blink to show I'm ready.

"Oil blend," Katerina calls out. "I'm pressing record with my fingers crossed."

"Okay, Mum. Breathe. Let the essential oils do their work."

If only my memories weren't as muddled as the oil mix. I examine Joey's worried face. If he's worried now, how will he cope with what happened? Perhaps children are never old enough to hear the truth about their parents.

Eventually I give in to the sweet-smelling calm. *"Lo farò per Joey,"*

Dermot nods, first at me, then at Joey. "She will do it, but just for you, Joe."

When I close my eyes and inhale deeply, my toes tingle as if memories are drawn from my extremities without permission. Some powerful *strega* witchcraft at work.

The room spins, but rather than fight, I spin too.

"Lo farò per Joey," I whisper as I leave for the past.

Chapter Four

Mariella, Italy, 1966

The shop door bells jangled a welcoming tone.

"*Buongiorno*," the old shoemaker, Signor Gallucci called.

I looked up from my sewing machine with a smile, and my boss Signora Giovanni beckoned for him to join us at the worktable.

Gallucci stared beyond us as he spoke. Something was on his mind. "My sister's been bedridden for almost six months." He paused and bit the skin around his thumbnail. "It's her birthday next week, and I plan to make her a special pair of slippers. I wondered if you have a piece of heavy-weight fabric, perhaps the end of a roll. Something pretty, but not too expensive."

I'd often stopped by after work and listened to the old man's stories. He'd never mentioned how sick his sister was. I looked at him questioningly, but he gazed at the floor. It seems men preferred keeping troubles to themselves.

"Take a seat, I'll be just a moment," the lovely

Signora Giovanni said softly. She rustled through her storage cupboard, eventually producing a piece of pink brocade. "I bought this at a fabric fair years ago. Much too fussy and flowery for today's more structured tastes."

As my boss spread the fabric across the cutting table, the Signor's eyes brightened. "I came in without a precise idea of what my sister would love, but this is perfect." The smile fell and he shuffled from side to side, his voice wavering. "I only need a quarter of this. How much do I owe you?"

"Nothing. You're doing me a favour by taking some off my hands. It's taking up valuable space." She cut a generous length of cloth and raised her eyebrows encouragingly in my direction.

It took a few seconds to realise what she was hinting at. I draped the fabric over my shoulders. "What about I sew your sister a bed-cape with the left-over piece? I can make it at home on the weekend, then she can receive birthday visitors like a queen."

His face coloured with embarrassment. "Thank you, but I can't accept charity."

"Wait," I said, thinking quickly. "Wait here." I ducked to the back door stoop and retrieved my old shoes. "Could you patch these? They're almost worn through. But only if you feel it a fair exchange."

Signor Gallucci's shoulders straightened. "Put them on. I'll check the fit."

Within minutes a deal was struck, and Gallucci marched proudly to the door; my shoes under one arm, the brocade under the other. He appeared younger and taller than the man who shuffled in. "Call in to see me after work. Your shoes will be ready," he said. "I'll squeeze some of the fresh orange juice you love. And maybe I'll have another legend to share."

Once he'd gone, Signora Giovanni hugged me. "That was thoughtful, Mariella. I wasn't sure what to say. You did a wonderful job. You are the best apprentice I could ever wish for."

"Thank you." I blushed and went back to my work.

"Finish the alterations on today's priority list and start on the cape. No need to do it in your own time, it will be valuable experience for your apprenticeship to work with heavier material."

As I cut the pattern pieces from the cloth, my shoulders bore the weight of Gallucci's situation. Like my father, Gallucci was getting old, and didn't have money to spare. He was responsible for his sister—but who would look after him when he could no longer work? Once I married Emilio, Babbo would have no need to barter, and my parents would be taken care of. When I made enough money in my own fashion shop, I'd be able to help the shoemaker, too.

In no time at all, I whipped up a lined bed-cape and a pair of matching bows to add to the slippers.

At five O'clock, the Signora flipped the wooden window sign from *Aperto* to *Chiuso*. I packed up my parcel and waved goodbye,

I had half an hour until the cobbler shop closed. Enough time to detour past Emilio's grandparents' house. He was taking care of their house by the sea while they holidayed in Roma. My bare feet flew over the smooth, well-worn cobble stones, some still hot from the afternoon sun, and some cooler cobbles shaded by the high terracotta roofs. I criss-crossed to the hot ground and cooked my feet until they were tender, then skipped back to the shade where they almost sizzled like a hot pan dipped into water.

Before I entered Emilio's grandparents' lane-way, I checked no one could see me, then I checked again before knocking on the tall gate protecting the vine-covered court-yard. I untwisted my hair tie, shook my head, and set my curls free.

Emilio looked up in surprise and set down the watering can to give a long, low, whistle. I gazed at the man I loved. I'd never learned to whistle, but if I could have whistled at Emilio, in his open white shirt, it would have been a breath-less, throaty affair. As I appraised him from head to toe, he did the same, smiling at my messy hair and laughing at my bare feet.

"I'm light-headed all of a sudden," he said. "My heart has diverted the blood flow from my brain."

With my hands on my hips, I swayed side-to-side. He clasped my wrist, pulling me towards him for a firm, insis-tent kiss.

"I've good news," he said, when he released me. "I've convinced father to take me with him on the buying trip to Florence."

I pouted. "Getting away from me is good news?"

"I'll have father alone for the entire drive. It will be the perfect time to tell him about us. I will ask permission to marry you. I promise. I'll be back next Tuesday."

I ran my fingers over his chest and wrapped my arms around his neck for another kiss. He pressed me against the grape-vine trellis, lifting my skirt with one hand and caressing my neck with the other.

I forced myself to move away. "Stop. Not yet, Emilio. First, the commitment."

He grazed his lips against mine. "Meet me in your fami-ly's olive groves Tuesday after work."

My whole body smiled as I headed to the cobbler shop. There'd been so much waiting but at last he had a plan and an opportunity to talk to his father alone. Soon our relationship would be out in the open and I'd be holding Emilio's hand along the main street for everyone to see.

Signor Gallucci's shutters were down, so I peered through the square glass peep-hole and rapped on the door. He appeared from the back and unlocked the door, then gestured towards the worn wooden bench inside the workshop.

"I have a surprise," I said, thrusting the black-and-white striped carry bag towards him.

"Not another." Gallucci shook his head, so I wrapped his gnarled hands around the handle, studying his face as he unwrapped the tissue paper. As he unfolded the cape and draped it across the counter, his eyes glistened.

"It is beautiful. Golden embroidery fit for the shining spirit Theia." He touched the tips of his fingers to his lips then opened his hand in a chef's kiss. "Sit. Sit. Sit," he said urgently. He lifted a pair of shoes from the shelf. It took a moment before I realised they were mine. Along with replacing the soles, he'd re-coloured and polished the leather to a burnished shine.

"Thank you. They're perfect." I slipped them on.

He smiled for a moment, then hesitated. "Many afternoons when I finish work, I stand at Castello Ruffo, reminding myself to marvel at the beauty around us. I've seen you walk out of town all prim and proper, then run like the wind when you think no-one can see. You, Mariella, are a fleet footed goddess, but I have concerns. Who are you looking for, when you look behind?"

"No one real." I smiled at my feet and paced around the room. "These shoes feel different."

"Good. Because God only gives us one pair of feet. I've given God a hand by adding cushioning to the sole."

I danced around Signor Gallucci's cramped shop. "These are a miracle."

He gave me the same concerned look Uncle Tonito sometimes wore. "Are you sure there's no one following you?"

"No. It's just a game. There's an imaginary wolf who nips at my heels. I make sure I always stay a little bit ahead."

We sat for a short while, me admiring my shoes and the Signor marvelling at the cape.

When we left the shop together, he walked towards the cliff, and I wandered up the lane in the opposite direction. Once on the unpopulated road, I looked up at the ancient castle perched on the cliff and waited for the tiny figure of the shoemaker to appear.

After waving thanks with both hands, I ran towards home.

I zoomed and zig-zagged until I was exhausted, then bent to clutch my knees, waiting for the stitch in my side to ease. But my feet were in heaven; the remodelled shoes like angels' wings. When I ran my hands over the supple leather a promise passed through my fingers. *With these on your feet you can run from the wolf or leap into a lover's arms.*

Next Tuesday. I would be ready to leap.

Chapter Five

Joe, Present Day

It's been at least thirty years since Mum whacked my hand for cracking my knuckles. Once, she used the slotted pasta spoon out of the boiling pot and claimed it was shock therapy. "It's for your own good, Joey," she'd said. "You'll thank me one day. It'll cause arthritis and it's annoying to women."

Until today, Mum's punishment proved effective. But the sight of her head covered by a towel, being asked to remember what happened in Italy when she can't remember the only language she's spoken for over fifty years, is difficult to watch. Beyond difficult.

I crack my knuckles one by one, listening to the disturbing rise in Mum's voice. With each finger tug I question my motivation for pushing her to reveal her past. Am I being selfish? I hope not. There's only Mum and I left. With her mind slowly dying, recording her stories seems a way to keep her alive.

Following a particularly worrying outburst, Dermot

makes an on-the-spot translation. "Her memories are disconnected, especially when there are associations to the Ndrangheta."

The mafia? A new question forms in my mind: was Mum a victim or a gangster's moll? I try crushing my knuckles again, but they've run out of snap.

"Time to change the essential oil," Katerina says. "The next one is a scent particular to southern Italy."

She hands Dermot another of the brown glass bottles and the room fills with an unusual aroma.

Almost immediately, Mum smiles.

We all lean in like parents and grandparents waiting for baby's first steps, but Mum doesn't take one. Her breathing falls out of sync and she cries as she reaches out her arms.

I jump up to help but Katerina beats me to it. "I'm here, Maria," she says gently. "I'm here."

Izzy touches my shoulder and asks me softly, "Are you okay?"

"I shouldn't be putting Mum through this. She's already frightened by memory loss."

"She's fine," Izzy says. "Watch her feet, they're like a litmus test. When she's really anxious, her toes jiggle as if she's getting ready to run. They're relaxed, now. Maybe she's right into her virtual visit back in time." Izzy tilts her head and smiles at me, then takes Mum's hand. "This will be so good. I wish I could travel back in time with you."

Izzy and Katerina soothe Mum better than I can. Dermot is needed for translation. I rub my throat. I'm what Granny Blake used to call the fifth wheel. Surplus to requirements. I squeeze my arm through the gap and touch Mum's elbow. "You don't have to do this."

Mum looks at me, her eyes brimming with concern.

"She'll be fine, she'll be grand," Dermot says. We look at

each other man-to-man. I believe him. Perhaps because I need to.

"Dermot..." Mum pulls him close to whisper. After she's finished, he asks her a question in Italian and she looks at me intently before giving him a go-ahead-nod.

Dermot takes a deep breath. "This smell evokes powerful memories. Maria's afraid. Not afraid of what happened to her, but that you, Joe, are waiting for tales of light-hearted skipping through bergamot groves and splashing in the sparkling Tyrrhenian Sea. And although she says her life has all that, it's also taken her along darker paths." Dermot makes steady eye-contact. "You're expecting sing-along-musical, but will you be okay if her performance is more Greek tragedy?"

I nod and Dermot conveys my agreement to Mum then signals for Katerina to press record.

Mum starts talking and during each break Dermot translates.

"She's on her family farm," Dermot says. "Oranges. Mamma's marmalade...perfume from a young man. She can see a picture of the perfume bottle in her head, but can't remember the name."

Without being asked, Katerina passes Mum a pencil and her trusty drawing pad.

We crowd around, watching her sketch a square squat bottle with rounded edges and old-fashioned lettering. *Acqua Di Santa Maria Novella. Firenze.*

"Firenze," Dermot says. "I'm surprised, I thought your accent was southern. Did you live in Florence?"

She shakes her head.

Dermot sighs. "Ah. It was a gift from him?"

"Hmmm. *Sì.*"

Katerina fans more of the scented air in Mum's direction. "It's working."

"Mum picked the scent then?" I check the label, dabbing some on the back of my hand, inhaling the smell. "Bergamot?"

"*Dimmi tutto bergamot*. Tell me everything bergamot." Dermot doesn't disguise his zeal.

Mum's voice is suddenly song-like and happy. Like a bird ready to fly back in time.

"*Bergamotta di Calabria*," Dermot repeats excitedly. "So many things are running through her head. She feels the sunshine and remembers his kiss."

Katerina, Izzy, and I huddle near the window. "She seems happy now," I say.

"I can't wait to write this story," Izzy says. She prods Katerina's arm and laughs. "It's definitely not in the category of cocoa or knitting, eh?"

A sharp knock on the door interrupts and before anyone opens their mouth to say, 'come in', Bettina bursts through, pausing to study my polo shirt and jeans, ending her inspection with a shrug. She's either disappointed in my casual outfit or the body underneath. I feel uncomfortable either way. It's much better travelling through life incognito.

Bettina does the one-hand-clapping wave, lulling me into believing our polite nod- hello routine's back on track. Then she speaks. "Fewer clothes now than when you arrived yesterday."

I touch my torso as if checking. "Yes. I was hot."

She winks as if agreeing, then peeks through fanned-out fingers. "Should I shield my eyes for tomorrow's attire? Who knows what you'll peel off next?"

I wince with fear at her painted talons, keeping my eyes on the door. "There'll be nothing to see here. Do you need something?"

"Oy!" Mum mutters harshly under her breath. I shudder with visions of the slotted pasta spoon.

"Not right now, Mr Blake." Bettina says, ignoring Mum and holding a note towards Izzy. "Your beau, the handsome doctor, left this at reception."

Izzy pockets the note, but I don't miss her blush or Bettina's smirk. I bet Bettina's read it.

Mum starts complaining. Seriously this time. The couple of Italian words I recognise are unsuitable for translation.

"She wants you to stop whispering," Dermot says. "Her memories are difficult to anchor, even without the interruption. Especially you, Joe."

After Bettina leaves, Mum and Dermot have what sounds a serious discussion. Izzy looks at me hopefully, as if I might magically understand what Mum's saying. I shrug and mouth 'no idea'.

Izzy exhales in response—I feel deflated.

There's a see-sawing of English to Italian, then Dermot translates. "She hates me echoing back to you guys. Says you can't stop commenting. And she feels self-conscious. If her brain worked better, she'd control her stories and present a highlight reel. But the memories will tumble out without thought for anyone's feelings."

Katerina, Izzy and I look at each other, lips pressed tightly, scared to talk. Then Mum passes another message to Dermot.

He clears his throat and suppresses what could be laughter. "How old are you, Izzy?"

Dermot's a braver man than me.

I knuckle-crack again. Women seem to hate the age question as much as knuckle cracking. If I had to guess I'd pick between thirty and forty.

"Thirty-six," she says. "Why?"

"Maria just called you and Joe children. She wants you to go and play outside."

I kiss Mum goodbye, then wonder if I can't do something useful with my time. "Mum? Should I research the Ndrangheta for your memoirs? I could look up some local history."

Dermot begins to translate, but Mum clearly understands, she swears more than the time I stole pearl-headed pins from her sewing room. I only needed three for a beetle collection. She didn't hit me, but the look she gave me, made it feel like I barely escaped alive.

"No investigation," Dermot says. "She'll stop the stories if you do. She's only doing it for her grandchildren and great-grandchildren."

Mum grabs every opportunity to mention grandchildren. It's an obvious prod. No. It's more. It's a full-on stab.

"I'll stay for a minute," Katerina says. "Go on, you two."

I race to catch Izzy who's disappearing down the corridor. "I'm sorry for getting us thrown out. It was my fault for talking."

She laughs. "I'm used to it. Teachers made me sit outside class all the time. Come on, I'll buy us some pink fizzy drinks from the vending machine. We might as well, Kiddo." Izzy searches through her purse, then turns her giant handbag upside down trying to find loose change. "You don't happen to know any shifty moves, do you?"

I stare blankly. "Sorry?"

"You know? Where you make your selection from the machine, give it three elbows and a sideways kick? The machine here only takes cash to cater for the oldies who think debit cards will steal their identity."

"No fancy moves but I do have old-fashioned money." I

hand her the coins and watch her make a selection without asking my preference.

"Is your mum right about you wanting to fix the world?" Izzy hands me a soft drink. It isn't pink.

"Doesn't everyone want to fix things?" I pull the drink tab and cola sprays onto the floor. I am a kid. "Where can I get a mop?"

"Here." Izzy produces tissues from her bottomless bag, throws them on the floor and wipes the mess with a deft foot move.

It's almost a dance. I tap my fingertips lightly against the vending machine glass, matching the musicality of her heels on the hospital floor. Usually, Izzy wears comfortable nurse's shoes, but today she's wearing beaded sandals. She has polished toenails.

"So, tell me about the grandchildren your mother mentioned. How many children do you have, Joe?"

"Technically speaking, none," I say wistfully, preferring not to think about the child who would have once called me Dad.

"Technically speaking? What a funny way to answer."

"Sorry. None."

"I'll let you buy me a chocolate, too and you can tell me all about it," Izzy's smile is contagious. I can't help but join in.

She leads me to the sunny nook. I wouldn't normally tell anyone about my life, because what's not personal is boring and what is personal is private, but it feels hypocritical expecting Mum to spill her secrets while I keep quiet.

I take a sharp breath. "I was married once. Mum made tiny dresses for the baby girl we were expecting. I thought things going wrong in childbirth was something from the Middle

Ages. You'd know these things happen still, being a nurse, but it was a shock to me." Grief strangles my throat and thickens my voice. "It was a long time ago. Nearly twenty years."

"Oh," Izzy says. "Chocolate won't fix that, and we're in deep shit if you tell me any other sad stories because my tissues are all in the bin."

"Mum mentioning grandkids was a not-so-subtle hint about me remarrying. She never gives up."

Izzy gives me a sad smile. "You could meet someone."

"I don't know. Even my housemate hates me, even though I feed him and look after him."

"Don't stand for that. Kick him out."

"I can't. It's Mum's dog, Biscotti. I call him Scotty for short and I'm pretty sure he calls me the bastard who kidnapped his owner and won't bring her home."

Izzy's eyes soften for a moment, then she narrows them. "Call the poor boy his proper name. No wonder he doesn't like you."

"Me and Scot—Biscotti. We have to put up with each other. I'm too set in my ways for someone else and besides, who'd have me?"

She giggles. "Your chances are greater if you've got a yacht or a penthouse."

I'm thankful she's making light of the situation. I'd hate Izzy to become maudlin and start looking at me as poor-old-Joe.

"No impressive bait here, wealth or otherwise."

She pinches me lightly on the arm. "The good news is, even though you're older than me, men have more wiggle room. An old bugger on the TV last night was bragging about fathering a child at eighty! Whereas for women, thirty-six is almost game over."

I have no idea what to say. Izzy must be picky. I can't picture too many men turning her down.

We sit quietly while she reads the note Bettina gave her. She turns her back to tap something on her phone and the atmosphere changes.

"Are you okay?" I immediately regret asking. It's none of my business.

"The man I'm meeting has changed the time. Which is okay, except he's told me rather than asked me. One strike for him. Do you mind if I get something from my car?"

I take out my phone while she's gone. Until my dog learns how to text I'm unlikely to receive any messages. I play solitaire instead.

When Izzy returns, she's wearing a smug expression. The doctor must have apologised.

"Do you think we can sneak back in and sit quietly without your mum noticing?"

"We can give it a try."

We're heading back down the corridor when Katerina wheels towards us, making an exaggerated stop sign. "Go back. Wrong way," she says. "That's me thrown out now. Maria says I'm too distracting, but honestly, I didn't say a thing."

"Sorry, Katerina," Izzy says. "Maria's grumpy when she's tired."

"That's putting it too kindly," I say. "Mum can't ban you, Miss Katerina." I move past her. "I'll go talk to her."

"Stop, Joe. I'm not worried. In fact, it gives me permission to escape. I've decided to read your mother's story all at once, like a novel. My daughter invited me for a holiday in the Blue Mountains. She found a wheelchair accessible Airbnb, and although it looked fabulous, I said it would have to wait. I thought Maria needed my calming influence, but it seems Dermot's charm and the essential oils are doing their trick, so I'm free to go."

"Are you sure? You're not just saying this to make me feel better."

Katerina holds eye contact for a long moment. "Don't think of my help as a favour. Feeling useful at my age gives me great pleasure." She spins towards the lilac wing, then turns back, taking a Manila folder from the wheelchairs' side pocket. "I almost forgot. These are for you, Izzy; notes from Dermot—he's written up the translations so far. Have fun."

Katerina disappears and Izzy clutches the folder to the chest. "Katerina is a darling. Don't you just love her?"

"Of course, and I'm always impressed. Online bookings for an Airbnb." I shake my head in wonder. "You expect an old lady to call it a guest-house."

"Next minute she'll be saying Y.O.L.O.," Izzy chuckles.

Even though I have no idea what she's talking about, I cough-laugh politely. Realising laughter might be the wrong response, I ask, "What's yolo?"

"Oh, Joe. You only live once."

"I know. That's why I'm asking, now."

"An acronym. Y.O.L.O. You Only Live Once."

"Y.O.L.O," I say, trying not to look at her eyelashes. When I knew her as a nurse, I never noticed them being so long and fluttery.

"I'm off, too," she says. "I'll see you tomorrow."

No point going back in to see Mum and be thrown out again. Instead, I sit amidst the residents and people watch. There's nice old George who's obsessed with puppies like Mum. He's doing his usual thing, offering to help. The world needs more Georges.

One resident, a tall man who looks healthy enough,

walks non-stop in straight lines, even when he bumps straight into walls. I don't know the man's real name, but in my head, I call him Rick O'Shea. I chuckle at my own joke. A dad joke, for a man who will never be a dad.

I'm ashamed to admit I've never taken much notice of the other residents. Sad that. They're all unique, like Mum and Katerina, but I lump them together as *the others*.

Next time I walk through The Figs with Izzy, I'll ask their names and say hello.

I hover at the doorway of the old kitchen, waiting for Mum and Dermot to take a break. Eventually she looks up, but waves me away.

I gesture for Dermot to come over. "Thanks for today. Tell Mum I love her and I'll be back tomorrow.

"She's doing well. I'll keep recording while she's eager."

To avoid another conversation with Bettina, I creep around the back of The Figs. Hopefully, by tomorrow, I'll be invisible again.

I'm almost at my car when I spot Izzy leaning against hers playing with her phone.

"I thought you were out on a date?"

"Waiting for the Royal Auto Club to arrive. They're busy. An hour's wait."

"Won't start?"

"Flat tyre." she says.

"Want me to change it?"

"Do you know how?"

"Sure." The look Izzy gives me makes me stand taller.

I watch her open the boot and unload boxes of clothes and food, loose shoes, jackets and books. The pile in the empty parking spot looks larger than the space it left behind.

"Going on a holiday?" I ask.

"It's my back up stuff," she says. "I'm prepared for floods, pestilence and famine."

My smile isn't well received. She obviously misinterprets it as being judgemental.

"Don't give me that look, Joe. You've probably got a Swiss army knife and a car full of lifesaving tools."

Unfortunately, I don't have anything worth showing. With no decent comeback, I concentrate on the job. When I drop the spare tyre on the ground, I'm relieved it springs back. "Good to go."

"Why'd you bounce it?"

"To make sure it has enough air."

As I'm loosening nuts with the wheel brace, she crouches beside me. "Anything else I can get?"

"It's okay. I'm good." Sliding the jack under the wheel arch, I realise she's late for her date. "Isn't someone picking you up? If you want, I'll finish up by myself and drop your car keys into reception."

"No, I was meeting one of the doctors. We were driving separately. I'll meet him when you're done."

Izzy's phone rings and she walks around the car park, balancing one foot in front of the other on the garden edging as she talks.

I swap the wheel and tighten the nuts. "May as well cancel the R.A.C." I repack her stuff in the boot. "I'm done. But don't drive too far on this spare tyre."

"I'm going home now, anyway. He doesn't feel like waiting even though I've had a flat tyre. Typical. Men can be bloody selfish. That's strike two."

"One more chance then?"

"Not with Izzy's rules. Two strikes means out."

Chapter Six

Mariella, Italy, 1966

A heavy-lace curtain screened our workroom from the street, but I could make out the stocky form of Nino DeLuca arguing with Signora Giovanni on the cobble-stone path outside. Nino's hands mirrored his words—and his hands were swearing. No doubt a made-up complaint about the fit of his suit. Something only I could fix.

I glared with the hope he'd sense my daggers and go away. My boss was strong and she would do her best to get rid of him, but Nino was persistent. There was only so much she could do when the DeLuca family dominated everything and everyone in Scilla.

My boss and Nino paced the pavement, screened by the window display of bride and groom. The male wore a suit copied from last year's spring wedding fair in Milano— narrow waisted with double pockets. I had draped the female form in an original design of my own; delicately embroidered, beaded-silk, a boat neck, and half sleeves. A

Mariella design. Signora Giovanni often stopped customers and bragged about my creations. "Check out the workmanship and style," she would say. "Mariella is a talented seamstress."

My mother warned me pride was a sin, but the drive and dreams of being a sought-after designer didn't allow for false modesty.

When the bells jingled, I angled my chair to peer between the mannequins and see how successful the Signora had been. She didn't enter alone, but she hadn't given up arguing.

"Mariella is busy," her voice as curt as she dared. "If the matter is urgent, I can help."

"I want the girl. She has a distinctive style."

Not wanting to put Nino DeLuca offside, I pasted on a professional smile, but held back all warmth. It wasn't wise to give him further encouragement.

From the time I was small, Babbo cautioned about getting on the wrong side of anyone connected to the Ndrangheta, the Calabrian Mafia. Nino DeLuca was the Don. When I met Emilio, I hadn't realised Nino was his uncle. Even if I had, I'm not sure the universe gave me much choice. It wasn't as if I stepped carefully into love. We tumbled and fell together.

"How can I help?" I asked.

"The pants for this suit roll at the waist." He lifted his jacket, sucking in the abdomen that moments ago had weighed heavily against the waistband. He coughed a loud, broken cough, causing his belly to quiver. "And I do not go along with your boss's suggestion to wear suspenders. My trousers should stay up like those in the magazine. Summer days are too hot to button a jacket."

The magazine he referred to showed American-Italian

singer Frank Sinatra wearing the latest style jacket while posing with Italian nobility. Nino had asked for an exact copy. "I must look like this," he'd said.

Nino and the singer were of similar age, but polar-opposites in charisma and body type.

Avoiding unnecessary eye-contact or unnecessary touching of bare skin, I inspected the offending waistband. Licentiousness oozed from Nino's pores.

I tugged the neckline of my dress, ensuring it sat firmly in place. "If you drop the suit in, I'll adjust it."

He closed his jacket, carelessly sweeping my meticulously placed pattern pieces off the worktable to take a seat. I clenched and unclenched my hands, hiding them behind my back.

"If I must," he snarled. "In the meantime, I have a proposition."

At the word proposition, Signora Giovanni stopped hovering behind and pretending to poke him with the pin she'd been holding in her teeth, to interrupt. "Mariella. The time! Your parents are expecting you."

"One moment," Nino said. "I want to show your girl a photograph of my cousin, Angelo. His wife died years ago, and he's ready to take a new one."

"How did she die?" Signora Giovanni asked.

"Sugar-cane fever, I think. Not important." Nino coughed, then smacked his lips together twice. My stomach responded with a double lurch.

"He has acres of land and a large house in Australia, but no one to fill it. You're older than his first wife, but..." Nino inspected me from head to toe. "Angelo was planning to live alone, but when I pressed him on the telephone for his bride wish list, he requested the near impossible: a proxy bride with the looks of his favourite actress Gina Lollobrigida." Nino licked his teeth. "You immediately came to mind."

"Mariella Borelli does not need anyone's help to find a husband. Besides, I need her here. She's indentured to my tailoring business, and I will not let her go until her years are completed."

A purple vein pulsed on Nino's forehead. "Think about it. Both of you. My associates are also your clientele." He headed towards the entry and muttered under his breath, "I'll drop the suit in next week."

He slammed the door so forcefully behind him the welcome bells fell from their hook. My mouth went dry.

I checked he was out of earshot, then I plonked myself into the chair. "What an awful, awful man. Thank you, Signora."

"Watch out for Nino. His family is well known for all the wrong reasons."

It was almost an hour's walk from the shop to home, and although I didn't want to be late for my meeting with Emilio, I dared not leave until I was certain Nino had driven off. My eyes wavered between the clock and the street outside. There were frightening rumours about the local mafia, and the Don was best avoided.

To be safe, I waited half-an-hour, but planned to make up time. Grown women who ran the streets were frowned upon, but I was barely out of town before I picked up speed. My fab new shoes carried me towards love like a storm-blown leaf.

Whenever I ran, I played a childhood game, pretending an Apennine wolf was chasing me. Imagining its sharp teeth snapping made me leap. Even at twenty-one, it gave me an adrenaline rush.

Outside our small farm, I caught my breath. Then as

usual, I climbed the broken wrought-iron gates in front of our tiny stone cottage, putting my toe into the scrolled letter 'B' for Borelli. My heart beat fast from the thrill of the run and at the thought of Emilio back from Florence. He would be hiding in the olive groves.

Creeping around the house, I took a wide berth from the kitchen where I knew Mamma was cooking and Babbo watching her from the table. They didn't approve of Emilio, but I couldn't rest until I knew how the conversation with his father had gone.

Emilio's last gift from Firenze was the perfume; *Acqua Di Santa Maria Novella*. I took the small bottle from my bag and dabbed intoxicating drops on my neck and wrists. I'd followed the constraints of society's expectations for long enough. Provided he'd spoken to his family and let them know we were to be married, I was ready to share more than a kiss.

My fuchsia pink dress billowed as I darted through the trees, knowing the silver-grey leaves were ineffective as camouflage. The fabric was as bright as the wild bougainvillea flowers Babbo claimed matched my personality. "Beautiful, with hidden thorns," he'd said. "Just like your mamma."

Emilio spotted me straight away, but it didn't stop the game. I dashed and hid and he did the same. Even though he kept track of me and I of him, we continued the game of hide and seek until we were out of breath. The most important part of our game was the chase.

With or without a smile, Emilio was movie star hand-some. On his more solemn days, he won over the nurturing side of my heart. When he smiled broadly, my heart leapt with desire.

"Where is my present?" I called.

"Oh no, *Cara* Mariella," Emilio gasped in mock horror. "I knew I'd forgotten something."

I unsuccessfully stifled a grin.

"My beautiful woman, forgive me." He imitated the accent of an American actor while making a peace sign with his fingers. Emilio closed his fists, then pretended to empty the contents into his pockets. He held out open palms. "Which hand?"

"You really have nothing?" I'd waited for days and secretly hoped he would present his gift on his knees. I wanted an engagement ring. A proposal.

Emilio lifted his shirt to reveal squished, brown paper parcels concealed inside the waist of his loose cotton trousers. "See I tricked you. I bought gifts. But you can't have them yet."

I pushed my lips to form a pout, and even though my expression was intentionally over-done, I hoped my mouth looked more sensuous than sulky.

He lowered his shirt over his tanned, lean stomach and his captivating smile reappeared. "Catch me and I'll share everything I have."

Emilio wove in and behind the trees, stooping to pick fallen olives and tossing them near my feet. He continued to hide and reappear, laughing hard as I hopped from foot to foot. I raised my skirt above my knees and turned it into a dance.

"On one less lovely, your moves would be comical," Emilio said.

I swatted his arm and followed him up the narrow track.

We side-stepped tomato and chilli bushes bordering the Borelli land, and fell against each other to catch our breath. I inhaled the scent of bergamot oranges ripening in the wild orchard where fertile land ended and stone-strewn hills began.

Emilio kissed me quickly, then hauled me up the hillside. He hoisted me onto a cleft overlooking the valley while he stood near the niche in the rocks below. I thrust my hip sideways, a signal for Emilio to catch me as I jumped into his waiting arms.

He pressed his lips to mine, and I flung my arms about his neck. But before we got carried away in the kiss, I needed to hear the news. I leaned my head backwards and flicked my long, dark curls. "Anything to tell me?"

"Open your hands," he said. "I have gifts. But you can't have both today."

"Which will I enjoy the most?"

"It's a game of chance."

I ran my hand down his shirt, tickling the exposed skin between gaping buttons, and selected the smaller parcel. The one most likely to hold jewellery. He lifted my face to claim the awaited kiss, and I smiled as I leaned into him, waiting for him to say the words I'd long waited to hear. A wave of awareness rolled up the hillside like a dark cloud. I pulled away and wiped my mouth.

"What's wrong?" he asked.

"Your car. I didn't see it on the road." If his parents knew, there'd be no need to hide it.

"Mariella. Kiss me. We can't stay long past dusk."

I wriggled free, finding footholds in the sandstone and climbing above the lover's niche onto the rocky ledge.

"Mariella," Emilio implored. "Climb down. Let me hold you. I've thought of nothing but kissing you."

I looked to the west, across father's olive fields and to the road. Emilio's car wasn't there. It took a moment to find it deliberately hidden from view behind the house.

"You didn't talk to your father in Firenze?" It was both statement and question.

Emilio swallowed hard and produced the other parcel. "Mariella, take both."

I threw both parcels at his feet. "Keep your gifts. I take your avoidance as no. You did not have the discussion as promised."

"I tried talking to Papa."

I sat on the rock, head on my knees. "Unless one of those gifts at your feet is an engagement ring, there'll be no kissing today."

Emilio climbed and sat beside me, dropping the presents on my lap. I ignored them.

He unwrapped the cylindrical package. "A fashion magazine. See? *La Donna*. One day, Mariella, you'll sew your designs, in your own shop and your creations will be featured on these pages."

I sighed. Emilio knew some of my wishes, but I avoided looking as he turned the pages.

"The woman on the cover is pretty," he said, closing the magazine. "But not half as beautiful as you."

"Is this supposed to impress me?" I asked.

"She reminds me of Gina Lollobrigida, as do you."

His words made me shudder. "Last week this might have been a compliment, but today you've broken your promise. And your uncle Nino came into the shop today saying the same thing."

Emilio laughed, but I detected uncertainty at Nino's name. "If you want people to stop complimenting you, you'll need to grow a moustache." He tilted his head, peering at my face. "Not even a moustache would make you ugly."

"Your uncle wants me to marry his Australian cousin.

What do you think of that?"

"You're all mine." Emilio's lids were heavy as he skimmed a hand over my ankle and spidered his fingers around my calf. "Neither the cover girl, nor Miss Lollobrigida has your perfect legs."

He offered me the other package, but I flicked his hand away. I refused to trade forgiveness for a trinket.

"It's almost dusk. Your parents will be waiting," I said, my voice flat and cold.

"Wait a few minutes longer. This is your favourite time of day."

In the evening, the Calabrian coastline softened and glowed, a veil of purple dropped from the sky. Today's lack of news ruined The Costa Viola's beauty.

"Open this gift, too." He tore at the wrapping. "You'll see why I picked it."

He draped the shimmering length of silk over my shoulders, the colours mirroring the Violet Coast. Graduated shades of the melting sun merged with cool aquamarine to create a heavenly mauve.

"You'll make another eye-stopping garment." He winked. "But to be honest, I'd find you more beautiful wearing nothing."

He lowered himself to the lover's niche. "Climb down, Bella. Join me."

"Not today, Emilio." My throat tightened. "Your trip to Florence was the ideal opportunity. You promised to explain to your father."

"In my family, bloodlines rule everything. Even marriage. I must handle this carefully. On this occasion, my father was entangled in tricky business propositions. My plea would have ended in a certain dismissal. You are too important for me to gamble."

I held the gifts close. Was this tangible proof that Emilio believed in me and my dreams? I wasn't there on the trip; I didn't know his father—but I'd been patient for so long. "If your father doesn't accept our relationship, you can walk away."

Emilio slumped, resting his head unhappily near my feet. "I'm afraid of losing my standing in the family. But I'm more afraid of losing you."

I dangled my bare toes onto Emilio's shoulder, and he covered them with kisses, then slithered up to kiss my lips.

I stared towards the ocean. "Have you ever been to Sicilia?"

Emilio gazed at my mouth. "No, I haven't." His voice was thick with desire and another emotion I couldn't place. Perhaps fear.

"When I was small, I asked Babbo and Mamma if we could swim across the Strait of Messina. Babbo said it was too dangerous. Signor Gallucci explained what our ancestors believed. Men were warned of monstrous goddesses: Cariddi, who guzzles the sea like wine and swirls it around her mouth, spitting out both ships and sailors. Scylla, who waits in her underwater lair to swallow the drowning men."

"Legends. Again?" Emilio turned away from the water. "You should stay away from that old man. He talks rubbish."

I ignored Emilio. "Gallucci believes if we never take risks, we'll never experience the life we are meant to live."

Emilio nodded. "New experiences? For you, I will brave the consequences."

I pointed my foot towards Sicily, jutting proudly from the sea. "If Italy is a boot, what is Sicilia?"

Emilio stroked my leg, and despite my mood, his touch left a frisson of pleasure. "I do not care about Sicilia; I am more interested in lands found in the north." He tickled the base of my foot. "Catanzaro, Lido." He traced a path around to my calf drawing a circle. "Napoli is somewhere around here, now on to Roma."

I laughed off the tickling, but things didn't feel the same. He paused at the back of my knee, poking the skin. "Here we have Firenze, Rimini." He crossed to the front of my thigh, tapping five fingers. "The Cinque Terra: Monterosso, Vernazza, Corniglia—"

"Stop." I pushed his hand away. "You care too much about geography and family rules."

"I want to breach the boundaries," he said.

I shook my head with forced conviction. "Until you are brave enough to face your family, you'll never cross into the North. Those pleasures will forever remain unknown."

Chapter Seven

Mariella, Italy, 1966

After closing up shop, I wandered aimlessly between the charming stuccoed, terracotta-roofed buildings of Scilla. I couldn't imagine living anywhere else.

Like a knife to the chest, I realised that if Emilio didn't marry me, living near him in such a small-town would be torture.

Once past the houses, I half-walked, half-ran and forced my mind onto the other dream for my future. The thrill of starting an exclusive clothing boutique. I'd bring all my creations to life; I'd also have the luxury of locking the shop door to unsavoury clients. Nino DeLuca and the like could be damned.

I dashed along the strip of land which hugged the bougainvillea-covered cliff and overlooked the bejewelled sea. When I ran out of breath, I stopped and assessed my situation. Working for the Signora had many perks—it had gifted me the second meeting with Emilio.

A few weeks after we connected over the shoemaker's rescue, he came into the shop to be measured for a suit. He'd insisted on several fittings, and soon we began meeting in private.

A couple of weeks later, Emilio wrote a thank you on the back of picture. Him wearing the suit at his brother's wedding. My workmanship was good, but he was the perfect model. He attached a small gift: perfume from Firenze with a secret note inside the wrapping. He asked me to meet him at the tunnel. But begged me not to tell a soul.

Soon, the secrecy would be behind us. Emilio would drive his Alfa Romeo down Scilla's main street, me by his side, not caring who saw. The wind would whip my hair against my face and he'd brush it away with the open display of affection I'd craved. When we walked hand in hand the world would be blinded by the diamond on my left finger.

Buoyed by my daydreams, I raced home, leapt over the gate and burst into our tiny stone cottage.

Mamma and Babbo exchanged a troubled look. They were seldom this serious.

"What is it?" I asked.

"Later," Mamma said. She dropped cloves of garlic into my hand. "Whatever needs to be discussed can wait."

I knew not to argue, so I fastened an apron around my waist ready to help. "What's for dinner.?"

"*Pesce spada alla ghiotta.*"

My mouth watered at the thought of the sword-fish and I rubbed my tummy in exaggerated circles. Babbo occasionally traded eggs and jars of Mamma's bergamot orange marmalade with the local fishermen.

I kissed my father's cheeks. "Babbo. Thank you for the fish. What are we celebrating?"

"Only our luck in having a beautiful daughter."

I forced a laugh.

While peeling the garlic and chopping the sweet onion, I chatted about my day. How Signora Giovanni and I had completed last minute fittings on a bride and three brides-maids. I exaggerated as I imitated the way they'd paraded around the workspace in their gowns and elbow-length gloves, jostling for position in front of the single mirror. But Mamma didn't smile.

When I related the part where Signora Giovanna told the wedding party they were extremely lucky to have me design their clothes, neither Mamma nor Babbo looked impressed. "Do you understand? Signora Giovanna told our clients that I'll be more famous than Yves Saint Laurent...and..."

Mamma's icy frown cut my story short. I stared into the cast-iron-pot and watched olives, cherry tomatoes and sweet red onion bubbling away. She held up the sword-fish ready to throw in the hot pan. "Mariella, go out to the garden for extra chilli. Lots of them."

I was relieved to leave the kitchen. The wood fire stove was hot and Mamma was stone cold. Before going back in, I rested against the kitchen's outer stone wall and caught drifts of my parents' conversation through the window.

"Can't we let her be?" Babbo sighed. "Our own parents disapproved... they came around."

"It's not just the young man." Mamma's voice was unmoving. "Mariella needs to accept what she can and can't have. Even if we had money, we couldn't change everything."

I burst into the kitchen clutching a bouquet of red chilli. "What can't you change?"

Mamma patted the seat of a chair. "Sit down."

"Why isn't Emilio right for me? We plan to get married." I looked pleadingly at Babbo, hoping for an ally.

"Any love affair kept in the dark, signals something amiss," he said.

"Oh, Babbo, I'm not a child."

"No, you aren't, which is why we are discussing this rather than telling you." Mamma wiped her brow with her apron. "I was already worried, but your comment about the Signora bragging of your talents sent me into a spin."

"Aren't you proud of me?"

"You're talented, but showy. Coupled with your association to Emilio's family this combination is risky. The Carbone and DeLuca families have reason to be feared."

"Whatever are you talking about?"

"My own vanity robbed me of having other children. Everyone in Scilla remarked on your beauty. Emilio's mother was desperate for a daughter and envious of my beautiful baby girl. Provoking jealousy in anyone is serious enough, but envy from a Strega has terrible consequences. Emilio's mother, Strega Carbone, gave me Il Malocchio, the evil eye, and there were no more children."

Mamma wasn't teasing. Her voice shrank to a fragile wail and Babbo held her close, stroking her hair. "I'm so sorry I never gave you a son. Now you must work in the fields even when you're too old."

"No, Mamma, don't cry." I hugged them both, holding my cheek against hers. "There's no such magic. Not everyone has a son."

Mamma's voice was heavy with terror and superstition. "Two babies died in the womb. Then my youth dried up before its time."

My heart beat faster. I'd never known that about my mother. She'd kept it a secret to protect me. Now I needed to help her. "We will be fine. I'll make money from beautiful dresses," I said. "I'll pay workers to help with the farm."

"Pride. Again. It is dangerous. When Strega Carbone finds out Emilio is seeing you behind their back, she'll cast her eye on you, too."

"How did you know I was seeing him?"

"A Mamma knows everything. And you are not careful enough." She dried her tears and silently knotted the bright red chillies with string to hang around my neck. "Here, this will ward off *Il Malocchio*. If I could afford it, I'd buy you a necklace of red coral and gold, but this should protect you. Tuck it under your clothes if you must, but wear it. For me."

I slipped it beneath my blouse in respect for my parents' beliefs. Superstition governed their generation and some of that superstition had filtered down. "Yes, Mamma." My right hand instinctively made the sign of the horn; middle fingers pressing my palm with the index, thumb and pinkie extended. A sign Babbo taught me could ward off evil.

I looked at the large crucifix and picture of Jesus on the wall, then back to the chilli around my neck. My parents' belief in both magic and a Catholic god was conflicting. Yet, in the pit of my belly grew a sadness and fear.

Mamma was so often right.

Chapter Eight

Joe, Present Day

For three days in a row, Mum's asked Izzy and me to leave
the remembering room. But Izzy's still smiling as she leads
me through the residential care's back door to a weathered
picnic table under one of the enormous spreading fig trees
that must have given this place its name.

She plonks herself on the bench seat, then throws me a
grave look. "I've obviously picked the wrong friend."

What is she on about? I'll never understand women.

I attempt a light-hearted tone. "Wrong friend?" My
voice sounds like a worm crawling from beneath the fallen
fig strewn ground.

"Got you there." She hits her chest and laughs. "Being sent
outside takes me back to my school days. I regularly got sent
outside for talking. One day, I blamed the girl next to me. The
teacher said it was my fault for picking the wrong friend."

When Izzy smiles, her hazel eyes look green.

"These last memory sessions have taken me back to school, as well," I say. "It's the icky smell. The room's full of it."

"Smell?" Izzy sniffs the air, then buries her nose in her armpit. "It's not me, is it?"

"The bergamot," I say. "Katerina claims it's an ingredient in expensive perfumes, but it stinks like old oranges left to go mouldy in a hot school bag." I offer Izzy the back of my hand. "Here, I accidentally spilled some as I added drops to the diffuser."

"You're dead right." She wrinkles her nose. "What a pity for us. When we're old and forgetful and somebody's flinging essential oils around to jog our memories, you and I will be telling stories of dirty school bags while other oldies are dancing around in French perfumeries or skipping through groves of bergamot oranges in Calabria."

"I wouldn't know a bergamot orange if you threw one at me." I pick up a fig and aim for the yawning-mouth knothole in the tree. It misses by a mile.

"Your parents never took you to Italy, then?"

"Dad discouraged Mum from most things Italian. He was definite about Mum never going back."

"He wouldn't let her go? Seems mean."

I shrug, not knowing why Dad stopped Mum talking about the old country. "She got Christmas cards from her uncle Tonito, but her parents died long ago."

Izzy collects her own figs and squints an eye as she takes aim at the same tree. She throws three figs in rapid succession and bulls-eyes them all. I try again, hoping to redeem myself, biting my tongue for better concentration. When I miss the tree completely, I avoid looking at her. I can bear annoyance, but pity cuts too deep.

"What about this Emilio fellow?" she asks. "Could he be your real father?"

I cough to release the knot in my throat. I'd never thought of my mother being with a man other than my father. "No chance. The Emilio encounter took place at least ten years before I was born."

"How old are you?"

I frown, probably adding extra wrinkles in the process. "Forty-five."

Izzy nibbles her lip using her teeth like she's using some sort of mouth abacus. "Yep, 1966 is too early for that—but sex isn't a one-off deal. Your mum and Emilio could have been at it for years."

My shudder is involuntary and makes me feel immature. I try for a cover-up and stick my fingers in my mouth to make a gagging sound. May as well play it up.

Izzy laughs and I'm relieved she's laughing with me, not at me.

"The words sex and parents should never be used in the same sentence." I make a clenched teeth grin.

She stands and turns her back towards me, stroking her own shoulder while moving her other hand over her bottom. It actually looks as if she's hugging someone else. She caresses and croons, "Emilio. Emilio. Emilio."

I go for a second gagging, wanting her to laugh again. I'm not as opposed to female attention as I thought. It's sad and ridiculous. Maybe I'm high from inhaling the bergamot oil. Izzy's a gorgeous young woman who must have men lined up down the street, badgering her to notice them. After rejecting a handsome, and no doubt witty, doctor for being thoughtless, she's stuck with my company, a plain old average Joe whose sharpest move is pretending to throw-up.

Izzy stares for a long moment. "Why are we both single?" she asks.

"No secret here. Look at me." I wave my hands from shoulder to hip. "Even if I tried to socialise, I'd never be a chick-magna—" I regret my choice of words before I finish, but stopping part way through chick magnet is a mistake. *Chick Magna?* If there were posters illustrating what HOT men are like, I'd be on it. Not as a positive example. I'd be the man in the red circle with the diagonal line. NOT HOT captioned underneath. I'm an example of LUKE-WARM AT BEST.

To my surprise, Izzy's eyes light up. "I'm going to take on a side project." She clicks her fingers. "I'm on leave to write up your mum's memoirs, but there's not much to write up at the moment. I'm going to make you my project, Joe."

I crack my nervous knuckles wondering what I've missed. "Can you give me more information?"

"I'm setting you up on a dating site."

Izzy isn't asking my permission; she's already scrolling through her phone.

"I've tried it already. Got zero interest." I shrug. It took me years of being alone before I was ready, then months to work up the courage to sign on. A waste of time. No one amongst the crowd of other singles was desperate enough to try me.

"Okay. Dating site name?" Izzy doesn't look up.

"Cupid4U.com."

"Joe, Joey, or Joseph?" she asks seriously.

"Joe, just Joe Blake. But it's inactive." I consider doing the gag thing again. I liked it better when Izzy was laughing. But I've flogged that one to death.

"No, it's not." She turns the screen towards me while

screwing up her pretty nose. "Is this your profile? Seriously? You know nothing about marketing, Joe Blake."

I laugh at her saying, *you know nothing Joe Blake*, instead of *you know nothing Jon Snow*. Her fake British accent was perfect. I wonder if I should let her know I got the Game of Thrones reference. But she's already moved on.

"What do you do for a job?"

"I take proposed building plans...then I use measurements and materials to estimate cost. It's all done on a computer these—"

"Joe, what are you wearing in this picture? Red caps are not a good look. They give a subliminal message about your political leanings."

"It has a Nike tick on it—"

She holds her phone closer and squints. "I can't tell what's on it. In fact, it's so bad I couldn't pick your face out of a line-up."

She groans and I half shrink under the picnic table, watching her scan the rest of my bio.

"Don't read it out loud." I beg.

"I need to, for your sake: *I'm fairly shy and an average bloke. I enjoy most things. I'm a steady man who'd like to meet a woman.*" Izzy sticks out her tongue. "This tells me nothing, Joe. First an out-of-focus picture, then a bio without any heart."

"Stop, I spent hours crafting that." I aim for a jokey hurt smile.

"Cruel, but kind," she says, unperturbed. "Okay, Joe. Close your eyes. You're browsing in a bookshop. You pick up a book with an unappealing cover. What do you do?'

"Put it down," I say.

"You're feeling generous and you read the back cover

blurb, but it tells you nothing about the book. What do you do?"

"Okay, I get it. I put it down."

"There are thousands of books, Joe. You only read those you find interesting. We're going to give you a new cover and a catchier blurb."

"What if we write: 'Nothing special here, move on?'"

"You'd get more hits from that than from this airy-fairy waffle." She slaps the table emphatically.

Ouch. Disappointment now has a sound.

"Give me a minute," she says. "I'll be back." Izzy grabs her handbag and disappears before I get the chance to ask why.

While I wait, I flick a few figs towards the tree, hoping to improve. Who would have thought that instead of estimating building costs while waiting for a lottery win to pay for my dream trip, I'd spend my entire holiday in an aged care facility? Even more unbelievable is it turning out to be the highlight of the last decade of my life. My mother's tales are interesting, and I'm enjoying everyone's company. Especially Izzy's.

I need to come up with an interesting personality trait for my personal blurb. I'm excellent at guessing the time. Can guess within five minutes. Night or day. I shrug at my luke-warm superpower and chuck another fig. This time I hit the bullseye. Pity she wasn't here to see.

Izzy creeps in a second too late and picks up her phone. She takes up where we left off. "You've put no age range either. Who are you aiming the ad at?"

"A woman?" I shrug.

"You're forty-five. I'm going five either side. Female forty to fifty."

After Izzy writes the bait to hook me a woman, she

pushes me against the fig tree, moving my arm onto a branch, and twisting my head in several poses until she gets a suitable shot. I'm a plasticine man in the hands of a demanding mistress, which should feel completely emasculating, like it did when Bettina was checking for an Italian designer label. But it doesn't feel the same. Not at all.

Chapter Nine

Mariella, Italy, 1966

The Signora opened the shop door just as I was about to walk away. It was a ridiculous decision to arrive at work so early.

"I wondered who was knocking at this hour."

"I hope you don't mind, but there's a garment I'd like to complete before Don DeLuca's wife and daughter arrive to collect it."

She stooped to catch her breath. "I raced down the stairs too fast for a woman of my age, especially when my morning espresso hasn't yet reached my legs."

She tilted her head and regarded me curiously. Are you sure everything's okay?"

"Yes. Last time they came in two hours early and made a dreadful fuss about the garment not being ready."

She blew out a long breath. "Ugh. I remember how well-mannered you were. You explained the appointment was for two, not twelve, but Signora DeLuca wouldn't have it."

"You start work, and I'll put myself together. I look frightful."

"Thank you. And sorry again."

Signora Giovanni gripped the handrail to climb the stairs to her private quarters. She was as 'put together' as ever. The few grey streaks through her dark locks were natural highlights. Surely, she didn't wake up with hair styled in an impeccable French twist?

I poured a glass of water and took a sip. In truth, there was only a little finishing on Signorina Isabella's dress. Isabella's hard-to-please mother had allowed me to deviate from the book of patterns. I'd experimented with the fabric, taking inspiration from Yves St Laurent. An A-line dress with hand-appliqued block colour. The graphic black lines were hand stitched. Although I wanted to ensure everything was perfect, it wasn't my only reason for coming in early. Yesterday when I slipped on the shoes after work, my toes crunched a folded piece of paper. Emilio must have snuck into the laneway.

He asked me to meet him. He had something important to say.

True to form, the DeLuca women arrived before their appointment, but I was in such high spirits about meeting Emilio, I couldn't care what the mother said.

I greeted them politely and enthusiastically. We relied on word-of-mouth recommendations to keep the business open.

While Isabella changed behind the screen, I studied Signora DeLuca. Mother and daughter were alike. Nino had chosen a beautiful woman for a wife, but her lack of smile lines told an unhappy tale.

Isabella, on the other hand, paraded around the salon, joy in every step at her new dress.

"You look fabulous." I clapped my hands with genuine pleasure. Then I checked myself. Too much pride.

Signora Giovanni beamed, but Signora DeLuca looked down her nose. "It is too short. I can see her knees."

"But I love it, and it's the fashion," Isabella said, admiring her reflection.

"Surely you won't wear those knee-high boots?"

Isabella winked at me, unaffected by her mother's disapproval. She strutted as if on a catwalk, twirling in front of her mother and giggling until the older woman's harsh expression softened. "Who knows Mamma? With your legs we might get you wearing the latest trends."

Signora Giovanni inspected the dress seams then folded the dress in tissue paper. "The style and workmanship are exquisite, but Isabella's beauty is the icing on the cake. We couldn't ask for better advertising."

"She is stunning." Signora DeLuca agreed.

"She's the image of her mother," Signora Giovanni said. "Do you mind taking blank appointment cards to hand to your friends? Someone is sure to ask."

The mother peeled notes from a roll of cash, and Isabella wandered through the back room, stopping to flick through a clip-board of my design sketches. She stopped at a drawing of a wedding gown. "Who's this beautiful dress for?"

Shrugging my shoulders, I said, "Just ideas." I wasn't going to tell her or anyone it was my own dream gown.

"One of Mariella's unique designs," Signora Giovanni

said, wearing a smile so haughty Mamma would surely disapprove.

Isabella took her mother aside, but her stage whisper echoed around the walls. "When I get married, Mariella must design my dress."

"You can't be a bride without a groom," her mother snapped. She curled her lip and turned to my boss. "It's a pity so many men left Scilla after the war."

Signora Giovanni rested her palm against her chest. "I'm thankful that a prominent family such as yours has honoured a local business. As for you, Signorina Isabella, I'm sure there's not a man alive who could resist you."

When the cuckoo clock chirped four, the Signora said what I'd hoped to hear, "Go home early. While you're walking, you can dream up your next design. We will hang it in the window as bait for more wealthy customers."

I skipped my way to Emilio's grandparents' house. His note explained they were on another jaunt, this time in Venice. But just in case they'd come back early, I opened the courtyard gate tentatively.

Emilio stood facing the corner wall, his muscled arms above his head, picking grapes. I took a moment to admire him. He balanced a bare foot against his other leg; his navy shorts rolled to reveal a pale upper thigh. If I could capture him in my sketchbook. I'd take care to draw the muscle definition in his calf, the way his shorts hugged his bottom, and beneath his gauzy white shirt, the outline of his tapered torso.

I licked my lips. Emilio was *delizioso*.

When I crept up behind him and circled my arms

around his waist, he jumped, then relaxed against me. As my fingers drew patterns over his chest, his muscles quivered.

"Mariella." Emilio flashed the whitest of teeth; a slightly chipped tooth highlighting the perfection of the others. He took a deep breath. "You came. And we're all alone. Don't be angry, but I have an ulterior motive. I'm setting the scene for a seduction."

"We can't. We aren't married. If you abandoned me, I'd be left with a ruined reputation. I'd no longer be able to work in the shop."

Although these were genuine concerns, it was increasingly difficult to believe my own arguments.

He pressed a plump grape to my lips, and I bit into the sweet juicy flesh. "Besides, it's dangerous. I could get pregnant."

"It's all taken care of." He produced a small package. "My cousin bought these on an overseas holiday."

"What are they?" I asked. It was clear they were not something approved by the Pope.

"A sheath to prevent you from conceiving."

I closed my eyes to slow my breathing. "Emilio. I want to, but I can't."

He led me to a canvas-covered swing with a mattress larger than my bed at home. "You know I plan to marry you, Mariella. I've waited so long."

"My parents don't believe you will. They say neither the Ndrangheta nor your mother will consent." I sat upright, smoothing my dress, covering my knees. "My parents think I'm in danger."

"You are in danger," he said, pulling me sideways to lie with him. "In danger of discovering how much joy a man and woman can share."

"But the stories I've heard about the Ndrangheta." My voice was barely a whisper, and I closed my eyes as his hand crept further up a thigh than a good girl would allow.

"Your parents are fond of stories, but that doesn't make them true. An evil Ndrangheta is infinitely more interesting than the truth. The word Ndrangheta itself means heroic or valiant. There are minor indiscretions, but we are a protective group, an *onorata societa*."

"But—"

He kissed away my words and persisted in exploring my body, running his hands along the lace trim of my underwear, then cupping the cheeks of my bottom.

"The touch of your skin drives me crazy," he said, short of breath. "I might actually be crazy. I'm willing to leave everything behind for you if I have to." His fingers fumbled with the knot on my chilli necklace, but couldn't untie it. "Trying to ward away my advances?" he asked with a nervous laugh. Emilio abandoned the necklace and traced a path between my breasts.

I held him at arm's length, looking for signs of untruthfulness, but found none. I leaned my head back exposing my neck and décolletage, encouraging Emilio to kiss me. As he lifted my dress above my head, I murmured a weak objection.

He stopped. "If you aren't sure, I won't force you." I could see the desire in his eyes, but he sat up and held my hand. "I love you, Mariella. Please be mine?'

The craving in his eyes made him look drunk. And he wasn't the only one intoxicated with desire. I wanted him as much as he wanted me.

"I intend to marry you," he said, "with or without the blessing of my family.

My fingers trembled as I unbuttoned his shirt. "Kiss me before I change my mind."

We lingered over the kiss and fell back onto the swing bed.

"Emilio!" a man's gruff voice yelled from inside the house. "Emilio? Are you here?"

Emilio lifted me from the swing seat and rolled me underneath. "Stay there," he whispered. "It's Uncle Nino. I'll get rid of him."

Although I was frightened to look when the back door opened, I was even more frightened of not knowing where Nino was. I barely breathed as I stared at Nino's two-tone black and white shoes.

"Gardening without your shirt on?" Nino said, tapping one foot. "Tanning for your bevy of young ladies, eh?" Nino DeLuca's laugh, followed by that filthy cough, made me feel unclean.

"No, Uncle," Emilio laughed. "I love the sun. But I've been out too long, and I'm hot and thirsty. Let's go inside for a drink."

With my knuckle pressed against my teeth, I willed Nino to agree.

"Good idea. We've business to discuss." Nino's feet waddled towards the door as he spoke. "Your mother and my wife are up to something."

Chapter Ten

Maria, Present Day

My eyes are closed when Dermot calls me. "Maria. Maria."

I'm unsure whether I want to come back to the present. My heart is beating rapidly at the memory of how long I waited under that swing for Emilio to tell me I was safe. He did not give me the signal he'd promised. I'd dressed behind a large potted plant, then opened the gate to the laneway.

"Signora Maria."

The old kitchen at The Figs is cool, but sweat beads on my lip and forehead, just as it did that day so long ago.

"*Hai bisogno di una pausa?*" Dermot asks.

"*Sì.*" He's right; I need a rest.

"I'll find Joe," he says.

"Joey and Izzy have been gone a long time," I whisper in Italian.

"You told them to leave," Dermot replies.

"Did I? I can't remember." I reach for the bottle of water beside the chaise. "Why am I so warm?"

"You were remembering the Italian sun," Dermot explains.

I'm still trying to recall what I told Dermot when Joey strolls back in with Izzy.

"Ask them where they were," I murmur.

He ignores my request. "You're back. Perfect timing. We're just taking a break."

I tilt my head from one side to the other, trying to interpret Joey's expression. He looks happier than he has in a long time. I nudge Dermot with my elbow. "Tell Joey that spending time with Izzy agrees with him."

"Your mother thinks fresh air agrees with you," Dermot says.

"You're changing my words," I say in Italian.

"Don't worry, I'm paraphrasing." Dermot smiles.

"Why? Did I insult someone?"

"No. But it wouldn't hurt most of us to pass our words through a filter. I didn't want to embarrass Joe."

Joey catches me staring and shrugs questioningly. "You all right, Mum?"

"*Sto bene qui. Grazie, Joey.*"

Joey nods his head. He can't interpret the words, but he understands the tone.

Izzy huddles with me and Dermot. She whispers conspiratorially. "Do you mind translating something juicy? You will love it, Maria. I know it's important to you that Joe is happy, so I've set him up on a dating site."

"I can hear what you're saying and I'd prefer you to stop," Joey says. "Mum doesn't need anyone giving her ideas."

I raise my hand to shush Joey, then talk to Dermot. "A dating site? Tell Izzy that my Joey's too good looking to need that kind of help."

Dermot winks at me, then makes up his own version. "Maria's very interested. How does the dating site work?"

"I took a profile picture for Joe." Izzy scrolls through her phone and holds it far enough away for me to focus. A thoughtful young woman. Perfect for Joey. But the picture won't do.

"Joey won't get enough interest looking like that. He looks *molto* handsome wearing glasses. Take another photo."

This time Dermot translates properly and I give him an encouraging thumbs up. You catch more flies with honey than you do with vinegar.

Izzy hugs me. "I'll redo the pictures, Maria. But I'm not sure Joe wants to find someone."

"He just needs to put himself out there," I say. "We all have events that break our hearts."

I study Izzy's face as Dermot translates—she looks at me with concern.

"Challenge accepted, Maria," she says. "You and I will help Joe find a wife. When women express their interest by hearting his profile picture, I'll show you first so you can vet them."

I elbow Dermot. "Ask Izzy if she's got a man. Joey and her would be good for each other. Save themselves advertising to strangers. Men can be dangerous. Especially for a woman."

Dermot raises an eyebrow, then asks Izzy, "Maria wants to know if you are on a dating site, too?"

"Ask her about being matched up with Joey!" I prod Dermot's arm.

He shakes his head and mouths an unmistakable, "No."

"For what it's worth," Izzy says. "I am on a dating app."

My Joey spins his head so fast it nearly falls off. "Really. Why didn't you share?"

"We already had one example of an ineffective bio. That was yours. There'd be no benefit in viewing two crap bios."

"Ask Izzy if she has a suitor. If not, what is she looking for?"

"Have you found the dating app successful?" Dermot asks casually, ignoring me again.

Izzy brushes her arm as if ridding herself of terrible memories. "No. Enough said."

"So, it's the blind leading the blind," I say. "Has anyone in this room found love?"

"Me," Dermot says. "When I met you last year at Katerina's big event, you asked if me and my lady friend Claudia were lovers."

"Did I? I can't remember. Did you order your woman on a dating site?"

"I don't think it's legal to order a woman, and I can't imagine men wanting to do such a thing."

What does Dermot know? Bad things happen in this world, and the people who do them do not care whether they are legal.

Dermot smiles to himself. "Claudia fell into my life and almost fell out because I was slow to act."

This is exactly what I mean. Men need a push. It looks like Izzy does too. "Tell Izzy to open her eyes. There's a perfectly good single man in the room."

"Can't do that," Dermot says in Italian, then in English he makes up his own version. "Maria hopes you both find love."

I gesture with my hands, swearing like a true Calabrese. "*Merda.*"

"What's going on with Mum?" Joey asks. He turns to Dermot. "I can tell Mum's annoyed. Why aren't you translating?"

I tell Dermot I agree "*Sono d'accordo.* Why aren't you doing your job?"

Dermot ignores my question. "Maria is frustrated. She says you can go outside again if you like. It's time to get back to the story."

He's right about one thing. I am frustrated. I can understand much of their English, so why can't I speak it? I growl from the back of my throat, worrying about poor Joey being sent out again so quickly, then I notice he's smiling and already holding the door open for Izzy.

I'd like to tell Joey that he needs to catch love while he can, but I doubt Dermot would translate. If I had my wits about me, I'd push these two together so hard, they'd bounce to the floor in each other's arms.

I hear both of them laughing as they walk down the corridor. Perhaps Dermot is helping. He's letting nature run its course.

Chapter Eleven

Joe, Present Day

I recognise the scheming glint in Mum's eyes. If I'm not careful, she'll start match-making me with Izzy, and I'll have to fake my own death to avoid embarrassment.

Once in the garden and well out of Mum's ear-shot, I summon the courage to question Izzy. "You kept that information close to your chest."

"What information?" Her plea of ignorance is almost believable.

"Being on a dating site and not mentioning it. Seems unfair not to have shared"

Izzy picks dried leaves off the picnic table, scrunching them in her fingers, avoiding both my question and my gaze.

"Sorry," I say. "I'm getting as bad as my mother. You don't have to show me."

"Nah. You're right." She wipes her hands on her jeans.

"But showing you my mess can wait. Maria wants a photo with your glasses on. Get them out."

"Mum thinks everyone looks more intelligent with glasses," I say. "She reckons it makes men look less threatening. Says that's important in a man."

Izzy watches me finger comb my hair, then quickly wipes my glasses with a cleaning cloth. "Hurry," she says.

I put them on. No point arguing with a woman who knows what she wants.

"Oh, Joe." Izzy whistles. "Maria is right. The glasses add something for sure. They define your jawline and frame your eyes."

I wait near the tree like a helpless child, expecting her to arrange me in her preferred pose like she did earlier, but she raises an impatient eyebrow. "Surely you remember? Stand the same way as before."

She positions the phone to take a photo, and I try not to look disappointed in case it makes me seem creepy. I'm not creepy. At least I've never been creepy before. But I liked it when Izzy touched my arm and moved my head. It's been a long time since I was that close to a woman.

Chapter Twelve

Mariella, Italy, 1966

After weeks of slow-to-no dressmaking business, Signora Giovanni and I created a new window display. On one side, bridesmaid gowns hung against a riotous background of ribbons and flowers. The other window showcased one of my designs all on its own. The dress was a blend of fashions from glossy magazines. The jovial display hid the bleak truth. We needed something to drum up new clients. The Signora didn't say it, but I knew she wouldn't be able to continue employing me, when there was barely enough work for one.

She was sorting fabric and I was blocking pattern pieces for a new design, when the entry bells announced a customer. Signora Giovanni leapt impressively to her feet, smoothed her hair, and adjusted the tape measure around her neck so it hung symmetrically. I imagined her uttering the mantra she lived by, 'Presentation and attitude are the variables we can control.'

We waited like mannequins, then our shoulders slumped in unison when the door closed again. The mystery customer had changed their mind.

"It must have been the wind." I went back to my drawing.

Minutes later, the bells jangled again.

This time Emilio entered the shop, checking over his shoulder nervously to make sure he was alone.

What was he doing here? We'd agreed to stay low. I fixed my anxious gaze on the paper pattern pieces.

"How can we help you?" the Signora asked.

"I'm looking for a new Summer jacket," he said. "Perhaps I can browse the sample catalogues?"

Signora Giovanni shot me a questioning look, then handed him the catalogues. "The table and chairs outside are perfect for perusing. There's a refreshing sea-breeze."

"Oh, no. The sun makes my eyes water. May I sit inside near the fan?" He pointed to the noisy table-fan oscillating between my workspace and where the Signora was arranging the fabric by colour.

She raised an eyebrow. "If you wish."

Emilio made a show of struggling to balance catalogues on his knee. He let them slip several times. "Do you mind if I clear a small space at the end of the workbench?"

He moved his chair next to me. "Which of these should I choose?" He pointed out almost identical jackets from different collections.

"Whichever you choose, you will forever mourn the opportunity of the lost choice," I said with a wry smile.

Signora Giovanni cast a puzzled look in my direction, then a light bulb of an idea brightened her face. "Mariella is right. Why not have us make both jackets in different colours?"

"Both it is. I have a meeting to attend, but I'll return in a few days to choose fabric." Emilio spun his chair so his back was to the Signora and puckered his sensuous lips in a kiss as he shoved a squishy parcel under the catalogues and stood to leave.

"Wait a moment," the Signora said. "I have swatches upstairs for you to take home. You should view the colours under different lighting. But be careful of the sun or you'll damage those sensitive eyes of yours."

I took advantage of the Signora's absence and threw my arms around Emilio's neck. Jingling bells zapped us apart like an electric shock. Nino DeLuca filled the doorway. By his expression, we hadn't moved quickly enough.

"Mariella," the Signora's voice almost pierced my eardrum. "You might be an excellent seamstress, but how many times must I show you how to take a collar measurement without dropping your tape?"

I never dropped things, and she'd never complained about my technique before. I looked down at the Signora's distinctive orange tape measure pooled on the floor at Emilio's feet. How did it get from her neck?

"Step back, and I'll show you again." She picked up the tape and ran it through her fingers before wrapping both arms around Emilio's neck in a measuring method which looked much like an embrace. She smoothed his clothing before barking out measurements. "Fifteen and a half inches." Then, without missing a beat, she feigned surprise at Nino. "Signore DeLuca? I didn't see you come in. How long have you been standing there?"

He furrowed his brow, presumably reflecting on the pantomime he'd witnessed. "Too long," he snapped. He narrowed his eyes at me, then at Emilio. But I could see he wasn't sure.

"We're in a hurry, Emilio. The family is waiting."

The Signora wore the pasted smile she reserved for difficult customers. "Do come again. Two of my favourite clients."

Don DeLuca answered with a hacking cough, then spat on the pavement outside.

The door had barely closed when the Signora grabbed my shoulders and thrust her face inches from mine. "Mariella, the war might have robbed our village of eligible young men, but any of those left in Scilla would be a better choice than Emilio."

She shook me. "Emilio and Don DeLuca are members of the same 'Ndrine. They are a blood clan of the Ndrangheta. Do you know how they deal with those who refuse to fall in step?"

I started to cry and she pressed her lips shut then passed me a handkerchief. "I will resume this conversation when you are calm. I have an errand to run."

Once she was gone, I sobbed and pushed aside the catalogues to rest my head on the worktable. My hand touched the package Emilio had hidden. The inside of the wrapping was covered with scribbled words of undying love, an invitation to our next private meeting, and a small jewellery-sized box wrapped in white paper. My heart pounded as I opened it, but it wasn't the engagement ring I hoped for. Another tiny bottle of my favourite perfume.

I pressed it to my nose. Notes of bergamot. Scents of Scilla. This time it held the fragrance of disappointment.

When the Signora returned, I challenged her. "Most of the Mafia talk is hearsay."

Her reply was low, but far from soft. "You are wrong. The obligation of *omerta*, the silence, prevents the initiated from revealing criminal and immoral activities, and actual witnesses amongst our community are too terrified to speak."

"But Emilio told me the Ndrangheta is like the Greek and Roman myths. It is all hyped-up legend."

"Listen. *That* is part of the *omerta*. Denial of its existence. The Ndrangheta recruit members from bloodlines, and Emilio is marked. I'm telling you; he's destined to become a 'made man'. You've heard the whispered stories of illegally made money, political blackmail, extortion, and murder. Multiply those stories a hundred-fold and you're closer to the truth."

I stared in disbelief, but her eyes spoke with such certainty. What could I do? First my parents and now my boss?

"If this is true, then why don't the wives object to husbands involved in such crimes?"

"Power and money, Mariella. The dazzle of status and the glitter of expensive gifts blind them to unpleasant truths."

Chapter Thirteen

Mariella, Italy, 1966

Emilio's note asked me to meet him on Wednesday afternoon at Castello Ruffo. I'd arrived early, then waited for hours. I only gave up because it was long after dark and my parents would be frantic.

I'd heard nothing since.

By Sunday morning, I was beyond worried.

As Mamma and Babbo dressed for church, I prattled on to quell my fears. When it came to her only child, my mother worried enough to earn a place in the Guinness Book of Records. I didn't want to fuel her concern. The umbilical cord might be cut at birth, but an invisible bond between us transmitted my fidgety angst. Babbo looked on amused and confused, like the time we'd both eaten fermented blueberries and become tipsy.

"Mamma, let me sew you a new church dress." I lifted her bell sleeve. "This one's too heavy for such a warm day."

"This is fine," she said. "I have a winter dress and a

summer dress. You can make another once they wear thin. What would I do with three?"

I shook my head. Mamma's church clothes would never wear out. The minute she got home from the regular post-mass lunch with Uncle Tonito, the dress would be hung in the shade and get four airings before seeing soap and water.

Mamma flapped her arms like a burgundy-grey winged wood pigeon. "Tonito will be here soon." She shooed me and Babbo onto the stone path.

Outside, Mamma waited on the wicker bench in the shade of an ancient olive tree planted by my great-great-Nonna. I sat beside her, and she dismissed Babbo with one of her not-so-subtle looks.

As he was leaving, he pinched my arm. "What's all the fuss? Does your mother think your uncle Tonito will drive off if we're a minute late? That man is as patient as a saint."

Mamma stared with darkened eyes and said, "Women's talk."

Babbo wandered into the olive grove out of earshot.

Taking my face in her hands, she lowered her voice. "I've heard things."

I jumped to my own conclusion. "Signora Giovanni told you, didn't she?"

Mamma's eyes clouded. "Not at all, it was Emilio's mother. She stopped at my market stall to hiss: *Your daughter will never see my son again.*"

My chin trembled, but I held it high. "Emilio's mother is wrong. He's asked me to marry him."

"That woman said more before she spat at the ground and walked away, Mariella." Mamma looked around before whispering. "Strega Carbone reported your goings-on to Nino DeLuca and he's called an assembly of the clan. The Strega might not be invited to these male only meetings, but she has a voice. Without a doubt, that witch calls the shots."

They'd threatened him. This almost explained why Emilio hadn't turned up for our meeting. My nostrils flared with anger. "Is Emilio in danger?"

"You must forget Emilio. We've been warned."

Tonito's car appeared over the hill, and Babbo walked towards the car, pausing to pat my head like he'd done when I was a child. But my heart wasn't comforted.

Uncle Tonito wound down the car window and flashed his usual grin—he often looked as if he was laughing at a private joke. My usually happy mother didn't return her brother's smile.

We exchanged solemn greetings and climbed in, then Tonito set off in the direction of town. After a few miles of our grimness, he pulled over onto the rough grass verge and turned to mother in the back seat. "God will forgive us missing church for one Sunday. I think it's better to take this mood elsewhere."

Although Mamma squeezed my hand and nodded yes, I couldn't imagine what solution she expected by missing mass. She believed in nothing more powerful than prayer.

Tonito said, "I know a private place where you can speak freely and tell me what's going on."

Tonito stopped in Palmi, a neighbouring town, and ordered us to wait while he shopped for food.

He returned with fully laden paper bags which he handed to Babbo who stared glassy-eyed through the window. "We can think better on a full stomach. I've bought delicious meats, cheeses, olives, bread and wine."

I forced an appreciative *Mmmmm*, but my parents were sombre. Our silence continued on the winding drive from the town centre, past the houses and scattered farms, and was only broken after Tonito veered off the road straight into the woods. Only when he'd rounded a couple of bends did I realise there was a track. Half a mile into the wooded area he parked under a shady tree. "Down this way," he said. "Follow me."

Babbo carried the food while Tonito fetched a basket, picnic rug and chair from the boot of his car. Fresh air, the earthy smell of composting leaves and tiny rays of sunshine filtered through the trees provided unexpected peace.

Despite being overdressed for both place and occasion, Mamma relaxed on that rickety chair in the middle of nowhere.

Uncle Tonito put his arms around his sister. "Mother Nature's cathedral. We can say a personal prayer. God would approve."

This place was safe. I felt it in my gut. No Apennine wolves chasing us here.

Mamma watched from her chair, while I sat on a dry, silvery log while the men wandered off to explore the river.

My father lingered on the crumbling bank both hands behind his back, his weight shifting from foot to foot. The way he kneaded his lower back and rolled his torso forward then back; it was clear his body wouldn't be up to working the fields for much longer.

Tonito returned to organise the picnic. He arranged the food on paper-bag plates on a large rock and produced leather-cased aluminium tumblers for the wine from the basket. "Okay," he called. "After we eat and drink you unload whatever it is that's plaguing you."

We ate slowly and without a word, when we'd finished, Mamma packed everything into the basket while I closed my eyes. I opened them to find Tonito regarding me over steepled hands.

"Trouble with a young man?" he asked.

"Strega Carbone, again," Mamma said, her voice high-pitched. "She doesn't want Mariella in her family and passed on a warning from the Ndrine."

"Your young man is a Carbone?" Tonito let out a low whistle.

I shrugged.

Mamma brushed crumbs from her Sunday dress. "Mariella thinks she, and Emilio, and love, are free to make their own decisions. But there's no choice at all. She must stop seeing him."

Uncle spoke calmly to me. "What do you want to do?"

"I love him and he loves me." I avoided eye contact. "When Emilio and I marry, I will have my own shop and we won't have to worry about money." I didn't say out loud that Babbo was getting too old and weary for farm work. "I will employ workers for the heaviest farm chores."

Babbo kicked at leaves with his worn shoes. "It is the parents' job to worry about their children, not the other way around."

"How can I not worry? Everything I've dreamt of depends on Emilio."

When Mamma repeated her concerns about Strega Carbone to Tonito, I buried my head in my hands. She reminded him of many previous curses the Strega had cast.

When she'd finished, Tonito prodded my arm. "Have you seen Emilio since his mother sent this warning?"

"Other than a note, no. Emilio might not be the most punctual, but he's never disappeared before."

Tonito lifted my chin. "Mariella, if your heart cries out for Emilio, and you'd both be happy distancing yourself from the Ndrangheta clan, then find a way to see him. Leave Scilla if you must."

Mamma wailed and sent a shudder rippling through my body. "But what of Strega Carbone?"

I threw my arms around her shoulders. "I won't go. Not if his mother will curse my family."

"You have to live your life without fear," Tonito said.

"But how will I look after my family if I'm gone?"

"You say 'my family' as if they are yours alone. They are mine, too. My sister, my brother-in-law. If you get a chance at happiness, you must take it. We will all be here together, looking after each other."

Babbo pulled Mamma close and I nodded to Tonito, but the choice to grasp happiness wasn't entirely mine. Surely Emilio could have pushed a note under the shop door?

On the walk back to the car, Mamma kept her eyes on the trees ahead. "Talk to Emilio, but stay away from members of the Ndrangheta and avoid the Strega as if your life depends upon it."

The branches rustled and my skin prickled. I couldn't see it, but I could feel the Apennine wolf snapping at my heels.

Determined to get a straight answer before the week was up, I stopped by Emilio's grandparents hoping to catch him alone in the courtyard.

Despite the solidly built high wall, a fortress of limestone rocks and stucco, male voices cascaded into the laneway. I leaned against the wall, re-tying my shoelaces while desperately trying to steady my breath.

I tilted my head, hoping to catch strands of conversation. Emilio was pleading. "I can't do that. I don't want to."

"You will stay away from her."

"But—"

"Your mother can be wrathful." Nino sniggered. It was definitely him—his characteristic cough punctuated the laughter. "One woman is as good as another when the lights are out."

I jumped to my feet, ready to open the gate and drag Emilio away, but fear bit deep. I pinched the tip of my nose to stop the tears.

Aimlessly, I rounded the corner, then crouched at a set of stone steps to collect my thoughts. Emilio made a promise to marry me with or without his family's blessing. What about our love? My reputation?

Uncle Tonito's voice startled me. "Are you okay, Mariella?"

It was too late to hide my tears.

"Problems with Emilio," he asked.

"No." I fanned my face.

"Whatever it is, it won't be as bad when you know the full story."

I took a long slow breath. "You think it might be a misunderstanding, uncle?"

"Many things we dwell on are misunderstandings." He pulled me to my feet. "Come, I'll give you a lift home."

Chapter Fourteen

Joe, Present Day

I finish reading the transcript of Mum's story so far, and shake my head. Some things don't add up.

"What do you think?" Izzy taps her hands impatiently on the outdoor table. "When I read it last night, I decided your mum should've got rid of that Emilio fellow. She gave him too many chances. First, he was too gutless to stand up to his family, then he didn't bother letting her know where he was."

"His wasn't an ordinary family, they were mafia, and dangerous."

"Worse then. The bastard should've checked to make sure she was safe."

"The two strikes and you're out rule, eh?"

Izzy chuckles. "Talking about my disastrous date... seems I dodged a bullet there. Bettina told me he almost burst a blood vessel yesterday. Stormed into reception complaining a flock of birds had shat on his shiny new car.

Wanted Bettina to put an order in with maintenance to have the fig trees cut down. Demanded someone wash his precious paintwork immediately."

"Did she?"

"Course not. Can't name a care facility *The Figs* then get rid of one of two trees. We'd have to chop the S off. No. Bettina handed him a bucket and pointed out a tap.

"I wish I'd seen it," I say.

"When he's back next week, I'll sprinkle sunflower seeds around his car in a re-enactment. More effective than the Strega's curse at bringing in birds." Her eyes twinkle with mischief.

"You wouldn't really?"

"Nah. My feelings for him aren't strong enough to waste time getting even."

So, Izzy isn't in a relationship. I lean against the seat and tilt my head to catch the weak rays of sunlight. My cheeks are warmed by either sun or pleasure. Then I remember my earlier concerns. "I'm slightly sceptical about Mum's memoir. Do you think she is telling her own story? Or is this a dementia thing where she saw an old movie and now thinks it was about herself."

Izzy takes the folder from me and shakes her head. "This is set in the right place, Italy. It's about a woman around the same age. Why question it?"

"The name Mariella. I checked with Dermot, she definitely said Mariella not Maria."

"Then you must be right, there's no way she could have shortened her name. For example, someone with a name like Joseph would never call themselves Joe or Joey?" Izzy stretches the eeee at the end of my name, infusing it with sarcasm.

"What about Borelli," I say defensively. "Her maiden name wasn't Borelli either. A different last name too?"

"What was your mum's maiden name?"

"I can't remember. I went through a box of her stuff last night to dig out her old passport, but couldn't find it."

"Could it be your mother's parents never married and she didn't take her father's name?" Izzy suggests.

"Anything's possible, but they were strict Catholics, I can't imagine them not marrying."

"What was your Uncle Tonito's last name?" she asks.

"I've already checked. It doesn't match either."

"But Tonito was your uncle?"

"Yes."

"Tonito doesn't sound too common a name. When you go home, have another look through those boxes, but this time try not to do a 'boy look'."

Chapter Fifteen

Mariella, Italy, 1966

After a week of frayed nerves, I sewed at double-speed to push away the disappointment of Emilio's absence. I couldn't allow the claws of doubt to take hold.

To drum up business, Signora Giovanni wheeled a clothing rack onto the pavement, selling ready-to-wear garments made from the fabric she'd bought at discount fairs. I sewed, while the Signora chatted to passers-by on the street.

She came inside, her face pink from the heat, and fanned herself with a handful of notes. "I've sold four more dresses. It seems people are more willing to spend if offered a willing ear. I make more money smiling and listening to gossip than I do sewing," Signora Giovanni laughed, then stopped to yawn. "Apparently the grocery store in Catanzaro sells soap-powder for fifty liras less than in Scilla, even though both stores are owned by the same family." She raised her eyebrows and cupped her hand to whisper, even though we were alone. "I've heard intimate details about how Sofia's lady parts are not the same since the baby. And... Grumpy Mauro Labrazzio has been seen talking to his sister-in-law when his brother's not home. He's now called Happy Mauro. He skips down the streets while he whistles—if you believe the rumours."

The Signora recounted the goings-on as if part of a melodrama: swooning and covering her eyes all while fanning herself with the cash.

While she pressed creases out of a newly finished garment, I opened my mouth several times to ask a question playing on my mind, but my words stuck.

"Five o'clock," she announced. "You've worked hard, Mariella. Thanks to you we've made money today."

I covered my workstation with a sheet. "Signora." I said, then hesitated. "Did anyone out there say anything about the Carbone family?"

Her face clouded. "No. So, it isn't the lack of clientele worrying you?"

I shook my head.

"Mariella, I don't believe anything's happened to Emilio. Someone would have told us. Bad news is the hottest of currencies."

I reached for the chilli necklace under my blouse. I wanted to prevent bad things happening to Emilio, yet I had conflicting thoughts. If he'd abandoned me without explanation, I hoped for him to suffer.

The weight of fear slowed me down and every step towards home was an effort. Neither the fresh aroma of bergamot oranges nor my fabulous running shoes could lighten my heart. I yelled into the wind, "Come for me now." My message was for the ears of my imaginary wolf. I had no wish to outrun it. Without Emilio, without answers, I welcomed the sharp toothed beast.

I shuffled up the dirt road leading to home, only lifting my head when I heard the soft 'thud-thud-thud' of olives raining on the ground near my shoes. My heart pounded with hope as I searched for the source.

Emilio peered from behind the gnarled great-grand-mother olive tree, a finger pressed to his lips. Urgency hardened his handsome face. "Mariella, I can't stay, so I'm asking you to trust me. There'll be a time for a full explanation, but that will have to wait." Emilio crouched on the ground, his long fingers forming a fist around fallen leaves. "I love you and want you to run away with me."

"You're frightening me."

"Come." He grabbed my hand, pulling me up the hill-side. I held back, but he stopped to kiss me, giving my tired feet wings.

We flew up to sunset rock.

"Listen, Mariella, this is important. What was the name of your school friend? The one whose family moved to Roma."

"Sylvia."

"Do you still write to each other?"

"Not very often. Why?"

"We need an alibi to explain where we've gone. Tell your parents Sylvia has invited you to stay next month. She's asked you to help with something, make up a reason, perhaps you're going to visit the Colosseum."

"Are we running away to Roma?"

"I don't know yet, and if I did, I might not tell you until it's safe. We need a cover." His dark eyes pleaded beneath thick lashes.

"I can say Sylvia has asked me to make her a ball gown. When will we go?"

"Tell your parents you're leaving in exactly two weeks. On a Monday."

"Must it be such a complicated story?"

"If we are to get away without suspicion, we need a believable lie. But the fewer people involved, the safer we'll be."

Once Emilio left, I refused dinner and disappeared to my bedroom. I slid the wooden box from under my bed and reread Sylvia's last letter. I'd shared it with Mamma. It was all about Sylvia meeting the man of her dreams. My heart fluttered as I studied the handwriting. I wiped my sweaty palms between each careful imitation of each word. When my style was similar enough, 'Sylvia' wrote a new letter telling of her romantic, whirlwind engagement. She asked me to be a bridesmaid and help embroidering her wedding dress. My parents knew I'd never refuse such a request.

I tore an old envelope to mask the postage date, then practised my lie until I fell asleep.

"Mamma. Babbo," I said over breakfast. "I picked up a letter from the post office yesterday and read it last night in bed. My friend Sylvia's getting married and wants me to be her bridesmaid. If you don't mind, I'd like to catch the bus up to Roma?"

My voice cracked twice, but my parents didn't notice; they looked over their coffees and smiled, first at me then at each other. I covered my eyes with my long fringe to hide the guilt.

"A trip away will do you good." Mamma nodded rapidly; her eyes bright.

"Of course," Babbo agreed. "Of course."

"A wedding?" Signora Giovanni smiled when I asked her about taking leave. I imagined wheels turning inside her head. "You must design and create the most beautiful bridesmaid dress. I will sew a matching purse and we will fill it with appointment cards."

What had I done? Now Signora Giovanni hoped this wedding would revive the failing business. I searched for words to make this right.

"Too tacky?" she asked.

"It's not that," I said. "It's just that Sylvia's already chosen a bridesmaid dress for me. It won't be perfect, but it's her wedding."

Signora Giovanni held her hand over her mouth. "How terrible of me. Of course ... could we make her a going-away dress? A present from both of us."

I had mistakenly thought, by practising and preparing, I'd be ready to answer all questions without wavering, but it wasn't a matter of remembering words—emotions came into play. I squirmed in my seat; it was far from easy lying to the face of someone who trusted me to tell the truth.

Over the next week, I worked extra hard for Signora Giovanni, supplying more dresses than she could sell from the rack outside.

"I'm going to miss you, Mariella," she said. "We're quite a team."

I wrapped her in a bear hug, holding it too long.

She narrowed her eyes. "Are you okay?"

"Of course," I lied.

The one thought easing my guilt was Signora Giovanni not having to agonise over the shop-takings or worry about covering my wage. I doubted she'd have sacked me. Instead, she would continue paying me out of her own savings, leaving herself with less for retirement. Departing was an easier option. Once she discovered I wasn't returning, she wouldn't replace me.

Four days, three hours, and twenty-two minutes before I was due to leave Scilla and meet up with Emilio, I watched the Signora show the latest batch of dresses to an older woman, full of broad smiles and bubbly chatter. The Signora peered at me through the window display, a frown was etched in her usually smooth forehead.

When she came inside and headed straight for my work-bench, I busied myself. "Did you recognise that woman?" She leaned on her elbows; her mouth twisted in a way that didn't bode well.

"No," I answered honestly.

"She just bought a lovely dress for her granddaughter, Sylvia. It's her birthday. She's visiting Sylvia in Roma this very weekend. A birthday get-together. Does any of this ring a bell?"

The Signora touched the side of my neck with her index finger, but may as well have wrapped her hands around my throat.

I could barely whisper, "I promised. I promised Emilio not to tell."

"You are lucky Sylvia's grandmother isn't blabbing to the whole town. The Ndrangheta have ears."

I dropped my shoulders, resting my head on the pooled fabric. "Does she know I lied?"

"Sit up," she said, shaking my arm. "I didn't tell her or anyone about your make-believe trip. But someone will find out. They always do."

Chapter Sixteen

Maria, Present Day

Dermot tries to give me his phone. "Maria, it's your Joey. He wants to know when we're taking our next break."

I look around for my son. Didn't Dermot just say Joey was here? He shakes the phone and my mind finds sense where moments ago there was none. "Joey is on the phone? Has he been reading the story?"

"I'm not sure. I always give the transcript to Izzy. You can ask him yourself. He's waiting outside."

I'm about to say no, but Dermot heads for the door.

Will this turn out badly? Will Emilio let me down? I run my hand over my blouse, trying to grasp the chilli necklace Mamma gave me. Instead, I catch my reflection in the window. I'm an old lady now. Mamma's protective necklace has long turned to dust.

There's no more Emilio. Instead, Joey stands with his hands in his pockets and looks from me to Izzy, then

Dermot. "Mum? I have a question. I'm trying to find photographs and documents to add to your memoirs, but the only thing I've found is this."

He holds up a black-and-white photo of the ancient olive tree. My Italian family smiles at the camera. He points to a lovely young woman. "Is this you?"

"*Si.*"

He points to my parents. "What are their names?"

"Mamma. Babbo."

"Their real names?"

I clutch at my empty chest again. There is nothing to protect me from the lies I have told. The lies I keep telling. "Mamma. Babbo." I repeat with a shrug. I know I'm hiding something, but I'm not sure what.

"What was your last name?"

I wait for Dermot to translate, even though I know exactly what Joey said.

"Blake," I reply.

"Your name back then?" Joey points to a carefree young woman in a picture. "Your maiden name?"

"Maria Blake. I am Maria Blake."

Joey sighs and looks pleadingly at Izzy.

My mouth wants to say my other name and the deception makes me feel helpless. I rub my chest again.

Izzy presses fingers to my wrist. "You feeling okay, Maria?" she asks gently. "Pulse is normal... Dermot, can you ask her if she has chest pain?"

"*Non!*" I say.

No pain in my chest, but a pain burns my soul.

Colour leaches from Joey's face and he cracks his knuckles. I reach to comfort him, but Izzy gets there first. Good. At least Joey has someone to turn to.

"*Sto bene.*" I say. I am good. Maybe it's not a sin if deception is for a good purpose. To protect my son.

Izzy smooths my hair. "You're probably just tired, but
I'll get the duty doctor to check you out."

Chapter Seventeen

Joe, Present Day

Izzy flops into the chair to read her memoir notes. At first, I think she's tired, then I worry her creased forehead is concern for Mum.

"Do you think my mum's okay?" I ask.

"I'm not worried. Her colour and vital signs were good. The doctor will check her out thoroughly."

Although I'm not religious, I make the sign of the cross on the palm of my hand. Mum would appreciate that.

Izzy sits upright. "The big pity is, I didn't get a chance to ask Maria more details. She didn't describe the Calabrian marketplace at all. I'll have to invent bits."

"Mum told me a little about it. Long time ago."

Izzy clicks the pen, armed and ready to write, then stabs it in the air towards me. "Spill."

"It was a long time ago." I close my eyes to remember. "I imagined a medley of spices, riotous colour, and a patchwork of voices competing with each other as they yelled to customers on the dirt walkway between stalls."

Izzy stares. At me. Not with glassy-eyed boredom, but with a jaunty, interested eyebrow. It's not every day an average Joe like me gets a look like that. Especially not from a woman like Izzy.

"What?" I ask.

"You're rather poetic."

"A fluke." I shrug, disappointed in myself. "A bit like numbers coming up in the lottery, a lucky combination."

"I'm not buying it, Joe." Izzy waggles her finger. "You've got essential anecdotal information, and you've a nice way of saying it."

Blood rushes to my head and I re-tie my shoelaces so she won't see how red my ears are.

"Do you know what the Strega looked like?" Izzy asks, scribbling furiously.

"Not a physical description, but Mum was terrified of her. She told me of the curses, and how she felt rather than saw the Strega's evil. She reckoned it trespassed throughout her body like a thin bony hand stealing the joy."

"That's it," Izzy says throwing the pen then squeezing her fist at her chest like a thumping heart. "We're banned from the room anyway, so let's tell Dermot and Maria we're working offsite. I think we should write this memoir together."

I tie my shoelace again. This time to hide the smile.

Chapter Eighteen

Mariella, Italy, 1966

My feet were restless whenever I was forced to sit still, but they were much worse the day I waited outside our farm gate for Uncle Tonito. It was as if Gaia, our Mother Earth, quaked the ground.

I gripped my suitcase handle, eyes on the road, waiting for my uncle to drive me to work. From there I would catch the afternoon bus out of Scilla and into my new life.

"You must be excited." Tonito said, stowing my case in the boot. "Young ladies love weddings. Perhaps, you will catch the bouquet?" He winked and tugged at my hair like he used to when I was small, making my forced laughter a more uneasy betrayal.

Fortunately, he spent the entire drive talking about soccer, and Italy reaching the finals in the Intercontinental Cup. While he chatted happily, I went over my plans. I'd walk to the bus stop at four and catch a one-way trip to Palmi. There, Emilio would meet me and take me to the secret picnic place by the river where we planned to hide overnight. Only then would he reveal the next leg of our journey.

Scilla's main street was barely wide enough for scooters, so Tonito parked his car a block away from the shop. He insisted on carrying my suitcase to the corner.

As we hugged goodbye, he said, "Have a wonderful trip. You deserve it."

I slipped him an envelope. "Please keep this safe. Open it and explain everything to Mamma and Babbo the day before I'm due back."

I walked off quickly, suitcase in hand, but Tonito followed.

"Mariella, I don't know what you're up to, but secrecy is rarely a good idea."

"I have no choice."

"There is always a choice," he whispered. "Talk to me."

"I can't tell you. Not yet. But you'll understand when I do."

Tonito was still arguing when Signora Giovanni opened the shop door. He closed his mouth, waved goodbye, then turned away. She raised her eyebrows questioningly and beckoned me inside.

"So?" she asked. "What's going on? I told you secrets don't stay hidden. I've never seen Tonito look so concerned."

I shrugged without answering.

"I know this is about you and Emilio? What excuses, erm...lies, has he given his parents and boss?"

"Signora," I hung my head. "I am sorry for not telling the truth. I don't know what Emilio told his family, but he seriously begged me to be careful about saying anything at all."

"I bet he did. You're not just dipping your toes in the Ndrangheta pond now, Mariella. You're jumping in feet first and eyes closed. You won't know what you've gotten into until the water is over your head."

"I'm sorry," I repeated. "I know you disapprove of dishonesty, but I didn't want to involve others in my lie."

"I might not approve of what you're doing," she said gently, "but I understand completely. It's been twenty years since my husband died and I would tell a thousand lies to spend another day in his arms." Her voice cracked, and she covered her eyes.

My chin quivered. "Oh, Signora, that is so long to grieve."

"Grief never ends." She wiped away her tears, then rubbed her hands brusquely, as if moving on. "But we can live life beyond grief. Come on, let's make this a good day."

I unrolled swathes of fabric across the workbench and took out my design sketches, showing the Signora a simple shift dress I'd sketched during my anxious, sleepless night. "This pattern is so straightforward I can cut two at once and have them finished before I leave."

Signora Giovanni sold clothes outside while I put in a mammoth effort to leave her with extra dresses to appease my guilt.

"It's lunch time," she said, surprising me. "Pack away your stuff."

I studied her face as she took a handful of lira notes from the cash box. But I couldn't read her emotions.

She flashed me a smile. "Go to the Pasticceria. For me, you can buy the cannoli as usual. You choose whatever takes your fancy. Extra strong espressos coming up."

I pushed the money away and she eventually gave in, winking as she pushed me out of the shop. "Okay, you're taking care of the cakes. I'll crack open the special bottle of black coffee liqueur."

The bluest of skies smiled over multi-coloured buildings and flower-filled window boxes as I walked slowly around the block. My chest heaved at the thought of being away from this beautiful, familiar view.

With stacks of sweet treats balanced in my arms, I left the Pasticceria and detoured along the back alleyways. I had two lots of cannoli for the Signora, a slice of limoncello torta for me, and bags of almond biscotti for my parents and uncle. I stopped at the accountancy office where Tonito worked.

He was with a client, but stood as I entered the building. I pressed a finger to my lips, then pointed to the sweet packages left on the table, mouthing, "Thank you. For you, and Mamma, and Babbo."

He held his hand to his heart then blew me a kiss goodbye.

I backed into Signora Giovanni's shop using an elbow to lever the door handle, pasting on my widest smile, pretending this was pure celebration. "I bring wondrous deliciousness. I hope you've poured—"

She raised her eyebrows and cast a sideways glance. "Morning tea will have to wait. We have clients."

I turned to find Nino DeLuca and his daughter Isabella flicking through my wedding design album. My smile disappeared, but I quickly rearranged my face into what I hoped passed for agreeableness, and put down the cakes.

Nino DeLuca coughed onto the back of his forearm, then patted his belly. "None for me, I'm hoping to shed a few pounds."

Isabella prodded her father with obvious affection.

"Don't worry, you will look handsome in the wedding photos."

"Someone getting married?" I asked.

Signora Giovanni turned away, but not quick enough to hide a troubled frown.

"I am." Isabella's face was aglow with more beauty than the sunset over the Tyrrhenian Sea.

"Congratulations." I took a sharp breath.

Nino's mouth skewed into scorn. Widening his stance, he placed his hands on his hips like an arrogant general gloating about sending soldiers to their death.

"Do you want to know the details?" he asked.

I ignored him, pulling more wedding albums from the shelf. "Isabella, you might find the perfect style in one of these."

"Are they your own designs, Mariella?"

"No, but—"

"My daughter insists only you can make her dream gown, that's why we raced over. One of my men told me you were taking a holiday. He saw you with your uncle this morning. Said you were carrying a suitcase."

"Only for two weeks," Signora Giovanni said too loudly. "It will take longer than that to order whatever silk or lace Isabella chooses." She flicked so rapidly through a catalogue; she tore a page. "What style do you have in mind?"

It wasn't just Nino's presence. Something was wrong. The atmosphere hissed of danger.

Isabella fidgeted, looked at her father, then me, before glancing around as if searching for an answer without knowing the question. I felt sick for myself, but sorry for her too.

Nino strode towards me, not covering his mouth as he

cleared his throat. "You haven't asked the name of the groom." Baring his yellow canine teeth, he coughed again.

I desperately wanted to hide, but I resisted the urge to curl up under my workbench. Instead, I lifted my chin, clenching my own teeth to keep them from chattering.

I knew the name of the groom before Nino spoke.

"Emilio Carbone," he spluttered—face thrust at mine— full of foul breath and spittle.

Isabella, ignorant of the unfolding drama, leaned towards me with the conspiratorial familiarity of an old friend. "This is so exciting. I'm marrying Emilio. You must have seen him around Scilla? Don't you think he's the most handsome man you've ever met?" Her sweet whispers were suffocating, but there was no escape. "You know, he's never shown interest in me before, but his family came to dinner last Monday night and left us to talk alone."

She giggled and fluttered her eyelids, covering her pretty mouth like a child.

I wondered if she knew who or what her father really was? And what had she heard about me?

"Perhaps Mariella is feeling jealous?" Nino DeLuca lit a cigarette. "Remember—I have a cousin in Australia you can marry. You must be desperate to be a bride after designing for so many others."

"Outside. Now." Signora Giovanni shooed him towards the door. "Your smoke will discolour the fabrics."

Breathing a half-sigh of relief, I veered the conversation back to the dresses, then using the bookmarked designs for inspirations, I sketched something new. Isabella watched in silence while the power of the pencil carried me away.

By the time Nino coughed his way back into the shop, Isabella had her potential design and a bag filled with swatches of silks, brocades and lace.

I fell into my chair when they left. "There isn't enough time for us to share our farewell afternoon tea. I need to leave."

"You're still going?"

"Yes." I shut down the voices in my head. "This is one of Nino's tricks. I'm not falling for it."

The Signora bit her lip and hugged me. "Take care."

I could barely muster a smile as I waved goodbye. Emilio had failed to confirm our plans. I dragged both my suitcase and feet to the bus stop in town, feeling the weight of Nino, Emilio, Isabella, and the whole blasted Ndrangheta on my shoulders.

Chapter Nineteen

Mariella, Italy, 1966

Once seated at the back of the bus, I scolded myself and forced myself to banish unwelcome thoughts. Emilio would never let me down. He'd made a promise, and he would explain the misunderstanding. He'd meet me at the bus stop in Palmi, and I would direct him to the riverside picnic spot. While it was true that Emilio hadn't told me where we were heading afterwards, I believed he had good reason for his secrecy and for not warning me about Isabella.

I squeezed my fingers until they hurt, but it didn't strangle the doubts.

I'd followed the rules. Surely, he'd follow them, too. Emilio had been definite about me not telling my parents of our plans. I hadn't said a thing to them. I'd written a cryptic message only Tonito would understand. *I'm attending a picnic at Mother Nature's cathedral before travelling on to 'Sylvia's wedding'. I don't know the actual venue, but I'll let you know when I arrive.*

"Excuse me, Signorina, ticket please." The moustachioed conductor took ages to check my ticket even though I'd bought it from him moments ago. "What are your plans in Palmi?"

"I'm changing buses and travelling to Roma."

Uncomfortable about repeating any more lies, I willed him to go away. He stood close until the bus lurched onto the road.

Once he was gone, my thoughts went back to Emilio. He'd been uncharacteristically tight-lipped. I was throwing away my life without hearing the final plan—without knowing exactly what we were up against, or why we needed to hide.

Perhaps Isabella and I were both victims. I felt sorry for her. The euphoric young woman would soon face the worst of deceptions. An arranged marriage that would never take place. She was the perfect mafia wife. Kind and beautiful, yet naïve.

I ran my fingers through my hair and tugged until my scalp hurt. What if Emilio found Isabella too agreeable? She would be the sort of wife who came with a ticket to promotion within the Ndrangheta ranks. I had no plans to become his hidden Mafia mistress while he adored Isabella in public.

The bus followed an ancient tractor, and we travelled slower than I could run. It suited my mood to crawl. With every bend of the road, I grew fearful of reaching Palmi and facing the truth.

Just in case the worst happened, I swallowed my pride and took out my purse to count my savings. If Emilio didn't show, I'd need a back-up plan. I'd search for a cheap hotel and spend a few nights crying to myself before returning home and owning up to the lie.

As we slowed to a stop in the Palmi town square, the bus conductor approached. "I'll carry your bag, Signorina," he said with a wink. "A young woman with your obvious assets should have a man doing *everything* for you."

His emphasis on the word 'everything' made my skin crawl.

A grandmotherly figure struggled with multiple parcels at the front of the bus, and I pointed to her. "I'm strong, Signor, but the lady over there needs help."

Unperturbed, he shrugged and winked. "I have an apartment in Palmi. A comfortable place to stay the night." He cast licentious eyes from my head to my feet.

I had to restrain myself from poking them.

"No need to look at me like that," he said. "I was planning to sleep on the couch."

I pushed past, muttering a silent prayer for Emilio to be waiting on the pavement.

Once I had crossed the road, I spun slowly, scanning the piazza for any sign of him. He wasn't there.

When I could no longer bear the weight of disappointment, I settled on a park bench.

Before long, the bus conductor sauntered over and wiggled his walrus moustache. He'd obviously never tested this gesture in a mirror, or he wouldn't have shown it in public. "I'll keep you company."

"I'm fine, thank you." I looked away in the hope he'd do the same. Instead, he sat beside me. If not for my suitcase, it would have been too close for comfort.

"Many women enjoy my charms."

Deciding he wasn't the hint-taking type, I spoke firmly. "Please go away. I'm waiting for my fiancé."

He pouted his lips into a sloppy half-kiss. "You aren't frightened at all, are you?"

"Yes, I am. I'm terrified. Terrified I'll hit you with my suitcase if you don't stop bothering me."

"No wonder your fiancé stood you up. Your mouthy, snooty attitude would put any man off. I should've known by your fancy clothes you were a woman who doesn't know her proper place."

He snarled and made a rude sign with his hand as he took off. My skin kept crawling long after he disappeared down a side street.

The shadows lengthened and my doubts grew. I spotted a sign advertising *Albergo* hung from chains above a run down *taverno*. The price would be as cheap as the décor. I sighed—there was no point in waiting—it was time to pick myself up and move on.

I'd just grabbed my handbag from my knees when teeth grazed the back of my neck. I whirled, using my bag as a weapon.

Emilio shouted, "It's me." He held his hands in surrender.

"How long have you been in Palmi?" I pressed my palms against my eyelids, trying to stop the welling tears. Deep down, despite telling myself Emilio would come, I'd given up hope. I sagged against my suitcase and sobbed.

"I'm sorry for leaving you alone. I've been hiding since before you got off the bus."

"You left me waiting?"

"I almost ran over to punch the man bothering you, but you, my *Bella*, seemed to have the upper hand. I had to make sure you weren't followed. I'm sorry." He gently kissed each of my fingertips, repeating his apology with every kiss. "*Mi dispiace, mi dispiace ...*"

"I thought you'd abandoned me. Nino came in with Isabella—"

He covered his mouth then pulled me to my feet, taking my suitcase. "Come see the tree where I was hiding."

I braced myself. There wasn't much fighting spirit left. "I'm not looking at anything with you until you explain. Why does Isabella believe she is marrying you?"

He sat down again, his arm around my shoulders. "The DeLuca and Carbone families called a meeting and announced my marriage to Isabella without consulting me first. The poor girl was thrilled, and everyone was hugging and shaking hands. I didn't have the heart to make a scene in front of everyone, so I wrote her a letter and slipped the note under her door."

"Well, she didn't get the message."

Emilio's shoulders sagged. "That's unfortunate, but I'm more concerned about you. Come see the tree."

Carved into a gnarled branch, amongst older graffiti, was a heart with our initials: E.C. and M.B. We smiled at each other through tears.

"Come, we'd better hurry," I said. "I might not be able to find our special spot if we don't get there before dark."

Emilio opened the car door and I sat sideways in the passenger seat, lifting my skirt slightly to show my legs as I swung them slowly inside. His eyes followed every move.

Once out of town, Emilio squeezed my knee. "There's more to tell you, Bella. After the DeLuca's left, my grandparents took me aside. My Nonno said, 'Members of the Ndrangheta follow a strict code. Your grandmother wasn't part of the Ndrine. I could only marry her because she was carrying my child. It is dishonourable to cause a young woman's loss of reputation. The clan would not allow an innocent baby to be born a *bastardo*.' I was never more pleased to follow their rules."

Was Emilio suggesting I become pregnant? I held out my hands in a question.

He nodded. "My grandparents encouraged us to follow the same plan. My Nonna has told my parents I'm taking her to see an eye specialist in Napoli. She'll hide in her bedroom until it's too late for anyone to follow."

Emilio took a hand from the steering wheel and reached to stroke my cheek, his voice low and uncertain. "What do you think? Could your dreams of opening a fashion design business wait?"

I didn't need to think. "Yes. And. Yes."

He weaved his fingers through mine, then squeezed my hand in a silent *ti amo*—I love you.

A rush of love filled my heart and some of the tension floated away. Emilio and I would marry and have children, then later I would open my shop.

I almost missed the camouflaged turnoff, but I didn't care. I loved Emilio, and he loved me and at that moment nothing else mattered.

We drove carefully along the track, parking the car near a clearing at the edge of the stream.

"This place is heaven," Emilio said, as he pulled a blanket from the car. "Even if they realise we're gone, no-one would look for us here. We can camp, and sleep, and ..." He winked at me before continuing." I've brought food for at least two days."

"Where will we sleep?" I asked.

Emilio peered at the night sky through a gap in the canopy. "There are a few clouds, but I don't think it will rain. We can sleep on this blanket under the moonlight."

"Isn't it dangerous?"

"The only predator out here is me."

I turned my head towards the breeze to cool my

blushing cheeks, then, my voice quivering with anticipation, I said what I should have been too scared to say. "I'm not planning on much sleep tonight."

Emilio picked me up and carried me towards the stream.

"Put me down," I said, squeezing his upper arm. "You'll tire yourself."

"I plan to exhaust us both." He flexed his bicep under my fingers and nibbled my ear.

After setting me down on an enormous, flat-topped boulder at the water's edge, he unbuttoned his shirt. He pulled it over his head, and I leaned back onto my elbows, biting my lip as I watched him undress. As he removed each item of clothing, he kept his eyes firmly fixed on mine, and a flush of warmth radiated from my thighs.

The moonlight cast lacy shadows over his naked flesh. In my mind I sketched this demi-God.

His muscular arms lifted me to my feet, and the boulder became my stage. My breathing grew ragged as I slowly removed my clothing, performing to an audience of one. Emilio's enthusiasm for my routine grew blatantly obvious.

We didn't make it to the blanket until much, much later.

"We should sleep," I said, closing my eyes, feeling anything but sleepy as Emilio rested his body against me. Where his skin touched mine, I felt a delectable frisson of pleasure.

"But it's stirring again." His voice was breathy with desire.

Eventually, we slept.

Chapter Twenty

Joe, Present Day

Izzy shows me a photocopied drawing taken from Mum's sketchbook. "Joe, look what we've got today. A real treat. Words and pictures."

The shadowy outline of a naked man makes me not want to know what Mum described.

"From what I can see, this man's in pretty good shape." She laughs wickedly. "Unfortunately, part of his body's obscured."

I angle the picture towards the window of the sunny nook, and grunt. "So, if I'm reading your smile correctly, you're saying this man would get plenty of hits on a dating site. Especially if he displayed this as his profile."

"I'd probably stop for a sneaky look." Izzy winks.

I force a low, throaty laugh. "You haven't shown me your profile picture, yet." I'm pitching it as a throwaway witty line, but it comes dangerously close to lewdness.

"If you're asking me if my profile picture is revealing, then you're completely off track."

I've unintentionally touched on a nerve. I have a talent for not thinking things through. "I'm really sorry. I would never imagine you naked, and not for a minute would I expect you to have a sexy photo."

"Joe. Shut. Your. Mouth. You've already put your foot far enough in it."

I reflect on what I just said. It sounded as if I don't think she's attractive. Best I do as I'm told and shut up.

"Here." Izzy passes me her phone. "You can look at my dating profile. At least then you won't have to imagine it, or block out images that aren't there."

The photo shows a head shot with Izzy wearing a broad-brimmed hat and dark sunglasses. My first thought is—she's trying to go incognito. I keep my opinion to myself. "Can I read your bio?"

"It's in front of you."

I scroll through Izzy's list, pressing my lips in a thin line as I read. I'm speechless.

Hi to all possible matches, I believe it best to be up front and not waste anyone's time.

1. *I'm a nurse, so I'm not your tribe if you believe scientifically proven medical treatment is part of a government conspiracy.*
2. *There are three different forms of 'there/they're/their'...check your grammar before messaging.*
3. *If you need to know my Myer-Briggs personality type to check compatibility, we aren't compatible.*

4. *Finally—Fuck off now if a specific body weight or bra cup size is included in your perfect life partner wish-list.*

I search for words to describe her profile. "It is very honest... Direct... Very straightforward."

"You don't think it's off-putting to be so upfront?"

"Depends on the man or woman reading it. Maybe you could soften it. Just a bit."

She tilts her head to one side. "How?"

"Add some activities you enjoy doing. Like you could write—love Thai food and binge-watching British TV police dramas."

"Do you?" she asks.

"It was an example." I should have made up something unrelated to my own interests. British police dramas probably seem old and odd, and for all I know Thai food is out of fashion.

"Oh, that's a pity. I love Thai food."

My heart does a clumsy somersault. "What about tonight?" I ask, summoning bravery I didn't know I possessed. "We could share Thai food and read through Mum's latest addition to her memoir. It would be a double duty..." I bite my tongue just in time to stop myself saying the word date.

"Why not make it a triple duty event?" she asks. "We can eat the food, read the pages, and practise our first date questions in case anyone ever clicks on our profiles. That's unless you have to be home early to watch episodes of Inspector Morse, or feed Biscotti?"

I rack my brains for something witty to say, but take too long and the moment's lost.

"I've an idea," she says. "Take a picture of the dog. Animals improve your chances with women. My kooky aunt once argued Hitler wasn't all bad because she'd seen a picture of him with his German Shepherd, Blondi." Izzy laughs until tears sparkle on her fluttery eyelashes.

It takes effort to keep my voice steady. "About tonight. Name the time and place." I sit straight-backed and composed. Then her smile does a crooked little quiver, and I melt.

Izzy marches down the corridor, throwing words over her shoulder. "I'll text you."

Chapter Twenty-One

Mariella, Italy, 1966

Wearing only a sated smile, I reached for my lover, thinking he'd called my name. But he was still sleeping. Then I heard what had disturbed me. A rumbling along the track.

I sat bolt upright to the bright lights cutting through the leafy darkness and shielded my eyes.

A car.

The headlights went out, and I frantically pulled on my dress. "Wake up. Wake up, Emilio," I whispered.

He stirred and reached for his clothes while my eyes adjusted to the dark. I sighed. Uncle Tonito's car, soccer-team flag dangling from the aerial.

Emilio hastily dressed. "What's happening?"

"Just my uncle," I said. "He's read the note and come to talk us out of it. I'll send him away."

"Mariella! He wasn't supposed to open it."

Instead of stopping to argue, I stormed to Tonito's driver's door, shaking my fist. It took a second to register the fear in his eyes and the blood-stained handkerchief tied around his head.

From the back-seat; a hacking cough and flashing blade. My uncle mouthed a single word. "Run."

I was stuck in terror-induced paralysis, until Emilio's voice sliced through the dark. "Mariella!"

I heard and felt his footsteps behind me. Then, with a fierce grip, he seized my arm. The pain jolted me into action.

He towed me towards the stream and we ran into the water. Nino followed along the bank, moving quicker than his physique suggested.

We side-stepped boulders with nothing but moonlight to guide us. Nino, never far behind, yelled at us to stop.

Emilio lost his footing and fell into the water. I pulled him up by his shirt, painfully aware of Nino gaining ground.

"Stop!" Nino called. "You can't run forever. Your mother demands you come home."

We kept moving, losing sight of Nino upstream, where the bushes grew thick and impassable. My lungs burned as I gasped for air, but I didn't dare slow down. I had no intention of letting that *bastardo* catch us.

Nino's voice boomed through the dark. "I wouldn't like to be Mariella's uncle. He's already lost half an ear."

An image of Tonito's bloodied ear twisted my heart strings. I crouched to splash water on my face. I caught my breath and my thoughts. "We have to go back."

Emilio rubbed his knees as if he was in pain. "We can't. Nino has a knife."

I scrambled around to find a weapon-worthy stone. "If we cut through to the road without Nino seeing us, we can loop around to the track and the cars. Back to help Tonito."

"What then?" Emilio raked his fingers through his hair.

I choked on a tearless sob. "We have to do something."

"What if your uncle Tonito has already driven away?"

"He wouldn't. He would stay and die rather than abandon me."

"You go, but take care," Emilio said. "I'll distract Nino while you help your uncle. Drive him to Palmi, and wait for me there."

"But what about..."

"Go. Once Nino has followed me upstream, I'll double-back to my car." He kissed my forehead and pushed me gently towards the river bank. "Wait for me in Palmi, behind the tree with our carved initials."

Twigs and leaves gave way to a harder surface, moonlight illuminating the road ahead. Rough gravel scoured my feet, so I moved to the spindly grass growing on the shoulder. There, I broke into an easier stride, all the while clutching my rock.

Once along the track leading to the river, I slowed. Uncle Tonito's car hunched in the shadows near Emilio's. Under the dim light, I made out the shadow of a man slumped over the bonnet.

"Tonito." I gasped with relief when he stood and groaned. "Get into the car. I'll drive."

I draped one of Tonito's arms around my shoulder, ready to help him to the passenger door, but he shrugged me away and stumbled backwards.

The car door opened from inside. "You are not going anywhere." I recognised her voice before I saw her. My head boiled with fury at the shrill sound of the Strega.

"Out of my way," I said, the rock above my head ready to smash her skull. I had no intention of allowing her to hurt Tonito again.

"Don't, Mariella." Tonito's voice bled into the night. "Get in the car. We're leaving."

"You can't get away from me," Strega Carbone snarled. "I curse you. I curse your family." She pushed me as she climbed out, and the blood in my veins ran cold.

I lunged for a handful of her greying hair, twisting it to hold her still. The rock in my other hand poised to strike. "There will be no cursing when you're dead."

"Drop it!"

I looked up to find Nino and Emilio less than ten feet away, Emilio's hands bound behind his back. Nino shoved him forwards.

Emilio struggled, but after a sharp kick to the back of his knee, he fell to the ground. Nino yanked Emilio's head back and held the knife to his throat.

Blood pounded in my temples, making me dizzy. Desperately, I ripped at the Strega's hair and threw the rock wildly at Nino, striking his shoulder.

He barely flinched. Instead, he skimmed the tip of the blade over Emilio's face. "I won't kill him," he shouted. "But Emilio will carry the mark of his defiance for the rest of his life."

I opened my mouth to cry, but the flash of the knife near Emilio's face paralysed my voice. I fixed my eyes on Nino. As if in slow motion, he slashed my love's forehead and ran the blade across his cheek. "Pretty girls won't chase him now, and his eyes won't be tempted by a *puttana* like you."

Emilio lifted his face, and shook his head slowly. "Go with your uncle, Mariella. Go home."

The moon shone on blood dripping from Nino's blade. "Tomorrow I'll lay down my terms. Don't worry, girlie. You will agree."

My shoulders sagged, and I released the Strega. Then I clutched my chilli necklace with trembling hands.

Strega Carbone's light-coloured eyes were filled with malice. "Your amulet is useless; I've already won. Ask your mother. She knows my power."

"You've paid an enormous price, too," I said. "I may not get to keep your son, but you have lost his love."

I dropped to my knees and started crawling towards Emilio, but Tonito lifted me by the waistband of my dress and hauled me to the car. When I kicked him to get away, he slapped my cheek and shoved me into the passenger seat. The engine squealed into life and drowned my whimpering.

I forced myself not to look back.

"I am so sorry." Tonito's raspy voice was barely audible. "Threats towards me meant nothing, but I couldn't ignore it when they threatened to kill your mother and warned of what they would do to you."

I closed my eyes, wishing I could open them to a different reality. "Nino's men must have seen you holding the note," I said. "I should have listened to Emilio, and kept our secret."

"Even without a note, they would have hounded me. They would have cut off both ears. Then what?"

We drove to Scilla in silence.

A few miles before my parents' farm, Tonito made the turn to his own house. "I'll phone a doctor and change out of my blood-stained clothes. No need to alarm my sister more than we need to."

As we waited for the doctor to arrive, neither my uncle nor I spoke a word, but my mind spoke plenty. It shouted echoes of guilt. My actions had endangered the people I loved.

"What have you done here?" the doctor asked, carefully removing the dried blooded handkerchief, revealing Tonito's partially severed earlobe. "I can't guarantee the success of re-attachment, but I can clean it up and stitch it back. I will leave the rest to God and Lady Luck."

Once the doctor had gone, Tonito swallowed the pain killers. "Come, Mariella, it is almost dawn and we need to catch your father before he sets out."

I took deep breaths as he approached our family farm. From behind the mountains, a hint of pink sunlight burnished the stonework of my home. Tonito swerved to avoid my suitcase in the middle of the driveway. It looked as if it had been thrown from a distance; the clasps had broken, the seams were burst open, and its gaping mouth had vomited my belongings.

"They've already been here." My voice shook.

Tonito shook his head. "No, they hurled it from the car."

I wanted to race to the door, but at the same time I wanted to run and hide.

"Mamma. Babbo." I called. My clammy hands slipped from the door handle.

"Is that you, Mariella?" My mother's voice hummed above the pounding in my ears. She tightened the belt of her old dressing gown. "Why are you here? What happened?"

"Sit, Mamma. Uncle and I have something to tell you."

Babbo crept from the bedroom, his shoulders trembling. Mother's eyes widened as she stared at Tonito's bandaged ear.

"It is Strega Carbone," Mamma said. "I can feel it."

She set her face for revenge and Babbo tried to hide his weeping. They listened silently as we explained.

"Nino DeLuca will be here soon," I said. "He has a proposal."

"A demand." Tonito bared his teeth.

Babbo clung to my hand as I sniffled. I gripped him tightly, never wanting to let go.

Mamma stood. "I will make breakfast." Her outward calm would have fooled most people. We knew otherwise, but we followed her lead, bumping into each other to help in the tiny kitchen, busying ourselves during the nightmare wait.

When Nino arrived, he was alone, and he wore the same superior expression on his mission to ruin people's lives as he used when demanding a minor alteration to his trousers. His voice was firm with the knowledge he couldn't be refused.

"You were given poor advice," he said, coughing over the basket of bread in the middle of the table. "Emilio's grandparents are living in the past. Fifty years ago, Emilio might have been allowed to marry a pregnant woman outside the family, but not these days. Let's hope you aren't with child."

I stared first at my feet and then at the serrated knife. If I sliced Nino's throat, would the others help me carry his body up the mountain?

"Are you listening?" he asked, reaching into his shirt pocket to pull out documents and a photograph I'd seen before. "My cousin, Angelo Morellini. He is still in the market for a wife, and now I have one to offer."

Babbo pushed back the chair. "No," he emphasised his second, "No" by pounding a fist on the table.

Nino sneered. "This is not negotiable. Mariella must

leave Scilla. In fact, Emilio's mother will not settle for anything less than her leaving the country."

Despite my revulsion, I grabbed Nino's hand. "But I promise I will never speak to Emilio again if you let me stay with my parents."

"If not for Signora Carbone perhaps I could be convinced, but she would rather you die. I've convinced her a move to Australia is as good as death. It's the only way."

Nino unfolded the papers. Permission for a proxy marriage, dated for one week's time.

"It will take months and months to organise emigration paperwork," I said.

"I have contacts. You will embark on the voyage to Australia soon."

I blinked back tears and held my chin high. "It seems I'm attending a wedding after all."

Chapter Twenty-Two

Joe, Present Day

I check my reflection in the Thai restaurant's front window. I pull my polo shirt out of my jeans, only to tuck it straight back in. In the quarter hour I've waited, I've done this several times. "Joe," I warn myself. "This is not a romantic date, so why do you care what Izzy thinks?"

My inbuilt clock tells me there's ten minutes until our meeting time, but I check my phone, anyway. Eleven minutes. My brain is running fast.

It is unthinkable for me not to arrive early—my dad's mum, Granny Blake, was a font of life advice. *A man should never keep a woman waiting. It sends a message of abandonment.* I remind myself, it's not a romantic date. But I do feel protective of Izzy.

I fiddle with the shirt again and hear Izzy's voice from several metres away. "Shirt's better out," she booms.

"Hi." I hold out my right hand, hoping she can't see my red ears from this distance.

"A handshake? This isn't a job interview, Joe. What about a platonic hug?"

I consider a full bearhug and hearty back-slap, but opt for the cardboard-cut-out version—me resting a self-conscious hand on her shoulder, standing too far away to lean in. Being hug-phobic is like standing on the edge of a cliff, where there's a niggling impulse to leap off. What if my body gets too close, and I have the urge to squeeze her—or worse—kiss her?

Izzy's staring at me. Oh, God. I hope she can't read minds.

"I'd offer a penny for your thoughts," she says, "but then I'd sound like the old people at The Figs. I've picked up heaps of their sayings."

"If you have an actual penny, I'll tell you. But I don't accept modern currency."

Izzy laughs as she shrugs. "I don't have a penny, so your thoughts are safe. For now, anyway."

The server leads us to a table in the corner. I read somewhere it's less intimidating to sit beside someone instead of opposite, so I take a seat next to Izzy and immediately regret it. We're the only people in the restaurant not facing each other.

Izzy doesn't seem worried. She's busy studying the menu. Her eyelashes look longer up close.

"I've no idea how to pronounce half these dishes," I say. "Or the name of the restaurant."

Izzy smiles, so I pull out the opening conversation I'd rehearsed earlier. I figured word puns might be a hit with a writer, so I Google searched amusing names for Thai eateries. "They could have given the restaurant a wittier name like *Suit and Thai* or *Tongue Thai'd*."

She chuckles. "Funny and clever. An excellent combination."

Accepting Izzy's compliment is dishonest, but I do it with a nod.

"What first, Joe? Your mum's memoirs or practising dating questions?"

I'm jolted back to reality. If Izzy improves her dating profile, this dinner will be the first and last. "Let's get the questions over and done with."

"Izzy sits up like it's an official interview. "Right. What do you do in your spare time?"

"I visit my mother in the nursing home and..."

She holds her hand up so fast it's a blur, like in those old martial art films. "Stop! If there isn't a rule about grown men not mentioning their mother on the first date, there should be."

"Okay. I've started growing pesticide-free veggies. And it seems I've got a green thumb."

Izzy's mouth twitches, then she forces a smile. "Does gardening run in your family?"

I twist an invisible key, locking my lips shut before chucking it dramatically over my shoulder.

"What are you doing?"

I shrug. "You said not to mention my mother."

Izzy slaps the table and cracks up, laughing. I join in and the server stares at us as if we're on drugs when he plonks the shared platters between us.

Izzy piles food high on her plate. None of that silly pickiness or denying herself the pleasure of eating. Mum would approve of Izzy filling her belly. Italians love food-lovers. But I won't mention Mum.

Between courses we swap roles and I ask Izzy the question I thought up in the shower. "What qualities does your ideal partner have?"

"The same things everyone likes, I suppose. Tolerant, cares about other people, can laugh at themselves, and mature enough to look after their own finances. That's mostly it, except I have some petty hates."

"Like what?"

"Really annoying habits. Might be harmless, but get right under my skin."

I wonder about the knuckle cracking, but push it away. "For instance?"

"I went on a couple of dates with a nice enough man who said he was always romantic, not pacifically on Valentimes Day. Pacifically? Valentimes? I could have overlooked one, but two mis-words in one sentence was a deal-breaker."

I come up with an annoying example and smile to myself as I speak. "I borrowed a book from the lie-berry this morning. You might enjoy it; it's all about new-cu-lar energy."

Izzy splutters and chokes on her food as she laughs, so I give her a seriously good back slap. "Should I give you the Heimlich manoeuvre?"

She giggles and coughs intermittently but holds her hand in a clear stop signal. Then her face clouds over. "In all seriousness, I have a deal-breaking nasty habit of my own."

Expecting another joke, I get ready with a high-five hand, but she bites her lip and leafs through Mum's memoir papers.

In the minute and a half where I wait for her to speak, I run through an inventory of possibilities for this habit: Talking through the important bits of TV shows. Biting the end of someone else's pencil. Staring into the fridge for ages and letting cold air escape.

Izzy sighs and looks at me seriously. "I'm a smoker, and I'm not trying to give up."

"Oh." I crack my knuckles under the table and wonder what to say. "At least you're not a quitter."

Izzy's smile returns. "Four cigarettes a day," she says. "And I thoroughly enjoy each one of them."

The smoking doesn't bother me, but my gut churns thinking about her health.

"Don't look so worried, Joe. I had a friend who was a fitness fanatic, and he died from a heart attack at thirty-three. When your time's up, it's up."

My eyebrows raise involuntarily at the thought of a nurse having such a blasé attitude towards health. I pat my stomach. "Speaking of fitness, I better not eat another bite."

Izzy laughs. "We've both done enough eating and more than enough pretend dating. Is it too late for the memoirs?" She reaches for her phone.

"10:15 ish, I reckon."

Izzy checks. "10:19! Did you just look?"

"No. Lucky guess."

Izzy gives me a seated bow. "Greetings, Time Lord."

The server hovers, then clears the table when I give him a nod.

"The bill, please," Izzy says loudly, then changes to a whisper as he disappears into the back. "They want to get rid of us. We better not stay and hold them up while reading Maria's stories."

"Tomorrow, then."

The air is cooler outside and I rub my hands together. "Can I walk you to your car?"

"I'm fine. I live around the corner."

She probably walks alone all the time. I check the

streets—they're well-lit and no one's around. "If it's okay, I'll watch you and wait for a text telling me you're safe."

Izzy smiles. "You know what? Come with me, we can read the memoirs at my place."

Despite my overfull belly, I walk along the street with a spring in my step.

At the bottom of the apartment complex stairs, I ask, "Am I allowed to mention Mum once we're inside?"

"Do whatever you want. There's no need to impress me. We're not dating."

Ouch. I fill in the awkwardness with a running commentary on the amount of metal needed for stair-rails, the non-slip quality of the tiles, the longevity of window tinting. I'm a monotone version of David Attenborough expounding the quality and quantity of building materials.

Izzy smiles when she steps inside. She fills her entire apartment with a glow that leaves no space for disappointment.

She flops into an oversized, overstuffed armchair. "I'm dying to know what prompted your mother to draw a naked man."

I pull a dining chair next to her. "I'll skim read the love scenes, thanks. A lot of Thai food went down, and I wouldn't want it coming back up."

We read side-by-side. Izzy finishes reading her copy before I'm halfway through. She rests her hand on mine. "Maybe you shouldn't read the rest, Joe." With a different tone, this could be a come-on. But this is an unmistakable warning.

"I can't stop now. Mum and this Emilio fellow are in the middle of running up a stream to escape a Mafia boss."

Izzy grimaces.

"I've already survived reading a love scene between my mother and some thug. What could be worse?"

She hesitates a moment, then stands. "If you're sure. I'll go make coffees."

My fingers tremble as I read the last page. "No wonder Mum kept it to herself," I call into the kitchen. "I'd be happier if she was retelling a movie. The thought of her living through this is tough."

Izzy hands me a mug. "Mmmmm. Your father isn't Emilio. But he's not Angelo Morellini either?"

"No. Dad was Australian."

"I'm invested now, Joe," she says. "Let's hope Dermot gets the rest of the story."

Chapter Twenty-Three

Mariella, Italy, 1967

My final days in Italy were unbearable—hours were filled with Mamma crying about me going away, and Babbo cursing the unfairness of it all.

Over the years, Babbo saved the largest branches pruned from great-Nonna's olive tree. He'd planned to build a family table from the seasoned wood. There'd be no large table to feed his future grandchildren. Instead, he turned it into a seaworthy trunk, a vessel to carry his dreams away.

Babbo called me over to show me the finished box. His eyes glistened.

My throat tightened as I touched the waxed timber. I wanted to climb inside and hope someone on the ship would push me overboard.

Nino originally placed me under house arrest on the farm, but I begged him to let me go to work. Preparing myself mentally for an unknown future was exhausting enough without putting on a brave face for them.

When he agreed, I uttered a soft thank you to God. But there was cruelty in his change of mind. Every morning for weeks, Nino picked me up from home and delivered me to the dress shop. He posted a soldier outside. There was no way Emilio could get to me, or I to him.

My heart raced with grief as I pinned intricate lace sleeves to the ruched bodice of the wedding dress. When I compared the garment to my original sketch, a fat tear landed on the page, causing the ink across the bride's face to bleed. My drawing of a woman in mid catwalk twirl, once resembled me, but now all I could see was Isabella. With every stitch the garment became more hers than mine. My tear-blurred eyes made sewing more difficult. After the tenth attempt to thread a needle, I collapsed into sobs on the workbench at the betrayal.

Signora Giovanni touched my shoulder gently and swore, "*Maledetto bastardo*, DeLuca is damned."

I almost laughed through tears at such bad words leaving her mouth.

"Forcing you to make a dress for your own proxy wedding is bad enough. Sewing Isabella's gown, too, is despicable."

At the mention of the proxy wedding, a knot formed in my stomach. I'd hoped for a private closed affair, but the Ndrangheta considered a public spectacle the perfect opportunity to advertise the dire consequences of disobedience. Those *bastardos* had ripped my dreams of an intimate wedding from my chest. I felt desperate and hollow.

Signora Giovanni wrapped her arms around me. "Put the sewing down. Leave Isabella's dress for me to finish. As for your gown, wear the one from our window display. No one else could look as beautiful in it as you. After the wedding, I will burn it and imagine Nino DeLuca as a devil in the fire. Use your last days here to sew yourself an outfit. You may as well be the most stylish woman in Australia." She kissed the top of my head. "Wait here."

The Signora hurried upstairs, and I listened to her tapping footsteps on the floor above.

She returned holding a parcel. "I have a gift. I've thought about this whole situation—too much, if I'm honest."

"You've done enough for me already."

"It will help you." She undid the string and showed me the pile of textiles—a folded length of silk, pieces of Chantilly lace, gauze bags of miniature pearl beads, and reels of golden embroidery thread, the whole tied with white ribbon. "I can't bear to think of you forced into a marital bed with a man you've barely met." When she fanned out the fabric, I saw the makings of an Angel's gown. "Tell Nino's cousin, Angelo, that to be truly happy you must fulfil your wedding dream. This includes sewing your own dress and marrying him properly in the local church. It will buy you a little extra time."

I ran the pearl beads nervously through my fingers.

"I'll miss all your talk of Greek and Roman gods," Signora Giovanni said. "I chose the pearls because of the story you told of Aphrodite."

"Aphrodite?" My throat tightened.

"Forced by Zeus to marry someone...?"

"Hephaestus," I said.

"Why was she forced?"

"Jealousy. Aphrodite's carnal desire for men interrupted peace between gods."

The Signora took a long slow breath. "What was this Hephaestus like?"

"Unpleasant, cunning and deformed."

When she began to cry, my stomach heaved, and I raced past Nino's guard in the laneway to throw up. I would be forced into the bed of a man I didn't love.

I begged Mamma to stay away from the proxy ceremony. The sight of her only child being sold and transported would be too cruel to bear. My own pain lessened when she agreed. I'd have a better chance of staying composed without her attendance. And I had no intention of allowing DeLuca to claim mine and mother's tears as a win.

As I climbed out of Uncle Tonito's car, Signora Giovanni rearranged the lace train of my dress. The Signora was right. The many townsfolk stationed outside the church eyed me up and down like seagulls ready to pounce on a crust of bread. Emilio wasn't among them. No knight in shining armour to save me.

I took a deep breath and imagined the wedding gown as a suit of armour, then I readied to march into battle.

Babbo opened the heavy ecclesiastical door, then offered his arm for the walk down the aisle,

It was a relief to find the church unadorned: neither ribbons nor flowers. Babbo whispered as we walked over the flagstone hearth, "Shine, Mariella. Shine."

Last Sunday, our priest preached about light, explaining how it could illuminate the good or cast shadows for evil to hide. The trick was to shine your own light bright enough there could be no darkness.

I nodded hesitatingly at Babbo. I didn't think it possible, but I would try.

Lifting my chin high, I conjured my most dazzling smile

—one I hoped screamed *I will not allow darkness to win.* God, alone, knew the light wasn't real.

The guests turned and whispered to their friends. The fallen woman had arrived.

Babbo's arm trembled as we walked slowly—one foot in front of the other, to the beat of music more fitting for a funeral. The murmuring crowd grew silent when the priest made the sign of a cross.

My proxy groom stood at the altar. Nino DeLuca. This choice was calculated heartlessness, but I refused to dim the light.

"All stand." The priest raised his arms. Most of his words were a blur, until he said, "If anyone objects to this marriage, then speak now or forever hold your peace."

The congregation quivered as one, shuffling their feet as they turned to the church doors. But the only objections were those screaming inside my head.

The ceremony continued, and I repeated when prompted: offered my solemn vow to be a faithful wife, a partner in sickness and in health, in joy as well as sorrow. I promised all this to a man I'd never met.

Nino coughed as he pushed the wedding ring over my finger, his proximity and his touch bringing bile to the back of my throat. I forced back my fear and hoped God forgave my dishonesty when my voice echoed. "For as long as we both shall live."

Chapter Twenty-Four

Mariella, Italy, 1967

Before catching the ferry from Italy's mainland to Sicily, my family and I attended church together—for the last time. After the service, Signora Giovanni and Signor Gallucci hugged me goodbye. I held them far too long, delaying the inevitable loss of losing my friends.

The Signora sighed. "I saw Emilio."

My heart raced with hope. "Did he send a message?"

"He didn't speak, but I saw his scar. Not too horrific. Typical—the man's punishment is always lighter than the woman's."

I didn't respond. She never liked Emilio and didn't understand the depth of our love. No point convincing her, or anyone, now.

Signor Gallucci sheepishly handed me a patchworked leather handbag. "A small farewell present." He unbuttoned one of the two compartments to show a collection of shells and salt crystals. "There's a letter in the other side, a card, too. Instructions on appeasing Poseidon in case of rough weather. There's a chant to say as you throw the shells overboard."

I choked back tears. "Thank you."

As we boarded the ferry, my heart beat high in my throat, with hope of Emilio turning up with a miraculous plan to rescue me—or at least a goodbye.

Mamma, Babbo, Tonito, and I acted as players in a pantomime, each voice artificially cheerful. We pretended this was a grand adventure, with me setting off to explore the world. But when we reached Messina, and the blue funnels and white stars of the Achille Lauro passenger ship loomed, the performance ended. Mamma wept in public, and Babbo trembled like a lost child.

"Don't cry Mamma. I'm sure Angelo will be kind." I touched my nose to hers so she wouldn't see the doubt. "Once we're married, perhaps we can complete immigration papers. You and Babbo can move to Australia."

Mamma kissed my cheeks twice, but her crying worsened.

"My new husband and I will make grandbabies." I held her tight, feeling her sobs against my chest.

Babbo held us both, until Mamma broke the hug and forced a brave face. "The wind is ruining your beautiful curls." She smiled sadly, combing my hair with her fingers.

Babbo pressed his cheek against mine and I wasn't sure whether the tears were his or mine. "We will write to each other."

The deep horn of the Achille Lauro vibrated in my chest. This was both the dreaded call to walk up the gangplank and a call that couldn't come soon enough. I didn't want to leave, but I couldn't delay the deep hurt that was the inevitable severing of family ties.

I clutched my passport and papers as the horn blasted again. "I'll wave from the deck."

Clenching my teeth in a self-protective smile, I watched my parents through binoculars as they searched for me along the crowded railing. Flocks of paper streamers unrolled and flew through the air, everyone screaming as they tried to catch the particular strip of paper thrown by loved ones. A fragile connection for both those leaving and those left behind.

My heart almost stopped when Emilio appeared, standing a head taller than my family. The scar, though red and angry, did not ruin his beautiful face. I scanned the crowd for Nino DeLuca. What else might he do to Emilio if he found out?

His eyes locked on mine and a blue streamer unravelled from his hand and twisted its way towards me. I lunged, desperate to grasp the paper thread joining me to Emilio's touch. The breeze changed direction, whipping the streamer beyond my reach. I leapt across the deck, eyes closed and arms desperately outstretched. It brushed against my palm, my hand snapped shut, and I landed in a crouch, bringing the paper ribbon to my lips. One last kiss. My tears flowed freely, releasing blue dye which trickled over my hand and dripped onto the deck, forming a wobbly blue heart.

The beast of a ship exhaled its dieselly breath, the engine growled from within its bowels. My feet shook as the vessel began to stir. I pulled myself quickly up on the railings, waving with one hand, gripping the precious streamer with the other.

The paper-thin connection pulled taut.

When it snapped, my heart broke, too.

Arrivederci, Italy, my beautiful Italy, home of everyone I've ever loved. Farewell.

Chapter Twenty-Five

Joe, Present Day

Whatever Mum revealed in today's session with Dermot has taken its toll. She drags her chair to the window, a signal for me to leave her alone.

I try to cheer her up, but she waves me away. Poor Mum. She's frustrated when she can't remember, and emotionally exhausted when she can.

After a few minutes, Dermot approaches her, his voice as soothing as an Italian lullaby for a fretful child. She wipes her eyes and offers a weak smile. It's more than just the language. Dermot is calming, while I'm a disappointment.

I'd like to make Mum happy, but for her, that means me meeting a woman. I better bring out the big dogs and post a picture of Biscotti on the dating site.

"Do you mind if I take Maria for a walk around the grounds?" Dermot asks. "She needs it. When you read today's account, you'll understand why. I'm no expert in emotions, but I wouldn't be surprised if retelling a trauma is almost as bad as living it."

There's a heaviness in my chest as I hug Mum goodbye. I feel I've let her down, haven't done my job. I want to protect her from things that happened before I was even born, even though that makes little sense.

"I'll transcribe it tonight and get it to you in the morning." Dermot waves, then walks Mum away.

I skip breakfast and find Izzy waiting in The Figs car park. "Let's sit outside for a while," she says. "I've been reading yesterday's transcript. As you know, I'm a dirty smoker, so we may as well sit here. Unless you find it too revolting?"

"I'm fine with it. Granny Blake used to smoke inside the house, if you can believe. I always thought her walls were painted yellow, but Dad told me they were white under the nicotine stains."

Izzy sticks out her bottom lip. "You're staring again. Glad I don't have any pennies for your thoughts, cos I reckon you're imagining my lungs stained like your granny's walls."

"Not at all." I can't tell her what actually flashed through my mind. It shocked me, so it would definitely shock her. I thought about waking up with her beautiful face on the pillow next to mine.

I clear my throat. "Don't worry, I don't mind cigarette smoke, it reminds me of the kindest, smartest woman I've ever known...anyway, Gran didn't die of lung cancer, she died of old age."

Izzy holds up the latest memoir episodes. "I've had a

quick look. Do you want to read it yourself before you go inside, or will I give you a summary?"

"Summary, please."

"Mariella went through with the proxy wedding." Izzy's eyes glisten with tears. "I desperately hoped she'd have a last-minute reprieve like in the movies. She boarded the boat for Australia, leaving everyone and everything behind."

I squeeze her arm. "Come on, it must've turned out okay. Maybe this Angelo was an understanding bloke and helped Mum cancel the contract?"

She stubs out the cigarette, buries the end in a large plant pot, then offers me a mint as we walk through the main doors.

Bettina whistles under her breath as we sign ourselves in. "You two don't spend much time in 'The Remembering Room'." She puts air quotes around the words. "Maria's covered the former residents kitchen sign with something in Italian. Dermot, the honey, translated it for me. He's cute and clever. Pity he's taken."

Once we get through the security door, Izzy pokes my arm. "You've missed your chance, Joe. The cougar's found other prey."

I wipe my brow dramatically and laugh. "Alas, my broken heart."

"Alack... or something similar. I'll find you a suitable wench. I want to please Maria."

We stop outside the kitchen to admire Mum's perfect lettering '*La Stanza Del Ricordo.*'

Dermot grins. "It's good, eh? The Remembering Room."

"I hope that means Maria's recovered?" Izzy says, then wraps her arm protectively around Mum.

Mum makes hand signals to Dermot and chatters at triple speed, pointing at me as she talks.

Dermot whispers, "Your mother insists on me asking about any women you've matched on the dating site."

"I haven't even checked it."

"Checked what?" Izzy pokes her nose into our huddled conversation.

"Women who've contacted me through the dating app."

"Oh, I've checked." She pulls out her phone and swipes. "You got three love hearts the other day, but none of the women were suitable."

I'm not sure Izzy should be deciding who's suitable for me. "How can you log into my account? I thought the account holder was the only one who could see?"

"Oh..." Izzy blushes. "Hmm... hmm...remember I helped you set up the password. I didn't think... I'm so sorry."

Dermot's voice echoes in the background, a backward and forwarding of English and Italian, presumably letting Mum know what's going on. My mother jumps out of her chair to wrestle the phone out of Izzy's hand. *"fammi vedere!"* she says.

No need for Dermot's translation. She wants to look.

There's a saying about three being a crowd, but what about four? Mum, Izzy and Dermot ignore me to look at the hits on my dating profile. My dating profile. Mine.

"I need to translate the bios for your mum," he explains, looking sheepish.

There's too much laughter for my liking, and I'm sure a chunk of it is at my expense.

"Enough," I say. "I'm not happy choosing a life partner from a photograph or having other people choose it for me. It's unnatural having my life decided by others."

Izzy and Dermot stare with wide-eyed shock, and I knit my eyebrows in complete confusion. "What?"

Then it hits me. My mouth hangs open, unsaid words

hanging in mid-air. I wrap my arms around Mum. "I'm so sorry, here I am complaining about being set up with a woman, when you had no choice at all. A young woman forced across the world..."

My throat tightens and I hug her like she held me was as a little boy. Mum protected me, and here I am complaining about a situation I can walk away from. She couldn't escape from her circumstances in Italy, and she can't walk away from dementia, now. "Is this all too much for Mum?"

"She seems fine today," Dermot says. "When we got back from yesterday's walk, she tipped out the essential oil and cursed, 'No more *bergamotta di Calabria*, that part of my life is over.'"

"So, that's the end?" I ask.

"Not at all. We tested some other scents and settled on Peppermint oil."

"Start the diffuser," Izzy says. "Let's see where the slick of peppermint oil leads."

Chapter Twenty-Six

Mariella, The Achille Lauro, 1967

I stared at the shore until those I loved were blurred ants on the horizon. Long after land disappeared, I felt the pull of my parents and knew they were still crying. My old life lay behind me, and an unthinkable reality stretched ahead.

When the queue of people being directed to cabins dwindled, I abandoned watch. The purser showed me down the stairs and left me to explore the musty space I'd be sharing with a stranger for the next five weeks.

Not even a porthole in this space. I could have watched a small circular patch of the Tyrrhenian Sea. The same sea I'd looked across almost every night to watch the violet sunset. Except I was trapped in a claustrophobic holding cell.

If only I could open a porthole to let sea spray reach my face and rid the smell of fermented vegetables. I refused to think about the origin of such a stench.

Place-cards allocated passenger berths on the double

bunk. Mrs Mariella Morellini was welcomed to the tightly blanketed bed above—an unfamiliar and unwelcome name change. I clenched my fist. This was not the married name I'd wished for.

The place-card of my cabin mate, Mrs Stella Pansini, appeared untouched, and nothing in the cabin hinted at her presence. Hopefully, Mrs. Pansini had missed the boat.

I stowed my carry bag and shoes, then climbed into bed, cocooning myself with the blanket. If I hid and cried out every tear, perhaps I'd wake as a butterfly.

After midnight, a woman disturbed my emotionally exhausted sleep. The purser shushing her as he handed her the key. Either the rocking of the ship or too many glasses of *vino* made her stumble as she undressed.

I feigned sleep when she giggled and slurred in English.

Slammed cabin doors from up and down the passageway announced it was morning, and I peeked at the woman in the bunk below. Mrs Stella Pansini was sound asleep. Her dark wavy hair, spreading in wanton abandon against the pillow, was much like mine except shorter. and tied back from her face with a black-and-white scarf. Ridiculously, I'd assumed from the title Mrs, that my cabin mate would be an older woman. She was my age, maybe a little more.

Was she a woman on holidays? Was she running away from, or to, another life? The ship cruised from Southampton, England, stopping to pick up passengers in ports along the way. Now that the Achille Lauro had left the hazy shores of Italy, there'd be no change of passengers until we reached Australia.

I lowered myself over the edge of the bed, making as

little noise as possible. Collecting my clothes and toiletries, I headed for the cabin door.

She yawned and spoke a husky-voiced English.

I half-smiled at the language barrier. The perfect excuse not to talk.

"*Ti sei svegliato presto*," she repeated in Italian.

"*Si*." My shoulders drooped. I'd need a better reason to keep to myself.

"Wait for me," she said in Italian as she bounded out of bed. She stretched her arms in a yawn, then ruffled her hair. When her fingers tangled in the scarf, she shook with laughter. "Oops. I don't usually wear a scarf to bed. Perhaps I had too much to drink." She smiled. "I'm Stella."

"Mariella," I said.

Stella smiled again, then covered her mouth with her hand before dropping her head to her knees. She shook as she took long, deep breaths.

I started to the door, but she sprang to her feet, her tongue hanging out. "I'm good. False alarm. I'll feel better after breakfast. I usually do. A cold shower, a cup of coffee and plenty of food. A laze by the pool should do the trick."

I tried not to stare, but I was drawn to this Stella, who promised an interesting voyage.

She led me to dining area number three, which I could have found on my own, but Stella took charge, even signing us in for breakfast.

"Stella, my Stella," a young man yelled in Italian as we walked towards our table. Unfazed by his public display, she smiled and curtsied.

My stomach dipped—uneasy with the lurching waves. "I'm going back to the cabin," I said. "I'm not hungry."

"Eat. You need to eat. This is my third voyage and food settles the queasiness."

I nibbled the edges of a slice of crusty bread, but the smell was all wrong. Stella poured pineapple juice. "It's not fresh, it's from a can." The metallic taste tingled my tongue as if the tin had added flavour. My stomach performed awkward somersaults. "I've got to go."

"Here, try this." Stella dabbed a serviette with oil from her bag. "Peppermint. Hold it to your nose."

I closed my eyes, inhaling the smell until my queasiness eased.

The young man who'd yelled from the entrance pulled a chair from a nearby table and joined uninvited. "You didn't tell me about your sister when we danced last night."

I was about to say, "No, we are not sisters." But a wave of nausea forced me to clamp my lips shut.

"Sorry," I heard Stella say. "It's jealousy. My sister Mariella's always been the prettier one."

"Well, hello, Mariella. Pleased to meet you." He lifted my hand to his lips. "I'm Danny."

"Hi." I shuddered, remembering Nino DeLuca holding my hand at the proxy wedding. This young man seemed harmless, but my reactions were set to high alert.

I looked closely at Stella while she chatted about last night's music. Yes, her hair was similar, but what about the rest? About the same height, narrower in the hips and a little thicker in the waist, but from years of measuring up bridesmaids I could tell we'd wear the same size clothes.

"Guess which of us is older?" Stella moved beside me; her face next to mine.

"This is a trap," Danny replied with an easy laugh. "Your skin's a little more tanned, but your nose and your mouth are the same. You're not identical twins, but you're definitely family."

Stella and I raised our eyebrows at each other. The

young man wasn't making idle conversation. He genuinely believed we were sisters.

"One more thing," he said. "You're both beautiful."

I barely made it back to the cabin in time to cradle the empty wastepaper bin in my arms. After vomiting for an hour, I wobbled my way down the passageway to the shared bathroom, emptied the bin and washed it clean, hoping I wouldn't need it again.

Once back in the cabin, the sickness returned. It seemed never-ending.

Stella looked in on me every now and again, bringing individually wrapped packets of dried biscuits and flip-top carafes of boiled water. She reapplied her lipstick, often changed outfits, and always sprayed a liberal amount of perfume. The sickly sweetness barely masked the vinegary odour of my stomach's contents. I now knew the source of the stench permeating the cabin.

For three days straight; I threw up, slept, cried, and stared at the ceiling, bemoaning my loss. On the fourth day, I ventured to the deck, hoping a view of the ocean would lift my spirits, but it was immense and threatening, with none of the jewel-like beauty of my beloved homeland. I leaned over the railing, wishing I could reach the water. If I could dip my fingers in the waves, it would be like swimming with Emilio, pretending to ignore him as he splashed and tickled the bare skin of my midriff.

Like a sunflower seeking light, I angled my face to the sun. Rainbow splotches danced across closed eyelids, and I touched my lips, remembering his kiss.

One day I would forget him. I tried to picture his beautiful face, but all I saw was the scar.

I returned to the cabin and sobbed.

When I'd cried myself out, I searched under the flap in my suitcase for my stash of sketchbooks and pencils. I needed to preserve my memories. I drew Emilio's scarred, but handsome face, Mamma smiling as she held a spoonful of sauce for me to taste. Babbo's tears as he said goodbye. I sketched the Port of Messina as our ship sailed away. The golden statue of *La Madonna Della Lettera*, a twenty-foot-high welcome to the protected harbour. I cross-hatched the hills of the Italian mainland, trying to capture how they'd shimmered and winked from the horizon.

Then I found more tears to cry. Enough to send me to sleep.

I woke up when Stella pulled the blanket from my bed and sprinkled peppermint oil around the cabin. "Enough. Get up. The place stinks and you can't spend five weeks wallowing in misery."

She pushed me down the passageway and into the bathroom. "Here." She handed me a pile of unfamiliar clothes. "I didn't want to rummage through your suitcase, so you're wearing these."

The shower cut out before I'd rinsed my hair and I had to finish the job using a cup over the basin. After drying myself, I donned Stella's clothing—her navy white striped shirt wasn't a style I would have chosen, but it was a relief to step into someone else's life. Perhaps some of Stella's exuberance would leech into my miserable skin.

Back in the cabin, Stella had dressed in a navy and white outfit not dissimilar to the skirt and top she'd loaned me.

She adjusted my collar, looking awfully pleased. "I bought presents from the ship store. Extra strong peppermints and new sunglasses."

"Thank you, but I have my own sunglasses."

"Not like these, you don't."

Her laugh made me curious and I managed a half-smile. Stella seemed on a never-ending mission for fun.

She held up identical dark-lensed sunglasses and handed a pair to me. "These are one of a kind—well... in our case, two of a kind. I studied your face. The major difference between us is around the eyes."

"Thank you," I said. "You are very kind. They should block out the sun."

"These aren't for sun protection, they're part of our new persona. This voyage will be one to remember."

Who was this woman sharing my cabin? I was unsure of Stella's plan, but took comfort in knowing that whatever it was, it might fill in some of the dark emptiness.

"We can even change our names... you're probably not brave enough," she spoke at twice the normal speed. "No... that could be a problem. I've already met a few people... A new last name, at least. We'll have to share one if we're sisters."

An hour ago, I was sure every scrap of happiness had dried up. Maybe Stella's clothes *were* infused with joy. It didn't matter where the spark of hope came from, just that it came.

"Loren," I said. "Stella and Mariella Loren."

Chapter Twenty-Seven

Mariella, The Achille Lauro, 1967

Stella burst into the cabin and fanned a pile of women's magazines across the bed. "Look what I found in the library. They're from all over the world."

She handed over a magazine written in English. *An Australian Women's Weekly*. "If we read them together, by the time we dock in Sydney, you'll be speaking the language like a native. Choose a page."

I closed my eyes, waving the pages like a butterfly and allowing its wings to settle open. A series of letters.

"Perfect," Stella said. "Short and personal."

"*Dear Aunt Gladys*," she read, holding her hand to her forehead in a mock swoon. "Come on, Mariella. Your turn. Read after me."

Pointing to individual letters, she explained, "Most of the English alphabet makes the same sounds as Italian. But watch out for 'ch' which makes the sound 'c' makes when followed by an 'i' or an 'e'."

Stella may as well have asked me to understand nuclear fission. "Slowly," I said. "Read it slowly and I'll copy."

We alternated between her reading, me repeating, then her translating. Finally, I read the entire letter myself.

Dear Aunt Gladys,

My shyness is dreadful. I blush whenever a stranger speaks to me and doubly blush if said person is male. I'm almost twenty-two and fear I'll become an old maid if I don't meet someone soon. But how will I learn to talk to them? Please help.

Yours sincerely,
Miss Bashful.

Once I finished, I used my sketchpad to help remember the meanings. 'Letter' confused me. I drew the alphabet and an envelope.

Stella's patience grew thin while I illustrated the phrases, and she closed my sketchpad with an *oomph*. "You're drawing as if you're sitting an art exam. Stick figures from now on. That's enough for today."

I laughed with relief. The lovely Stella was no saint.

"Hang on," I said. "We haven't read the reply."

To speed up the process, she translated directly to Italian, "*Join a club or engage yourself in group activities where conversation develops naturally.*"

"I have an idea." She tore pages from my sketchpad and folded them into quarters. "A smaller booklet to carry around."

I refolded the pages neatly, but Stella tugged my arm. Come on, we'll find some English people to practise on.

"No. No. No. Keep it slow and simple," I begged.

"Okay. But you'll have to talk to people eventually." She pulled me to my feet and curtsied. "How are you?" she asked.

I wanted to tell her she'd asked me at least ten times that day. Instead, I answered, "Good."

Stella put one hand on her hip and waved the other in the air like a magician's assistant. "No. Repeat after me: I'm more than good, I'm fabulous."

I laughed, but I didn't copy. Mamma had warned about pride bringing bad luck. Ignoring her advice had not worked well.

For a fortnight, I was the sole subject of Stella's attention. Making me parrot and remember English phrases became a game. Stella lolled about on either a deck chair or her bunk, reading a magazine, and found words and phrases for me to practice and write/draw into what she called my Bible. Mamma would have had a conniption at the blasphemy, but Stella's praise helped me push away thoughts of Scilla and all I'd lost.

One morning she yawned loudly then prodded my mattress from below. "I thought up a new plan while you were snoozing. It's time to practise conversational English with other people."

I drew my knees up to my chest. "I can't. I'm not ready."

"I'm not taking no for an answer. You've lots of words now." She leafed through the Bible to prove it. "You can carry this with you. May as well say yes quickly, because I won't give up until I wear you down."

I nodded reluctantly and she gave me instructions. "We'll stop on the deck between groups of people and pretend to fasten our shoelace so we can eavesdrop." She threw her arms into the air like an opera singer. "We are on a human treasure hunt for native speakers of the English language. Preferably men, pleasant, but not sleazy."

"Men? Please. No," I said in English.

"The first of us to find such English tutors shall have the other as a slave for a week."

Framing it as a competition weakened my resolve. So much for being humble. I wanted to win.

After discounting several groups, I found two men who spoke non-stop. I couldn't understand a word they were saying, but their appearance intrigued me. I'd never seen men like them. Hair, long and shaggy with chopped fringes, white trousers, dark belts and patterned jackets like members of British music bands.

They laughed and cheered competitively as they used a forked pole to slide pucks across the ship's deck onto numbered, painted triangles. I bumped into Stella in my hurry to tell her.

"I found a pair of candidates," she said.

"Me too."

"What were yours doing?" she asked.

"Playing shuffleboard. They look like members of the Rolling Stones, except I'm pretty sure they're not famous."

Stella rolled my sketchbook pages telescope style and checked them out from afar. "They'll do. It's easier to start conversations when people are doing something. Mine are just drinking."

"I'm not sure."

"Trust your old Aunt Gladys." Stella laughed, then outlined a complicated scheme which involved her tripping over and me calling for help. I was to yell once in Italian, then again in very poor English, "Help! I no speak the language."

She convinced me this would have men begging to teach me English.

The planning was unnecessary. As we approached the shuffleboard deck, the competing team walked away and one of the long-haired men called in our direction. "You two birds wanna play?"

"Sure," Stella answered, dragging me by the hand.

"Birds?" I asked.

"Hard word, that one. It means the same as *uccelli*, but the English use words differently," she whispered, "Birds is also a word for women, but only the young and attractive."

I crossed my eyes and poked out my tongue.

She whispered in my ear, "Remember. You are banned from speaking Italian." She turned to the men with a dazzling smile. "Are you Australian?"

The darker-haired fellow stared at his feet as he spoke. "No. Cockney. A particular part o' London."

"You sound Australian," Stella said.

The blonde man chimed in, "Well, it's hotter 'ere than England, init?" He looked straight at the sun and squinted his eyes. "'Ere, watch this." He stared at the sun and repeated himself. "Well, it's hotter 'ere than England, innit?"

His friend laughed. "Yer right. Yer sound like an Aussie."

I couldn't hear the difference at all, just thought he looked silly with his face all screwed up.

He did it again. "See Aussie. Full Dinki-Di. My theory is the convict accent changed cos they pulled a bloomin' face lookin' at the sun. The Londoners wondered what that bright yella thing was hangin' about in the sky, made a squint-eyed face, and Voi-bloody-la they sounded Aussie. Try it yourself. It works."

Stella acted all coy. "No, I won't. I am not taking part in silly games with men whose names I don't even know."

The light-haired man winked. "Mick."

The other fellow shook our hands. "And I'm Terry."

Mick bowed. "You're twins, right? Non iden'ical, but close enuff."

Stella draped her arm around my shoulder, pulling me so close I lost balance. "Stella, and my clumsy sister, Mariella."

"Hi," I whispered, hoping I'd said my one tiny word clearly.

"So, where are Cinder-Stella and her definitely not at all ugly step-sister 'eaded?" Mick asked.

"Sydney," Stella said, "and don't think me rude when I occasionally talk to my sister in Italian. She's only recently started learning English. Very recently."

I held out my embarrassingly curled-paged phrase book-let. "English—Italiano. Learning."

Terry looked on kindly and spoke slowly. "We. Will. 'Elp. You. Pleased. Ta. Meet. Ya." Then he turned to Mick. "We gotta 'elp a girl in need."

"Yeah. Write in 'er book. Some'ing useful like, *Give us a drink, thanks*."

As Stella scribbled; *Can I please have a drink?* Mick turned his attention to me, framing his face in his hands. "Me, 'andsome." He then trapped Terry in a headlock. "This git. Right Ugly."

The two men began sparring and barking out peculiar things like. "Ya given me a dead leg now, ya pillock."

They reminded me of puppies fighting over a stick, and I laughed, but Stella hooked her arm through mine. "We'll play our own game of shuffleboard."

Terry licked his fingers and flattened his fringe. "'Ang on, we'll play the game and I'll teach 'er the number names."

"That's 'ow we started our lessons in French class," Mick said. "Un, deux, bloomin' trois right up to soixante-neuf."

"So, you speak French?" Stella raised her eyebrows. "How clever."

She wasn't purely asking Mick if he could speak French. There is more to communication than words. She was having a go at him. Putting him in his place.

Mick looked as if he was about to be tested on a pop quiz of French verbs. "Not really. I'll set up the game. It won't do it itself." He moved the pucks back to the starting line.

I pushed the puck with a shuffleboard stick and it skittered across the deck, landing inside a triangle near number fifteen.

"Fif-teen." Terry tapped each digit with his pointy-toed shoe.

"Fif-teen," I repeated, and everyone laughed.

By the end of the fifth match, the Italian Birds were ahead of the Cockney Lads. Stella was talking to Mick while I studied my Bible full of scruffy numbers and scribbled sayings accompanied by hasty illustrations.

A deep horn sounded and Mick held his hands over his ears. "What's that bloomin' noise?"

"Storm warning," a uniformed officer called. "Everyone inside."

Down in our cabin, despite major rocking as the ship lurched and waves crashing against the hull, my stomach remained calm. Stella and I both inhaled peppermint-oil-soaked handkerchiefs and chatted from our designated bunks.

Stella's speech got faster; her tone grew higher as the weather worsened. I leaned over the edge to check. "Are you okay?"

"I'm... I'm scared."

"Of the ocean?" It surprised me when she nodded; Stella seemed unbelievably brave. The sea was such a part of my life I found its moodiness fascinating—playful, comatose or downright dangerous. I loved its unpredictability.

"What if the ship sinks like the Titanic?"

"It won't. There aren't any icebergs this close to the equator."

I remembered Signor Gallucci's gift and his advice to appease the ocean God Poseidon. "Let's sneak out on deck," I said. "If anyone asks, we need the fresh salt air, but we must be careful. Bring your longest scarves."

Up on deck, we were the only people braving the storm. Stella trembled as she tied a scarf between us. I tied the other to the handrail.

"We're safe, but we better be quick." I opened the bag, grabbing a handful of salt crystals and shells for Stella, and another for myself. "There's instructions somewhere in this bag."

Turning my body so the wind was at my back, I fumbled for Gallucci's directions, then flung my shells into the air, letting the wind carry them over the waves. "Poseidon!" I yelled dramatically. "God of the sea, protect us from harm."

I held Stella's arm as she threw hers too and laughed as she repeated the chant. We untied ourselves and edged inside, struggling to close the door behind us.

She flopped into one of the empty armchairs at the bar while I returned the card to the bag. Another envelope peeked out from between the leather partitions. Signor Gallucci must have slipped it in without saying.

I turned it over in my hand. *Mariella* —the handwriting unmistakably Emilio's. I pushed it back in, swallowing hard and gripping my throat.

"You okay?" Stella asked. "You need a drink. I'll get one if the bar's open."

Once alone, a wave of sickness passed over me, but not from the rolling sea. It was a painful yearning, and a fear of reading Emilio's farewell. I put my head in my hands.

"Hey, you," a male voice shouted. I readied myself for a stern warning from a ship's officer about us going outside.

I was relieved to see Terry and Mick waving from the stairs, and Stella smiling as she hurried back carrying a tray of pink creamy cocktails with long-stemmed cherries.

"We've looked everywhere for you lot. I even slipped a fiver to an unfortunate lookin' geezer in a white uniform. He checked the passenger list for a cabin wiv sisters. Sent us on a right goose chase dint 'e Terry?"

While Mick squawked and slapped his thigh, Terry smiled uncomfortably and looked at the ground.

"Wish I'd 'ad me camera to take a pic of Terry's mug when two old ducks in their sixties opened the door. They looked way too happy to see us." Mick took the cocktail glasses from Stella and draped his arm around her shoulder. "'Ere let me. Looks like the wevver is 'avin a right old knees up. I reckon we should join it."

Stella lifted a drink to her lips and smiled. But I slid my glass back to her. I couldn't afford to spend money on drinks. I didn't want to touch my small nest egg. I whispered in Italian. "No alcohol for me, thanks. I'll drink lemonade. I'll try to make myself understood at the bar if you write it down."

"No need," Stella said. "The waiter was born in Rome."

I found the bar unattended, but clinking glasses and

tuneful humming let me know there was someone out back. I didn't call out. My brain felt squished inside the envelope of Emilio's unopened letter. If he professed his love for me, I would be heartbroken. I clutched my temple, feeling echoes of Don DeLuca's threats. I couldn't ever see him again. If Emilio was glad to let me go, I'd feel worse. I decided not to read it.

The bar steward appeared and scratched his chin. "Back again already?"

I bit my lip. *"Non Capisco."*

"Ah." He shrugged, and switched to Italian. "I'm paid to speak whatever language you like. Another Pink Squirrel?"

"No alcohol for me, thank you. Just a lemonade."

He creased his brow. "Changed your mind? Less than five minutes ago you asked for two Pink Squirrels with double shots. Quite a kick in those squirrelly tails."

I glanced at Stella. She was wearing blue while I wore green, but he'd mistaken me for her. "That was my sister," I said. "People confuse us all the time." For a split second my headache eased and the mood dial turned up a notch, but my half-smile slipped away as I balanced the tray of drinks on the way back to the table.

Stella and Mick were laughing, but Terry was staring through the windows, scowling at the squall.

"Stella," I whispered. "The bar steward thought you'd changed your mind. He thought I was you."

"See, I told you. And we aren't even trying."

"Wot's she sayin'?" Mick asked.

"The bar steward thought Mariella was me."

Mick laughed so much tears sprung from his eyes. "Bar steward," he said, laughing again. "We called our mates that in front o' our mums so we wouldn't get a clip round the ear for sayin' bastard."

Terry laughed at Mick's joke, but his ears turned red.

"Ta muchly." Mick sipped his beer and grinned at Stella, who gulped a huge mouthful of her second cocktail. "This'll go down a treat."

The ship lurched and I reached to steady my lemonade. Terry's glass knocked against his teeth before spilling beer over the table "I think we should go back to the cabin. It's getting rough," he said to Mick.

Mick glared at him. "No gen'leman wud leave birds alone wivout buyin' 'em a drink."

He winked and picked up Stella's glass, touching it to his lips as he raised his eyebrows. "Wan' anuver one, luv?"

"Yes, please," Stella giggled, and looked around the lounge bar. "Pity there's no music."

"Leave it to me. See wha' I can do." Mick stood and gyrated in a rhythmless dance, rocking his arms with an empty glass in each hand. "I'm a beast on the floor."

Stella raised an eyebrow and he winked again. I did not like Mick's mannerisms. They reminded me of Nino.

I linked my arm through Stella's. "We should go."

She tried to shrug me off, but I leaned in to whisper. "This storm's getting worse. We'll be safer in the cabin."

Her eyes widened and she gripped my hand.

"What you two prattlin' on about?" Mick asked.

"I've got to go," Stella slurred slightly. "My frien...sister is scared. And it's hard for her not speaking English."

Mick widened his stance and crossed his arms. "Come on. Stay."

Stella wobbled, so I wrapped my arm around her waist. "We'll meet you tomorrow at dinner," she slurred.

Terry brushed the long fringe from his eyes and gave a tiny wave goodbye.

Chapter Twenty-Eight

Mariella, The Achille Lauro, 1967

Stella dabbed her face with the napkin and scanned the passengers eating breakfast. "Let's move to another dining room for a coffee."

Another move? We'd already eaten fruit in one and a cooked breakfast in another. My guess was Stella hoped to run into the Cockney Lads.

"I'd rather stay here." I anticipated her next suggestion, "and the weather's too rough for shuffleboard"

Stella twisted her mouth to the side. "What can we do today?"

"Read more Aunt Gladys letters? They're fun, and I'm picking up extra words."

Stella looked around once more. "Come on then. Nothing happening here."

In the cabin, Stella flicked through magazines. "I'm looking for something to brighten the day."

A few minutes later, she slapped her hand on the open

page. "This letter doesn't have expressions to use over dinner, but it's interesting."

Dear Aunt Gladys,

I'm unsure whether my husband's carnal desires are normal. Other than kissing, he agreed to wait for sexual relations until we were married. He impressed me with his gentlemanly behaviour.

My mother warned me that once married, I'd have to submit to my husband on a weekly basis, but she was wrong. After the usual honeymoon night, my husband wanted 'it' again the next morning.

Now, months later, he doesn't even wait until dark. I put him off as often as I can, but he's insistent. The whole thing has me worried.

I can't ask Mother, as she will label him a sex fiend. Your advice is my last hope for reassurance.

Yours faithfully,

Tired and embarrassed.

By Stella's third reading and my imitation, her laughter bordered on hysterics. She told me she found the letter funny, but something about her smile was amiss.

"If only women could do whatever they wanted without having to write to magazines for advice," Stella sighed.

She was right. Men called all the shots, at least in Italy. I wondered if Australia would be any different.

"You've never had a wedding night, Mariella. Do you understand what the letter's about?"

I tried to hide the heat in my cheeks.

"So, you do understand... You've experienced men and their..." Stella looked around the cabin as if searching for the right words.

"Carnal desires?" I suggested.

Stella nodded. "Without reading Aunt Gladys's response, I can tell you what I've discovered. All men are different. I've only had one man myself, but you don't have to look far. For example; Terry and Mick. I bet they're both opposites in bed."

"You're married, aren't you, Stella?"

"Yes. A proxy bride. Sent to Australia with Lena, a girl from my village."

My ears pricked. Stella had real experience with an arranged marriage. She could be my own Aunt Gladys.

"Lena and I compared photographs and letters from our future husbands while onboard the ship. We agreed she'd drawn the short straw. Her man was stocky and dressed in old work clothes, while mine was tall, handsome, and immaculately stylish." Stella frowned.

"Wasn't it a real photo? Was he ugly in real life?" The photo Nino had given me of Angelo showed him as pleasant. Not exactly good-looking, but his looks weren't my main concern.

"Yes, it was a real photo. My Lorenzo is kind and very handsome," Stella said.

"You don't seem entirely happy?" I was curious. Not just for her, but for what might await me.

"Lena and I met in the city a month after we'd met our husbands. She'd rarely smiled since I'd known her, but in that little café, her smile was wider than the Sydney harbour. She put her arm through mine and whispered, 'Help me pick a new bed.' Then, she giggled and told me how she and her husband had broken the bed from making love so often."

"Lena didn't think him a sex fiend, then?"

"Not at all. She didn't seem the least bit scarred." Stella

stared at the ground, then continued. "My Lorenzo and I weren't in the market for a new bed. An entire month and we barely creased the sheets." She brushed her dress over her hips and closed her eyes.

I closed mine, too, and thought of Emilio, of our night in the woods. I didn't want to make love to another man. Thinking of him wasn't helping. I shook myself. "Come on, Stella, let's leave the English lessons and get some exercise. It will clear our heads."

"Exercise?" Stella poked out her tongue.

"I like exercise. When I was a bambino, I pretended to outrun imaginary wolves." I took a deep breath, filling my lungs with stale air.

"Might bring a few real wolves out a-hunting if you prance about on deck."

She was right, but I'd never survive this trip unless I moved about outside. "I don't mind going alone."

Stella exhaled dramatically. "Not on your own. You'll need me for protection."

I looked on incredulously as she selected a pair of kitten-heeled shoes and buckled the fine strap around her ankle.

"What?" she asked.

"Can you run in those?"

"They might not look comfortable to you, but I've shopped every store in the Sydney centre wearing these babies."

"I'm warning you, there'll be no stops for window shopping, and deck four is more than half a mile long. We'll run up and back in time for the last round of lunch sittings."

"You're on," Stella said. "I might be sore, but I'll work up a seafarer's appetite."

Up on deck, Stella held my hand, and we dodged sunbathers and ocean-gazing passengers.

"Avoiding a shark?" someone yelled. "Is it the rare land variety?"

"I'll protect you, Mariella," Stella said, short of breath.

A woman tutted, "Females running? What next?"

Even though running hand-in-hand was impractical, her grip firmed like a pact, and I returned the grasp. We would protect each other.

I blocked the blur of spectators and commentators, pretending instead to run in the solitude of the Calabrian countryside. I inhaled the imagined scent of bergamot, waved back to Signor Gallucci standing at the castle, and salivated, thinking of the delicious meal Mamma was preparing.

A familiar voice stopped us in our tracks. "Cor, look at them pins move. Poetry in bloomin' motion and I've not even started chasin', yet," Mick whistled, as if calling dogs.

Stella laughed, but I cringed.

"Headin' for some grub. Wanna join us?"

Stella looked at me hopefully and although the voice inside said *stay away from this man*, I had to go. I'd squeezed Stella's hand in a promise and I intended to keep it. That meant staying close.

The drinking began during lunch and continued throughout the afternoon. I couldn't make out everything Mick said, and it was he who did most of the talking, but I understood enough body language to know he was bragging. Stella told me he had a vast collection of single records, played in a band, and planned to leave his job as a mechanic's assistant to become a DJ.

He yelled across the table, "The Aussies are lookin' for a

with-it bloke to play the right tunes. Ya know. Shake things up on the dance-floor."

While I understood the attraction of bodies moving in time to music, I was glad Terry didn't ask me to dance. We watched in uncomfortable silence.

He stared at Mick and Stella. I couldn't tell whether he wished he was dancing with her, or, like me, didn't trust his friend.

He pressed his palms together and imitated opening a book. "Your English Italian phrases?"

"In the cabin," I said, carefully and slowly in English.

"I can help you. D'you want to get it?" He stood as if to accompany me, but I gestured for him to wait.

When I got back, Stella and Mick had gone.

"Where is Stella?" I asked.

Terry pointed down the stairs to the cabins below. "Collecting a new single. A hit song on a 45." He patiently acted out playing music until I understood.

My mouth felt like sawdust. I pushed the drink coasters aside to clear room for my Bible. Drawing calmed me. And I needed calming.

Terry flicked through and became absorbed by my drawings. "You're fab, can you draw me?" He framed his face with his hands.

I sketched his slightly asymmetrical face—crooked nose, squarish chin, one ear larger than the other. I wondered if he'd noticed, or if only girls agonised in front of mirrors searching for imperfections.

I'd barely completed the outline when he reached for my pencil to write the names for lips, eyes, nose, teeth, chin and ears. "In Italian?" He pressed the pencil into my hand.

Carefully, I wrote under the English words. *Labbra, occhi, naso, denti, mento, orecchie.* Terry read them out loud, touching each part of his face and laughing.

My return smile was shaky. Beneath my outward calm, I wanted to run. But why? Terry seemed harmless.

I let out a low whistle, then tapped the glass face of my watch. "Long time," I said.

Terry's lopsided ears turned red and he squirmed.

"Which cabin?" I asked, my voice firm.

"Orright." He got to his feet. "We can try. But they might not open the door."

With each step down the grand, winding staircase from the Sorrento deck, I weighed my decision to chase Stella. She was a grown woman and could do whatever she wanted. I should leave her alone. I turned to climb up again, but immediately spun around and clutched the brass banister for strength. I was stuck halfway—both on the stairs and in my choice. I took a few hesitant, clattering steps down the utilitarian stairs to the bowels of the ship, and stopped again. Up or down?

"What d'ya wanna do?" Terry asked.

I tried to make eye contact, hoping to see what he was thinking, but he wouldn't look at me. In that moment of avoidance, I knew. Mick was a wolf worse than those I'd escaped, but this time, rather than run, I needed to chase. Stella and I had sealed our promise with a handshake.

I grabbed Terry's shirtsleeve and pulled him down the remaining stairs. He led me past doors and through deserted hallways. This side of the ship looked much the same, but a sharper scent overpowered the vaguely familiar aromas of diesel fuel and seaweed. Danger.

Terry stopped at the door and I froze at the sound of a woman crying. He had the key out of his pocket and into the lock before I'd shaken myself back into action.

As the door flung open, Mick screamed, "Get out!"

I pushed my way into the cabin. Stella cowered in the corner covering her face, while Mick, his face contorted with fury, held a blanket over what I assumed was his naked lower body.

Stella sobbed and shook, her neck red where she'd struggled from his grip. Two bloodied bite marks on her shoulder suggested violence. The terror in her eyes confirmed it.

I comforted her and wrapped her in a sheet while the men argued. Terry pushed Mick against the wall, and turned to Stella. "Are you okay?"

Mick punched him in the back of the head.

I expected Terry to fall, but he spun, leg high, kicking Mick in the face.

"Come on," I said to Stella. "We'll report this to the ship's police."

"No." Stella muttered something incoherent.

"You want me to kick him?" I pointed at Mick holding his bloodied mouth.

"No. I want it all to be over. Take me back. I need a shower."

Stella's legs wobbled as I helped her to the bathroom. She hid there as long as she could while I waited outside, keeping watch.

Eventually she came out with a glassy-eyed stare and an unconvincing smile. "Scrubbing away my sins."

"From what I saw," I said, my voice trembling, "they were Mick's sins, not yours."

She gagged, covering her mouth, and I led her back to the cabin where she curled up on the bed, her face to the wall.

"Stella," I called several times, but she shut me out.

I was at a loss. When Mamma's friends faced problems,

she stayed by their side. She took jars of olives or marmalade and helped people pray through terrible times. Babbo and I left her to it. She would have known what to do with Stella. I had no idea what to say that wouldn't make things worse, and I could no longer ask my mamma for advice.

My composure crumbled, but I couldn't let Stella hear me cry. With nowhere safe to sit alone, I took a long shower of my own.

First, I cried for Stella, replaying the mixture of terror and relief as we'd barged in to save her, and the impotence of not being able to undo what had already happened. Then I cried for my Mamma. I needed her hugs right now, but I'd never see her again. I sat on the shower cubicle floor and cried buckets for all the things I couldn't change.

Chapter Twenty-Nine

Joe, Present Day

Izzy watches from her armchair, waiting for me to finish reading. I put the memoir document down without saying a word. Then I pick up our coffee cups and take them to the small kitchen nook in the corner of her apartment. I need a moment to myself after reading Mum's latest episode.

"You, okay?" Izzy asks.

"God. I need a drink after that." I crack my knuckles. "Poor Stella. Awfully unlucky to be stuck on a ship with such a man. I didn't see that coming."

Izzy squints as if she's having trouble seeing. "You mean you didn't get an inkling of what was about to happen?"

"No. Mick sounded friendly. One of those fun-loving, witty guys popular with girls."

"Men can be both charming and dangerous. A lethal combination."

"But it makes little sense. Women flock to his type. He

shouldn't have needed to force her. I suppose sex before marriage was unacceptable back then."

"We're talking about the swinging 60s, Joe. Surely, you've heard about free love? The pill? The sexual revolution? This has nothing to do with him not being offered sex, and everything to do with him taking it."

When I shrug, she juts her head towards me, signalling me to respond.

I'm way out of my depth, but Izzy's waiting. "Yeah— James Bond movies. He was pretty sleazy, but the women seemed to love him." I throw my hands casually in the air, but Izzy throws a look that turns me to stone. Granny Blake told me to shut up when I don't know what to say. I should have listened.

"What exactly is your point, Joe? What happened to Stella wasn't a bloody movie. It was a real-life problem then, and it's a real-life problem now."

I decide to shut my mouth, but Izzy's eyes burn holes in my forehead as she waits for me to say something. "Well, at least Mick was on a ship and it's not as if he could hide. I'll be glad to read the next chapter. Officers will definitely arrest him."

"You can't be serious?"

"Sexual assault is against the law," I say.

Izzy's pulls at her hair. "Yes, it is, but he'll get away with it."

"At least the ship's full of people. There's safety in numbers."

Her eyes fill with tears. "Where do you think most sexual assaults happen, Joe?"

Things have taken a turn and I don't know how to make everything all right. I open my mouth, then falter and shake my head.

She slaps her hands on her hips, but her trembling arms make her seem fragile rather than menacing. "I'll tell you what most men think. They think rape happens when a woman's carelessly alone in the dark, that the perpetrator is a masked man who appears from nowhere and drags her into the bushes. Well, it's not like that. It's often a 'nice' bloke. Someone she knows well—a colleague who makes a pass but when she turns him down, he decides 'no' is a codeword for 'yes'."

I crack my knuckles again. I don't mind Izzy being annoyed, but I'd rather Mum's wooden spoon than witness Izzy's sadness.

She speaks slowly. "Some men, and I'm not talking about you, think women play hard to get because they don't want to seem easy. They think women like to be 'convinced' like the actresses in old movies."

"I'm really sorry. I didn't mean to upset you."

"I'm not just blaming men. I'm angry at women who think coquettishness is cute and feminine. *Oh no. Oh gosh, I really should stop you, but you're so attractive and powerful.* Fuck that." Izzy's volume rises, but her words feel less angry. More a cry for help.

It takes a lot of strength to stop myself throwing my arms around her and trying to protect her, but I'm afraid it's the wrong move. I shuffle ever-so-slightly closer. "Do you want me to leave?"

Her voice breaks. "No..."

"What can I do?" I ask, watching her shoulders heave under the weight of sobbing.

"Sit here and wait."

She disappears through a door I imagine leads to her bedroom. Absent-mindedly, I scan her bookshelf, but all the titles blur into one.

A realisation sparks my stupid man brain. Izzy's speaking from personal experience. I take a deep breath. *SOME BASTARD SEXUALLY ASSAULTED IZZY.* Days ago, when reading Mum's memoirs, I wondered why anyone would join the mafia. Now, I'm wishing I had a connection with the clan. I'd arrange a cruel misfortune to befall a man I've never met.

By the time Izzy reappears with washed face and dried eyes, I've arranged her books in alphabetical order. "Sorry, I say. Sorry for everything. And I shouldn't have touched your books, but I felt useless."

"I'm fine, Joe." She's replaced her usual easy smile with one that takes effort. "The memories hurt, but I survived. And I'm sure, like countless women in the same boat, your mum's friend Stella did too."

"Did you report what happened? The Police should know."

"No. I didn't put myself through that. Statistics don't favour the victim."

Pulling my shoulders up and out, I try to appear stronger. "I wish I were a tough guy with a gun. I'd go looking for him."

Izzy splutters and sighs. This time, the hands on the hips mean business.

"I wouldn't kill him," I explain, "but I would scare the shit out of him."

"Stop. I don't want you to rescue me."

I drop my head. "I've never held a gun and I've no idea where I'd get one. I just wanted to help."

"I wouldn't like it if you went all Rambo, Joe. I like you exactly the way you are."

Izzy's comment warms me from the inside, melting corners that have been cold for years.

I think of positive action I can take. "Would you rather we work on Mum's memoirs in a public place from now on? We could go to the library?"

"I've told you—stop. I feel safe with you, so don't worry. But I'm tired now. It's time for you to go home."

I drive the long way home, replaying the conversation and adding this key puzzle piece to what I already knew about Izzy. No wonder she avoids men. Her straight-forward, off-putting attitude on the dating website isn't her being irritable. It's self-protection.

My eyes blur under the threat of tears. I want to shelter Izzy and stop her from being scared.

Chapter Thirty

Mariella, The Achille Lauro, 1967

Over the next week, I kept watch on Stella day and night, only venturing from the cabin to collect our meals.

Once she showed signs of improvement, I primed myself to confront Mick. I needed him to stay away and not even look in Stella's direction.

My legs trembled as adrenaline raced through my body. I stumbled through the dining room and scanned the lunch patrons for the rat. My plan did not include a fully developed idea of what I'd do or say when I found him. Especially not in English.

Mick was nowhere to be found, but I eventually discovered Terry, in a corner, dining alone.

I sat opposite and slammed my hands on the table. He knew I was there, but didn't make eye contact. Instead, he focussed his attention on the serrated knife he was spinning around his plate.

We stared at the circling knife until it slowed to a stop.

Terry looked up. "How is she?"

I shook my head. I didn't have the English words to explain how broken Stella was. "Asleep."

"I made... a complaint." Terry tripped over his words. "But I don't think they're takin' it serious. Them laws aren't clear. There's no copper on board and the steward can't make 'is mind up wevver we're ruled by the nearest country's legal system or followin' laws of the flag our ship's flyin' under. Eiver way, nothin' can be done until we dock."

I understood less than half of what he said, but I understood this much; Mick wouldn't be punished. I wanted to snatch the knife and ruin Mick's face, DeLuca style, for stealing Stella's joy.

"I asked crew to move 'im to anuvver cabin. 'E's gone."

I nodded my understanding. "Grazi. Thank you."

Terry dropped his chin to his chest, then unexpectedly lifted his head to smile. "The ship's doctor can't fix his teef." He burst into nervous laughter. "I 'ope they give 'im new choppers made of yellow plastic."

We laughed together, our shoulders shaking, tears in our eyes. There's a fine line between laughing and crying.

I stood to say goodbye. "What...Mick's... name?"

"Sorry, I don't understand."

I wrote my name and address in my language Bible and pointed at my last name before asking again. Eventually, he wrote Mick's full name and address in England.

"*Grazie*. Thank you."

I gripped my book tightly as I walked back to the cabin. Such details might come in handy. Inside, Stella pretended to sleep, and she didn't answer when I offered her food. Although she lay still, her shoulders quivered as she fought to suppress oceans of shame filled tears.

I moved the small tub chair in the corner and propped

myself higher with a pillow on the seat. The regular rocking of waves soothed me. It reminded me of one of Babbo's sayings, "We can alter the ship's sails, but we have no control over wind and waves."

I racked my brain until I thought of something I could control. I took out my battered toffee-tin filled with thread, needles, and a sharp pair of dressmaking scissors. Then I found the dress I'd made using the fabric Emilio bought in Florence. It would be a gift for Stella and a way of removing myself from my own pain.

Shortening the dress provided leftover fabric for a scarf Stella had admired in one of the English magazines. Stitch by stitch, I tried to sew my friend back together.

She cried all over again when I gave it to her. "It's beautiful. I don't deserve it."

"Come on, get up, have a shower, and try it on."

It surprised me when Stella did as she was told. I guessed she didn't feel she could turn me down after my effort. I didn't care what motivated her, as long as she got up.

It felt like forever before she came back to the cabin. While she was gone, I flicked nervously through a magazine and stopped at an advertisement for hand cream. A man held the woman's silky-smooth hand to his lips for a kiss. In profile, he looked like Emilio.

I ripped out the page. Stella returned as I was throwing shredded paper into the bin.

She'd hidden her new dress under a bathrobe, and even in the safety of our cabin she hesitated about taking it off. "I can't wear it, Mariella." She touched the hemline. "It's too short, especially after what happened."

She rummaged through her trunk and pulled out a plain black shift.

I plucked it from her hands. "No, you're not in mourning, and I won't allow you to hide. You could strut around this ship naked and your body would still be off limits. What you wear or don't wear is no one else's business."

She rested her head on folded arms. "I shouldn't have followed him. Not alone. I'd had a few drinks, and I enjoyed his company."

I lifted her head. "Did he invite you to his cabin for rough sex? Is that why you went? Look at me, Stella. I know that's not what happened."

"No! Of course not. We were talking about my husband and I told him how Lorenzo has a recording company in Sydney. Mick said he'd made a demo of himself singing with his old band. He wanted me to listen. He thought maybe Lorenzo could help him break into the Australian music field."

"*Bastardo*." I knocked my sewing tin from the bed to the floor. "If I knew Calabrian curses, I'd throw every one of them at that excuse for a man."

Stella's face paled. "But what if I was putting out mixed signals? I enjoyed his attention." She sank to the floor and sobbed.

"Still not an excuse!" I squeezed her hands until they turned white. "Would your husband think a woman being pleasant an excuse to rape her?"

"No. Never. My Lorenzo's a respectful man."

"See. You know in your heart that this isn't what good men do."

Stella stuttered as she whispered. "Lorenzo and I laugh and dance together, but I rarely share his bed."

My eyelid spasmed in a nervous tic. There must be something dreadfully repellent about Lorenzo? What if I found the same of Nino's cousin, Angelo? Would I have to submit to a man I found repulsive? "I hope Angelo accepts my refusal of his advances as well as Lorenzo does."

"Stop creasing your forehead," Stella said. "You're on the wrong track. It's not a fault with me or him. Lorenzo isn't interested in any women."

My hand flew to my face. "Why didn't you have the marriage annulled? The Pope would have agreed. You could've returned to Italy and found a more suitable husband."

"Our agreement worked for everyone. My family home had seven crammed into nothing more than a garden shed. By marrying Lorenzo, my family had one less mouth to feed, and the extra money Lorenzo sends each month stops my younger brothers and sisters from going hungry. He's generous. I have lots of freedom, and my life is better than it would have been if I'd stayed behind."

"Why did he take a proxy bride, then? Why didn't he... he could have just lived with... kept living on his own?" I struggled to find the right words. I knew some men preferred other men, but I'd never met one. At least not one who admitted it.

Stella cleared her throat and twisted the scarf around her fingers. "His close friends know it's a sham, but for business deals he must put on a front. I accompany him. Play the role of a dutiful wife. And help him sign contracts. I rarely see those people again, so it's an easy pretence."

I softened my voice and leaned closer. "Will you tell Lorenzo what happened?"

"I don't know. Oh, God." She shook her head. "How bad would it have been if you and Terry hadn't arrived?"

That night, I lay awake thinking about what Stella had said. She'd told me intimate details about her life while I'd kept mine to myself. I'd avoided her questions about my proxy marriage and she'd stopped asking. After running it over several times, I decided to share the difficult subject by disguising it as an Aunt Gladys letter.

It took three drafts before I was happy with my English sentences. Then, as quietly as I could, I slipped the letter into a magazine, planning to surprise her during daily reading.

After breakfast, we returned to the cabin for my daily English lesson. "I found another Aunt Gladys letter. One we must've missed," I said. "Do you want me to read?"

"You're going to read it out in English? You'll be teaching night school to Italian migrants by the time we get off in Australia."

I turned the pages until I came to my letter.

Dear Aunt Gladys,

I have been lucky enough to make special friend. We been through wonderful times, but crazy bad as well. She ask me my reason for leaving Italy, but I not tell.

My story is no happy, and I afraid it make my friend sad.

Should I still tell the truth? Or should I make up happily ever after fairy-tale?

Yours sincerely,

Little Red Riding Hood.

I covered the magazine with my arm, and Stella frowned. "You're trying to tell me a letter like this escaped my notice? I don't think so."

I ignored her. "Before we read the answer, I thought we predict what Aunt Gladys might advise."

"I know you wrote it, Mariella, or should I say, Little Red Riding Hood. But I'll go along with the game."

Stella leaned back on her bunk, one raised leg pushing into the mattress above. Her hand massaged her forehead as if giving the question careful thought. "A genuine friendship is about sharing. If only one helps the other, it's out of balance and not a friendship at all. So, spill the beans."

"I haven't told you about my proxy marriage because I'm having difficulty coming to terms with it. I'm going off to live with a complete stranger."

"You can get a sense of someone's character from letters. What has your husband said about where he lives and what he enjoys doing? Lorenzo used to send me a letter every fortnight. I learned a great deal after twenty-six letters. It was like a courtship. He left out 'minor' details, but I got to know him through words."

"Angelo's cousin cut through bureaucratic red tape, so our approval took less than a month."

"You know his cousin? What did he tell you?"

"That Angelo preferred his women on the younger side, and that he'd put in an order for one who resembled Gina Lollobrigida—his favourite starlet."

"Ugh." Stella looked as if she'd accidentally eaten goats' shit. "No wonder you're unhappy. No photographs of him? Not even a phone call?"

"He sent one letter. It arrived the day before I left Scilla. I opened it but haven't read it. It's in English."

Stella waved her arms and jumped up. "Show me! Quickly!"

I knew exactly where Angelo's letter was, but I feared finding out what sickening things he'd written to his promised bride. I'd considered finding a translator, but in all honesty, after Nino's description where Angelo sounded like a slave trader with expendable wives, I didn't want to know more.

I bit my trembling lip and handed over the blue aerogram, its lightweight paper folding back on itself to form an envelope. "I'd rather not read it myself."

Stella checked both front and back, reading his name and address. "*Angelo Morellini, Lot 561 Cane Cutters Way, Ingham, Queensland, Australia.*"

She hovered her free hand over the words. "His handwriting isn't shaky. At least you're not gonna turn up to an eighty-year-old. If we can find a detailed map, we could look up the town."

With my throat too tight to speak, I jerked my chin towards the letter, indicating for her to read on.

She nodded and patted my arm.

Dear Mariella,

I am nervous about meeting you, especially after the phone calls from my cousin Nino. International calls cost an arm and leg, but that didn't stop him calling several times to tell me about the woman I needed to marry. You.

Don't take this the wrong way, because I've never met you, but I initially declined his offer, telling him I wasn't looking for a wife. He was very pushy. He told me you looked like my favourite actress and offered to pay a professional photographer to take pictures and send them to me, but I refused.

It wasn't until Nino's fourth phone call that I sensed you'd be safer here with me than staying in Scilla.

Ingham, my town, isn't large, but it has a thriving Italian community where I hope you'll feel at home. I work hard on the cane farm, but by the time you arrive, the sugar should be harvested and we can get to know each other face-to-face.

Yours,

Angelo.

Stella smiled as she finished reading.

I tapped my head to stop the cogs in my brain from breaking. "This doesn't add up. Nino told me Angelo asked him to find a wife. One who looked like Gina Lollobrigida. Angelo's written the opposite."

Stella glanced at the letter, then at me, then back again as if his words contained secrets only she could see. "Maybe Nino tried to make you feel better by telling you his cousin is very picky and that you're one in a million? You know— that kind of thing."

I snorted a pig-like laugh. It wasn't joyous. "Nino wouldn't do anything out of kindness."

She pulled a cardboard box from her suitcase and shook it. "I've been holding out. My Nonna's gave me some home-made almond biscotti. Every bite, the taste of kindness. Have some. It makes everything better."

Shaking my head, I took the letter instead.

"Maybe your parents asked this Nino character to find you a husband?" Stella suggested. "Perhaps, like me, your marriage will feed your brothers and sisters."

"I'm an only child," I said too harshly. "Mamma and Bubba would never do such a thing. They avoid Nino DeLuca at all costs."

Stella ate a biscuit, then brushed away the crumbs. "Angelo sounds kind, and Ingham sounds like a winner." She took another biscotti and inhaled the smell. "I'd love to live in an Italian community. I bet they have the food I love. In

Sydney, Italians are outsiders." She offered the box again. "Are you sure you don't want one?"

I relented, choosing the piece with the most almonds and read Angelo's letter as I ate. I could think of no explanation for Nino pushing this marriage before he discovered I was with Emilio.

"If your family don't need the money, and you don't want to get married, why did you agree?"

"It's a long story," I said.

"Oh, that's a pity. If only we were stuck on the ship with nothing much to do." Stella rolled onto her belly, propped a pillow under her chest and smirked sarcastically. "Get on with it."

I continued extolling Emilio's features until Stella interrupted. "I get it. Emilio is tall and muscular and sounds like a veritable God. I know you love him, but what happened?"

"His family found out we were seeing each other."

"How long had you been together?"

"Almost three years." My chest sunk with realisation. It was a long time to keep it a secret.

Stella stared. "So, he didn't tell his family at the beginning?"

The collar on my shirt was suddenly tight and I cleared my throat. "No, he didn't tell them." I wanted to rationalise, to add extra details, because the truth didn't paint Emilio in the light he deserved.

Stella closed the biscuit box. "Food doesn't cut it. We need the big guns. I bought three bottles of Marsala in Sicily when I got off the boat. After a drink, you'll happily tell me."

Stella poured, and the black-red liquid sloshed to the bottom, then whooshed up the sides of the clear plastic tumblers like a tsunami bringing memories of grapes and my homeland. I took a steadying breath and downed my drink, pressing my damp lips on the back of my hand. "Emilio belonged to the Ndrangheta. They restrict marriage to people within the mafia, but I wasn't a member. Not even close."

"So, you accepted you'd never marry and were happy to keep the romance secret?"

"No, he planned to marry me anyway. He was trying to bring his family around."

"Oh. I see," Stella said.

I could tell she didn't see at all.

I took another sip. "We tried to elope." The Marsala wasn't helping.

"You mean marrying, then telling everyone it was a done deed?"

"No... More of an escape."

"From what?"

"*La Famiglia* had organised a different bride for Emilio. Behind his back. He was promised to Nino's daughter, Isabella, and he wasn't happy."

Stella tilted her head as if studying my face. "What did Nino's daughter look like?"

I reached for the bottle. "That's a strange question. She was lovely. A beautiful girl, but naïve."

"So, Emilio told you about the proposed wedding and wanted to get you away?"

This was almost what happened. "Not quite. Isabella told me about it first. She came into the bridal shop where I worked."

Stella sat upright, then abruptly crossed her legs and arms. "Sorry to break this to you, Mariella, but it sounds awfully dodgy. Tell me, did your parents like this Emilio?"

I felt a little dizzy. I'd drunk more than I meant to but it wasn't the alcohol. "They warned me about him, but they didn't know him as I did, they only knew his family and the stories they'd heard."

Stella topped up my drink. "Anyone else warn you?"

Shifting uncomfortably in my seat, I took a gulp and stared at the tumbler. My tears created a sad rainbow. "My boss thought I should stay clear."

Stella grasped my hand. "You know him better than anyone. If you thought they were wrong, you're probably right."

I let out a relieved breath. At least Stella understood.

"Tell me the rest of your story," she said gently.

My heart hurt as I spoke. "I didn't get to say a proper goodbye after they caught us. My uncle and I escaped. Soon after, in fact the very next day, Nino arranged my proxy marriage."

Stella's perfectly arched eyebrows flattened, the expression around her eyes at odds with her encouraging smile. "You need to step me through it if I'm to understand. You were courting Emilio in secret? The only people who knew about it were your parents and your boss? A mafia boss called Nino organised for Emilio to marry his daughter and for you to marry his cousin? And his cousin is the Angelo who wrote this letter?"

"Yes. All of that is correct."

"But you missed the part about running away?"

I didn't want to remember, let alone retell, but part of me hoped sharing would ease the pain. I steadied myself and started from the beginning.

"Emilio asked me to meet him in a neighbouring town. From there, I was to direct him to a location only I knew. He worried about being questioned by Nino. Said he couldn't tell what he didn't know. Other than my uncle, I was the only person who knew where we planned to hide."

"How did your uncle find out?"

"I gave him a note to let my parents know I was safe."

Stella scrunched her nose. "But despite this care, you were discovered?"

"Yes." My heart pounded at the memory.

"How did they find out?"

I pinched my earlobe between my thumb and forefinger. "Someone in the village must've seen me giving the note to my uncle."

"Was Emilio angry about you leaving a note, especially when it was a secret?"

I took another sip of the fortified wine. "No, Emilio wasn't angry. Neither of us thought we'd be found out." The wine sloshed in my stomach, making me seasick. "It was terrifying, Stella. You should have seen the horrible thing Nino did to Emilio."

Stella wrapped me in a hug and gave me a few minutes. She wiped my tears with her scarf. "I'm sorry for asking. But what happened next? Did Nino hold a gun to Emilio's head?"

"Not a gun." I shuddered. Remembering the experience was a nightmare. "After we escaped, I ran back through the forest to help my uncle. He was trapped in his car, bleeding where Nino had sliced his ear. Nino had forced him to surrender the note.

"So, Emilio ran for help?"

"No, he ran up river to lure Nino away. I got back to the cars and planned to collect Emilio from the road. Instead, Nino captured Emilio and dragged him back to camp. He slashed my love's face in front of me." I paused and held my chest to stop the sadness growing. "He slit his cheek, just missing his eye."

"That's the last you saw or heard of Emilio?"

"He was at the dock when the ship departed, but I only saw him from a distance. I found a farewell letter hidden inside a gift from someone else."

"What did it say?"

"I was too upset to read it."

Stella screeched. "Get it out! Read it now."

"I can't."

"You will. You're making me face people outside the cabin. You can face a letter!"

My hand trembled as I retrieved Emilio's letter from the bag.

Dear Mariella,

If I can get away without being seen, I'll wave goodbye from the Messina docks. It will be a last farewell because it's the only way I can ensure your safety.

Don DeLuca has made his expectations clear. My marriage to Isabella is set in concrete. He told me it would be a pity if I ruined the arrangement. You are going all the way to Australia with a chance of a better life. He's promised no harm to your parents unless I refuse to marry Isabella, or you refuse Angelo. Then Nino will contact his Australian cousin, and make sure you are also punished. If you run away from your husband, whatever punishment he has in store for either you or me will be reassigned to your parents.

They can stop us from seeing each other, but they can't stop love. My love for you is everlasting.

Emilio.

. . .

After I finished reading, I expected Stella to understand how bad things were for Emilio. Instead, she drummed her fingers against the empty bottle.

"What?" I asked. "Emilio wasn't let off lightly."

"Emilio was tall and strong? What was Nino like?"

An invisible band round my midriff tightened. I wanted to throw up. "Short and overweight."

Stella's mouth twisted to one side. "Was he healthy? Strong?"

"He had a persistent cough." Suddenly, I felt short of breath. "There's no air in this cabin." I held my hand to deflect further questions, but Stella ignored me.

"I don't understand how a smaller, unfit, older man chased and overpowered an athletic man, then dragged him along a river bank, getting back to this camp before you took off?"

Stella's voice sounded from afar and the truth squeezed my heart like a vice. Emilio knew. He was part of the plan. Pinpricks of light flickered before my eyes and I collapsed.

"Mariella. Mariella." Stella slapped the back of my hand and trickled bottled water over my forehead. "I'll fetch the ship's doctor."

"I just need to be alone. I'm cold."

She spread a blanket, carefully tucking me inside. "I'll be back with a doctor."

"But I don't need—"

"You do. You passed out." She paused at the cabin door to cast me a worried glance, then Stella disappeared.

What a fool I'd been. Emilio being part of the deceit was the only feasible explanation. But if Emilio was not who I thought, then I couldn't trust myself to ever love again.

I had the overwhelming desire to run and keep running, but I was stuck on a blasted ship.

Footsteps sounded in the passageway, and a key turned in the cabin door. I rolled to face the wall.

The doctor and Stella were silent, but I felt their eyes on me. A hand patted my back. "You can stay up there," he said. "But turn towards me and open your mouth."

I faced the grey-haired man with the white button-up coat and stared at the stethoscope around his neck. He put a thermometer under my tongue. "Your friend said you passed out. Just nod. Yes, or no?"

I nodded.

"Pain?"

I shook my head because the pain wasn't physical. I angled a pillow between myself and the doctor. I'd believed Emilio. I'd given him love and my body, but it was all a game for him. He'd pursued me for pleasure, without ever intending marriage. Doctors have no medication for fools.

"98.6. Temperature normal." The doctor hesitated. "Is there a possibility you're pregnant?"

"No," I said. "I'm not ill. I don't need medical help."

"But, Mariella," Stella said. "You collapsed."

The doctor looked from me to her. "Stella and Mariella? Oh, you must be the sisters a recent male patient complained about."

Stella wilted and steadied herself on the rail of my bunk.

"Don't worry, I did my best *not* to save his teeth," the doctor said. "But if you repeat this information, I'll deny it. I've sworn the Hippocratic oath."

Stella's voice was barely a whisper. "You didn't help him? Why not?"

"This was the second incident involving the punk. The first only two days into the voyage. A poor woman came to me with savage bite marks. Having his teeth knocked out seemed fitting. And I thought leaving him without them might put him out of action. I did it for the safety of other female passengers, but also to look my wife and daughters in the eye."

My strength restored, I sat up, indignant on Stella's behalf. "What did that *uomo cattivo* complain about?"

"He claimed you both lured him into his cabin, then beat him up." The doctor shook his head. "I knew no such thing happened."

"Thank you." I slid off the bunk and wrapped my arms around Stella's trembling shoulders. "He bit her, too. And would have done worse if we hadn't stopped him."

The doctor sighed. "I apologise for that man and all the other bad eggs. But don't be put off. There are plenty of fine men left in this world." He repacked his medical bag and headed for the door. "I'll be revisiting the thug for another check-up. Considering he was *the victim of an attack*, it would be negligent not to provide him with the full scope of precautionary treatments. I must inject a very large needle of antibiotics into a tender part of his anatomy... and I have a notoriously shaky hand."

Chapter Thirty-One

Joe, Present Day

Izzy points at tables on the pavement. "Let's sit alfresco. We can pretend we're in Italy."

"We'd be warmer inside the cafe," I say.

"Come on. We're made of sterner stuff." She walks back to the car and retrieves a chunky knit jumper from her boot, then holds up a picnic blanket with North American Indian design. "Want to drape this around your shoulders."

"No, thank you. I don't want to look like C-grade movie extra in a black and white cowboy and Indians movie."

"Suit yourself." She pulls the old jumper over her head. "Toasty. Just ignore the pulled threads." I grab a loop of yarn and she slaps my hand away. "It's not a cartoon, Joe. You can't pull a thread and expect all my clothing to unravel."

I keep my thoughts to myself.

While Izzy types up the transcript, I nurse my coffee. The buzz of sounds within drift around our table. Coffee machines and patrons' chatter mingle with lyrics. Someone sings about feeling as if there're only two people in a crowded room. The song sums up how I feel. There's nothing I'd rather do right now than watch Izzy's hands fly over her keyboard as she adds notes to the memoir document.

She pauses to sip her coffee, then looks up and smiles. I realise I'm not cold at all.

Bettina teeters along the footpath in heels that could double as weapons. "What a coincidence us all being here," she says.

"Why?" Izzy asks, without looking up from her laptop.

Bettina leans over the table and I shuffle my chair back a little. "Why what?" she asks.

Izzy folds her arms. "It's hardly a coincidence to be at the one café anywhere within cooee of The Figs."

"Well... I'm here because the geriatric health specialist, Dr Bryson Kent-Jones, dropped me off at the door. Sweet of him not making me walk. Invited me here on a second date." Bettina hoola-hoops her hips. "You know Bryson, don't you Izzy?"

"Geriatric health. How useful..." Izzy's eyes ooze with such wicked intent it almost drips to the floor.

There's a momentary pause, where I pray Izzy doesn't verbally connect geriatric to Bettina's age, but she ends the conversation with a can't-be-bothered shrug.

Dr Bryson appears and taps Bettina's elbow. "I don't have much time." He rolls his eyes in Izzy's direction, then steers Bettina to a table inside, his voice auditorium loud. "I found a parking spot down the road. No trees to mess with the Beamer. In my opinion, all street trees should be given the axe. A waste of ratepayers' money."

I try to keep my eyes on the memoir, but I'm caught up

assessing Bryson. Well-dressed, good-looking, luxury car, prestigious career—all those things, but mostly opinionated wanker. He's also obviously stupid. If he'd changed Izzy's tyre, *she'd* be with him right now. I lift my coffee like a tequila shot and drink to stupidity.

After they've eaten, Bettina points to her shoes while mouthing something about the car. Bryson leaves and she totters toward us.

"You guys, you've gotta keep quiet about what I'm gonna tell you." She holds a finger to her lips. "I have a bit of... erm... goss... erm pillow talk. The medical team assigned to Maria's care are seriously considering giving the Irish translator his marching orders. They aren't pleased with The Remembering Project. Too tiring and exploitive." Bettina sighs dramatically. "Thought I'd give you the heads up."

Izzy's expression remains neutral until Bettina leaves, then she wails like Biscotti when I don't feed him on time. "What's our back-up plan when the only person Maria likes, *and* can understand her properly, is cut from the project?"

As I drive home, I think about inviting Izzy to my place for the next memoir reading. Away from Bettina and her geriatric doctor who ruffled our comfortable calm.

I'm fiddling with the keys when the dog's growls an ungreeting.

"Time to stop acting as if I'm an intruder." I flop onto the sofa and rustle the packet of dog treats I keep on the side table.

Biscotti doesn't wait for a 'Here, boy.' He sits by my side salivating for a beef strip. I dangle a second to stop him cowering under the dining table. "I need your help. Man to man." Biscotti covers his head with a paw. "Not interested? This involves your human mum. My mum too. Whether you like it or not, we're brothers."

To my surprise, he angles his head as if offering a sympathetic ear. "Sorry mate, I understand Mum's Italian as much as your barking."

"Woof. Woof." He wags his tail.

"That's a first. You're telling me you want another treat?" I throw him two and watch him wolf them down. "I'm an old dog, like you, but I'm learning. Meet me half way."

Biscotti stands proudly and I notice his resemblance to a wolf. Mum used to say he was a husky-bitzer-cross.

"Why did Mum choose you when she was terrified of wolves?"

Biscotti doesn't run off, but tilts his head from one side to the other.

"I wish I knew what you were thinking. Are there training courses in dog whispering?"

He shakes his head and only flinches slightly when I pat him.

I ignore him in the hope he'll stay, but he half-heartedly snarls and skulks away.

I turn on the TV and flick through every channel, but can't relax with the worry of wanker Bryson and his crew stopping Dermot.

I arrive at The Figs before Izzy, so I let myself into The Remembering Room where Dermot is writing up notes and Mum is resting.

After I kiss Mum's cheek, I lean back to gauge her condition. "You okay, Mum?"

She nods.

Dermot asks, "Do you need me to translate?"

"Yes, please."

I hand Mum her old handwritten recipe book. "I need your opinion, Mum. I'm thinking of inviting Izzy to my place to type up your memoirs. We'll get more done that way. I'm going to cook dinner using one of your old recipes, but don't know which one?"

Mum tilts her head with obvious interest and lifts the corners of her mouth in a smile. Her eyes twinkle as she speaks, and her rapidly moving hands match the rhythm of her Italian words.

"Your mother loves knowing her cooking is still appreciated, even if it is second-hand," Dermot says.

I'm certain Mum said much more. "What else did she say?"

Dermot shifts uncomfortably in his seat. "She wants to know if it's a date? And she's insisting on inspecting any new women chasing you on your phone."

I shrug, resigned to being worn down. I open Cupid4U, but before I hand it over, the advertising banner across the top of the app changes from *Hair Plugs*, to *Ramp Up Your Sex Appeal*, to *Italian Language Lessons Near You*. "Maybe the computer chip is listening to my thoughts and offering me a solution? Language lessons? Worth a try."

Dermot points at the unopened messages. "Three women have shown interest in your profile. Do you mind if your mam checks them out?"

"Go right ahead."

Mum taps and nods, all the while muttering in Italian.

"This is the woman your mam likes best," Dermot says.

Mum points out a ridiculously attractive woman. I take back my phone and study the photo. This woman can't be for real. Her hobbies rank low on my favourite things to do: entertaining guests, playing tennis and wine tasting. "Hang on." I follow Izzy's security instructions, copying the woman's photo and posting it into Google's reverse image search. Eleven matches—all with different names, occupation, and birthplace. "It's a scam," I say. "A woman like that's not going to look at an average Joe like me. Lucky Izzy warned me about catfishing."

When Izzy had said it, I'd made a joke about not knowing cats could swim and she'd chuckled. Her laughter warmed my heart, so I'd tried another joke. How would one cook a cat if one hooked one? Izzy had shaken her head and told me I'd gone too far.

Mum snatches my phone and taps and swipes, trying to find someone else. When she babbles in rapid-fire Italian, I rub my chin and look to Dermot for help.

"She wants to close your profile and open Izzy's."

I pretend I don't know Izzy's password and fumble with my phone. Izzy changed both of our passwords to *Biscotti6*, because it was easy for her to remember and keep a regular tab of the traffic on mine. Since then, I've visited her page quickly. Even though I don't mind Izzy checking my profile, I feel guilty checking hers.

Mum yells what I assume is *hurry up* and I decide Izzy probably won't mind Mum having a look. I watch Mum scroll through a queue of interested men.

Ever since Izzy told me of the prevalence of date-rape, I've been scrutinising men's faces everywhere. Screening these matches on the website is akin to reading tea leaves. I squint and speculate about their intentions. Eyes too far apart and they look devious; too close together and they're the sort who don't know right from wrong. In short, anyone interested in Izzy looks like a predator.

My heart pounds uncomfortably in my chest, so I leave Mum and Dermot to it. "I'm getting a drink. Back in a minute."

I'm on shaky ground. If Dad's mum, Granny Blake, was alive, I'd tell her how I feel about Izzy. She'd give me advice —she dished it out like broth in a soup kitchen. Most of it good.

Cross to the other side of the road when you pass a woman alone, especially at night.

Friendship is more important than romance.

Don't go for looks. Looks fade.

If a woman doesn't want to talk about something, let her be.

What would I ask Gran now?

As I walk back into The Remembering Room, Dermot waves me over. "Your mam says Izzy's changed her profile picture."

I check it out. Izzy's smiling at the camera. She's beautiful.

Sorry, Gran. Is it okay if a wonderful woman also has a pretty face? Am I bad for wanting both friendship and the other? I reckon Gran would say yes to anything if she met Izzy.

Izzy's bio has changed too. It sounds softer—more open to meeting someone. My stomach burns with an emotion I don't want to own. These profile changes are signs that Izzy is ready to date again, and that's ...good. Good for her, anyway. If I'm to keep her friendship, I'll have to bite my tongue about unsuitable matches.

Mum complains in Italian to Dermot, and I watch over their shoulders as Dermot reads out Izzy's list of interests. "She loves family history research. And she wants to learn

Italian. Your mother says Izzy sounds like your perfect match."

"No, Mum." I point out Izzy's desired age range. "She wants a younger man. See? I miss out."

Mum argues, and I try to shut out her voice. Her tone is either tired, or tired of her son for being such a loser. I shake my head when Dermot starts to translate, and I hand Mum the recipe book. "What should I cook?"

"She's already decided," Dermot says. "Lasagne. But she tells you to practise first. Make it for yourself, then try it. You don't want to ruin an opportunity to impress a good woman."

Chapter Thirty-Two

Mariella, The Achille Lauro, 1967

For the last fortnight of the voyage, Stella and I got up at first light and took daily runs around the deck. By eating breakfast at first shift, we avoided the crowds of younger passengers who'd spent the previous night drinking and dancing.

We took turns choosing our table companions. Whenever it was my turn, I sought people who reminded me of my parents. Something as simple as Mamma's grey streaked hair and hunched shoulders. I even found comfort in a pair of weathered hands like Babbo's.

Many older couples were on their way to Australia to live with grown-up children. Each time someone said this, my heart sang with the hope of my parents doing the same.

Stella, the school ma'am tyrant, pushed me to make conversation and practise my English. "Do you mind us joining you for breakfast?" She forced me to say each morning until it felt natural. When we left the table, she elbowed me until I said, "Have a very nice day."

After leaving the African coast near Madagascar and sailing the Indian Ocean, I became more confident, and with Stella's help, my language skills skyrocketed.

"Time for me to cut the reins," Stella said one morning, as we headed to the cabin below.

"What do you mean?" I pressed a hand to my chest. Was Stella letting our friendship go?

"No more falling back on Italian. English only from now on."

"But—"

"No excuses. Spies become fluent in less than the time of our voyage. In a week, you'll be greeting Australians in their own language."

"Does this mean I can't ask for help when I get stuck?" I asked in Italian. My heart raced at the thought of talking to people and standing like a mute.

"I do not understand you. Speak English."

We swapped magazines in the library, then returned to the cabin where I slowly read to myself, whispering sentences under my breath. English wasn't as expressive as Italian, but I grew fonder of my new language. Stella helped when asked, but mostly she made me flounder in the deep end until I found the courage to swim.

The day before we docked, I flicked through my magazine, wanting to impress Stella with my spy-like dedication to learning, when an article warning unsuspecting women caught my attention.

"Stella?

She rolled over and sat cross-legged, her head almost touching the bunk above. "What?"

"I've been reading this." I held up the page to show her the headline. *How to Spot a Rogue.* "It's about avoiding the wrong type of men. Want to hear it?"

Stella scratched her nose. "No. It's time for me to put Mick, and you to put Emilio, behind us. I think we should listen to our gut. We know when things don't feel right."

"I could find another article?"

"I have a better idea. We'll paint each other's fingernails."

We sat cross-legged on the floor and Stella opened a faux crocodile-skin cosmetic case, setting out a manicure set and three bottles of nail polish. She then produced some jewellery from a zip up compartment under the lid and put it on.

Stella held out her hands, showing a diamond solitaire on the left and an unusual ring on the right hand—smaller baguette diamonds with a sinuous gold setting snaking around a blue-green stone.

"Your rings are exquisite," I said. "What's the larger stone?"

"An Australian opal," Stella shrugged. "Lorenzo gave it to me for our anniversary. What does the shape remind you of?"

I squinted at the gold outline. "Is it a musical instrument?"

"Yep. His lover plays the French Horn."

Stella remained silent while we painted each other's nails. Once they were dry, she reclined on her mattress, her right arm under her head as though sunbathing. I hung down from the bunk above to talk with her, but there were clouds in her eyes.

She looked at the ring on her left hand and let her arm flop over the edge of the bed.

I cleared my throat. "Stella? I don't have a camera. I'm worried we might not see each other again. Sydney to Ingham is a long way. Can I draw you?"

Her eyes filled with tears. "Go ahead. I'm not moving. Please draw me beautiful and strong."

I sketched the shape and tilt of her head, the angles of her shoulders, and her flexed knees. I drew every detail of her beautiful face and the poignancy of her dangling hand, the disappointment of the opal ring, the fingers yearning to touch and be touched.

When I finished, I held the portrait to my chest.

It took a moment before I was ready to show her. I put on my brightest voice. "I'm done."

"I'm done too," she said. "I wish we had more choices in life."

"I agree. Imagine how different our lives would be if we weren't controlled by men?"

"What would you do?" she asked.

I didn't need to think about the answer. "I would definitely not travel half the world to play dutiful wife for a man I might not like."

"At least your relationship has prospects," Stella said. "You'll likely have babies and become part of an Australian-Italian community. I'm sentenced to existing with my darling prison cellmate, a husband who may as well be my brother."

Chapter Thirty-Three

Joe, Present Day

Yesterday, while my practise dish of lasagne was bubbling away in the oven, I researched language lessons. By the time I found beginner Italian classes close to home, and enrolled for two—starting tonight, my lasagne had crisped around the edges. The one thing I'm good at is knowing the time. It's like there's a clock ticking permanently inside my head. Unusual of me to lose track of time, but I was caught in a dilemma—tossing up whether to sign up for the discount classes offered for couples.

Couple simply means two. No insinuation of romantic involvement.

My finger hovers near Izzy's phone number. But I have second thoughts.

"What do you reckon?" I ask Biscotti. "Will I tell Izzy how much I appreciate her writing up Mum's story and ask if she'd like to come over for a taste of Mum's famous lasagne?"

He hits his head with his paw.

"I could tell her the lasagne could be useful for adding detail to the story?"

Biscotti turns on the spot, tail between his legs. He looks at me as though he isn't impressed. He spins again as if telling me my house isn't much chop.

I'm not trusting a dog's opinion on décor, but after reviewing the room myself, I rethink the plan to invite Izzy over. My place is clean and organised, but there's not much else going for it. If my house was a person, he'd be an accountant called Nigel—stringy vertical blinds for hair. Nigel's colleagues would avoid sitting next to him in the lunchroom because he's...boring and awkward. Izzy's apartment is the popular girl. But not the mean girl, the one who offers money to people short of change at the checkout. She's the person who makes everyone feel special.

Izzy matches her house—and unfortunately, I'm bland like mine.

Biscotti nudges my knee.

"What mate? I can't redecorate!"

He nudges the phone this time. I take it as a signal to dial. When you look for signs, you find them. I might well be going mad, but I press Izzy's name in my contacts.

She answers straight away. "What's up?"

"I'm cooking lasagne. If you like, I can bring it over."

"I'd love some. I've a fondness for good food."

"Then... instead of the memoir reading and writing, I was wondering if you'd be up for going somewhere afterwards?"

"Where?"

"I'll tell you after dinner?"

"A surprise? Why not?"

If Izzy likes the lasagne, I'll try more of Mum's recipes. The way to a woman's heart could be through her stomach.

When I park in the visitor's space at Izzy's, I glance at the dashboard. Fifteen minutes late. What's happening to me?

Tucked under my arm is the hot lasagne wrapped in an insulating beach towel. A bottle of Prosecco with a bag of salad ingredients dangle from my wrist. I readjust my stance to press her apartment buzzer with my elbow. Three times, I buzz, but Izzy doesn't answer her door.

I've known women who might ignore a man who turns up late, but Izzy seems more the—throw open the door to yell, 'did you get lost?'—type. Maybe the doorbell's drowned by sounds on the TV.

Leaning against the wall and balancing one foot on the other knee to support the lasagne, which now feels ten times heavier, I manage to knock. It sounds sharper and louder than intended. I hope I don't sound impatient, especially since I'm the one who's late.

Izzy's sticks her head through the door without a hint of annoyance. "Sorry," she says, her hair dripping wet. "I lost track of time in the shower. Hope you haven't been standing long."

I smile at my good fortune. "Not at all."

She excuses herself to dry her hair, so I make myself at home, putting the lasagne in the oven, assembling the salad, and opening the Prosecco.

When she returns, Izzy closes her eyes and inhales deeply. "Yum. Dinner smells delicious."

"One of Mum's favourite recipes." I pour the wine, feeling pleased with Izzy's praise. Then, whoosh—I have an out-of-body experience. I'm looking down on an average man who's gone to too much trouble. If this were a movie, the audience would cringe in their seats. They'd cover their eyes to avoid the moment where the man is turned down. I modulate my actions to show clear, yet false, platonic intentions. "Eat first, then the surprise." As soon as I finish speaking, my head bounces around like Biscotti's. Please, dear God: Greek, Roman or otherwise, stop me from saying *woof woof*.

"I'm a quick eater," Izzy says, "and I'm even wearing a new dress."

I hope she doesn't notice I'm wagging my tail.

Once we've cleared our plates, I reach into the carry bag and brush a stray lettuce leaf off the envelope. My hand shakes as I slide it across the table. "A gift. I hope you're not offended. I should have asked, but I had the idea and got carried away—"

"You're over-explaining. Give it to me."

She smiles at the shiny certificate I took ages to print, then unfolds the downloaded PDF brochure, running her finger over the class description. "Joe! Italian lessons with old movie clips, songs, and role-plays. Perfect!"

I sigh and breathe at once, turning to hide my nervous giggle. She didn't notice the printed word *couple*.

"You're coming, too?" she asks. "Please tell me it's for both of us."

The Italian tutor answers the door, red lipstick accentuating her broad smile. "*Parli Italiano?*"

Izzy's look is as blank as mine.

"*Si,*" the tutor says, cycling her index fingers. This is a familiar gesture. Mum used it whenever she demanded an answer.'

She wants us to speak Italian before the lessons begin? Not me. I'm a deer caught in headlights.

"*Si*," she repeats. This time, the action is more urgent.

"*Si*," we echo obediently.

Izzy bragged on the drive over about spending the afternoon practising with the Italian translator app, which helped her with Mum last year. Wanted to get a head start. But all she manages is a clenched-teeth smile. Her practised phrases seem to have evaporated under the heat of pressure.

Our tutor rests one hand on a curvy hip and smiles. "I am Dorotea. Don't look so worried. There'll be some English. Follow me. My language studio is out back."

Izzy and I sigh with relief as we follow Dorotea along a pathway around the side of the house. We weave through a thriving vegetable garden—tomatoes, capsicum, zucchini and numerous unlabelled leafy patches. Down the back there's a blue-painted weatherboard cabin with a sign over the door: *Ciao Bienvenuti*."

Dorotea poses in the doorway, angling her body first to Izzy and then to me. "*Mi chiamo Dorotea*." This time she pairs her hand roll with a dark chocolate stare; sweet enough that I don't run, but the tang of 80% cocoa is strong—she's not to be taken lightly.

"*Mi chiamo, Joseph Blake*." I immediately wish I hadn't used my full name. Not only does it sound formal, but if Izzy says a different name, Dorotea might say something like, 'so you're not married then?' and Izzy will say, 'No. Why would you assume that?'

The 20% discount no longer feels like a good deal.

"*Mi chiamo, Izzy*."

My shoulders relax, and Dorotea chatters in a sing-song

voice as she directs us to a low table pushed up against a kitchen workbench. A large flat-screen TV hangs in front of us, and the side wall is one giant whiteboard, full of unrecognisable words.

I run my hand over the smooth surface, checking for seams.

"Special paint," Dorotea explains. "It changes any wall into a whiteboard. Magnetic, too." She points to the chairs. "Please sit. We'll wait a few minutes for the other student to arrive."

In front of us, workbooks and pencils are set on exactly the same angle, equidistant and parallel to the table's edge. Arranged by someone very particular.

While Dorotea twiddles with her laptop and projects her slideshow through the TV, Izzy whispers, "Do you think she's beautiful?"

I mouth, "I hadn't noticed."

Izzy elbows me. "Joe! You need glasses."

I tilt my head to check Dorotea out. Almost fifty, a snug black hat covers most of her brown hair. She wears a close-fitting unadorned dress, suggesting military precision, but when she flashes a lipsticked smile, the effect is easy-going and pleasing.

An intercom chimes, and she presses a buzzer to speak. "Signora Dorotea will meet you at the side gate."

The second she steps outside, Izzy starts talking. "What do you think of her, Joe?"

"She seems very organised."

Izzy pouts playfully. "I wonder if she's single?"

"Why? Do you fancy her?" I ask with a laugh.

"No. I was thinking about you. How good would it be if you found yourself a woman who speaks Italian? Your mum would love it."

"She's probably married."

We straighten up and shut our mouths when the door opens.

A man in his thirties, with Nordic features, follows Dorotea inside and bows toward us. "*Mi chiamo, Denzel.*"

Show off.

"Are you related to Denzel Washington?" Izzy giggles at her own joke.

Denzel ruffles his white blonde hair and flashes toothpaste advertisement teeth. "No, but I get asked that a lot."

He laughs a little too long. Then he shakes Izzy's hand a little too long.

There's a hint of colour in her cheeks when he lets go. "I'm Izzy."

Dorothea assigns each of us five minutes introduction time. Denzel takes up ten minutes regaling us with his extensive world travels. He shakes a keyring holding gold 'country' disks and larger rings for 'continents', saying he 'earned' them.

Imagine driving with that rattling on your key ring? Walking with it in your pocket could put a hip out.

Denzel seems to have a bottomless pit of travel money and is starting his second world tour. "This time I want to speak the language because I intend to *blend in* and communicate with the *natives.*" He smiles from Dorotea to Izzy. "My extensive tour of Italy will be *expensive,* but what better to spend our money on than experience?"

Every time Denzel puts stressed words into air quotes, I clear my throat like a cat coughing up a fur ball. Izzy gives me a sideways warning glance, then turns back to Denzel, smiling as he drones on and on.

Dorotea raises a perfectly arched eyebrow towards the digital clock displayed on the TV. I don't need to look at the time, I know Denzel's taken our share. For that, I'm thankful. I've got little to say.

When it's Izzy's turn, Dorotea says, "We will run over-time a few minutes. I like to keep to a tight schedule, but I can break it this once."

"Joe and I are learning Italian to help his mother, Maria. She has dementia, and has forgotten how to speak English, but still understands Italian."

Dorotea pushes my workbook aside and sits on the table in front of me, her dress creeping upwards. "So, you're Italian, Joe? I thought you had the look of Italian men. An earthy attractiveness."

My face flushes with embarrassment and I stare at the table. "Most of my features are from my father's side. Australian."

"Ah, well. We'll be speaking Italian in no time. *Parli Italiano?*" When she makes her hand signal, we all answer '*Sì*' like Pavlov's dogs. Denzel sounds supremely confident, Izzy less so, and mine is an unmanly squeak.

Dorotea holds a workbook identical to ours and opens it to the first page. "Common words and phrases," she says. "First column: Italian, second column: phonetic pronunciation, and the third column—which we'll be folding and hiding after ten minutes—has the English translation."

I've barely read through once when she rings a bell. Surely the time can't be up?

"Now you've practised alone, we'll pair up. There's no point knowing a language and not speaking it. For this session, it's Izzy and Denzel. Joe, you're with me."

I ignore Izzy tugging my hair like a teasing schoolgirl, but check her progress several times during the lengthy session. Instead of moving back to her own seat when it ends, she sits with Denzel to watch video clips of Signora

Dorotea asking questions to the camera. Without help from our notes, we're expected to respond when pre-recorded Dorotea does the hand action.

On the screen, Dorotea's wavy hair is loose and clipped to one side. She looks less like a teacher and more like a celebrity. My mind gets lost, unsuccessfully wondering who she reminds me of. I consider passing Izzy a note to ask her who the tutor looks like, but there's already note-passing happening. An exchange between her and sun-bleached Denzel.

I can't wait for the lesson to end.

Izzy fastens her seat belt with an obvious click. "Well, well, Joey. How interesting?" Her use of the name Joey doesn't escape me. Mum is about to come up.

"Tomorrow, when we see Maria, we're both going to speak Italian. I'll say *Parli Italiano* and you'll say *si*."

"Will you do the Dorotea hand actions?" I ask.

"Perhaps. You'd probably like that."

I can't watch Izzy's face while I'm driving, but I've memorised enough of her expressions to fill in the gaps. In my mind, she's doing an animated eyebrow jiggle. Teasing me again.

"Maria will be impressed," she continues, "then when we've exhausted our tricks, I'll ask Dermot to translate. I will tell your mum all about the stunning Dorotea and how her son was the teacher's pet."

"Is this a bait and switch?" I ask. "You shining the spotlight on me so Mum doesn't ask about you and Denzel?"

"What?" Izzy sounds genuinely shocked.

"The love notes," I remind her, rolling my shoulders back in what I hope is a nonchalant move.

"Love notes?"

Izzy is quiet for a moment, then she splutters with laughter. "Denzel wrote to ask if I wanted to practise the phrases with him during the week."

"And?" My shoulders slump.

"If I tell you, you must promise not to get annoyed or offended."

My shoulders are overdoing it now, pulling out their whole damned chirpy repertoire, when they'd rather brace themselves for bad news.

"I wrote: *I can't because my husband is the jealous type.* I added at the bottom, *He has hot Italian blood.* Then I pointed at you."

Offended? Annoyed? I feel ten years younger and ten times as dangerous. "Hot Italian blood? We'll have to keep up the pretence," I say with a smile. "It will be difficult, but I'll try."

"What about Dorotea? It might ruin your chances with her?"

"I have a confession. I signed us up for classes using the couples discount code. It was 20%. I felt bad not telling you."

Izzy flares her nostrils. "So, Dorotea thought we were married, yet she plonked herself in front of you—all lipstick and stocking tops. I'm not keen on that woman. Her name, for starters. People who talk about themselves in third person frickin annoy me. But her name was worse than annoying. Every time she said Dorotea, my brain heard *Diarrhoea.*"

I chuckle out loud.

"Don't laugh at me, Joe."

"I'm laughing with you. Whenever she said Dorotea I heard *Dirty Ear*."

Izzy squeezes my hand on the steering wheel, laughs, then unfortunately lets it go. Probably wishful thinking, but my finely tuned sense of timing says she held it a second longer than usual.

When I park at her apartment, she reaches for her bag. "I hope I didn't sound ungrateful. Thank you for the lessons. It was good surprise."

"We don't have to go back for the rest," I suggest. "We could learn together online?"

She warms me with her smile. "Good idea, Joe. My favourite part of this evening was driving there with you."

Chapter Thirty-Four

Mariella, Sydney, 1967

The Australian landmass grew larger and crowds of passengers cheered from the deck. When we cruised under the Sydney Harbour Bridge, the voices grew deafening.

Stella pointed out the passenger wharves at Barangaroo. "Look at the people waving at us."

I gripped her hand, my mouth too dry to talk. For the past six weeks I'd still felt connected to home. But what if I descended that gangplank and by standing on Australian soil, I cut all connection to my Italian homeland?

"Are you okay?" she asked.

I wasn't.

Stella elbowed me playfully. "Look how blue the sky is. Just like Italy."

It felt wrong to be greeted by a familiar shade of blue. Everything about this place was supposed to be different.

She leaned over the railings. "Look! Lorenzo's waving at

..." she stopped mid-sentence. "How will you recognise the man Angelo's sending to meet you?"

I scanned the sea of people. "He'll be holding a sign with my name on it."

But there was no one with a sign. Not yet. I had a name and address just in case, but this didn't stop my knees shaking. This stranger would put me on the train that travelled up the east coast from Sydney to Ingham—a distance greater than Rome to London.

"Don't be nervous." Stella hugged me. "He'll be there." She pulled me towards the disembarkation queue, but I dragged my reluctant feet. In Sydney, I would say goodbye to Stella, and although we'd promised to write, we'd be more than a thousand miles apart.

Clutching the suitcase with my most precious possessions in one hand, and passport and documentation in the other, I struggled along the gangplank. Stella had left all her luggage in the cabin, trusting porters to collect it. But I couldn't bear to lose another piece of my life. The back of my throat ached with dread. "Will you wait with me until this man collects me?"

"Of course." Stella kissed my cheek and took my paperwork. "You need both hands for that heavy suitcase and if you lose your papers, the authorities will lock you up in the old stone convict barracks."

I knew she was joking, but a shudder ran along my arms and tingled in my fingertips. It didn't stop until Stella draped her arm around my shoulders. I tried to absorb some of her self-assurance. I needed all the strength I could muster for what lay ahead.

Stella went through the checkpoint first. The man from customs looked from her face to the picture on the passport, made a quick check of her entry documents and waved her through.

She passed me my papers. "I'll be waiting over there. Just past the roped-off area."

As I handed my open passport to show the officer, Stella's face stared back from the tiny photograph. I waved my arms frantically. We'd mixed up the paperwork.

I tried to attract her attention, but Stella disappeared into the crowd.

Chapter Thirty-Five

Maria, Present Day

Dermot helps me upright. He's good like that. He senses whenever I grow tired.

"Look who's here, Maria," he says.

Katerina grasps my hand. "Maria, how are you?"

"*Amico mio.*" I've missed my friend.

"Are you okay?" Katerina turns quickly to Dermot where they begin rapid-fire question-and-answer time. The chatter sets my head in a spin. It's all noise. An upturned pile of scrabble tiles—lots of letters and sounds, but I can't form any words.

I throw my hands up and press them over my ears. "Can you translate for me, Dermot. I must explain to Katerina how I haven't been sleeping, but there's lots I need to do."

After Dermot translates, Katerina asks, "Have you told Joe or Izzy how you're feeling?"

"I don't want to worry them." I don't tell her that if I stop my stories now, it might be too late. Recently my fractured memories have become harder to catch. With so little time and a mother's work left undone, I need to hurry if I'm going to help my son.

Katerina's eyes glisten with tears. "I'm so sorry. I was the one who insisted on the Remembering Project and suggested bringing in Dermot." Her chin quivers. "I wish I hadn't joined my daughter on a holiday. I must tell Matron how tired you are."

Before I can argue, she disappears. I raise an eyebrow at Dermot, hoping he'll race after her, but he tugs at his collar with guilt.

"It's not her fault or yours. It's no one's fault," I say.

"But I kept prompting you. I've lost count of the number of times I told you not to give up and asked you to keep going."

"*Una porcheria*," I say, and it is bullshit. "I didn't want to stop. I know my own mind, even when it's broken."

"But—"

"No. I won't have it. Have you noticed how much closer Joe and Izzy have become? They think they're happier because they're finding out my life story and learning to speak another language, but I know differently. It's because they have each other."

I massage a pulse, pulse, pulse in my temple. "If I stop the stories, Joey will go back to his lonely, monotonous life and Izzy will come back to The Figs with me and Katerina. Joey needs her more than I do. Izzy doesn't realise it, but she needs Joey, too."

Matron stamps both feet announcing her arrival. It puts me in mind of an army sergeant. "I've called the doctor. Until Katerina told me, I'd been arguing with your care team and telling them you were fine."

After a backward and forwarding between Dermot and Matron, she beckons him to follow and I'm left alone.

An hour later there's a re-enactment of the entire conversation when that doctor with an arrogant air arrives. This time I don't care whether they're talking about me or to me.

The doctor's gaze rests on everyone in the room—except me. "I'm concerned stress has exacerbated her dementia."

"He's concerned your dementia's getting worse," Dermot translates.

I shake my head in denial, but I know the doctor's right. I've known since Dermot began repeating tales from the previous session, trying to tease out missing details and I couldn't find what he was fishing for. From under my sea of tiredness, I sensed a swoosh as the memories swam away.

Matron sandwiches my hand between hers. "Maria, listen. The sessions with Dermot must stop. At least until you're back to your old self."

Which old self does she mean? The carefree Italian girl I once was? The frightened young woman sent away from all she loved? Or, the one abandoned in an unfamiliar country, stripped of everything?

While Matron marches away to collect the prescribed sedatives, Katerina and Dermot lead me back to my room.

Within seconds of swallowing the medication, I battle to keep my eyes open, but they droop without permission.

"Matron phoned Joe," Katerina whispers. "I'll wait for him."

I concentrate on the whirr of her wheelchair vanishing down the corridor, and I fight sleep with all my might. Dermot kisses my cheek. "*Arrivederci*, Maria. I'll come back as soon as I get the doctor's permission."

I grip his shirt-front and force my heavy-eyelids open. My mouth is thick with sleep, but I speak deliberately, emphasising the importance of my message. "I might not get better, Dermot. Catch up to Katerina. She must tell Joey and Izzy something. If they want to know what happened, they must find Stella."

Chapter Thirty-Six

Joe, Present Day

I'm surprised to find Katerina waiting in the garden out front of The Figs. I press my face against hers for a cheek-on-cheek kiss. "You're back. I hope you had a glorious trip."

"It was wonderful. I'll tell you all about it later."

"Have you seen Mum, yet? She'll be excited. She's asked after you a few times."

Katerina hesitates. "Yes... I've seen Maria and Dermot, and I've got the last... latest batch of translations."

She smiles, but I've known Katerina long enough to know something's up. "What's wrong? Spill!"

Izzy rounds the corner, tipping a mint into her hand from a small metal box. I don't need detective training to know she's been smoking. We all know she smokes, yet she still tries to hide it. She gives Katerina one of those big genuine hugs we all need. "Welcome back."

"Thank you." Katerina sighs. "I suppose it's best to tell

you both together. Bettina's bound to blab as soon as you step foot in reception."

"Blab what?" Izzy asks.

"The doctor visited Maria yesterday. He's convinced that day-after-day of remembering is having a negative effect on her health."

"Is Dermot with Mum? I'll get him to translate." I start for the door, but Katerina puts a hand out to stop me.

"Wait a minute, Joe. The doctor's sent Dermot away."

Izzy puts her hands on her hips. "What's going on?"

"Apparently, she hasn't been sleeping. And none of the night staff thought to mention how unsettled she is," Katerina growls. "This wouldn't have happened if you'd been here in a nursing capacity, Izzy."

Izzy's shoulders sag, and Katerina quickly pats her arm. "That came out wrong. I was acknowledging your skills. I pushed you to write the memoir. I wasn't thinking. First, I robbed Maria of the best nurse, then I took off on a holiday."

"Neither of you are responsible," I say, kicking stray pebbles off the path and back into the garden where they belong. "But poor Mum..." I should have watched her more closely. I would have done if I hadn't been so preoccupied watching Izzy.

"Did the doctor say anything's wrong medically?" Izzy's high-pitched voice ties a worry knot in my stomach.

"Doctor Bryson said it's exhaustion. He'll reassess in a month, but we might not get any more stories."

"No. No. No. He doesn't know how tough Maria is." The certainty in Izzy's voice is reassuring.

Katerina's hand trembles as she holds out the folder. "Here's what Dermot translated overnight. I'm not sure which of you to give it to."

"We're working together, now." Izzy smiles. "We have a system. I scan it onto my computer and type, while Joe reads the hard copy. He's better at decoding Dermot's tricky handwriting. I add in extra details to bring it to life, and Joe makes wonderful suggestions. We make a good team, don't we Joe?"

Katerina looks at Izzy with a curious smile before turning to me. "I believe you do make a good team. I'm looking forward to reading this personalised piece of history."

I pull out my phone. "Where's Dermot now?"

"Flew home last night to see his lady. He'll come back *when* your mother's given the all clear to continue."

Katerina's *when* has more the tone of an *if*.

"I'll go see Mum. Unless I see her face to face, I won't know she's all right."

Katerina lifts her shoulders then drops them in a sigh. "The doctor ordered sedation. She'll be asleep for most of the day."

Izzy takes my arm. "Come on, Joe. We can type up these notes and come back when she's awake."

"Dr Bryson has limited visitors to one at a time. One per day and half an hour max. But before you go, Maria asked me to pass on a message. I'm not sure what it means or why, but she needs you to find her old friend, Stella."

Izzy's apartment has warmth, her floor to ceiling shelf-unit displays a collection of first edition books and vintage cigarette lighters. If you can tell a lot from what people collect, what do odd socks and mismatched Tupperware lids say about me?

After the first read-through of the notes, I shuffle them around, looking for missing pages. "Where's the rest? We've got Mariella landing in Australia and losing both her immigration papers and her friend. Then it ends?"

Izzy stops typing and takes a deep breath. "How are we going to find out what happened if Maria stops telling the story?" She moves the computer mouse in circles then faces the laptop towards me. After closing the memoir document, she pulls up a search engine. "Well, we're both still on leave and the story has stalled. It's not ideal, but it gives us time to look for Stella."

"Where would we even begin? All we have to go on is Stella from Sydney."

"Hang on." Izzy has an ah-ah expression. She opens a previous chapter of the memoir document. "Here, sit with me, I'm looking for where Maria/Mariella first meets her cabin mate. I'm sure Stella's name was on the welcome card or was that just my—"

"Stop. There," I say, pointing at the screen.

"Bingo." Izzy highlights the name. Mrs Stella Pansini. "And her husband's name was Lorenzo. Surely his name and record company must be searchable."

Sure enough, a check through Google throws up several archived newspaper articles containing the name Lorenzo Pansini. Izzy and I read the screen, head against head. I'm not sure what's more thrilling, following a trail to find Mum, or the faint scent of Izzy's herbal shampoo.

"Restive Records," I read out loud. "Gave a start to lots of budding musicians. He seems like a good bloke."

"Skim through them, Joe. We're not doing a character study; we're looking for Stella."

I take the mouse and flick through the articles, reading

headlines and scanning for names, when Izzy yells. "Stop. A picture."

Her hand wrestles mine for control as she zooms in. A smiling Lorenzo handing a framed gold record to a chart-topping pop star. On his arm, his lovely wife, Stella.

"Notice anything?" Izzy asks.

"1966. The year before she met Mum."

"Yes, but not just that. Look at Stella's face. She looks so much like the photo you showed me of Maria holding you as a baby."

I tilt my head and squint the screen. "Mum wasn't exaggerating, they looked very alike."

Izzy stands and takes out her phone. "You keep looking through the newspaper archives. I'll try all telephone listings of Pansini in Sydney and surrounds."

I scroll through and scan pages for relevant references. Except for another picture of both her and her husband attending Go-Set magazine's music awards, there's no further mention of Stella.

I need caffeine and food. Trying not to interrupt Izzy's phone calls, I make my way quietly about her kitchen. She's mid-way through dialling when I hand her a mug and two ginger biscuits. "It's all I could find in your pantry," I whisper. "I'll buy lunch if you want to keep calling."

Izzy cradles the phone with her shoulder then holds a shhhhing finger to her mouth. "Hello," she says. "I'm looking for a relative I lost contact with years ago. Lorenzo Pansini."

For every phone call, Izzy creates a slightly different backstory. She winks and smiles, and I sink into the seat happy to listen. But she mimes eating and waves me on my way.

By the time I get back with the burgers, Izzy's flat out on the sofa.

"I found a cousin." Her pretty mouth is down-turned. "Lorenzo divorced Stella many years ago, and we can no longer ask Lorenzo where she went because he's been dead ten years."

I take a chair and unwrap my burger. "It's impossible to find Stella now, we may as well give up."

Izzy usually loves her food, but she dumps the burger on the coffee table, half-eaten.

"They looked better on the menu board," I say.

"Nothing wrong with them. It's the disappointment nicking my appetite."

The cogs inside my head are unsuccessfully searching for something to say, when she sits up and takes a bite of her burger. Between mouthfuls she says, "Maybe we can find more by researching the town of Ingham? Even if the details we find aren't specific to your mum, knowing about the town would add texture and colour to her memoir."

"Sure, where do we start?"

She grabs her laptop and minutes later rotates the screen. "There's a Facebook page, a Wikipedia page and stories from Ingham back in the sixties."

"Your pick."

Izzy clicks an entry. "Nearest city is Townsville. It's a sugar town."

When she smiles, I can taste the sugar. "I like that. Sugar Town."

"Sounds like a song," she says.

If I were a musician, I'd write a song called Sugartown. It'd be all about Izzy.

"Look!" She claps her hands. "Every year, Ingham holds an Australian–Italian festival."

I move closer to read the screen, even though I could see it perfectly from where I sat. "More than half the town's population are of Italian descent." I nod my head. "And look at that, the weather is wonderful, too. 26° to our 16°."

Izzy switches websites before I've finished reading. "I'm going to check out this festival. Home-made Italian food, traditional and non-traditional music, stalls, and beautiful Signorinas" she stops reading, mouth agape. "Joe. It's next weekend! We should go."

"It's too late to organise that," I say. "I don't want to be a downer, but accommodation is probably booked out a year ahead."

Izzy bites her thumbnail. "If I ring around and find a cancellation, will you come?"

I cross my fingers behind my back hoping she can find something. "Of course, I will."

I watch Izzy doodle in the margin as she rings each caravan park, hotel and motel. She scratches each name off with increasing disappointment. By the end of the list, I'm surprised there are no rips in the paper. When she's finished, she drops the pen. "Okay. There's nothing. You win the bet."

"This is more a lose-lose. I got hopeful there when one hotel took your phone number."

"He said he'd ring if anybody cancels. I could almost hear him roll his eyes. Clearly, no one ever cancels." Izzy flaps her hands like butterflies beating their wings against glass.

I restrain myself from calming those hands in mine. Too drawn to her hands for my own good, I stand reluctantly.

"Best go visit Mum. She's probably awake. Text me if the hotel gets back to you."

My car drives to The Figs on autopilot. The free head space fills with dread. This visit could be as difficult as the first time I saw Mum after dementia set in.

Before she got sick, Mum and I used to meet in the city for coffee and cake. It was her weekly chance to dress to the nines. That's what she used to say. Even past seventy, she made her own outfits, and always insisted on paying for high tea. Said it stopped her feeling guilty about choosing fancy places just so she could dress up.

In those days, Mum's English was perfect. Then boom. Life can change in an instant. I'll continue learning Italian from a computer program, but I need to hurry. Not too far in the future there's a worry of Mum not holding any conversation at all.

Chapter Thirty-Seven

Joe, Present Day

I'm sprinkling grated cheese over my toast, when the phone beeps.

A message from Izzy:

> Come over for breakfast?

ME
> An early start today?

IZZY
> Kind of. I've got news.

ME
> Good or bad?

I slide the toast under the griller; my eyes dart between the bubbling cheese and my phone. Please don't leave me hanging. I prefer Band-Aids ripped off quickly.

She doesn't text back until I've sat on the couch, food on my lap.

IZZY

Good news. Bet you can't guess.

ME

One of the Ingham hotels had a cancellation?

IZZY

Snowball's chance in hell.

ME

You going to tell me?

IZZY

No. Too busy making us some breakfast. See you at my place in half an hour.

After sending a thumbs up emoji, I take one bite of my cheese-grilled toast and hold it out for the dog. "Here, Scotty...I mean Biscotti. Food." He skulks towards me but stops half way. "Don't look at me like that. It's bread and cheese. Understand? *Capisci?*"

Biscotti turns up his nose. I sift through my brain for the Italian lesson on food names. "*Pane e formaggio.*"

He cocks one ear. Can dogs understand? He lunges and snatches the toast from my hand, but low growls when I pat him. "Righto," I say. "I'll leave you to it."

I grab my car keys, but do an about turn when I reach the door. Gotta change my shirt. May as well wear the one Izzy said she liked. I'll brush my teeth again, too. There's no law against getting your hopes up.

With my car on autopilot, I review the subtle signals Izzy's been sending lately. Not definite stuff, but signals I've interpreted as possible encouragement and tucked away in the optimistic section of my brain. I weigh up the facts. We've listed similar interests on the dating app, which isn't surprising since Izzy wrote both my profile and hers. On one hand, Izzy likes my company and wants us to hang out. On the other, she'd happily do the same with Mum or Katerina, and I doubt they brush their teeth in the highly improbable chance of getting close enough to kiss.

There's no concrete signal really, except when she smiles at me, I feel special. Like Luke-Warm-Average-Joe has been hotted up a fraction. And sometimes when we laugh at a shared joke, we hold eye contact for a moment longer than platonic friends usually do.

In Izzy's apartment parking lot, I take deep breaths and loiter in my car. Then I wait at the bottom of her apartment stairs, psyching myself into pushing the friendship into an ever-so-slightly romantic zone.

For a few seconds outside her door, I talk myself into it. But the moment passes.

She opens before I knock. "Why on earth are you standing outside? Your car pulled up five minutes ago and now you're out here dawdling. I hope you weren't about to make an escape?"

"Would you have chased me?" I ask, feeling unexpectedly brave.

"No. I'd have thrown a rock at you."

Izzy walks inside and I trail behind, wishing I had a witty come-back. I don't.

"Sit and eat." She pushes an omelette towards me. "I'm starving and the food's getting cold." She taps the table with her fork and flicks me a look. Not a good one. The perfect moment to show my feelings might not show up today.

In the kitchen, Izzy does a hot-potato-juggle getting dinner rolls out of the oven with bare hands. She butters them thickly, and hands me two on a plate. I nod thanks, even though the omelette sits like a brick in my stomach beside my foolish romantic daydreams. "Don't you want to know why you're here?" she asks.

"Yes, please."

She wears a wry smile. "There's good news and bad news."

"Put me out of my misery," I say.

"I contacted a librarian on an Ingham Facebook group. Her name's Annette, and she's their local historian. Guess what?" Izzy's eyebrows arch dramatically.

I whistle and pull my shoulders back, ready to be astounded. "You found Stella?"

She wiggles her theatrical eyebrows and laughs. "No. But almost as good. I explained through messages how we'd wanted to attend the Italian festival, then gave her our sob story of the booked-up accommodation. She offered us a small granny flat under her house. Although she doesn't rent it out to strangers, she's letting us stay so long as we assist her in setting up the Ingham historical society stall."

"Fantastic! What's the bad news?"

Izzy slides a folded sheet of paper across the table. "You owe me money for the flights and hire car because I've already booked and paid."

The booking details, her bank account number, and the dollar amounts are listed in black and white. I prefer it this way. Life would be easier if everything was set out in black-and-white.

As Izzy shoves in her last piece of bread, I transfer the money via a banking app. She points to my phone.

"What?"

"Can you log onto the dating app and give it to me?"

It's more an order than a question, so I hand over my

phone. "I won't bother logging in. You know the password because you made it up."

She swipes and taps the screen. "I'm changing your parameters. Initially, I set you up as seeking a woman in the range five years younger to five years older, but you're not getting enough hits. We need to widen the net."

My throat hurts when I swallow. Our friendship is more than I expected or deserve. For a foolhardy moment, I fantasised about Izzy wanting more. But she sees me as a project.

Chapter Thirty-Eight

Joe, Present Day

After surviving a cramped flight at opposite ends of the plane, Izzy and I disembark to blue skies and summery warmth. I'm suddenly optimistic. This might be my perfect day.

I'm captivated by the scenery on the drive between Townsville's airport and Ingham. Green mountains of the Great Dividing Range rise on the west of the highway. While on the east, all roads lead to beaches skirting the Great Barrier Reef. I'm tempted to flick the indicator and take us on a detour. Instead, I resign myself to daydreaming. *'The beach?'* I imagine myself saying to Izzy. She'd nod and say, *'With you? Yes, please.'* I'd smile confidently and pull her toward me. We'd wade barefooted at the water's edge and I'd caress her neck—

"I hope you're not falling asleep," Izzy says. "Maybe I'd better drive."

I shake myself back to the present. "I'm fine. We're almost there."

Giant banners advertising tomorrow's festival decorate Ingham's town centre. Izzy points out the motley collection of buildings standing sentinel on either side of the town's main road. The post office is painted a soft yellow, the colour of Izzy's blouse the day we started the Remembering Project. A sunny warmth sweeps through me.

"Look at that. Right there." Izzy points at a signpost directing us to the Hinchinbrook-shire Library. "Do you want to find our hostess, Annette, first, or have some lunch?"

"What about we go for a walk? Three hours on a plane has left me *feeling like a chair*."

"Is that an Italian saying?" She stares as if I'm an alien. "What on earth does feeling like a chair mean?"

"The shape. I've taken on a permanent sitting position."

"Right. Park in front of the sports store and I'll buy a baseball bat."

"A baseball bat? Are you matching my confusion and raising me one?"

"No, I'm planning to bash the kinks out of your legs."

I laugh like crazy as I pull into a parking spot. I decide against making a joke with the word *kink*. I've neither the comedic timing nor the charm to make kinky sound anything other than creepy.

Izzy studies me the way she looks at Mum when Mum's in a dementia blur. "It doesn't take you long to get jet lag, does it, Joe?"

"I'll recover." I hook my arm through hers as we walk. "Let me escort you through town and point out places of significance. See the old pub over there? I predict it does a great steak and chips for fifteen bucks."

"Reading from menu boards is against the rules."

"There are rules?" I ask.

"There are when I make them."

"Okay, since you've put your foot down." In a pathetic attempt at humour, I lift one leg and put it down. That's how desperate I am to make Izzy laugh. The sound is like a drug.

She groans. "Let's find Annette, but you'll need to let me do the talking. Either jet lag or unseasonal sunshine's making you giddy."

As she turns to the car, I mouth words behind her back. "I'm giddy because I'm with a woman who makes my heart sing." It doesn't matter that she doesn't hear. Saying it to myself feels good.

The library, modern and stylish, adds to the patchwork of buildings from multiple eras. I immediately recognise Annette from Facebook. I believe there are two types of people in this world: those who have fancy-dress wardrobes and those who wouldn't be seen dead in a feather boa. One look at Annette and it's clear she's a costume connoisseur.

"I won't be a minute," Annette calls over her shoulder. A second woman pins a Shamrock on one side of Annette's head to balance the rose clipped on the other.

"What's she wearing?" Izzy whispers.

"I think she's half-leprechaun and part Italian Tarantella dancer."

There's hushed conversation from the other side of the room, then the helper squeals, "Oh, Annette."

Both women burst into laughter at a joke we obviously missed.

Annette skips towards us, her arms dancing around. "Last-minute adjustments. Thanks for waiting."

"Your outfit looks great," Izzy says.

Annette holds both hands out. "Izzy? I wasn't sure it was you. Your profile picture doesn't do you justice." She releases Izzy and gives me a hearty back slap. "You must be Joe. You're a lucky man."

A blushing nod from me. I'd be the luckiest man in the world if what she's assumed was true.

Annette poses and shows off her costume. "I'm trying to represent the community making up this town. My mother was Irish and my father Italian."

Izzy gives me a thumb's up for guessing correctly.

"Gina," Annette calls to her friend. "Can you watch the front desk, please?"

We follow Annette to her office, but she ushers us inside and waits at the door. "Make yourself comfortable. First, I've gotta remove this get-up or the pins might do me an injury."

Once Annette's out of earshot, Izzy says, "She seems a lot of fun."

"Doesn't look as if she needs help to set up, though. She's got more energy than me." I crane my neck around the doorway, looking at the rows of bookshelves. "When you finish Mum's memoir, I reckon you should write a novel. We could visit libraries around the country together, slipping notes and pictures of you inside copies of your book. Which, of course, will be a bestseller."

"Thank you," Izzy says.

My cheek burns when she leans over to kiss it. She doesn't move away.

"What sort of novel should I write?"

Her face is so close I see flecks of extraordinary colour

in her eyes. Concentrate Joe. Words like love and desire swirl around my head. I will not say any of those. "You could write romance—"

"Hands above your heads. No sneaky kisses here." Annette's at the door, holding her fingers like a gun. She laughs. "I don't blame you, though. It's in the air. Lisdoon-varna, in Ireland, might be famous for its matchmaking festival, but the Australian-Italian festival in Ingham pumps Latin blood through the body, kindling many appetites... Aaah the food...and the music..."

I tug my shirt and blow out some steam. "I thought I was hotter than usual. Here I was thinking it was the tropical weather."

Annette smiles then glances over to her assistant, who's shelving books while answering the phone. "I better let Gina know I'm ducking out. You're probably both tired from the travel, so I'll show you to your room, then come back and help."

She bounces to the corner of the library, mumbles something, and grabs a box from a pile. "Do you mind carrying some of these?" she calls. "They're for the historical society stall."

"Of course." I race to take the box from her hands.

"We don't mind waiting," Izzy says. "We can walk around town."

"No trouble."

Laden with boxes, we plod down the wide stairs to the parking area. Annette balances one box on her hip and another under her arm, yet manages to open the boot of a bumble-bee yellow car.

Izzy unloads her cartons and laughs. "We won't lose this vehicle when we're following."

I wait to put mine in, but Izzy grabs them, moves

Annette's larger box to the side, and fits them together like a jigsaw.

"Your lady is not only gorgeous, but practical. As the young these days say, lucky you've put a ring on it, Joe."

Izzy smiles, but covers her hand.

We drive our hire car north and follow Annette into spectacular farming country. I smile at Izzy, but her eyes are glazed as she stares beyond the cane fields and mountains. She's biting her lip like she did when she told me about the bastard who assaulted her. I hope she isn't worried about Annette's off-the-cuff comments. First, telling us about the room. Singular. Then, assuming we're married.

I choose as reassuring a tone as I can. "I'm happy to sleep on the floor. Even in the car, if you prefer."

Although Izzy nods, there are vibes I can't identify. We cross a functional concrete bridge that spans the mighty Herbert River, and I try to make her smile. "Lift your feet!"

She looks blankly.

"Didn't your family tell you to lift your feet whenever crossing water?"

"No." She continues to gaze through the passenger window.

North of the river, we drive through a sea of sugar cane. Green stalks against a background of foliage draped mountains wave us on our way. The only colour breaking the green is Annette's yellow car.

"Sugar Town," I say. "Remember? We were going to write a song. I hope you can sing because I can't."

"Sorry. No singing talent here." There's a hint of a smile.

But Izzy, without a broad smile, still isn't Izzy.

I shrug. "Even if we find nothing about Mum, I'm glad we came. This trip with you is the best thing I've done in years."

She crosses her arms and says nothing.

Annette slows and parks in front of a house, which, like others we've passed, is set high off the ground on piers. This one has a room built underneath. She opens the downstairs door and hands Izzy the key. "If you don't mind, we'll leave the boxes inside in a corner to save us from carrying them up and back down the stairs in the morning." Annette waves her hands around the room. "Voila."

I step in after Izzy. The room's as charming and colourful as its owner. "This is nice." I'm relieved to see two beds separated by a desk. I won't need to sleep on the floor.

"Perfect." Izzy hugs Annette. "We appreciate this so much."

Annette opens a curtained sliding door. "To let in the breeze."

Izzy sucks in a breath. "The mountain view is spectacular."

"There are drinks and snacks in the little fridge, but if you want more, you'll have to drive back to town." Annette flits around, smoothing the already smooth bed sheets and wiping the table with her forearm. "That's it. I'll be back after five. You've got my number if you need me." As she opens the door, she says with a wink, "I don't mind you rearranging the furniture. But please move it back before you leave. Living alone means I can't move heavy objects." Then, like the busiest of bees, Annette flies off.

"This is great," I say to Izzy, "but what sort of guests would move the furniture?"

"She thinks we're lovers, Joe. It makes sense. It's what most people think of when they see a man and woman travelling together. Lovers would push the beds together." She perches on the bed closest to the door. "I knew I should have corrected Annette at the library, but she kept talking and there wasn't an obvious moment to blurt out we aren't married or together without making us all feel uncomfortable."

Is this why Izzy was quiet? There's something else I need to say, but I'm not sure what. I rub my brow and decide to say nothing. It's better for her to suspect I'm half stupid than for me to prove myself a complete idiot.

"You wait here, and I'll fetch our luggage." I head to the hire-car ready to lug both cases to the house, but Izzy appears beside me, picks up her own and scoots back inside.

While Izzy busies herself sorting through her suitcase, I feign interest in two bottles of water, a carton of milk and a packet of chocolate biscuits in the fridge.

Izzy rests her head on the pillow, so I take out my phone. It's been switched off since the flight. There are two notifications, both from Cupid4U. The first is from a woman living in Italy responding to the changes Izzy made to my profile.

You have wish to learn Italian. I spoke both language with fluently. Will teach you if you marry me for living in Australia. I crack my knuckles and stifle nervous laughter. This isn't the time to share. Izzy would find plenty of positives about the woman and before I could stop her, she'd snatch my phone and arrange for me to meet her. I don't want to contact this woman, let alone marry her.

I read the second notification, then blink. My eyes widen when I reread it.

The dating app has found a perfect match.

Izzy.

How could that be?

I scroll through my list of likes and dislikes, and then through Izzy's. She's broadened her age parameters and reworded many things on our interest list.

I don't know if the squished middle circle in the overlap of a Venn diagram has a name. But that's where Izzy and I both sit. Our desired partners, age ranges, and preferred interests live in that intersection of hope.

When she gets up to put toiletries in the bathroom, I study her from the corner of one eye. Although my hand shakes, I send a stream of kisses and hearts to Izzy's phone, holding my breath at the ping, ping, pinging of make-or-break notifications less than two metres away.

When she sits back on the bed to check, I close my eyes, wondering what on earth I've done. Maybe I should have waited until we're back in Sydney so she can avoid me.

Suddenly I'm a shy boy sipping a drink at my ninth birthday party, standing back, half hiding behind Gran's skirts. Gran's giving me a sharp shove. "Standing on the outside is fine for a while, but if you wait too long, you'll miss all the fun. Get in there now. It's always up to you, Joey."

I stride over to Izzy, watching as she reads my message. My beating heart roars in my ears.

She looks up, her smile a flash of pure delight. Gran was right. "Izzy August." I bow. "Where would you like to go on our first date?"

"I thought you'd never ask." Izzy pats the bed beside her. "Think carefully. I want it to be memorable."

I slide closer until we're touching. I'm tempted to lift my arm like an awkward teenage boy pretending to yawn. There's hyper-sensitivity in every place our bodies meet. My thigh tingles against hers, and my hand quivers where it rests on the smooth bare skin of her upper arm. I hope Gran's presence isn't hanging around because I have high hopes that this weekend will include footage unsuitable for anyone else's viewing.

"Sorry for being slow, I thought you weren't interes—"

"Stop talking, Joe. Now that you know—"

I press my lips on hers and for a delicious minute, we tentatively explore each other's mouths and tongues. Even though this is the stuff of dreams, I don't want to get too carried away. Not yet.

I break away, cradling her face in my hands. "That was the most unforgettable kiss of my life."

Izzy fans her face with a hand. "Perhaps we should go out on our first date soon?" Her voice is a breathless purr.

Chapter Thirty-Nine

Joe, Present Day

My palms sweat while I wait for Izzy to get ready. She asked for a memorable first date. Now I'm wondering if the choice I made while she was in the bathroom is too out there. She floats back into the room wearing a silky dress, and I take a deep breath. "You look beautiful. Maybe too fancy for the outing I've picked." I show her the Hinchinbrook tourism page displayed on my phone. "The perfect first date?"

"A cemetery?" Izzy laughs out loud. "Really? You want to take me to a cemetery?"

"It's a popular tourist destination." I wink. "I'm hoping you'll be afraid, so I need to hold you really close."

Despite Izzy's no-nonsense voice, her eyes sparkle. "I can't wait to post a picture on Instagram."

My stomach does a happy flip. She can't hide it. She likes the idea.

The thought of kissing Izzy at a gravesite doesn't seem unromantic to me. I'll happily lock lips with hers while ghostly figures watch. I offer my elbow. "Let's go, beautiful lady."

The drive to the New Ingham Cemetery is magical. Five kilometres of roads curving through sugar cane. These canes are taller than the others. There are fluffy feather duster flowers atop each stalk. The scenery is beautiful, but not as stunning as the woman beside me. On every straight stretch of road I steal another glance.

Izzy points to a pocket of rainforest trees. "Stop. Perfect setting for our first photo."

She moves me to one tree, then another, looking for the best backdrop. Then she positions me in silly poses like she did for my pics on the dating site. Except this time, my tingling at her touch is guilt free.

"Look, Joe. There! Through that gap in the trees. The cemetery gates. Want to walk?"

I take her hand in mine and we stroll along. I wouldn't care if the Ingham cemetery was kilometres away. I could walk like this forever.

Inside the fence, miniature gothic mausoleums complete with arched windows and doors stand row upon row. Izzy turns in a slow circle, checking out the ornate gravestones and family burial plots. "I reckon there's enough terrazzo to pave the streets of Sydney. Have you ever seen anything like it?"

"Nope. The mosaic tiling puts Pompei to shame." I inspect the intricate patterns and jewel colours. "Italians know how to live and they also know how to die."

We wander down the path and pause at a memorial headstone featuring a timeline of photographs of the couple buried beneath. I squeeze her hand. "Look at this one. From wedding to wisdom, their life is on display."

Izzy puts a hand to her mouth, eyes glistening with tears. "Aww. They're really old in the final portrait, yet still holding hands and smiling at each other."

I wipe a tear from Izzy's cheek. "Don't be sad. They shared a lifetime of love."

"I'm emotional because it's romantic." She points out the dates. "They died within weeks of each other. At least they didn't have to live without each other too long."

"See. A cemetery is a romantic first date."

She buries her head in my chest, and I cling to her. For today, at least, neither of us is facing life alone.

As we wander up and down rows of memorials, Izzy reads out the names. "I dare you to read this one out loud." Izzy laughs and points to a plaque. *Flavio Buttofuoco.*

"I won't even try," I say, "out of respect for the dead."

We snigger, but cover our mouths to stifle the sound.

Two rows up, a name on black-and-white mosaic head-stones catches my attention. "Panisi? Is that Stella's last name?"

"No. She was a Pansini. But we should look for a Stella Pansini? She could have followed your mother to Ingham." Izzy removes her shoes, looking ready to race. "It'll be quicker if we split up."

I wrap my arm around Izzy's waist. "I'm in no hurry."

Walking on grassy pathways with a bare-footed Izzy in the cool afternoon is heaven. I've never felt so high as I listen to Izzy's sing-song voice reading Italian names.

"Joe!" Izzy's screech makes me jump. "Look at this one. OMG!"

I rub my eyes and follow the inscription as Izzy reads:

Angelo Morellini
Entered this world in Reggio Calabria Italia on Aug 29th, 1938.
Departed earth from Ingham, Queensland on May 2nd, 2011.
Beloved husband of Ella. Father and Nonno to many.
Forever in our thoughts.

"Ella?" I ask. "Could Ella be short for Mariella? Mariella Morellini? Is it a coincidence?"

"Angelo and Ella? A fluke? Not likely." Izzy shakes her head, then snaps photographs of the grave.

I read it all again, then scratch my head. "Granted, it's a monumental coincidence, but they make TV shows about this stuff, so it can happen. Or Mum could have married Angelo, then divorced him before marrying Dad."

"Except the inscription says they have many grand-children."

"Had a child with Angelo, then left?" I wrinkle my nose in disbelief. "Mum would never abandon children. I know for sure that if she had grandchildren, she wouldn't be hiding from them. She'd kit herself up in camo gear and track them down."

Izzy chuckles, but the fun doesn't last. She sighs. "Maybe you were right when you thought your mum was telling someone else's story. It's happened once already, so it's not impossible."

I exhale to clear my head, then I read the headstone again. "I don't know what to think. Mum recalling Katerina's story was totally different. But if Mum was making it all up, then we have no chance of finding out how the story ends."

"We're not giving up that easily, Joe. I know research isn't romantic and we're on our first date, but could we try to get the bottom of this? Now?"

My heart pleads with my head. *Say yes to anything Izzy wants.* "Where should we start?"

"It wouldn't surprise me if Annette knows everyone in Ingham. I bet there are only three degrees of separation in a small town."

"But it's almost four," I say.

Izzy gives me a blank look. "Four degrees of separation? Why four?"

I laugh. "Four o'clock."

"Oh! Really?" Izzy checks her phone. "3:57! How do you know the time without looking?"

I shuffle my feet. We'll discover each other's quirks, eventually. "Probably because part of my brain is taken up by a clock. Nothing to write home about, but it's my only talent."

"I'm finding it very handy." Izzy's smile is bright enough to bounce off the mosaic tiles.

"If we hurry," I say. "We could catch Annette before she leaves work."

Izzy blows me a slow-motion kiss.

Marilyn Monroe has nothing on Izzy. Her sexy half-smile turns into a musical laugh. "I've a better idea, Joe. The mystery can wait. Let's go home." She throws me the subtlest of winks. "I'll send Annette a text telling her we were up before four this morning to catch the early plane, so we'll see her in the morning."

The North Queensland air cools, but my cheeks feel hotter than ever. I take a deep, steadying breath. We might end up rearranging furniture after all.

Izzy leans in to touch my forehead. "You're hot. It looks as if you caught too much sun."

The colour in my cheeks is unrelated to sun exposure.

"Do you want to go somewhere special for dinner?" I ask.

Izzy blushes as she shakes her head. "We'll pick up food on the way home."

We stop at an Italian delicatessen and buy olives, cheese, prosciutto, and bread. An armful of food, but not what I'm craving.

I point out a liquor store across the street. "Prosecco?"

"One glass. Maybe." Izzy bites her lip. She fastens and unfastens her seatbelt several times.

Is she afraid I'm trying to get her drunk? "We can give the Prosecco to Annette. I don't want you to feel uncomfortable around me. Not ever."

Izzy looks at me with soft, warm eyes. "Joe, I'm not scared of you. I'm nervous. It's been a long time since I've taken off my clothes in front of someone."

"I could promise not to look at you, but that would be a lie. I promise never to lie. We can turn the lights off if you'd rather. Not so I won't see you, but so you can't see me." My laughter falters.

She smiles. "Won't help. It's a full moon."

I cup her face in my hands. "Whenever I look at you, I love what I see."

My chest fills with song. I hope she hears it too.

Back at our room, Izzy takes a shower while I arrange the antipasto on a platter. It isn't a work of art, but the best I can do with trembling hands. I'm rummaging through the kitchen cupboard for glasses when she reappears.

Her tousled hair is damp and my breath catches in my

throat seeing the floaty sarong tied in a knot above her breasts. A single knot.

"I'll take the food to the table outside. Next to the giant tree," she says. "We've spent so much of our time together under a tree that when I saw it, it seemed to have grown here especially for us."

A voice inside my head tells me to calm down.

"Go on, Joe. Get changed or whatever you want to do."

As I gather my clothes, Izzy releases the door catch with her elbow. The sarong swishes over her hips and there's no sign of anything underneath. If I untie that knot, she'll be naked.

Calm? No chance.

I start with hot water, soaping myself up from head to toe, then I rinse with cold, cold water. I need the cold before I look at Izzy again. We've kissed. She likes me. This time I'm not dreaming. As I'm pulling on my shorts, I catch my waist in the zip. It saves me pinching myself.

The air outside is deliciously cool. Too cool for Izzy, who's tucked her hands between her knees. "You're shivering." I move my chair near enough to warm her.

She moves closer. "I'm enjoying your heat. What would Dorotea call it? Your obvious Latin blood."

I laugh and pick at the food. My body is ravenous, but not for food.

Izzy pushes an olive around the platter. "I'm not hungry."

"I'm not overly hungry, either."

We look at each other without speaking, then Izzy laces her fingers through mine. "Come on. We can eat later. I hope we both remember what to do."

I stand and pull her out of her chair for a kiss. Izzy's lips are soft, but our kiss isn't gentle. "If we forget," I whisper, "we'll practise more."

Izzy tilts her head towards the house. There's no uncertainty in the tilt. It's almost an order.

Once inside, I nuzzle her neck, inhaling the tantalising scent of soap and Izzy's skin. She traces patterns under my shirt with electric fingertips.

Using both teeth and hands, I untie the knot and watch the sarong fall to her feet. My eyes travel slowly upward until they meet hers. The fiery look on her face is as much a thrill as the lingering journey over her naked flesh.

With each item of my clothing, I cast aside any shyness. "Are you sure?" I ask, certain she'll say yes.

"Oh, yes." She closes her eyes.

I lift her from the ground and the silkiness of her skin against mine quickens my breath. I moan. "Izzy, I desire every part of you."

My fingers read her body for pleasure. The rise and fall of her breaths, accompanied by quiet moans, suggest my wish for her to want me as much as I do her, has come true.

I wake in the night with one leg awkwardly balancing on the edge of the single bed. Without moving the mattress, I edge myself into a sitting position. The full moon helps my hungry eyes revisit every one of Izzy's delicious curves. I creep across the floor to carry the small desk out of the way and drag the rug under the other bed until both beds are beside each other.

She turns and gives me a sleepy smile. "You said you would never lie to me, Joe."

"I haven't." My heart beats erratically as I search for an answer.

She pats the space beside her. "You told me only a few hours ago that your special talent was guessing the time."

"It is." I'm confused.

"Back into bed now," she growls, "you have a skill far more valuable than that."

Chapter Forty

Joe, Present Day

The sun peeps through a crack in the curtain and rouses me from a paradise of entangled limbs. A glance at Izzy's sleeping form, her hair strewn across the pillow, sends me into a breathless spin. Despite our lack of sleep, I feel refreshed.

I chuckle quietly · to myself, recalling Izzy's praise. Perhaps I'm a late bloomer in regards to my Latin blood?

From among the pile of enthusiastically discarded clothing, I find my shorts, then check my phone. Almost seven o'clock! I've lost all sense of time. We're leaving here at 7:45. My hand hovers millimetres from Izzy's naked back, but I stop myself touching her. If she's having second thoughts, waking up to me shirtless and leaning over, could be threatening. Would it be better to boil the kettle and call from a distance, offering a cup of coffee. Or is that too impersonal?

I'm still procrastinating when Izzy opens her eyes, her

smile deliciously wicked. "I hope you're not trying to sneak away?"

"No." I sit next to her and whisper, "It's time to get up. We've just enough time for breakfast before we help Annette set up—"

"Hush." Izzy throws back the quilt and I don't wait for a second invitation.

Afterwards, we grab a shared shower and hastily throw on clothes. Seconds into another kiss, we're interrupted by a knock.

"Ready?" Annette calls.

Izzy leaps up to open the door. "We've been up for ages," she says in a barefaced lie.

When Annette looks over at the beds with a knowing smile, my eyes follow. The way they've been pushed together looks haphazard and hurried. I pick up some cardboard boxes for the stall and walk outside so my flamingo pink face doesn't give me away.

We follow Annette into town. "I think she knows," I say. "Did you see that look she gave?"

Izzy taps my arm, her face serious. "She assumes we're in a relationship, Joe. We are in a relationship now, aren't we?"

"I hope so. What kind of boy do you think I am?"

She smiles a Mona Lisa smile.

The sign at the entrance of the wetlands complex where most festival activities are held says TYTO in giant letters.

"What does TYTO stand for?" Izzy asks.

"*Thank you* for last night's *turn on*." I try emphasising the keywords.

267

Izzy merely blinks. "Quick subject change, but thank you, too."

"You missed the acronym." I laugh. "Thank You Turn On. See? TYTO."

"Ah. I'd normally catch on. I'm blaming you for my sleep deprivation." She laughs and flicks through her phone.

I park next to Annette's car and lean over to kiss Izzy before getting out. She shows me what she was looking at. A picture of an owl. "It's not an acronym, Joe. Tyto is the name of a wetland owl."

"Is it nocturnal?" I wink.

Izzy chuckles. "Like us?"

We carry the boxes past rows of white-peaked tents, flapping flags and balloons. Their brightness contrasts with the green-grey foliage of wetland trees. "It's hard to believe we didn't see this when we drove past yesterday," I say.

Izzy's eyes sparkle. "The festival's appeared by magic. There's enchantment in the air."

I nod in agreement. Today, I totally believe in magic. If Izzy asked me, I'd search for unicorns or slay dragons.

At Annette's stall, we sort pre-packaged piles of photos and documents on the trestle table, then look to Annette for further instruction.

"The coloured stickers on each package match the stickers on the notice boards," Annette says. "Inside each envelope there are pictures of last week's test-run of the display."

Izzy works lightning fast, not wasting time matching coloured push-pins for each document. My method is more like my mother's. She couldn't hang clothes on the washing line without using identical pegs. Izzy's mixed selection is efficient, unpredictable and charming. Just like her. She finishes one board while I'm halfway through the first.

Before she starts on the next packet, she stops to wrap her arms around my waist as if it's something she's done every day for years.

I cross my fingers and hope she keeps doing it forever.

"Annette?" I ask. "Do you know much about Italian proxy brides?"

"A little. Why?"

"My mother came to Australia to marry a cane farmer, but married my dad instead. She has dementia now and isn't well enough to tell us what happened."

Annette taps her bottom lip. "There are several personal accounts recorded in a folder held at the library. But a few of the proxy brides are still alive. Maybe you should talk to one of them? I can look out for you. The old Italian matriarchs are like royalty at these festivals."

"Is Stella Pansini of them?" Izzy asks.

Annette creases her brow. "A woman called Stella used to run the Ingham bakery when I was a kid. Neither proxy bride nor a Pansini, though."

"Have you heard of the Morellini family?"

"Of course. Ella, Mrs Morellini, is a library regular. She's addicted to romance novels."

Izzy grips my hand and I feel the pulse of excitement. "How old is Ella?"

"Mid-seventies, at a guess. Though you wouldn't know it, she's sharp as a tack."

Izzy clutches my hand again. This lead has promise.

"Will she be here at the festival?" I ask.

"Can't keep Mrs Morellini away from anything. Look, we've almost finished setting up. Why don't the pair of you wander around before the madding crowd arrives, then you can come back and I'll see if I can find you a proxy bride to answer your questions?"

"Thank you." Izzy drags me out of Annette's sight and pushes me into a jewellery stall. "Ella could be Stella."

"Or, she could be Mariella. Or she could be someone totally different."

"Ella or Stella, I've got a gut feeling Mrs Morellini knows your mum."

While Izzy browses the back of the stall, I pick up a pair of owl earrings.

"Tyto. The eastern grass barn owl," the chirpy stall-holder whispers, with a sneaky glance at Izzy. "The owl's white face is distinctively heart-shaped."

"I'll take them."

Izzy sidles up to me as the stall-holder wraps my purchase. "What are you buying?"

"A gift. TYTO owls," I say.

She unwraps the earrings and her eyes shimmer. "Aww. A pair of heart faced owls to remember this weekend." She kisses me.

Arm in arm we stroll past gondola races, bocce bowling, and the rest of the festival circuit. Izzy plants a quick kiss on my lips. "I love looking around with you, but...do you mind if we go back to Annette? I'd hate to miss Mrs Morellini, our big lead. This was our original reason for flying here."

"Of course. I'm itching to get back to the Historical Society stall, too."

We round the corner to find Annette in full costume demonstrating a few steps of an Irish jig followed by some kind of Italian folk dance. Her audience, of one, is an immaculately dressed older woman, with enough gold jewellery to fill a small treasure chest. When Annette sees us, she cups her hands to her mouth and hollers, "I was about to send a search party. Mrs Morellini's here."

"This is Izzy and I'm Joe." I offer my hand, but Mrs Morellini pulls me in for a warm hug.

"Noi non possiamo avere una vita perfetta senza amici. We cannot have a perfect life without friends. Especially during festival time."

As she hugs Izzy, I look at her closely. Mrs Morellini's around the same age and height as Mum, and not dissimilar in looks. I interpret Izzy's pinch to my upper arm as a sign she's noticed the resemblance too. Could this be Stella?

"Joe and I are so pleased to meet you," Izzy says. "We're interested in Italian proxy brides who came to Australia. Joe's mum was such a bride, but she has dementia. We're writing her memoirs, and need info to fill in some gaps."

I bow my head with admiration. Women are clever in the way they get information. I would have come straight out and asked the woman if she was Stella. Straightforward blokey questions would have shut down the conversation before it began.

Mrs Morellini's quick smile suggests she'd love to help.

Izzy and Mrs Morellini decide a cup of coffee is in order and wander off arm in arm. I follow behind and we settle on a quiet table at the far corner of the festival food hall.

"Can you get us some drinks please, Joe?" Izzy asks. One of her eyes flutters with what is likely a Morse code signal only women can read.

I play it safe by lurking at the food counter longer than necessary. Izzy clearly has a plan and although this project is for my mother, I'd rather get useful information second-hand than have Mrs Morellini shut up shop. I only return when Izzy gives me the nod.

I hand out the drinks. "One ristretto for Mrs Morellini, an iced chocolate for Izzy, and a flat white coffee no sugar, for me."

They share a smile like girls who know a schoolyard secret.

"Your mother is very lucky to have a daughter-in-law like Izzy."

"Hmmm, uh, mmm..." I give up thinking of something to say and move my chair to the opposite side of the table.

Izzy's face is a mask of jokey indignation. "Joe hasn't proposed, yet."

"You'd better hurry or I'll grab her for one of my sons. My youngest is single."

Izzy sips her long glass of iced chocolate, licking her lips like the cat who got the cream. "Well, Joe, this is our lucky day. Mrs Morellini's invited us back to her house. She has pictures from when she first arrived in Australia."

Mrs Morellini finishes her drink, then picks up her handbag. "Better go now before you change your mind. It's rare to find people willing to wade through my old photographs and listen to me wandering down memory lane. Better follow my car. There are creeks running through cane-fields and roads winding around them, so it's too hard to give directions. I don't want to risk losing you. Not with the patchy phone reception out my way."

Once in the car, I lift a questioning eyebrow. "You didn't ask her about Stella, or tell her Mum's name was Mariella?"

"Nope. We need information about the proxy brides and how they settled into Australia. Mrs Morellini can give us that. If I'd questioned too deeply, I could have scared her away."

I narrow my eyes. "Is there anything else I should or shouldn't say once we get there?"

"Don't look at me like that. I haven't lied, I've just omitted details. She thinks we've been seeing each other for years, which is kind of true. I've seen you visiting your mother."

"Might be safer if I leave you to do the talking."

I pull up behind Mrs Morellini's car in the driveway of a small modern home on a parcel of land carved out of cane-fields. It's dwarfed by the high-set house next door.

"There's one more thing," Izzy whispers as she climbs out. "Ask if you can take a photo of me with her. It might come in handy."

In the front yard, I turn a full 360, admiring the view. "Lovely home," I say.

"Yes. My eldest son, Nick, took over the farm after my husband, Angelo, died." She points to a larger house. "I could live in that old place with them. They have the room. But I insisted on having my own house. It's good to have family close, but it's easier to get on when we have our own space."

"What a beautiful backdrop for two beautiful women. Mind if I take a photo of you together?"

Mrs Morellini beams when I position them in front of a hot-pink bougainvillea vine near the front door. "This was my mother's favourite plant. She taught me the name."

Her face lights up. *"Una buona mamma vale cento maestre.* A good mother is worth a thousand teachers."

Izzy gives me a sneaky thumbs up.

We follow Mrs Morellini's lead and slip our shoes off before going inside. The house is immaculate, like its owner.

"Make yourselves at home." She points to the dining room, then disappears down the hallway.

Instead of being packed with sentimental dust collec-tors, Mrs Morellini's house is minimalistic white. The only splashes of colour are houseplants so vigorous I'd be worried about them creeping out of their pots and strangling me while I slept.

Izzy rests her head against my shoulder, lifting it when a sunbird outside the window adds to its hanging nest. "Gorgeous here, isn't it? Do you like North Queensland?"

"Hard to tell." I kiss the top of Izzy's head. "I'm seeing everything through a loved-up-by-Izzy filter. Even cockroaches are charming today."

"You have such a way with words, Joe. I mean, who would imagine a man including cockroaches in his sweet-talking?" She sits up quickly when Mrs Morellini returns with an arm full of white photo albums.

"I'll fetch the rest," she says, "and you two can start going through to see which are from the right decade. Choosing all-white albums seemed like a good idea. They might look stylish on the bookshelf, but it makes it hard to find the one I'm searching for."

Izzy flicks through photos at lightning speed, only stopping at pictures of interest. She points out a recent picture of Mrs Morellini holding either a grandchild or great-grandchild. "How cute is this baby? No wonder your mum wants one of these."

"Watch out," Mrs Morellini says. "Your lady's getting clucky, Joe."

I blink, not daring to make eye contact with Izzy. We have a one-day romantic relationship and someone's already suggesting marriage and children. I don't want to comment in case I jinx things.

I risk a sideways glance. Izzy's looking at Mrs Morellini and making a slashing action with a finger at her throat. She mouths, 'Don't ask about babies.'

I hadn't thought that far ahead. But it's not a deal breaker if Izzy doesn't want children. At thirty-five she'd probably already have one, if she'd wanted one. With or without a man. Fortunately, Mrs Morellini doesn't comment further and continues sifting through photos. "Here's me and Angelo at our wedding. The happiest day of my life, although I never let Angelo know. A woman needs to keep her man on his toes."

I chuckle. "You were a beautiful bride. My mum used to sew wedding dresses and every time she completed one, she told me how honoured she felt helping the transformation from woman to goddess."

"Tell me about your mother. Where in Australia did she end up?"

Izzy and I shrug simultaneously.

"Sydney," I say. "But she was promised to a man in Ingham. I'm not sure she ever got here."

At this piece of information, Mrs Morellini's expression changes. Her lacklustre scrutiny makes me squirm. I don't risk looking at Izzy. Something tells me I should have left all the talking to her.

"You haven't told me your mother's name," Mrs Morellini says. Her voice has an undertone I can't decipher.

"Mar—"

Izzy flashes a warning glance in my direction and cuts me off. "Maria. Maria Blake."

Even though Mrs Morellini has already stacked the photos albums in a neat pile, she rearranges them, her hands lightly trembling. She grips the table edge to stand. "Well, you've probably had enough of an old woman."

"Not at all." Izzy places a hand on Mrs Morellini's shoulder, gently pressing her down into her seat. "Can you tell me anything about the voyage from Italy? It would help if I knew what ships were like in those days. Poor Maria's unable to remember much at all. The dementia's stolen many of her memories and what's lost is forever gone."

I pretend to study the tufted rug underfoot. We've heard plenty about the journey from Italy to Australia. Izzy's half-lie has the desired effect. Mrs Morellini relaxes and her smile returns. "Poor woman. How terrible for her."

I lean back to watch the performance.

Izzy circles, making small talk, strategising like a general while I, her obedient soldier, wait for the next command. "So, I bet the food was delicious? It sounds like a cruise we wanted to go on, doesn't it, babe?" Izzy beams at me. "We got a brochure once, didn't we? Some of those cabins had balconies overlooking the ocean. It was as luxurious as the Titanic. Before it sank, of course."

There's no half-lie in this. Izzy has gone full rogue. I don't mind though; it adds an extra level of interest. Now I can see why women are attracted to bad boys. It works in reverse.

"Oh no. My voyage was nothing like that. A basic two-person cabin with a tiny window. I shared it with a stranger."

"Another proxy bride?" Izzy asks.

Mrs Morellini taps her fingernails on the photo album. "Yes."

The tension returns.

Izzy turns a page. "Do you have pictures from your voyage? It won't help me with Maria's memoirs, but you were such a beautiful young woman and those sixties' fashions were to die for. I'd love to see you wearing them."

"I'm afraid not. And I know nothing about the woman I shared the cabin with, if that's going to be your next question."

Izzy traces her fingers around the album page, and I'm

like a spectator at a tennis match, watching to see which woman will hit the ball. "No need for me to ask," Izzy says. "I've already asked Annette about Maria's cabin buddy. Her name was Stella Pansini, but Annette assured us there aren't any Pansini families in Ingham."

Mrs Morellini stands. "It's been lovely meeting you; it really has. But I'm tired now."

"Of course. I insist you let us wash the cups. Help me, Joe."

Izzy ignores the head shake and clears the table. As soon as our backs are to Mrs Morellini, she does the cutest sideways mouth twist and whispers under her breath, "We're losing her. Do something."

I sit down again and hang my head. "I'm going to be honest with you here, Mrs Morellini. My mother has a prior history of repeating other people's stories and passing them off as her own, and we believe she's done it again. It's possible she heard a story somewhere, then passed it off as her own."

Mrs Morellini lets out a long, slow breath. "Has she really?"

"Yes," I say, glancing at Izzy, who's holding both thumbs up. "Last year Mum talked into a voice recorder, and we thought we were getting stories of her youth, but we had it translated, and it was a recount of her friend Katerina's life."

Izzy jumps in. "We were hoping to discover Maria is actually Stella Pansini and that you'd shared a cabin with her. Sorry not to have been upfront."

"I can't remember ever meeting anyone with that name. I don't know the name of the woman I shared a cabin with, but I swear to you, it wasn't Stella." She rubs her hands against her blouse as if she's washed her hands of us. I expect her to push us angrily through the door. Instead, her eyes fill with tears.

"Please don't cry," I say. "We've overtired you. Asked too much."

Izzy passes her a tissue.

"Thanks." She sniffs. "I'm sad you didn't find out what happened to your mother."

Izzy takes a pad and pencil from her handbag. "If it's not too much trouble, could I ask one more favour? We need a mud-map to find our way back to the festival."

"Of course." Mrs Morellini hastily scribbles a child-like map, then waves goodbye from the door.

As soon as we reach the car's cone of silence, I sigh. "Well, that's a dead end. An unsolved mystery, for sure."

"Joe. Look." Izzy holds the map in front of my face.

"I can't follow that. There's no sense of scale. Maybe she wants us to get lost."

"That's not my reason for showing you. We have our first piece of evidence." Izzy sounds serious.

"Evidence of what?"

"The identity theft."

Chapter Forty-One

Joe, Present Day

Izzy spends the entire convoluted drive to the Australian-Italian festival searching through her phone, and I worry she thinks badly of Mum. I'm sure my mother wouldn't intentionally deceive anyone, but a dementia impaired brain plays tricks. "I know the evidence is stacking up, and every son probably thinks their mum isn't capable of doing wrong, but Mum wouldn't steal Stella's identity on purpose."

Izzy runs her fingers through my hair. "I know she wouldn't. Once we get back to the stall, I'll check a few things to make sure, then I'll share my suspicions."

Our car parking space, this time, is further from the festival. Much, much further. But even from this distance, it's clear the festival is in full swing, with music blasting well beyond the grounds. As we walk along the road towards the entrance, a rough track cuts through the bushland. Izzy takes my hand. "A shortcut," she says.

I have my doubts it leads anywhere, but Izzy's in control, and I'm definitely following.

Gusts of wind rustle the trees, raining leaves on our heads. I brush them gently from Izzy's shoulders. "You are delicious, Izzy." I lift her hair, exposing the back of her neck and trail kisses across her shoulders.

"Would you rather go home?" she asks, without turning around.

"Honestly, yes, but we've promised Annette we'll pack up the stall, then we can leave and—"

She spins and locks her mouth onto mine. I take her hand and pull her off the track and into the scrubby bush of the wetlands, stopping only to kiss her.

Izzy drags me further away from the festival into the middle of nowhere, leans against a smooth-barked tree and closes her eyes. "Kiss me again, Joe." Her voice is breathy and eager, and it's the sexiest sound I've ever heard.

There's no need for further encouragement. We urgently semi-undress and act out the first part of a script that I've been pushing to the back of my mind for the entire day. Truth be known, love scenes have been writing themselves for months. The kiss and her touch get better each time. "We better stop now," I whisper.

Izzy rearranges her clothes. "Yep. There seems to be something about trees and my libido. I'll never look at one the same way." She sighs and pecks my cheek. "Do I look normal? Or do I look like a woman who's coming undone?"

"You look the best part of every splendid dream I've ever had." I kiss her gently.

"I hope we don't get lost." Izzy turns to walk in the wrong direction.

I take her hand. "Come on, let's follow the music."

We're out of breath when we arrive at the stall.

"Are you guys okay?" Annette asks. "You look like you've been on a cross-country hike."

"We have," I tell her. "It was supposed to be a shortcut, but we got lost in the bush for a little while." I wink at Izzy. "It was her fault."

Annette studies my face, and I concentrate on naming prime numbers to a hundred to wipe my tell-tale smile. "We've come to help pack up the stall."

"It's no bother. I can do it myself. It's a straightforward job," Annette says. "These display documents are only copies of the original, so I don't bother taking them down each night. I just zip up the cover and it's ready for the next day."

"We can watch the stall for you now, if you like," Izzy offers. "Go look around and get some Irish-Italian dancing in. If we're stuck, we'll phone you."

"Thanks. You're a dear. I wouldn't mind a break. How did you go with Mrs Morellini? Find anything useful?"

"We had a pleasant afternoon," I say. "Not much on Mum, though. I think it's a lost cause."

Annette looks disappointed. "I hope it hasn't been a wasted weekend."

I shake my head in a loved-up no.

She looks at me quizzically. "Good. I won't be more than an hour."

Once Annette's gone, Izzy looks around then whispers in my ear, "Back to Maria and Stella-Ella." She holds up the mud-map. "My first piece of evidence."

"I'm not sure what you're getting at?"

"Your mum's memoirs described Mariella as being an artist. Who, out of your mother and Mrs Morellini, has any artistic talent?" Izzy raises her eyebrows.

"Mum, without question, but we don't know for sure that Mrs Morellini has any connection."

"Ah... but there's more." She opens her phone to Mum's memoir document. "I found the description of Stella's ring. When I first read the transcript, I couldn't imagine what it looked like." She reads the entry. "Tubular gold, baguette diamonds curving around a sea-coloured opal, in the shape of a French horn. Are you visualising it?"

"Hmm," I say, even though the only baguette I know is a type of bread.

"Give me your phone, Joe."

She zooms in on the photo I took outside Mrs Morellini's house. "Look at her right hand. How would you describe that ring?"

The ring in the photo almost certainly matches Mum's description of the musically inspired ring Stella wore in 1967.

"And then there's this picture I sneakily took of her wedding photo when you were helping in the kitchen. Compare Mrs Morellini in her youth with the newspaper clipping we found of Stella with her record producer husband Lorenzo."

I slide backwards and forwards between the pictures. "I can't be 100% sure. They do look similar, but the woman also reminds me of Mum in pictures from the sixties."

"Well, there's a final and totally damning piece of evidence. Mrs Morellini's expression. She knew what was coming, Joe. You could see it written right across her face."

"Even if Mrs Morellini is lying, we can't go back and harass an old woman."

"We won't have to. When she cried for your mother, they were genuine tears of affection and guilt. Love and regret are the powerful driving forces in a woman's nature. We'll wait here at the stall—Mrs Morellini will find us."

Izzy and I share a loaf of homemade banana bread from the stall next to ours. "Delicious," she says. "I was starving." I clear our crumbs off the table so Annette doesn't come back to our mess.

"Don't look now, Joe," Izzy murmurs while pretending to read an historical society brochure. "Mrs Morellini's over there."

I'm not sure why I'm not allowed to look, but I keep my head down. "I don't know how you knew," I say. "How come, when women are operating on a higher plane and seeing stuff that goes over men's heads, they don't rule the world?"

"Men only think they rule the world. Women set the rules. Haven't you ever heard the saying: The hand that rocks the cradle is the hand that rules the world?"

I rub my forehead with the realisation of the truth in it.

"Excuse me." Mrs Morellini's voice is soft and sorry. She stands so forlornly I'm ready to forgive, no matter what.

I gently touch her arm. "Here, take my seat."

Izzy sets her arm around Mrs Morellini's shoulders and steadies her. "I'm glad you came."

She seems to have aged in a matter of hours; her body weighed down by whatever's on her mind.

"I wanted to tell you. Believe me, I did. But a dear friend and I made a promise many, many years ago. We promised never, ever to tell a soul." As tears stream down her lined cheeks, I stand protectively between her and the crowds.

"Is there anything we can do to help?" Izzy hands one of her endless supply of tissues.

"I couldn't bear Joe thinking his mother was an impostor, stealing another woman's identity." She forces the words between sobs. "Your mother is not a fraud."

Izzy and I exchange looks and I cross my fingers, hoping that instead of producing another tissue, Izzy miraculously knows how to end Mrs Morellini's heart-break.

"I have an idea," Izzy says, her face lighting up. "What if I call admin at The Figs and get them to put Maria on the phone?"

Mrs Morellini stops crying. "Will you tell her I've kept our secret?"

"No, you will," Izzy says. "Maria's forgotten English, so you'll need to speak Italian. It's time for good friends to reconnect."

Chapter Forty-Two

Maria, Present Day

My mind races as it searches for the source of a mechanical buzzing. I'm startled when I find it. This is the first time since I've been at The Figs that my bedside phone has ever rung. I stare at it for a moment, but my only effective communication is a series of charades or sketchpad drawings, and I can't do either of those during a call.

I race to the room across the corridor. Katerina looks up from her desk. "What's up, Maria?"

I stare for a moment, forgetting why I've come. She's writing a letter so I shift my attention to the new pictures tacked on the wall behind her desk. Katerina and a younger woman on a holiday. Her daughter?

Seeing them together makes me miss my Joey. He's away somewhere, isn't he? Or has he stopped visiting?

I hunch my shoulders and flop onto Katerina's bed.

"Are you okay?" Katerina wheels beside me.

I notice the phone on the bedside table. *That's it.* I grab it and point to the door.

"Do you want me to phone someone?" Katerina asks.

"*Non.*" I grasp the wheelchair handles and push Katerina towards the door.

"Good to see you're getting your energy back," she says. "You taking me for a spin in the garden?"

Instead of trying to explain, I charge into my room. But the phone has stopped. I wave my hands apologetically, throwing my palms towards the ceiling. "*Scusa.*"

"I'm not sure what you want." Katerina purses her lips in confusion. "But you can push me around the grounds if you're up to it." She runs two fingers up her arm like miniature legs. Our shared sign-language for a walk.

"*Un minuto. Scarpe.*" I am putting on my outside shoes when the phone rings again. "*Il telefono,*" I say, "*capisci?*"

Katerina answers, "Hello? Maria Blake's room." She nods at me, then continues. "Izzy, it's great to hear your voice. Are you enjoying yourself in Queensland? How's Joe?"

I study her face for clues. When she smiles, I let out a breath. It's not anything too serious. I couldn't bear anything bad happening to Joey.

Katerina puts one hand over her mouth as she listens, and I watch her sparse eyebrows dance. "You want me to put Maria on?"

Why on earth would Izzy ask to talk to me when she can't speak Italian?

Chapter Forty-Three

Mrs Ella Morellini, Present Day

I spin my diamond rings around wrinkled, knobbly fingers, and try to quell the sensation of time turning backwards. My hands are an anchor; a stark reminder of how many years have passed since I saw Mariella.

I clutch Joe's arm while I battle the urge to either fight or flight. Izzy is making the call to my dear long-lost friend, who now calls herself Maria. When Izzy speaks to someone in reception at The Figs care home, my gut does a nervous flip. She covers the mouthpiece. "They're switching me through."

I count in my head as I wait. *Uno, due, tre, quattro, cinque, sei...*

Izzy chats for a moment then gives me a thumbs up and hands over the phone.

"*Ciao. Questa e Stella.*" I barely have enough breath to get out my words in Italian, but I repeat them in English. "Hello. This is Stella."

Once the first tear escapes, a waterfall follows and I sit, unable to steady my legs. Mariella's voice starts old and shaky, but to me, she's the same young woman I met half a century ago. She remembers me and understands what I'm saying.

Maria, as she's been known for a lifetime, tells me in a steady, certain voice that it's time to break our promise.

I agree. Those with the power to hurt us have long gone.

Chapter Forty-Four

Joe, Present Day

I don't understand a single Italian word Mrs Morellini is saying, but it feels as if I'm witnessing a heart in the process of breaking. When the phone call ends, Izzy holds the trembling Mrs Morellini and I wrap both women in my arms.

I'm not sure if I'm using the hug to put Mrs Morellini back together or to stop myself from falling apart. Izzy's tears cool my hot cheeks and mingle with mine. I swipe my face with my sleeve, then bury my head in Izzy's shoulder, adding to the emotional mess rather than being the brave protector.

I'm surprised at how quickly Mrs Morellini regains her composure. "Sit, and I'll tell you what we talked about."

Izzy grips my hand. She's as nervous as me.

Mrs Morellini pats our shoulders. "It's okay. Mariella... Maria... knew me straight away and was thrilled you'd found me. When I told her how I searched for her for months, she cried. She lost track of the conversation for a bit, but she agreed it was impossible to both finish her memoir *and* keep the vow. She wants to finish her story for you, Joe. She's given permission to break our promise.

"Are you sure?" I ask. "You have the right to privacy."

"It's time. It's too late for reprisals, and it's not as if we intended to hurt anyone."

Izzy looks expectantly at Mrs Morellini. The festival lighting illuminates both faces in a manner reminiscent of a movie close-up. Young, clear eyes, next to cloudy old, both brimming with sentimentality and hope.

Mrs Morellini claps her hands, re-introduces herself as Stella, then begins to talk.

Chapter Forty-Five

Stella 1967, Sydney

My husband, Lorenzo, waved and called from the roped-off area of the docks. "Stella."

I held up one finger, mouthing I'd be another minute. Despite my reservations about our marriage, Lorenzo's boyish smile was so broad with welcome, it reminded me of our special friendship rather than the not-so-fulfilling aspects of our marital relationship.

I partially hid behind a small office building to watch Mariella. My misuse of her passport was an extension of the other gags we'd played together, like tricking the bartender. I was ready to bail her out by owning up to the mix-up.

She looked nervous, but I knew she'd laugh with me later.

Lorenzo waved again. He looked different. Wilder somehow, and definitely happier, as if he'd grown into himself, and accepted the person he was. Before I'd left for Italy, Lorenzo chose safe clothing, perhaps too safe, projecting the image of a straight-down-the-road business owner, but his style had flourished. A blousy shirt and long-line fur-trimmed vest hung over bell-bottom trousers. Suede pointy-toe boots indicated his new direction. He wore his hair wild like Jim Morrison, the musician Lorenzo dreamed of signing to his company, Restive Records.

He'd love Mariella, too, and would enjoy the tales of our practical jokes, but I had no intention of worrying him with the less pleasant events of our journey.

I watched Mariella stand at the customs' gate. As she scanned the crowd, colour drained from her face, her eyes were unblinkingly wide with terror. Suddenly, the joke didn't seem funny. As I lifted my hand to beckon her, fingernails dug into my arm and dragged me behind the building.

"Mick. What are you doing?" I fought the urge to scream. "Take your hands off me."

His missing teeth gave him the air of a feral animal. "Not 'til ya listen to my proposal." He pressed his thumb and forefinger hard against my collarbone, making me wince. I took a sharp intake of breath, worried the bones would snap.

"Introduce me to your 'usband or I'll tell 'im about your behaviour; drunken, flirtatious, you know the guff. Followin' a single bloke to 'is cabin is an obvious invitation."

I slapped his face. "You scum. They should have locked you up on the boat."

He shoved me hard against the wall of the hut, covering my mouth with his hand. I couldn't signal or yell. But this time I would not collapse inside myself. I'd find a way to attack. I was counting to ten inside my head and positioning my knee where it could do the most damage.

Unexpected rescue appeared from separate directions. Mariella, from my right, no longer looked like a frightened little girl, but a force to be reckoned with. Lorenzo strode from the left, adopting a wide stance, hands clenched in fists, as he breathed heavily through his nose. He looked battle-ready, which I would never have imagined. He was in control.

"Hands off my wife." Lorenzo's voice was unexpectedly deep. This aggression surprised me, but it had the desired effect. Mick dropped his hand as if my skin was molten metal.

"I was muckin' 'bout," Mick said. "She was just tellin' me she was goin' to introduce us. I'm lookin' for a break in the local music industry."

"After what I've seen, you won't get help from me. And I'll make sure you don't get help from anyone. Sydney's music scene is a tight-knit community."

"Then I don' imagine you'd want the music community knowin' about your whoring trouble an' strife." Mick brushed his clothes as if decontaminating, then flashed a toothless smirk as he waited for Lorenzo to make a deal.

A narrowing of Lorenzo's eyes and a shift in weight signalled a solution, but not the one Mick hoped for. Lorenzo became a tiger, ready to pounce.

It surprised me when Mariella stepped between them, brandishing an envelope like a weapon. "But there *were* witnesses? I was one. I've written about your vile, illegal behaviour."

"Waste o' time, ducky. The boat was in interna'ional wa'ers. Australian rules don't apply."

She waved the letter again. "This is not for the police; I got your family's address in England from the captain. When your mother reads this, it will break her heart. Imagine her discovering the terrible man her son has become."

Mick lunged for the envelope, but Lorenzo was faster, landing a blow on Mick's ear. I hoped Lorenzo had burst the bastard's eardrum.

The colour drained from Mick's face, but he looked more concerned about losing his mother's approval than the pain in his ear. He took another grab at the envelope, but missed, then scurried off, tail between his mangy legs.

"Out of the way, ladies," Lorenzo growled, lifting a fist and starting after him.

I grabbed his arm. "The *bastardo* isn't worth the effort." I wanted to cheer for Lorenzo and Mariella's bravery. I also wanted to run after Mick and kick out the rest of his teeth. Instead, I sobbed and cowered in shame. This would all need an explanation and it wasn't an event I wished to re-live.

Lorenzo wrapped his arms around me and rocked me until I calmed. "Shhh. Come on, we'll sort this out at home."

I remembered Mariella and collected myself. "Oh. Sorry," I said, "I haven't introduced you. Meet my friend, Mariella,"

Lorenzo hugged her, then shook her hand. "I'm Stella's husband, Lorenzo. We've met under unusual circumstances."

While they smiled and said their hellos, I recovered my composure.

"When did you write the letter?" I asked. "And how did you know you'd frighten that creep by writing to his mother?"

"There was no letter." She held up the envelope. "This is Angelo's address in Ingham in case his friend doesn't show."

"I'm impressed," I said. "Come, Mariella, let's find this

friend of Angelo's and see if he's okay with Lorenzo and me taking on the responsibility of getting you to Ingham."

I looked between Lorenzo and Mariella. They both nodded in agreement. We marched, arms linked, searching for a man holding a sign.

When I spotted the stocky, balding man carrying a blackboard with Mariella's name, I took out her passport and held it up. Playing with our identities this time was more than a craving for fun. Deep down, if only for a moment, I wanted to be her. She was off to meet a man who would no doubt look at her with both love and desire. Lorenzo was a kind husband, and I was happy with his company. But Mariella had a chance at a perfect life.

"Well, hellooo," he said, smiling and checking me out. He grasped my hand in both of his, while Lorenzo and Mariella looked on without saying a word.

I regretted the game immediately but needed to keep up the pretence. I explained in Italian, "My cousin, Stella and her husband Lorenzo are happy to accommodate me in Sydney until I catch the train to Ingham. I hope that's okay?"

He scuffed the ground while he looked at his feet. "But I promised to look after you. Put you on the train."

"I'll phone Angelo this evening and let him know the change of plan," I said.

"Okay. It's probably better for you to enjoy time with your family. I work long, long hours." He handed me a buff-coloured envelope. "The tickets."

"Thank you so very much for coming to meet me."

"Good luck with your marriage." He grinned. "Angelo will fall head over heels when he sees you."

We'd walked almost halfway to Lorenzo's car before he commented, "What was that all about?"

"On the ship, Mariella and I had fun confusing people. I wanted to do it one last time."

Lorenzo shot me a strange look, and I felt ashamed. I turned to Mariella. "I hope you don't mind staying with us?"

"As long as Lorenzo doesn't mind."

"Our pleasure," he said.

On the drive from the airport, I played tour guide, pointing out important landmarks. I was so involved in telling Mariella about the history and background of each site that I didn't notice we'd driven past the turnoff to the centre of Sydney.

"Lorenzo." I nudged his elbow. "We're going the wrong way."

Lorenzo smiled a secret-keeping smile. "I have a surprise."

He continued on to the quieter suburbs, eventually turning into a new residential estate and parking in the driveway of a brand-new single-storey brick house.

"What are we doing here?" I asked.

"This is for you. I had it built while you were away. I thought you might enjoy tending your own garden."

Mariella smiled at me, and I wanted to respond with joy, but I'd seen a glimmer of something in Lorenzo's eyes. He would not be sharing the house with me.

As we took our luggage out of the car, I thanked him with a hug and whispered in his ear, "Are you going to spend more time in the city?"

He shrugged. "Not all the time. Only for late-night events and weekend functions."

Lorenzo seemed pleased with the new arrangement, and

I didn't want to seem ungrateful. This man sent money back to Italy for my family and provided more material things than most women dream of. I swallowed everything I wanted to say. We left much about our marriage unsaid.

Mariella and I explored the house together. Brand-new furniture, tie-dyed scatter cushions on the floor, and macrame wall hangings. Lorenzo lit incense sticks, resting them in a brass burner, and filling the house with a sweet pungent smell.

"Frankincense," he said. "I burn these all the time now. The scent is food for the soul."

"I love the smell," Mariella said.

I pinched my nose. The stink overwhelmed me.

Lorenzo showed Mariella to the spare room and pointed me in the direction of a larger room he called the master bedroom.

Back in the living room, he reclined on the floor cushions; headphones on, listening to his latest demo tapes.

Mariella and I cooked dinner in the state-of-the-art kitchen.

"You're so lucky," she said as she admired the built-in cupboards and the sparkly laminate bench-top. "I'd be in heaven here, and your husband is a darling."

Everything in these surroundings was too new. There was no sign of Lorenzo's beloved collection of musical instruments. He wouldn't be spending much time here. I guessed from now on, he'd be staying overnight with his boyfriend. The thought of living alone set me more adrift than I'd been at sea.

That night, once Mariella went to bed, I cried alone in the master bedroom for hours. In the early hours of the morning, I worked up the courage to face Lorenzo, to discuss everything on my mind.

"Wake up." I prodded him until he yawned and stretched.

He made room for me on the sofa. "Come here, my girl. Welcome home."

My lip quivered, and he pulled me into his chest. "Are you okay?"

I wanted him to know what happened with Mick. I needed to explain how I understood that living this sham of a marriage was as hard on him as it was on me, but right then the overriding feeling was how unbearable it would be to spend my future alone. Instead, I said, "I missed you when I was away."

"Do you want me to come to bed?"

"No. It's almost morning. Go back to sleep." I kissed his forehead and pulled the knitted throw over his body, tucking him in like the child I'd never have.

On the way to my bedroom, I heard sobbing from Mariella's room.

"Let me in, please," I called through the door. The crying lessened as if she'd smothered the sound with a pillow.

Wiping her red-rimmed eyes, she opened the door. "I wish I wasn't going to Ingham, or we were going together. I don't want a husband." She rested her head against mine, and I stroked her hair.

We cried together.

Two young women stuck with our lot in life. If we had the power to choose, our lives would have been so different. I needed to use the one power I had—honesty. There was no point waiting to pluck up enough courage to tell Lorenzo. That moment might never come. I returned to the living room and sank to the ground near the sofa, whispering while avoiding eye contact. "Lorenzo."

"Yes?" He sounded wide awake.

"I know you love me like a sister..." I bit my fingernail, considering the kindest way to explain the things I needed to say.

"Come on, you can tell me. There's something serious coming and you may as well spit it out."

I swallowed, wondering how he'd respond. "This is difficult for me to admit. There are many nights where I dream of a man touching me all over, kissing me hard on the lips, then throwing me onto the bed with desire."

"Don't we both." Lorenzo half laughed; half cried. Then we held each other with a fresh closeness.

"I love you, Lorenzo."

"I love you, too, but it isn't enough, is it?" His eyes streamed with tears. "What can we do?"

"There's no way around it. You need me here for appearances, and my sisters in Italy depend on you. If my parents can't feed them, they'll be sent away like I was. Except they're unlikely to end up with a husband as considerate and sweet as you."

Lorenzo looked sadder than I'd ever seen him. "If the only reason you're staying with me is for the money I send to your family—"

"That's not what I meant. I've stayed because you're almost the perfect husband and you're definitely the perfect companion."

"But 'almost' is a weighty word." Lorenzo laced his fingers through mine. "Why don't you accompany Mariella on her trip up north? The poor girl could use your support.

If, while you're away, you decide you want to start a new life, I'll be both sad and happy, but either way, I'll continue sending money to your family."

"What will people think of a man whose wife runs off?"

"Divorce is more acceptable than the truth. Besides, I'll get sympathy." He stood and put on a flamboyant theatrical show of heartbreak. "I'll milk it for all it's worth."

I squeezed Lorenzo so tightly, he groaned.

"Remember," he said with a smile, "take time to think. The house and I will be waiting if you decide it's where you'd rather stay."

Chapter Forty-Six

Joe, Present Day

Mrs Morellini slumps in the chair, looking years older. "I need a break."

"Of course," I say. "I think we all do."

Izzy is visibly emotional and although I'm hiding it best I can, I feel the same. After the exhilaration of listening to what happened with Mum and Mrs Morellini when they were known by different names, there's now a lull; like the intermission of a play. One with a possibly disturbing second act. Mrs Morellini touches my cheek. She's trembling. "Your mother was a beautiful woman, inside and out."

Izzy wrings her hands, her expression entirely apologetic. "I'll go buy some energy snacks and drinks."

I'm usually uncomfortable with strangers, but Mrs Morellini is possibly the closest friend my mother ever had, and the connection feels as if it's been passed on through her DNA. Being with Mrs Morellini brings a little of Mum back. "Thank you so much for this."

Mrs Morellini gives me a long hug.

We look up to a loud "Oy!" and to Annette dancing back to the stall, her headpiece askew. "I wandered past earlier but didn't want to interrupt. You were deep in conversation, and Izzy was taking notes like a demon. It looks like the trip was worth it."

"Absolutely," I say. "This gracious lady has been a gem. She's told us about her younger days as a proxy bride. It's helped enormously."

Mrs Morellini throws me a relieved and thankful smile.

I move to make room for Annette, and a snack-laden Izzy returns. She unloads drinks and food on the table. "I didn't know what to buy, so I bought an assortment."

"None for me." Mrs Morellini shakes her head. "You young ones don't mind if I take myself to bed."

"Do you want me to drive?" I ask.

"No need. My car knows the way home. But if you don't mind, I could use a steadying hand as I walk to the car park. I'm okay on uneven pathways when the sun is shining, but low light isn't good for old eyes."

Annette tilts her head and studies our faces. "The pair of you may as well go home, too. I'm fine."

Izzy and I look at each other and nod. My head is so heavy it feels like it might drop off.

"Go on." Annette makes a shooing action. "Pop upstairs to my veranda early tomorrow morning, and I'll make you a nice fresh coffee."

As I hold Mrs Morellini around the waist, ready to catch her if she stumbles, I open my mouth to ask what happened next. But it's clear she's had enough for today. I don't push my luck.

Izzy doesn't have the same qualms. "Mrs M, I wanted to jump for joy when you and Joe's mum got back at that pig of a man, Mick. Too often, men escape without getting their comeuppance." Izzy hugs her, and I watch Mrs Morellini become the comforter, patting Izzy's back instead. Female intuition at work, again. I kick a pebble off the path, wishing my boot could strike the head of the bastard who hurt Izzy. I'd go to the ends of the earth to make her happy. We continue our slow meander and Izzy helps Mrs Morellini buckle herself in. "I've recorded everything you said, but I still don't know how you ended up here, while Maria ended up in Sydney."

"No need to beat around the bush with hints," Mrs Morellini says. "Tomorrow I'll bake some fresh cannoli, so the two of you better get to my place by eight in the morning. There's a lot to get through before you fly home."

We wave as she drives off, then hop into the hire car. I turn the key and the engine leaps into life. "Where to now?"

"Home." Izzy clutches the bag of food. "We've plenty of snacks and I haven't enough energy to go out for dinner."

I tuck her hair behind one ear. "You okay?"

"My shoulders ache and my head is spinning."

"They say there's nothing you can't learn from YouTube. Maybe I can do a speed course on therapeutic massage."

"Don't be daft, Joe. Your hands might intend to convey 'calm', but my mind would get the opposite message."

I snigger. "Would that be so terrible?"

"Wait and see." Her slow wink speeds up my pulse.

"There's something we need to take care of before the massage."

"What?" she asks.

"I want us both to remove our profiles from the dating app."

Izzy waves her hand dismissively. "You don't think I've

left the profiles up, do you? I took them down after our first kiss."

―――――――

Instead of the elegant woman in white from yesterday, Mrs Morellini greets us without make-up, wearing a red, white and green apron printed with the words *Baci Il Cuoco*. As she scoots us inside, she notices me trying to read it. "Kiss the cook," she translates. "I was planning to bake the cannoli for you, but I've decided you can help. Many an important conversation has unfolded over a cooking session." She hands out aprons. "Put these on and wash your hands."

Izzy sets up her phone on the workbench. "Hope you don't mind, but it saves me writing everything down."

"We don't have to rush. You've almost heard the whole story." Mrs Morellini pushes mixing bowls and spoons towards us and folds her hands in prayer. "Not long after we landed in Australia, your mother and I lost touch. Some months later I realised I'd made a mistake that's too late to set right, but your mother deserves to know about it. At the very least, I must apologise in person.

"You're planning a trip to Sydney?" I ask.

"My grandson helped me look up flights this morning. I need to visit Maria, but I wanted to check with you first."

"That's wonderful," I say.

"Yes. Now, give me your hands." Mrs Morellini inspects my fingernails. "Good, Joe. Short and clean. Give them another wash because you're making the shell dough."

She pushes a handwritten recipe towards Izzy. "Your job is the spicy cream filling. I copied this out. It will help when you want to make these for your mother-in-law."

Izzy raises her eyebrows but says nothing.

"Not like that, Joe. Rub the butter into the flour until it resembles breadcrumbs." She watches until she's sure we know what we're doing, then sits back in her seat and waggles her finger at Izzy's phone. "Switch it on, if you're both ready, and I'll tell you what happened all those years ago. But I want you to keep baking, and I prefer it if you don't interrupt."

Chapter Forty-Seven

Stella, Sydney to Ingham, 1967

Before Mariella and I caught the train to Queensland, Lorenzo rescheduled his appointments to ensure our last day was special. He insisted on buying us both new dresses to wear on the trip, and he waited patiently in the street while we tried every item in the store. Once we'd made our choice, we asked the sales assistant to pack our old clothes in the carry bags so we could parade our new purchases around the city.

Lorenzo slapped his leather-clad thighs with laughter when we came out. "I can barely tell you apart in your matching outfits."

He offered both elbows, and we took his cue, hooking our arms through either side, and we spent the morning promenading around the city, giggling at the mumbled comments and outright stares from passers-by.

"I'm like a book with matching bookends."

"Gorgeous bookends," I said.

Mariella laughed and patted Lorenzo's thigh. "And you're a hand-stitched, leather-bound special edition."

I'd never been happier with Lorenzo than on that bitter-sweet day.

———————

Lorenzo was quiet on the drive to the station and even quieter on the departure platform.

"Forgive me for not waiting until your train leaves. I'm not big on goodbyes." He handed me a gift. "I saw this in the jeweller's window next door to the dress shop. You'll understand why I had to buy it."

He stared at the cigarette-stub-covered ground, and I did the same. Even without eye contact, I knew his heart was as heavy as mine.

"Call me as soon as you can. I need to know you're safe." As Lorenzo turned toward the exit, he waved a hand over his shoulder and I mirrored the wave. I felt the connection pull, then weaken, breaking once he disappeared. There was a moment where I considered chasing him, but if I'd done that, I'd be promising to stay.

I needed to get on that train.

As we departed the station, I felt drawn from both directions. Although not by design, I'd taken a seat facing our destination, while Mariella faced the city we'd left behind. I longed for Sydney and Lorenzo, the man who'd cared for me, a place where I knew what to expect. But the pull of the unknown, with its promise of a new future, was the stronger force.

Mariella bit her lip. "Do you think we should've phoned Angelo again? Should I have let him know you're coming with me?"

She had already asked this at breakfast, but I answered again, "He knows you've been staying in Sydney with your 'cousin' and my presence will be easier to explain face-to-face."

She looked unconvinced.

"Don't worry, I'm not planning to stay with you at his place. I'll find a hotel and hang around in Ingham until you settle in. I want to make sure everything's okay."

Mariella creased her forehead. "Tell me to shut up if I'm prying, but when you said goodbye to Lorenzo, it felt as if you were saying an *Addio* instead of a temporary *Arrivederci*."

I blinked back the threatening tears. "We had a big talk about our feelings." I clasped my hands to my chest. "It's silly and girlish, but on the boat when I read your letter from Angelo, I was jealous."

"Jealous?"

"It's selfish complaining about a marriage because it lacks passion, especially when many women are trapped with brutal men. But I'm worried if Lorenzo and I stay together, we'll make each other miserable."

Warmth from the window beat against my closed eyelids as I tried to drive away the doubts. The train beat a clickety-clack on the tracks, lulling me almost to sleep.

"Stella. You haven't opened your present."

I opened my eyes to Mariella, pointing at the package next to me.

"Lorenzo's too generous for his own good," I said, peeling back the embossed outer wrapping to reveal a black velvet box. A note dropped onto the floor. Mariella picked it up and passed it back.

'It's time to give away my beautiful guitar. I hope someone takes better care of her.'

Swallowing hard, I removed the gold pendant encrusted with diamonds and fastened it around my neck.

Mariella scratched her temple. "A letter M?"

"I'm surprised you didn't read my real name during the passport swap."

She crossed her arms indignantly. "When your bloody photograph stared back at me, I panicked. I certainly didn't want to draw more attention by checking what should've been my own name."

"Good point." I gave a drawn-out yawn. "My real name's Maria-Rosa. A boring name I never liked."

"So, you just changed it?"

"With Lorenzo's encouragement. His inner-city flat had an entire wall covered with musical instruments. The centrepiece was a stunning guitar. 'This one's my favourite,' I'd said to him during my first visit. 'Can you play it for me?'"

"I don't play her. She's there for show." He took the guitar off the wall and handed it over. "She's a beauty. Just like you."

The product brand was emblazoned in gold across the head of the guitar. "She has a better name than me. Stella."

"If you like that name, there's nothing to stop you from taking it." He looked me up and down. "Pleased to meet you, Stella. The name is really hip. Like you."

"I used the name Stella from that day on."

Mariella blinked. "I don't understand. If you like the name Stella so much, why has he given you the letter M?"

"It's Lorenzo's way of setting me free. As Stella, I was too much like my namesake. Mostly kept for display."

We kept to our own worrisome thoughts during the Sydney to Brisbane leg of our journey. But once we changed trains and boarded the Sunlander, which travelled the thirty-hour trip north, the mood lightened. We laughed and chatted as we pointed out towns along the track. Mariella handed me a brochure which came with our tickets. "There's a map to mark off the towns."

It was quite an adventure watching the changing scenery roll past. The further north we travelled, the greener it became, and in places the rail line ran parallel to the coast, giving us blue ocean glimpses. The landscape, tropical and lush, embraced me and called me home.

"Mackay," Mariella said, marking off a major town.

"How long from here until Ingham?" I asked.

"We stop at Townsville in a few hours. Ingham is next." Mariella's voice rose. Not the raised tones of anticipation, more a squeaky plea for rescue.

I watched her rub a non-existent stain from the corner of her new dress. She kneaded and scratched it over and over.

"If you keep that up, you'll end up with a hole. Come on, it will be okay. I'm sure of it."

"How will I know if Angelo is kind and good? I wish we had that magazine article where Aunt Gladys told us what to look for."

"You'll see. You'll see it in his eyes, and his manner."

"That didn't work with Emilio. I was sure that man loved me. But, as you pointed out, he was complicit in the plan to get rid of me."

"I'll talk to Angelo and check him out. Then I'll stay as long as it takes to make sure you're safe. In fact, if I like the place, I might stay forever."

Mariella studied my face as if searching for the truth. "You think it will all be good?"

"I don't know everything. No one can." I smiled and attempted to project complete confidence. "But my intuition is first rate. I love you, don't I?"

Mariella shifted her attention to buckling and unbuckling the leather strap of her shoe.

"Stop," I said. "You're making *me* nervous now. Would it help if we were to practise?"

"Practise what?"

"The introductions."

For the next two hours, I coached Mariella on what to say, but she froze each time it was her turn to speak, leaving me to deliver all the lines.

She wrapped herself with trembling arms. "It will not work."

"That's okay. We'll do it a different way. I'll tell him you're too nervous, or you're feeling unwell, and I'll do all the talking until you're ready to join in."

Mariella flung herself across the seat and almost knocked me over me with her hug. "Thank you for sorting out my life. I wish I had half your bravery."

"It depends on the situation. You had no trouble summoning a truckload of courage to protect me from madman Mick. Best friends look out for each other."

***

As the train approached Ingham station, my fingertips tingled, and I realised I was nervous, too. I hoped I was right about Angelo. His letter to Mariella had filled me with hope, and I sensed the man she'd been sent to marry could be trusted. All this, gleaned from a single page of words.

Mariella gripped my hand as we disembarked, and we scanned the platform for someone fitting his description.

"Over there," she whispered. "Look. Do you think that's him?"

A man, twenty feet from us, watched a group of passengers leaving another carriage. He looked rugged, and eager, and different to any man I'd known, yet there was something handsomely familiar. I couldn't explain it. His familiarity had nothing to do with appearance.

Lorenzo had a friend in Sydney who claimed he could read auras. I'd laughed deep in my belly at the idea of goodness and wickedness, and everything in between, shining like a light from within. I'd chuckled even louder when he claimed only certain people could see this phenomenon. But, looking at Angelo, I saw everything wondrous in the world. There was so much good shimmering about his person.

He spotted us and walked tentatively in our direction, beaming with a whole-body smile. It was my turn to be lost for words. Angelo looked amused when he noticed our matching dresses, then he glanced at my diamond pendant.

Registering the letter M, he lifted his eyes to mine, and although my pulse raced too fast for meeting a stranger, I couldn't look away. I'd thought it impossible for his grin to get any wider, but his eyes became dewy as he gazed at my face. "Mariella," he said, his smile warmer than the sun. Before I could correct him, he enfolded me in his arms.

The world began spinning and my knees gave way until Mariella steadied me from behind.

Her stage-fright disappeared, her voice strong and calm. "Don't forget about me." She offered her hand to Angelo and shook hands, firm like a man. "I'm Stella, Mariella's cousin."

To my astonishment, word for word, she continued the rehearsed lines from the train trip, except this time, the role she performed was mine.

"I hope you don't mind me accompanying my cousin. She's been very nervous and is feeling unwell. I'll be staying in Ingham for a while, so if you can point me toward a decent hotel, I'd really appreciate it."

Angelo draped his arms around my waist and the warmth of his body heated mine. "Not at all," he said, his voice deep and low. "We're happy to have you, but I insist you come and stay with us at the farm."

I gasped, and he spun me around until we were a hair's breadth from a kiss. "Mrs Mariella Morellini. Mrs Mariella Morellini." He rolled the syllables around his tongue as if finally tasting an answered prayer.

I could taste it, too, and I swooned momentarily before shaking myself back to reality. Mrs Mariella Morellini wasn't my name.

The real Mariella grabbed my arm. "I need the bathroom. We'll be right back."

By the time we were out of earshot, I was faint-headed.

"It's okay," she said, propping me against a wall. "It's a change of plan, but it could be perfect."

I caught my breath and spoke slowly. "What on earth just happened? What have I done?"

"You did nothing wrong. This didn't come from earth; it was Eros taking control. His arrows pierced yours and Angelo's hearts. Now you're both in love."

"What will we do, Mariella?"

"For a start, call me Stella. That's my name."

I sat in the toilet cubicle with my head in my hands until she hammered on the door. "What does your heart tell you? That's what we must do."

Before we headed to where Angelo was waiting, Mariella, the new Stella, took off her wedding band. "This ring now binds you to Angelo."

I swapped mine, kissing the band and Lorenzo goodbye, knowing he'd understand. Then I tried to give her the opal ring he had designed.

"Keep it, Mariella," she said without hesitation. "Wear it on your right hand. Hurry, your husband, Angelo, is waiting."

The rough tracks through cane fields to Angelo's farm were so punishing it almost loosened my teeth. I hoped it wasn't divine retribution for our deception.

Angelo in the driver's seat had his thigh pressed against mine, firm and muscular from physical work. His masculine presence filled the car, impossible to ignore. I forced my eyes on the road ahead, not once daring to look at Mariella squished beside me in the front against the passenger window. I pictured her face and repeated Stella in my head, reminding myself this was more important than anything on a school exam.

Once we got out of the car, I spun in a panicky, giddy dance. Long stalks of sugar cane waved sweet hellos. Green-blanketed mountains offered protection. Even the clouds painted welcome messages across the sky in whimsical white. It felt too right to be wrong.

The farmhouse needed some attention, a coat of paint and some plants in the garden, but I was ready to grab a paintbrush and make this my home.

Angelo led us through the bright and scrupulously clean living areas, out the back door and into a veranda which had been enclosed with glass louvres, creating a room. He set one of 'Stella's' bags on the floor and gestured to a single bed. "I hope you'll be comfortable in the sleepout."

She nodded enthusiastically.

Angelo and I left her to unpack while he showed me around the kitchen, bouncing on his toes and touching everything. I smiled as he showed me how to turn on the taps as if running water was something spectacular. When he realised his absurdity, he laughed out loud. We giggled together and the fluttering in my stomach reached from my head to my toes. When he kissed my hands, they trembled, too.

He looked at the floor. "I can make up another bed in the room with Stella. I'm not sure what you'd prefer." His voice softened to a whisper so light it almost floated away. "We're legally married, but if you'd rather wait until we have a church wedding here in Ingham, I'll understand. I'll do whatever it takes to make you happy." He pushed a lock of hair falling over my forehead, then clutched his hands to his heart. "I did not know I could feel this way." His eyes met mine, silently begging me to feel the same.

"I intend to share the marital bed with you until the day we die, but please allow me a few days." This man was the one. I had no real hesitancy in the love-making department, but I feigned shyness in case the real Mariella changed her mind.

My pulse pounded through my body, but there was too much left unsaid. I buried my head in his shoulder and prayed. I prayed for strength and I prayed that when I told him the truth, as I eventually would, he'd understand and forgive me.

During dinner, I looked up several times when Angelo used the name Stella, but Mariella never faltered. She slipped into her new persona like her comfortable running shoes.

"I'm very tired," she said. "I hope you don't mind me going to bed."

Left alone, I stared wide-eyed in front of me, glancing at Angelo when I dared. Several times we caught each other smiling, but neither of us found the courage to speak.

"You probably need sleep too," he said, standing when I did. "I'll sleep on the sofa," he said.

When I shook my head no, his breath quickened.

Despite my quivering body, and a heart that raced twice as fast as it had ever beaten before, when Angelo took a step towards me I closed my eyes and nodded. Without a word, he carried me over the threshold of the bedroom.

I was sure of one thing. A night with this man would make whatever else we faced worthwhile.

Chapter Forty-Eight

Joe, Present Day

Mrs Morellini fans her face with a drink coaster, then points at the phone which is still on record.

"Time for a break?" I ask. "You want me to switch it off?

She nods. "Lusty memories and cooking have made this kitchen rather hot."

Izzy slaps icing sugar covered hands across her pink cheeks. "Oh. Em. Gee. I feel nervous for you, even though it happened over fifty years ago." She picks up a second drink coaster fan. "I'm quite warm myself."

Mrs Morellini smiles as she pours iced water into long thin glasses. "The cannoli shells are done, but they need a minute to cool, just like me." She blushes when she looks in my direction. "My apologies. It's probably a tad uncomfortable listening to an old lady's racy stories."

I smile and settle back into my chair. "I don't mind hearing about your love affairs, but I squirmed big time when my mother retold hers."

The women exchange knowing looks, reducing me to a teenage boy.

"Right-o, Let's finish our cooking," Mrs Morellini says. "Watch how this is done." She demonstrates squeezing cream filling into the sugary pastry tubes, and I fight the urge to snigger. Their looks were on the mark. I've reverted to adolescence these last few days. Now everything has a sexual connotation. When Izzy leans over the kitchen countertop, I impulsively slap her perfectly rounded bottom. She shoots me a warning, that is more 'we'll get caught' than 'stop annoying me'.

Mrs Morellini thrusts a plate of the sweet dessert in front of our noses. "Eat some."

I take a small bite. "This is heavenly."

"Come on, eat up," Mrs Morellini says.

We devour two each, then Izzy wipes her mouth with the apron. "So, did you read people's auras after that first meeting with Angelo?"

"Not auras, as such, but there's an atmospheric shimmer around the newly in-love." She stares at us. "I detected a special energy flickering around the pair of you at the festival."

For several beats, Mrs Morellini holds eye contact. I check the sky, muttering nonsense about impending rain, but immediately regret not watching Izzy to see if she feels the same.

My love for Izzy might not have developed at lightning speed as it did for the Morellinis, but I can't imagine deeper feelings than these. In lieu of prayer, I cross my fingers. Please let her love me.

The way Izzy moves her hands, stirring the air in a joyful dance, is mesmerising. I'm in love with calm Izzy, happy Izzy, and flustered Izzy. She settles back with a sweet sigh.

"I'm dying to hear the rest of your story. It must have worked out. You stayed married."

Mrs Morellini inhales slowly. "We enjoyed a glorious honeymoon week. Lorenzo accepted the news and congratulated me when I spoke to him from a phone box in town. A sadness grew between us, but it wasn't unexpected. Your mother spoke to him, too, and he said she could share the home with him in Sydney if she wanted to return. For a few days, there wasn't a single obstacle in our way. Or at least, I was too blinded by love to see any."

The colour leaches from Mrs Morellini's face as she remembers.

"And then what happened?" I ask.

"I'd pour myself a soothing Marsala and make myself comfortable and turn that recording gadget back on, but I've just seen the time. You'll need to pack up the stall then grab your bags and head to Townsville. If you don't leave soon, you'll miss your plane."

I smother a disappointed groan. "Sorry."

"It's okay. I understand you want to hear the rest. I'll get my grandson to organise a flight and I'll send you the details."

"Mum would love that and we'd love to see you again."

"We'll even collect you from the airport, won't we, Joe?" Izzy kisses Mrs Morellini's cheek. "It's been absolutely wonderful meeting you. Thank you for being so generous with your stories."

"I'll be there as soon as I can. There's something important I must deliver in person. A small parcel arrived here a year after your mother left Ingham. We'd lost touch. Angelo and I contacted Lorenzo, but he didn't know where to find her either. I eventually opened the package, even though I shouldn't have."

She pulls herself to a standing position and looks so fragile that I reach out to help. I hope she'll be okay. This has been an emotional rollercoaster.

"I won't come out, but on your way to the car, can you please pick stems of Bougainvillea flowers for your mother? Tell her they're from Stella with love."

Chapter Forty-Nine

Maria, Present Day

My good memory days are less frequent, and when they arrive, they're not always a blessing. Before I was brought to The Figs, doctor's visits were a rarity—now I'm poked and prodded and talked at. Feeling as if I'm no longer a person is hard to take.

I direct my harshest glare at the doctors discussing my case at the end of my bed. There should be laws ordering doctors to speak to the patient rather than about them.

"So, we agree," the female doctor says to her snarky colleague, "it's a permanent stop to *her* taking part in the memory recall mumbo-jumbo?"

"Agreed. It was over the top," the arrogant male replies. "Questioning *her* daily. It put *her* health at risk."

I stare at Dr Bryson Kent-Jones's name badge, wishing I had one of my own, which I would point at. *My name is Maria.* Surely with their superior brain power, they could remember that.

Instead, I put a hand in the crook of my elbow and fling my arm up in what I hope is the international sign to fuck off. There are other obscene Italian gestures and I intend to use every one of them each time they refer to me as 'her'.

He reaches for my wrist, but I slap his hand. "Families don't care about the side effects of stress. They've subjected *her* to this."

I flick my fingers from under the chin. "*Non me ne frega niente!*" *I don't give a damn.* At least not about the pair of you. Families do care. I'm not letting anyone talk about my son like that. I yell, "*Ho avuto una scelta.*" *I had a choice.* Joey gave me a choice. Why don't you realise that?

They blink without comprehending, then the female continues. "Restarting the sessions is a hard no from me. Poor old thing. *Her* family should leave *her* in peace."

Old thing. That's what I've become. A worn-out object, no longer human My brain is undoubtedly on-the-blink, but it isn't dead.

"Pity we can't stop family visits," Doctor double-barrel name says.

"We can't limit how long they stay anymore, but we can limit visits to immediate family. I'll write the order up in her charts."

"*Fuori!*" *Get out*, I scream, pulling my lower eyelid in a Mafioso warning. Stella told me she'd come and visit, but now they'll stop her. "*Fuori.*" I repeat, so loud they can't ignore the person inside the shell.

Their silent exchange suggests I'm making it worse.

I push past and escape to Katerina's room.

"You okay, Maria?" She pats the space next to her on the bed. "Here, sit with me."

When the doctors lurk in the doorway, her voice is calm and reassuring. "Maria is safe here."

Double-barrel checks his notes against the nameplate on Katerina's door. "I see. You're the resident driving *her* memoir-writing project."

"Not at all. We've been working together as a team. Maria has always been the driver."

"Well, we've done a follow-up health assessment. From now on visitors are restricted to Maria's immediate family."

Katerina puts her arm around my shoulders. "Ignore these people until they leave, Maria. They aren't related to you, so you mustn't talk to them." Through clenched teeth, she says, "Goodbye."

"*Dov'è Joey?*" Where is my son? Why doesn't he visit me? I rock backwards and forwards, trying to transport myself to a place of faith. I need to believe for a moment that everything will be okay.

Katerina takes a black-leather address book from her bedside drawer, then picks up the phone. "I'll call Dermot."

I listen as she tells Dermot what the doctors have decided. She hands me the phone.

"*Ciao*. My lovely Maria," he says. "I've missed our chats, but I'm glad you're doing okay."

"*Dov'è Joey?*"

"He just sent me a message; he'll be in to see you tomorrow. I'm looking forward to hearing what he and Izzy found out from Stella."

Stella? I dab at tears and hand Katerina the phone.

"Come on, Maria," she says after she hangs up. "Can you help me pack up the essential oil kit? There's no way the evil duo will let us use it again."

She slips the tiny brown bottles I once thought were poison, into square slots of a wooden case. I reach for a handful, removing a lid and taking a breath.

Cedar. I smell it again, then open another. Rose.

Cedar and rose together remind me of the talcum powder I used when Joey was a baby. Tears flood my eyes. My baby gave me so much joy but he is now grown. Poor Joey and his wife. The precious baby they wanted so much never took a breath.

His wife came to see me the day she left Joey. She explained how the air surrounding them was so suffocating with sadness—neither could breathe. They'd tried, but couldn't let go of their grief. They believed they had no right to be happy together.

Katerina hands me a tissue and I cry years of pent-up tears.

When I settle, I search through the box, craving a scent to shift my thoughts. Orange blossom, cinnamon bark, and peppermint.

Peppermint. Stella and me, on the ship to Australia.

I'm no longer afraid of the mafia. My only fear is Joey being lonely when I die. I've tried my hardest to push him into love, but some things aren't up to me. He has a friendship with Izzy and maybe that's enough.

The delicate bonds of love glitter golden, but we forge genuine friendships with links of iron.

The peppermint oil wafts to my nostrils. Stella. A friendship long lost, and the hope of reconnection now dashed.

Chapter Fifty

Joe, Present Day

During our take-off for Sydney, Izzy ignores the flight attendant's eyebrow warning. She's been talking throughout the safety spiel. "What a difference this trip made, Joe. On the way down I made a thousand guesses about your mother's changed identity."

I nod silently, but hide my face from the attendant by pretending to read the card showing crash positions and inflatable vests.

Izzy continues. "What were your theories? Did you have a favourite? All of mine were wrong."

I whisper, "I didn't have the brainpower to work out any reasons for the name change, except it being a mistake. If I'd thought about things more, it might have prepared me for hearing about Mum's past, and realising how sad I'd feel." My voice falters and I blink hard.

"Oh, Joe." Izzy squeezes my hand and pecks my cheek, prompting the woman in the aisle seat to tut. Izzy throws her a 'here's something else to look at' smile and kisses me full on the lips.

I wipe my eyes and smile. "Perhaps I should take up smoking with you. See if it relaxes me. A man with a cigarette is more acceptable than a cry-baby."

"Well, there's nothing wrong with crying. It has health benefits. But for someone who's been paying me a lot of attention, you're not very observant. I haven't smoked for two weeks."

"You're not stressed anymore?"

"Nope. I'm happy without it. Especially now we've almost solved the mystery. Running into Stella was pure gold."

A flight attendant delivers the pre-packaged airline food, and Izzy hoes into her sandwich with gusto. I have trouble navigating the packaging. Small plastic trays set inside a larger plastic tray, all smothered with plastic. "All this seems at odds with the message on the reverse of the safety card about cutting emissions to save the planet."

Izzy smiles at me and, as callous as it seems, I suddenly don't care about saving the world. Nothing beyond the two of us matters.

"Is there anything else your mum wants? Something to make her happy." Izzy stares intently as if she's peering inside my head.

I poke around in my brain, wondering what she's hoping to find. Nothing much comes to mind. "Like most mothers, she wants the best for her family."

"So? Is your life as good as you'd like it?"

I sense a hint of danger, but can't read the subtext, so I cross my fingers and hope I'm on the right track. "It's perfect. I don't want to change a thing."

She unfastens and refastens her seat belt, staring out the

window, her voice serious. "Your mother's desperate for a grandchild. What're your thoughts on the subject?"

Her shoulders tremble and she stops clicking. Something's up. I was right. Izzy doesn't want children. I need to let her know it isn't an obstacle. "I'm over the moon spending time with you the way we are. Just the two of us. My mother's dreams aren't necessarily mine."

"Okay." She reaches for headphones. "I just wanted to know."

She spends the rest of the flight staring blank-eyed at a movie.

Once I've built up enough courage, I ask, "You all right?"

"Sad movie, and I'm overtired. I need my own bed."

My gut tells me she's not okay, and although I want to make her feel better, I don't want to question her with the woman in the aisle seat half-listening.

When the plane lands, Izzy takes a deep breath then looks through me as if she's a boss preparing to announce a cut in a desperate employee's work-hours. "Joe, instead of giving me a lift home, I'll catch the train. You've got to pick up Biscotti from the kennels, and it'll save you going out of your way."

"Are you sure?"

"Yes. I have a couple of things to do in town."

Instead of pressing her for more information, I search through Granny Blake's pearls of advice. The most useful thing I recall Gran saying was: when people seem annoyed or upset, give them space.

"Okay," I say. "Phone me when you feel up to it."

Izzy pushes past the aisle lady and disappears without kissing me goodbye.

Chapter Fifty-One

Joe, Present Day

While navigating peak hour traffic on the drive to the kennels, I replay the plane conversation, eventually deciding I'm overthinking things. Maybe Izzy felt unwell. Not everything's about me.

When I try to pat Biscotti, he turns with his tail between his legs, then kicks as I lift him into the back seat of the car. "Come on, mate. Don't kick a friend when they're down. I can't be trying to work out why you're rejecting me, too."

The dog looks at me, one ear cocked. His eyes brim with sympathy, reminding me of Mum, who was always a great listener.

"I'll tell you all about it, eh? I don't know how I upset my lovely Izzy, but I ruined my marriage by asking too much about useless stuff and saying too little of the things that count."

When I climb into the driver's seat, Biscotti ignores my

command to sit in the back and joins me up front. May as well accept it and keep talking, even though he's not going to help. "Old Gran was big on advising men not to mansplain. She had that down pat before it was a thing. For the first time, though, I wonder if Gran's advice was wrong. A sixth sense tells me leaving Izzy alone won't fix our relationship. What do you reckon?"

Biscotti barks at the window, probably at his own reflection, but it's all the encouragement I need. I cut across lanes of traffic, then double-back towards Izzy's place.

There's a florist shop two blocks from her apartment, so I stop, taking Biscotti inside with me.

"I need a couple of things," I say to the florist. "These bougainvillea stems arranged into a bouquet. And I'd like to buy a lush houseplant. Something tropical."

The florist strokes Biscotti, and he pulls hard on the leash, trying to reach the plant display. She looks up. Not amused. "Better put him outside before he cocks his leg."

Biscotti answers with a disgruntled growl, so I tie him to the lamppost on the pavement. At least I'm not the only person the dog doesn't like.

Half an hour later, with Biscotti tethered to a dripping garden tap in Izzy's apartment garden, I stand outside her door holding a variegated fern similar to one she'd admired in Mrs Morellini's kitchen.

She opens the door wearing an indecipherable expression. "Joe?"

I'm not taking any chances of her shutting me out, so I hand her the plant and step through the door. "Even if it means leaving your place broken-hearted, I'm not going until you tell me what's wrong." I flop onto the sofa and pat the seat beside me.

She sits, cradling the plant to her chest.

"I'm hellbent on making things right because these have been the best days of my life, and I won't walk away without fighting for it. Not fighting for it. Fighting for you."

She traces her fingers over the lacy leaves and speaks softly. "It's not your fault. I didn't think things through."

Here it comes, the *it's not you, it's me* speech. "I don't understand, but if you tell—"

"Let me finish. Even though I hoped we'd become lovers, I wasn't prepared. I didn't prepare..."

Her words hang in the air like a slow-motion bullet, fired but yet to make impact. I clutch my chest instinctively. "Didn't prepare what?"

"I wasn't using contraception, Joe. We were living inside a romance novel and I didn't want to ruin it. On the plane, after you told me you didn't want children, I realised we'd had unprotected sex. More than once."

She sobs into the pot plant and I try to pull her into my arms, but she pushes me away. "Not now. We can be friends, but I need time to think."

Slumping like a discarded toy, I run through the conversation yet again. I didn't mean to say I didn't want children, but it seems I did. I swallow hard and am about to explain when a God almighty howl breaks the silence.

Izzy looks up, mouth hanging open.

"Sorry. Ignore the noise. It's bloody Biscotti. He's a naughty dog pretending to be tortured. He's got water and I've already fed him. He makes the same commotion at home to get attention. Then he promptly ignores it."

Still crying, Izzy runs outside. This time I chase after her. I'm stupid, but I'm not making the same mistake twice.

"He can be a mean bastard," I call. "Watch out for him."

By the time I catch up, Biscotti is sprawled on his back getting a belly rub. "Come on, you gorgeous thing," Izzy says. "Come inside. Naughty daddy leaving you tied up." He licks Izzy's hand and follows her upstairs, resting his head on her feet the moment she sits.

I watch her stroke his fur and wrap her arms around his neck. It really is a dog's life.

I tentatively reach for Izzy's tear-stained cheek. "I can give you as much time as you need, but I need to be honest. If by some miracle you are pregnant, I'll dance a happy jig from here to Ingham and back."

Izzy bursts into tears again, but this time through smiles. She throws her arms around my neck, and Biscotti wedges himself between us.

"Do you want me to stay with you tonight?" I ask.

She wipes her eyes. "I think it would be irresponsible to drive home just to drive back again tomorrow. We need to think about the environment."

Her slow wink turns my knees to jelly. Other parts react differently.

"You're a clever woman, Izzy. We can kill two birds with one stone. More time to make a baby while creating a healthier planet for our future children."

Chapter Fifty-Two

Joe, Present Day

At breakfast, Izzy's face is a combination of Snow White's dwarves: Happy and Sleepy. Although I haven't looked in the mirror, my guess is, I'm Dopey. It's the shock of this messy-haired goddess loving me. Me. Luke-warm Joe.

"What are you staring at?" she asks.

"Your breakfast," I lie. If it's possible to go overboard telling a woman you love her, then I well and truly dived into those waters headfirst last night. I pour myself a bowl of cereal, making a concerted effort not to suffocate her with affection. "Did you hear about the man who drowned in his bowl of Muesli?" I ask.

Izzy rolls her eyes before I answer.

"A strong *currant* pulled him under."

"Groan!"

"We should get dressed," I say reluctantly.

"What time is it?" she asks. "Come on, have one of your lucky guesses."

I've got better things on my mind than time, but I bite the side of my lip and concentrate. "7:21?"

Izzy reaches for her phone. "Shit. I can't check. I forgot to switch it back on when we landed."

"Better add a minute to my guess for the time taken to turn it—"

"Joe!" she interrupts. "Three messages and a missed call from Mrs Morellini."

I sit up straight. "Is she okay?"

"Well, we won't be going back to bed this morning. When she said she planned to visit soon, she meant it. Her grandson found a too-good-to-ignore last-minute flight deal. She's arriving this morning."

"When?"

"No details."

I rescue my phone from the jeans dropped hastily on Izzy's bedroom floor. "She's sent the flight number. Arrives at 9:45 am. An hour and three quarters."

Izzy taps a finger against her lip. "Fifteen minutes to get dressed."

"An hour to drop the dog home and get to the airport," I say.

Her wicked eyebrow raise is an invitation.

"How on earth will we fill the extra half hour?"

"Race you to the bedroom," she says.

I drop Izzy at the entrance of the arrival terminal, then drive off to park the car. This saves time and as soon as Izzy phones me, I'll drive through the passenger pickup area to collect her and Mrs Morellini.

While I'm waiting, I inspect the bouquet of Bougainvillea. It survived the night better than me. After tearing off a damaged papery petal, I use my fingernails to break off the thorns. I don't want them ripping into Mum's equally papery skin.

I'm wedging it safely back in the boot when Izzy rings.

"Be there soon."

With her all-white outfit, Mrs Morellini stands out from the casually dressed crowd.

"You cut a fine figure," I say, opening the passenger door. "Look at those people checking you out. I bet they're wondering which famous actress you are."

"Flattery will get you everywhere, Joe."

"Do you mind if we stop for a coffee?" Izzy asks. "Maria's doctors don't approve of her having visitors, but they usually finish their rounds by eleven, so best we stay away until then."

Mrs Morellini shakes her head. "Terrible stopping my Mariella from seeing the people she loves. But let's go somewhere quiet. I need to tell you what happened next."

Chapter Fifty-Three

Stella, Ingham, 1967

After dinner on the third day, Angelo put on a record and we waltzed around the lounge room. The 'original' Mariella danced with a broom, making silly conversation with her partner. "You barely touched your plate. You need to eat and put on a bit of weight." She twirled the broom as we laughed. "Don't take this personally, but your dancing's rather wooden."

Angelo joined in with puns of his own. "Mate," he said to the broom, "you need to brush up on dance steps if you're planning to sweep your lady friend off her feet."

With the weight of worry lifted from her shoulders, Mariella was quite the comedienne. We laughed far too much and made joke after joke.

Ominous ringing from the large black phone interrupted our banter. "Save those puns a minute," Angelo said, turning down the music.

"*Ciao*," he called into the mouthpiece, "Cousin Nino.

Yes, my bride arrived. *Bella Donna.*"

Mariella grabbed my hand, pulling me through the kitchen and into her room and closing the door behind us. She held a pillow over her face like a child playing hide and seek, and my knees shook so much I considered the possibility that an earthquake was moving the ground.

When Angelo knocked, my heart almost stopped.

"Nino wants to talk to you, Mariella."

For a moment, I forgot which of us Nino was asking for. But Mariella pointed at me.

I called through the closed door. "I'd rather not talk to him."

"He's insistent, and he rarely takes no for an answer."

I couldn't hold back the tears. My entire body trembled with terror. Angelo would discover the truth and my brief, but perfect, marriage would be over.

With both of us wailing, Angelo let himself in. His mouth hung agape with bewilderment as he looked between us, then he raced back to the phone.

I listened at the door as he spoke. "She's soaking in a cool bath. Might be a while. We'll call you back later if that's okay?"

Once he'd hung up, he called from the lounge room. "You better come out here and explain what's going on."

I walked to him slowly, covering my face to hide both tears and shame. Dropping onto the couch, I folded my knees to my chest before burying my head.

The real Mariella composed herself. "Your cousin's a despicable man and does not treat women fairly. I don't think anyone should speak to him."

"There's no way around this. You don't know Nino. When he demands a conversation, he gets one. Until he's certain that Mariella is planning to stay, he won't give up."

Angelo switched his attention to me. "Nino just warned me about you trying to escape when I turn my back." He flopped next to me, grasping my hands. "What's going on? My cousin is far from nice and on that point, you'll get no argument from me. But he's a powerful man. Used to getting his own way. My instincts tell me there's more to this than either of you are letting on. I want to protect you, but I need to know what I'm protecting you from."

"We're not cousins," I said, choosing my words carefully. "We shared a cabin on the boat from Italy to Sydney. After telling each other our disappointments and dreams, we felt like family. Family is more than blood. It's a feeling in our hearts."

Angelo sagged with relief. "Is that what you're worried about? Lying about being cousins? That's nothing. Nino doesn't even need to know."

I pressed my finger to his lips. "There's more. Much more, but before I tell you, you need to listen to what I'm about to say and keep it at the front of your brain." I brushed his forehead with my trembling fingers. "Before I met you, I thought movies and books about love were exaggerated and fanciful, but now I know they barely capture half the feelings. I loved you from the moment we met, and that love has grown every minute since."

He shook his head. "I don't understand."

"The love is genuine. I am real. But my name isn't."

The original Mariella took a step forward. "I'm the Mariella Nino is asking for. I'm the one he sent away. My lover was part of the Ndrangheta family, and Nino's clan had plans that did not include a *puttana* like me. To the man I loved, I was a mere distraction, a plaything, and became an inconvenience. Sending me to Australia solved his problem."

Angelo slid sideways, staring at me, his eyes pleading for the truth. "Then who are you? And why are you here?"

"While getting to know Mariella, I helped her read the letter you'd sent. I could tell you'd be a man who'd love a woman until the end of his days. I didn't consider switching places, but I thought about you and was jealous from the moment I read your words."

"It wasn't her fault," Mariella said to Angelo. "You mistook her for me, then I jumped in and introduced myself as Stella. We both wanted different lives and when I saw the opportunity, I seized it. Swapping identities was an impossibly tough decision for your wife." She patted my shoulder, then Angelo's. "For her, it was a battle between the head and the heart. You know how it ended, Angelo. Her heart won because the heart always wins. Your heart must win, too."

Angelo said nothing, and for a moment I sensed all hope of happiness crashing. Then, without looking up, his hand bridged the space between us, his fingers brushing my thigh. The electricity in that touch jolted me into action.

I turned to face him. "It was the woman you fell in love with, not the name. If you changed your name to Tom tomorrow, you'd still be my true love." I rested my cheek against his and closed my eyes.

I prayed with his skin against mine and hoped everything would be all right.

"Is there anything else I need to know?" he asked.

"Yes," the real Mariella said, "but that can wait another day. We have to deal with Nino."

Angelo gripped my hands too firmly for comfort, but I welcomed the pain. It screamed of him never allowing Nino to tear us apart.

Mariella paced the living room floor, practising what

she'd say to Nino. "I'll never be ready," she said. "There's only one shot at this, and it has to be perfect. This phone call affects the happiness of not only everyone in this room, but my parents' well-being, too."

Angelo fetched a bottle of Marsala from the cupboard. "Maybe this will help?" He poured three small glasses. "Just enough to knock the edge off our nerves."

We sat wedged together on the couch, knocking elbows as we sipped the Marsala. I, for one, hoped the potion was magic.

"Sorry," the real Mariella said. "I planned to sew you a beautiful wedding gown, but if my instincts are right, we'll need a dress much sooner than that."

Angelo jumped to attention, standing like an obedient soldier, eager to take orders from the general. "Tomorrow we'll drive to Townsville. There's a bridal shop in the city. What else do we need?"

"A Polaroid instant camera," she said. "Unless we absolutely have to, we won't involve anyone else in this plan. If Nino demands evidence, we must be ready to provide it."

Angelo hugged us both, then dialled Nino's number and handed Mariella the phone.

"Hello. Don DeLuca?" There wasn't a trace of nervousness as she addressed him. "I've kept my end of the bargain. In fact, it's turned out very well. Your daughter, Isabella, is welcome to Emilio. Angelo makes a far better husband."

Although I couldn't hear Nino's reply, the gruff, dark echo of his voice was enough to turn my stomach. Mariella twirled the coiled phone cord around her fingers like a defiant teenager ignoring her mother. I don't know how she summoned the nerve.

"Our wedding is next week," she said, "but there'll be no invitation. Angelo will send you a photograph, and I'm sure you'll agree it's best we never speak again. My parents don't want or need the extra burden, and I'm confident your daughter Isabella would feel the same. Imagine how emotionally scarred she would be if she discovered the dirty details."

There was quiet at the other end, then a muffled response stole the colour from Mariella's face. "Next month? ... I won't speak to whoever you dispatch, but perhaps my husband, Angelo, will agree to a brief check in."

She slammed the phone so hard it bounced from the cradle.

"Don DeLuca claims he's sending one of his Australian thugs to pay a personal visit. Surely, it's an idle threat. We're a long way from Italy, half a world from any mafia."

The expression on Angelo's face made me shiver. "There are members of every clan here in Australia. The old folk of Ingham still talk about *La Mano Nera*—The Black Hand. They terrified the Australians and the Italians. They practised extortion, kidnapping, murder and everything in between. The leader back then was from Palmi, Calabria."

"Palmi's not even a dozen miles from Scilla." Mariella gasped. "Where are they now?"

"The leaders of La Mano Nera are long gone, but we would be naïve to believe there aren't others."

"Then we must act quickly and have the wedding ceremony soon in case this *mafioso* asks around town. We'll stage the bridal photos, making them blurry enough that Nino won't tell us apart. It will be safer for everyone if I'm gone before he arrives."

Angelo held me when I started crying. There was a measure of relief at knowing this would soon be behind us. But a sizeable portion of my tears were from knowing I'd lose the best friend I'd ever had.

Chapter Fifty-Four

Joe, Present Day

Mrs Morellini retrieves a handkerchief tucked up her sleeve. "Excuse me, I need a moment to compose myself." She disappears into the ladies' bathroom, leaving Izzy and me alone at the café table.

"Now I understand why Dad didn't like Mum speaking Italian. Do you think there's still Mafia here in Australia?"

Izzy laughs a brittle laugh. "I'm sure of it. They're probably better at blending in these days."

"Yeah. Probably not wearing all black with white ties. And not carrying a machine gun helps." My joke falls flat. "Seriously. I thought it out of character for Dad, who was open to everything and everyone, to have a negative attitude towards Italy." I press between my eyes to stop them stinging. "All those years, he was probably protecting Mum."

Mrs Morellini returns and produces an old biscuit tin

from her oversized handbag. "I brought this with me, but I think it's rusted shut."

I try to twist it open, but it won't budge. Izzy wedges a coin under the edge and the lid pops off, spilling a wad of faded Polaroids over the table.

Mrs Morellini reaches for a couple of photos. "Oh! Here's your mum wearing my wedding dress, and here's me in the same dress with the same pose."

Mum and Stella wear a pearl-dotted veil to obscure their eyes and nose. Their exposed mouths and chins are so similar, the photos could be of the same person.

"In real life, your mother's lips were fuller, but we applied lipstick carefully until they matched."

She flicks through until she finds a photo of her and Mum wearing the identical dresses they'd bought in Sydney. "No wonder my darling Angelo looked as if he'd been struck by lightning when he met us on the platform."

Izzy stares at it, then clutches it to her chest. "When I heard Maria's stories about the pair of you tricking people on the ship, I thought she was exaggerating, but you look like sisters."

"We were bloody gorgeous, weren't we?"

"Stunning." Izzy holds it up to the light. "I can tell you apart, but only because I know."

I take Mrs Morellini's timeworn hands in mine. "Obviously, the mafia bloke fell for the hoax."

She slaps her hands together in a done-and-dusted. "Yep. We fooled Don DeLuca and his bloody henchman."

"Did you see Mum again after that?"

Mrs Morellini stares wistfully at the faded photographs. "Unfortunately, no. She left a few days later, taking my birth certificate, passport, and the Maria-Rosa identity. I promised to visit her in Sydney, but the train trip was long, and flying too expensive. I had my first son nine months after the wedding, and the second little 'un barely a year later. She made phone calls for a few months, but we were too terrified to put anything in writing. In hindsight, I imagine Don DeLuca forgot about us long before we stopped worrying about him." She closes her eyes and tears rest on the tips of her lashes.

Recalling painful memories has already taken a toll on Mum, and I don't want to add another casualty. "It's okay," I whisper.

Mrs Morellini sighs as she looks up. "So long ago, but it still gets me right here." She holds her hands to her heart. "I wouldn't undo any of it. Definitely not the ecstasy, even if I had to re-live the agony, too. Is that a movie?" She laughs and shakes herself, as if shedding the worst parts of her past.

When Izzy beams at me, I know exactly the ecstasy Mrs Morellini means. No matter what happens, love is worth all the risks.

When I reach for the sign-in pen at the reception desk, Bettina throws an inquisitive stare and holds up her hand. "Sorry, everyone. From now on, your mother's only allowed visits from medical staff and immediate family." She shrugs. "Doctor...Doctor Kent-Jones' orders." Her unusual pronunciation of Kent hints at a New Zealand accent, but I think Bettina is rhyming Kent with punt intentionally. Her body language suggests she's no longer being chauffeured in the BMW.

"What about me going in?" Izzy asks.

"Only in a professional capacity."

So, I'm the only one who can go in? I search the room for inspiration, but Mrs Morellini beats me to it. She flashes a movie-star smile and shakes Bettina's hand. "How rude of me. I'm Ella Morellini, Maria's sister."

Bettina clicks the screen, checking the background files. "Can't find you listed. Do you have identification?"

Quick as a flash, Mrs Morellini produces the photograph of Mum and her in their youth. "Non-identical twins."

"Of course," Bettina giggles. "I should have seen the likeness... but you really should be on the official list."

"Come on, "Izzy says. "Imagine if it were your mother in there."

"I do," Bettina says, "believe me, I do. My mother's ready for a nursing home soon and I'd love her to come here and have a nurse as caring as you." She exhales loudly, scribbles on a post-it-note, then drops it over our side of the counter.

I pick it up and hand it back.

"Where did this note come from?" She squints at it. "Hard to make out the writing. Looks as if it's signed by Doctor BJK. Permission for all of you to go straight through."

Once we're through the security door, Izzy doubles with laughter. "How about that? Bettina has a heart." She hooks her arm through Mrs Morellini's. "And you? You were so convincing. I bet you were enjoying a replay of the old sisters' game. You must've had a lot of fun back then."

Mrs Morellini winks. "We did."

I hide behind the bougainvillea blooms and crack open Mum's door. My camouflage is ineffective and Mum breaks into a smile. "*Joey. Tu sei qui.*"

She beams as she admires her flower arrangement, but

frowns when she touches the scars where I've removed the thorns.

"*Ringraziate che le spine hanno fiori, non disperate quando i fiori hanno le spine.*"

"I don't understand, Mum."

Mrs Morellini steps inside to translate. "Give thanks that thorns have flowers. Don't despair that flowers have thorns."

Mum drops the bougainvillea onto the bed and grabs Mrs Morellini by the shoulders, patting her, pinching her, and staring as if at a ghost.

"You remember me." Mrs Morellini says.

"Stella?" Mum drops her head into her hands.

Izzy rushes to Mum's side. "Maria? Are you okay?"

When Mum looks up, she's laughing, not crying.

Two pairs of expressive hands dance, and there's much laughter and tears as the older women launch into a frenzied exchange in Italian.

Izzy grabs my hand and we edge into the hallway, giving them space.

"*Vieni dentro. Grazie. Hai trovato i miei fiori preferiti e il mio amico perduto,*" Mum yells.

"Come inside," Mrs Morellini says. "Your mother thanks you for finding her favourite flowers and her long-lost friend."

Mum's flushed face is wreathed in smiles. She pulls me into their shared embrace.

Mrs Morellini gives me a wry smile. "Your mother says the bougainvillea flowers share a lesson about love. It's time to forget that one thorny relationship and notice the other flowers around you."

I shrug, pretending I don't understand.

"Your mother doesn't know about you and Izzy. Does she?"

Izzy and I shake our heads. "Not yet."

"Would you like me to tell her?"

"We can do it without words." Izzy pulls me close and kisses me so hard I think the woman in the aisle seat on the plane would have keeled over.

The torrent of Italian crying and laughter begins again. Mum shrieks, then pulls me and Izzy into a too-firm hug. I can barely breathe.

"I told your mum how I could see the aura of love," Mrs Morellini says. "She told me she'd already picked Izzy as your perfect match."

Mum starts again. My mouth drops open when I recognise the swear words.

"Don't worry about the coarse language. Your mother's never been happier. Who needs a dating site when you've got a mother? She could tell you were perfect for each other. Apparently, your grandmother Blake did the same for her and your dad."

"I've never heard the story about them meeting," I say.

"She's told no one what happened after she left Ingham, but she's eager to tell you now, while I'm here to translate."

Chapter Fifty-Five

Maria-Rosa, Sydney 1968

From the moment I arrived back in Sydney, Lorenzo used my assumed name without hesitation. Perhaps his own much-rehearsed deception made it easier.

He tilted the coffee pot over my cup, but I waved it away. "Are you ill, Maria-Rosa? Not having your usual top-up?"

"No." I glanced back at the morning newspaper and swallowed to ease the lump in my throat. The Mafia headline reminded me of the danger that lurked. Preserving links with Lorenzo maintained a discoverable trail between me and Stella. If Nino DeLuca's mob found the truth, they'd use it to get to my family in Italy.

"Come on. What's' up? This is the first time in the past year that you've ever refused coffee. Yesterday we joked about inventing a caffeine drip to pump espresso directly into our veins? This dashes that cunning plan." Despite his laughter, he scribbled his fingernail nervously over the flecked-orange laminate table.

The raw ache of saying goodbye to both my family in Italy and Stella in Ingham resurfaced. I readied my heart to lose another friend.

"Whatever it is, just tell me."

I stared into my empty cup, searching for the right words. "I owe you, Lorenzo. You saved me and gave me a home."

He pursed his mouth as if bracing for bad news. "I didn't save you. You saved Stella and me."

I folded the newspaper to frame the article, then pushed it towards him. "Read this."

"*Police Investigating Mafia Links to Australian Organised Crime.*" He looked questioningly.

"I've got a new identity, but it's not enough. The Mafia is everywhere. It's time to cut ties with you and Stella." I reached for Lorenzo's hand. "I should have applied for a city job months ago instead of relying on odds and ends from sewing. I'll look for a new place, closer to town."

"No need to hurry with the job. I'll give you money as part of our divorce settlement," he said.

"Divorce?" I laughed until tears ran down my cheeks. "We're not really married."

Lorenzo's laughter was thin. "We need something stronger than coffee." His shoulders sagged as he poured us each a glass of Amaretto.

I hugged him. "You are a marvellous man."

"Maybe not. It's time to own up, I've already filed for divorce. Time for me to care less about society's opinions and become the man I really am."

There was a ridiculous synchronicity to the idea of me

and Lorenzo getting divorced. I'd been jilted by a fiancé who had never bought me a ring. Married by proxy, then given away a husband to a woman pretending to be me. Divorcing a make-believe husband fit the ludicrous pattern.

"Lorenzo, I am so happy for you. It won't always be easy, but at least you don't have to hide."

My throat was painfully tight, but I refused to cry. This was good news. We were both ready to start the next phase of our lives.

Lorenzo left for work at eleven, and after packing most of my belongings, I collected coins from my jar. International phone calls were ravenous beasts, and with a serious topic on today's agenda, I expected the pay phone to devour countless five-cent pieces.

The nearest phone box was two blocks from home. I sighed as I fed money into the slot. This wouldn't be my neighbourhood for much longer.

Uncle Tonito was the only person in my family with a phone, and our usual arrangement was for me to phone at six am Italian time, then again at seven, giving him enough time to collect my parents for the second call. Midday in Sydney was only four in Scilla. It took two attempts before he answered.

"Ciao. Is that you?" Uncle rarely used my name. The houses in Scilla were so crammed together, we couldn't take risks of someone overhearing and passing information to the Ndrangheta. "Are you okay?"

"Yes. Sorry to phone early."

"I was awake. I'll talk to you in an hour."

Sitting on the kerb, I flipped through the newspaper, scouring the *situations vacant* and cheap *places to let*. After circling those of interest, I walked to the highway and checked the next departure time of the city-bound bus.

When I called Italy again, it was my father who picked up the phone.

"Hello. How is the weather?" He started every conversation with the same lively greeting and ended every call by begging me to stop sending money. But this time, Babbo's voice carried a sickening tone of concern.

"Is Mamma okay? Is she there?" I made the sign of the cross and prayed silently while I awaited his response.

"We're both fine. Nothing wrong at all." The tone of his voice told of his lies.

I could hear Mamma talking in Babbo's ear. I pictured her wrestling him for the phone. "Tell her one day we'll visit Australia."

"I better hand you over," he said. "Capo's orders."

"*Ti amo*. I love you."

"You too, *Mia cara*."

Mamma's soothing tones washed over me. "My *Bellissima bambina*. Your father's protecting you from the truth." She paused for a moment. "Hang on." I imagined the phone held against her heart and I could barely make out her muffled voice. "Shut up the house," she called to Tonito and Babbo. "Talk outside. I need to speak honestly."

Everything slowed except my pulse. There was a slamming of windows and doors, then Mamma returned. "Emilio's been here—determined to contact you. Apparently, he's phoned Australia. But he's being watched, and so are we. Nino has made threatening visits."

"But I don't want to speak to Emilio. Not now. Not ever."

"That's what your father and I told him, but he won't let go of the idea. We've decided we must sell the farm."

I ignored the man rapping on the phone booth's glass and rummaged through my purse for extra coins. "This is all my fault. I should've listened to your warnings. You told me what would happen, and I was stupid enough to think I knew better."

I heard Mamma's sharp intake of breath. "People in love see only the good, and it isn't a bad thing. But with Emilio pestering and bucking against the Mafiosi, we are living in fear. The last thing we want is someone from the Ndrangheta discovering you're not where they think you are."

My hands trembled as I scrambled to feed the greedy machine. "I miss you so much, and I want to move back to Italy. Somewhere other than Scilla."

"You can't," she said. Her voice quivered, then broke. "It will put you in more danger."

"What if I can't run away anymore?"

"You can and you will. I've watched you grow from a child into a strong, capable woman. Running is in your blood."

The man outside knocked impatiently on the phone box door. Reluctantly, I said goodbye.

Mamma's words fuelled my feet as I sprinted to the highway and caught the bus to town. Once seated, I checked the entries I'd circled on my newspaper. First, I would apply for the seamstress job at the Bond's clothing factory in Camperdown.

After racing from the bus stop to the factory, I took

deep composing breaths and straightened my clothing before introducing myself to the manager.

He showed me around, asked a few questions, and nodded at my broken English. "I'm willing to give you a try."

He sat me at a sewing machine along with a hive of busy women. The familiar smell of fabric and the buzz of machines put me at ease. When he returned an hour later to inspect my work, he smiled. "Fill this out." He handed me a clipboard of paperwork. "You can start full-time, next week."

I whistled as I walked to the flat I'd underlined in the classified ads. It was only a few blocks from the factory. Everything was falling into place.

But the 'To Let' sign was gone. In its place, a scribbled note said, 'No longer available."

Tired and teary, I crouched at the roadside, wanting to go home. Not to Lorenzo's house, but back to Italy.

I started to cry. "I need you, Mamma."

Inside my head, Mamma's voice snapped and snarled. 'You need a place to live. Now get up, my girl! Keep running.'

I crisscrossed half of the Camperdown streets, searching windows and fences for vacancies. When I doubled back towards the factory, I spotted a wooden sign wire-tied onto a letter-box. A converted garage, small, but close to where I needed to live. I whispered, "Thank you, Mamma," then knocked on the door.

After paying a deposit, I ran back to the main road. My feet light, Gallucci's shoes embracing them like a much-needed hug. Then something dawned on me I should have known all along. The imaginary wolf was not a menacing male, it was a she-wolf. She'd been protecting me, warning of danger.

My she-wolf helped me put one foot in front of the other. Her message was clear. Whatever life throws us, we must keep moving.

Chapter Fifty-Six

Joe, Present Day

Izzy strokes Mum's trembling hand. "I'm furious. First, that bastard, Emilio, sent you to the other side of the world, and as if that wasn't enough, he caused trouble for your family."

My Izzy looks dangerous. But in a good way. A fiercely protective she-wolf.

I take Mum's other hand. "So that's it? We never found out what Emilio wanted?"

"I can shed extra light on that situation." Mrs Morellini empties a faded brown paper bag onto Mum's bed, spilling a letter and a small parcel. "Emilio kept phoning our house, but Angelo repeatedly slammed down the phone." She bites her lip as she turns the yellowed envelope, checking the postmark. "1970. When this came in the mail, Angelo and I tried to find you, but Lorenzo had lost touch after you moved out." She whispers in Mum's ear, then turns to me and Izzy. "The letter is personal, but your mother doesn't mind me sharing."

Sentence by sentence; she reads the letter. First in Italian for Mum, then in English for us.

Dear Mariella,

I've written and rewritten this so many times, the words are engraved on my heart.

Part of me believed a clean break was best, but I'm weighed down by the heaviness of things left unsaid. Despite the awful, painful memories of our lost love, so much of our time was exquisitely beautiful. Like you.

I owe you an explanation.

When you doubled back to the campsite, Nino called up the river, setting the terms. He made it clear exactly what was at stake and repeated my mother's threat. Either you or I would feel a blade on the face. I returned to the camp knowing I'd wear a scar.

Your husband Angelo told me you don't want to talk to me. I understand, but I can't let this go. I need you to know I bought this present before we ran away together. I was waiting for daylight because I wanted to see the surprise in your eyes.

On our trip to Catanzaro, you threw a coin in the fountain. You were so annoyed, thinking I did not know what you'd wished for, but trust me, I did.

One of your wishes would've been an engagement ring as unique as you. You also would have wished for us to marry soon. I imagine you were worried about my mother, but I would have talked her around and she would have accepted you, despite your family background.

"*Dammi la scatola.*" Mum waves the letter away, clicking her tongue on the roof of her mouth as she snatches the box.

Mrs Morellini's shoulders sag. "I'm so sorry, Maria. If I

hadn't convinced you that Emilio was trying to get rid of you, you might have eventually found each other."

Izzy darts sentimental looks between me and Mum, eyes glistening with tears. Mum, on the other hand, doesn't seem at all upset by Emilio's words. Instead, she rattles the box. I watch her weathered hands peel yellowed, cracked sticky tape from the decades old wrapping paper. She opens the box and shows us.

A ring. A pink stone surrounded by diamonds.

Within seconds, the three women are speaking at once. It's difficult to make out what anyone is saying.

Izzy puts a hand to her mouth and sighs. "It's exquisite."

Mrs Morellini pulls a jeweller's appraisal from under the velvet base. "One and 3/4 carat pink sapphire. Twenty pave diamonds. Platinum setting."

Mum splutters and yells. Even if I spoke Italian, I don't think I'd understand this reaction. Surely there's some relief at knowing the man she loved, actually loved her. I hold my palms upwards, silently pleading with Mrs Morellini to explain.

"Your mother is scoffing at his choice of engagement ring. She can't believe the crassness of enclosing the valuation, and she's fuming at his comment about his mother. Says the man is an idiot. What was he thinking?"

I suddenly feel sorry for this man I'd decided to hate. Choosing any gift for a woman is difficult. Jewellery must be near impossible. "At least he knew Mum's favourite colour was pink."

"Italian girls wear yellow gold and white diamonds," Mrs Morellini explains. "Coloured stones are considered poor taste. I forgave my poor gay Lorenzo because of his craving to add colour to a dull life, but Emilio was nothing but a vulgar show-off. Totally wrong for your mother, who's always been 100% class." She throws back her head in a relieved laugh. "I wasn't mistaken when I told her she was better off without him."

"So, rubies and emeralds are tacky, too?" Izzy looks as confused as I feel. "Even royalty wear coloured gemstones. Anyway, I think the ring is striking."

I shuffle my feet. This must be the most discussed piece of jewellery since the scandal with Wallis Simpson. "Can we please hear the rest of Emilio's letter?"

Mum throws the ring box onto the floor, gesturing for Mrs Morellini to continue.

Everyone said you looked like a movie star. Even Don DeLuca understood my rebellion against Ndrangheta's orders. Who wouldn't be tempted by such beauty? Deep down, I believed you wished to be discovered by a talent scout and to end up on the silver screen."

Izzy interrupts, "Emilio was stupid. *Stupido."*

Mum's eyes blacken and she yells, *"Emilio! Sono stufo di questo lavoro. Ne ho le palle piene!"* She steals the letter from Mrs Morellini's hand and continues to shout.

Mrs Morellini's mouth drops open. "I can't repeat that in English. Let's just say, your mother isn't happy."

Mum's expression starts with stony seriousness, but as she talks with Mrs Morellini at length, the granite softens and eventually she laughs.

Izzy whispers in my ear, "Do you recognise any of these words from our Italian lessons?"

"Words? What words? There's no pause between them. It's all one-long-run-on-nonsensical-sound-to-me."

Izzy laughs, warming my heart. Her liking my corny jokes is nothing short of a miracle.

Mrs Morellini waits for Mum to finish, then translates. "Your mother is no longer angry with Emilio. She says he wrote this letter long ago, and you can't put an old head on young shoulders. She got many things wrong when she was young. For one, she believed in secret wishes. But wishes shouldn't be kept to ourselves. How can people fulfil them without knowing what they are?"

Mum thrusts her open hand towards me. "*Moneta.*"

"Coin," Izzy says.

I'm still searching my wallet when Izzy hands over a five-cent piece.

Mum flicks it high in the air and watches it land. "*Tre desideri.*" She makes eye contact with me as she talks.

Mrs Morellini translates. "Your mother doesn't care if her brain lets everything else go as long as when she closes her eyes, she can picture the sweetest memories. Her parents laughing and bickering in the kitchen, with Mamma threatening to smack Babbo with the wooden spoon. The day you were born, Joey. The joy on your father's face as he breathed the scent of your baby skin and brushed his lips against your downy hair."

The women chatter for a few minutes, then Mum holds up two fingers and taps Mrs Morellini, encouraging her to speak.

"Your mother took a while to work out her second wish. But she knows now. She wishes to speak with me regularly. She apologises in advance for repeating herself and says there'll be times when she won't have much to say because her thoughts are scrambled, but she reckons listening to me will be like the return visit to Italy she never made."

Mrs Morellini and Mum hug for ages. Izzy laces her fingers through mine and leans against me.

"Thank you," I whisper in her ear.

"For what?"

"Attempting to understand a broken woman and her average Joe son."

"Average Joe?" Izzy shakes her head, then stands. She holds her arm as straight as a sword and taps each of my shoulders. "I dub you Sir Well-Above-Average. No more of this luke-warm business. You, Joe, are hot."

Mrs Morellini smiles at me and winks. My cheeks burn hotter. "This is a win for me, too. At my age and living on my own, there aren't many people who want to listen to an old woman, especially not in Italian."

Mum laughs as if she understands, and starts another conversation, but she stops and takes a laboured breath before rubbing her eyes.

I squeeze her hand. "I think you need a rest, Mum."

"Wait," Izzy moans with desperation. "What about your father? When did she meet him?"

There's a brief exchange between Mum and Mrs Morellini, who translates. "She holds special memories of the day she met the Blakes—her Australian family. They helped her realise that family isn't defined by blood, but by love."

"Thank you for sharing your story." I kiss Mum's forehead. "Izzy and I will let you rest and we'll go write it up."

"*No, no. Aspettate.*" Mum gestures for us to wait.

"Better make yourselves comfortable." Mrs Morellini says. "She's determined to tell us now in case the doctors forbid further visits."

With a wildly sing-song voice, Mum begins, her hands accompanying the lyrics and bringing in every instrument of her emotional orchestra.

Chapter Fifty-Seven

Maria-Rosa, Sydney, 1969

My return to running took its toll on the shoes Signor Gallucci had repaired three years earlier. Although my feet needed more support than they provided, I couldn't bear to part with them. They were a comfortable, familiar reminder of my friend the shoemaker, and one of the few tangible connections to my Calabrian homeland.

Saying a prayer for them to last a little longer, I laced my shoe tightly

"Not running again are you, Luv?"

I jumped when Sheila spoke. I was unaware she and Judy, my workmates from the Bond's factory, were watching.

"Sorry to scare you. Just thought you might come out for a drink later?"

"Maybe next Friday. My landlord's making his three-monthly inspection this afternoon, and I want to do a final clean before he arrives. I need to keep him happy cos it's the only place I can afford."

Judy licked an imaginary pencil and made a cross in the air. "Next week then. It's marked on the calendar. We'll drag you along if we have to. I reckon you'd be a man magnet." She nudged Sheila with her elbow. "I wouldn't mind a few extra fellas hanging about."

"I'm not interested in meeting men," I said.

Judy giggled. "You one of them who prefers women?"

When I bent to lace the second shoe, Sheila pinched my bottom. "Look, Luv. Since I'm not doing well on the bloke front, I might reassess after tonight. If it's another dud, I'll jump the fence and hook up with you."

The women sniggered and blew kisses at me. They were always a jokey pair, but especially on Friday afternoons.

I pointed to the Chesty Bond mural; a muscular figure painted on the factory wall. "That's as close as I intend to get to a man."

Judy took a drag of her cigarette and looked unusually serious. "Be careful with your running, then. It's not something women do alone, and for good reason. I meant to tell you something at morning smoko. When my father dropped me into the city last week, we passed you on the road. There was a fella running behind you."

"I saw him. He's harmless." I kept my voice light, but couldn't stop the bile rising in my throat. I'd seen someone running, but I could outrun most men. He'd crossed to the other side of the road and given me a wordless wave before he disappeared down a side street.

It didn't take long for me to tidy my place, not surprising—considering the size. When I moved in a year ago, the bedsit had smelt worse than a ship's cabin after a vomiting spree. Whatever had been spilt on the moth-eaten carpet in the living area put up the dirtiest of fights. Multiple packets of bicarbonate of soda eventually neutralised the odour, but months passed before I could sit inside without holding my nose. The tiny, but now scrupulously clean, kitchen and bathroom were squished at one end. A new curtain screening the sleeping area from the living space.

My landlord checked things off his list, then ran his hand over the slipcovers I'd made for the couch to hide the musty stained fabric. When he took a deep breath, I started to worry. Perhaps I should have asked before making changes.

He tipped his hat at me, but wasn't smiling. "You're the best tenant I've ever had. The place looks grand."

"I haven't done much." I shrugged as if it had taken only minutes to make it look this good.

I handed him the last month's rent. "I love it here. It's perfect for me."

He pushed the money back and shuffled his feet. "I can't take it. Consider this as payment for the improvements you've made. My missus and I are very sorry to tell you, but we need you to move out. The mother-in-law's getting on and she's going to live here. It'll be nice and close so we can look after her."

"No trouble at all," I lied. "I'm pretty sure one of the factory girls is looking for a housemate."

"That's a tremendous relief." He sighed and scurried off. Presumably hurrying to give his wife the good news.

I threw myself onto the bed, but couldn't relax or read. My mind was crackling with miserable energy. Only an extra-long, extra tiring afternoon run would clear my head.

The streets of terraced houses with white-painted cast

iron lace trim reminded me of wedding gowns. Now that Mamma and Babbo didn't need money for the farm, I'd been putting money aside. One day I'd design wedding dresses again, then I'd save enough money for my family to visit Australia. Life in this unfamiliar country wasn't so bad. My parents would love the change of scenery and be thankful to get away from the Ndrangheta.

Instead of my usual route, I ran past Hyde Park and out along the track to the lookout where the new opera house was under construction. The multi roof design looked like billowing white sails. The brisk breeze blew salty air onto my face, and I imagined myself standing on a yacht racing for the finish line. Although I'd lied about the woman at work having a room to rent, I could easily ask around. There were so many workers; someone would know of a place.

On the return run, I skipped along the path, but as I checked the traffic to cross the highway and looked over my shoulder, I spied the running man, again. He was a long way down the path but heading in my direction.

I turned several sharp corners, my track illogical and unpredictable. But each time I stopped to catch my breath; he was there. The danger wasn't Judy's imagination or a coincidence. The stranger was following me.

My heart, already working hard, pounded a warning in my ears. Who was he and what did he want? Had the Ndrangheta caught up with me?

I sped up, taking a shortcut across a small park to hide behind a jacaranda in full bloom. I pressed my forehead against the huge gnarled trunk, staring at my feet as violet-blue petals fell over the tree roots and onto my shoes.

I calmed my breathing and hoped he'd run straight past.

"You okay?" His deep voice startled me.

I tried to conjure my she-wolf for help, but she wasn't around. When I leapt back on the road, my foot caught a tree root and my ankle buckled beneath me. I dropped heavily against the curb.

"Oh, God. I didn't mean to alarm you. Are you hurt?"

"No," I winced. "I'm not. Please go away."

To prove my fitness, I stood on my good leg, ignoring the pain as I gingerly tested my weight on the injured foot.

The stranger wasn't like the men from Southern Italy. His face was lightly freckled and his eyes brimmed with concern. "I'm so sorry," he said. "I didn't mean to frighten you."

"Why have you been following me?" I limped a step but fell again.

He hastened to catch me, then stared for a moment as if mute.

"Why have you been following me?" This time I yelled.

"It's hard to explain. I'd like to blame my interfering mother, but it doesn't make me sound manly." He gestured across the road.

There was no-one in the direction of his arm wave. I pushed him away. "You're lying."

"You can't see her, but she lives over there. Further down the street."

The pain in my foot made me light-headed. I grimaced. "Please leave me alone. I do not know you."

"I'm Jack Blake, and to be honest, I have no idea what to do now. From a practical standpoint, it would be easiest if I hoisted you over my shoulder in a fireman's carry and delivered you to your own house, but the voice in my head says if I try that you'll scream. Besides, after following you for what must have been more than nine miles, I'm not sure I can walk that far."

This man was admitting to following me. I waited to hear Mamma's voice in warning, but I sensed no danger. "Find me a stick and I'll hobble home. By myself."

"It's too far, "he said. "Put your arm on my shoulder. Looks like you'll meet my mother whether or not I want you to."

I raised my eyebrows. "What?"

"My mother doesn't have the answer to everything, but she'll tell you she does." He laughed affectionately and his pleasantly ordinary face lit up.

Jack might as well have carried me because my feet barely touched the ground as we travelled from the tree to a red brick house where a cheery-faced woman sat on the porch. She called out, "Brought a friend to dinner?"

"No, Mum. This is..." He stopped to look at me.

"Maria-Rosa, Maria will do."

"Maria. She hurt her foot, so I brought her here."

She laughed a deep belly laugh, and I joined in, despite the pain. This woman's welcoming manner comforted me, and I wanted to sit with her.

"Pleased to meet you, Maria. Sorry about Jack, but men don't come with inbuilt instructions. That's why women have to tell them what to do."

Jack murmured under his breath, but his mother gestured to the porch. "Make yourself useful and grab two chairs to set on the lawn. I'll look at Maria's foot."

She sat me in one chair and raised my leg onto the second. Then she went inside to make a cup of lemongrass tea, which she promised would reduce the swelling.

"When Jack was a kid," Mrs Blake said, "he brought

home cats he found stuck in trees. Other times it was dogs with thorns in their paws, even though I never found any evidence of said thorns." She chuckled again. "I told him to stop saving animals, but maybe I should've added that boys can't go around collecting injured girls?"

Jack kicked a clump of weeds, his cheeks and ears shiny and pink. "All right for Mum to blame me now, but she was partly at fault."

"How? Why?" I asked.

"During our weekly dinner, I told Mum about seeing a beautiful woman running." He kicked the weed patch again. "Mum said I should move to the opposite side of the road when a woman's alone. Never give them a reason to feel afraid."

I felt like Alice when she fell down the rabbit hole, except Jack was the mad hatter and his mother the queen. "What else did you say to your mother?"

"I told her I worried about you running alone and how I was scared a crazy guy might jump out from behind a tree and grab you."

"That's right," Mrs Blake said, handing me the herbal tea. She took a long drag on her cigarette. "I remember, now. I told him not to ignore his instincts. If a man suspects a woman of being at risk and does nothing to protect her, he might as well consider himself an accessory to the crime."

"So, you've been guarding me?"

Jack covered his face and shielded his eyes from the setting sun. "Well...not...well..."

"What Jack means to say is, we're about to have dinner and we'd love you to join us. I'm sure he was also going to offer you a lift home."

Jack uncovered his eyes and embraced me in the broadest of smiles.

Mrs Blake grinned at both of us and nodded as she stubbed out her cigarette.

"I'd like that," I said. "Very much."

Chapter Fifty-Eight

Joe, Present Day

Mum and Mrs Morellini chat amongst themselves and Izzy throws me her best come hither look. "Aww, come here, Joe. Your dad sounded just like you."

I pull back my shoulders and stand taller. "My dad was a good man. I hope I'm as kind as he was."

"Enough of that canoodling." Mrs Morellini says with a laugh. "Maria's just realised she's only made two of her wishes."

Izzy moves closer to Mum. "I'm hanging out to hear the last one."

Mum points to the corner where she chucked the unwanted ring box. Then she turns her finger waggle on me. While she babbles excitedly, Mrs Morellini retrieves the box. "Your mother believes..." she clears her throat. "Well... since Izzy absolutely loves this ring... ermm... you should take advantage and fulfil her last wish. She wants you to.... ask Izzy to be your wife."

"Mum?" I crack my knuckles right under her nose. "You're worse than the Strega and Granny Blake combined." I shake my head no.

"Oh, go on," Mrs Morellini passes over the ring. "It's obvious you love each other."

I glance at Mum, who's directing me to kneel.

I'm too nervous to look at Izzy as I lower myself slowly onto one knee. I hold the box in an unsteady hand. "Izzy. Will you please ..."

I look up and she isn't smiling. I stop and slump against my heel. This proposal isn't right. "Hold on, I'd like a rewind."

'Do something, Joe,' my inner voice screeches urgently. The only thing I can think of is to make an awkward comedic show of standing and undoing the actions I took to kneel.

But Izzy doesn't laugh.

My guts twist as I think about the almost disastrous consequences of our last misunderstanding. I have no intention of risking a repeat. "Izzy, can I please talk to you privately?"

Mum is adding her ten cents' worth as we leave, but I close the door and lead Izzy into the garden.

Instead of sitting under our tree, she kicks fallen figs into a pile. She doesn't look at me.

"I shouldn't have listened to Mum and Mrs Morellini. It was wrong to ambush you in front of them. I want whatever you want. Not what my mother wants. And if the idea of a second-hand ring is off-putting, you can pick your own. Anything you like."

She picks up a handful of figs and shoots them at the tree like bullets. "It's not that, Joe. I love the ring."

If it's not the ring, then it must be me. There's a pain in

my chest—she may as well have shot my heart. I turn away. Izzy doesn't love me like I love her.

"Do you have anything else to say?" she asks.

I shrug weakly, my body deflating.

"This makes you as feeble as Emilio! The last thing I need is a wimp." She marches to the door, then calls out. "Your Granny Blake was right about one thing. You men need bloody instructions. Being proposed to because of a weird family tradition where mothers tell their sons what to do, and who to love, isn't what I want. Or need."

"I'm sorry. You're right. "I put my head in my hands.

"Convince me, Joe. Convince me you aren't proposing to make your mother happy. Or to make me happy. Tell me what *you* want?"

Did I hear that correctly? I blink and think. But my brain is too muddled to form a sentence, let alone a coherent, convincing speech. I have a second chance to let Izzy know exactly how I feel, but what are the magic words? Women know everything, they make all the rules. Now would be the perfect time for someone, anyone, to share those rules.

There's no help coming. I'm on my own.

Izzy touches my shoulder, then runs her fingers down to my chest, soothing my floundering heart and reaching my soul. "Tell me from here."

My mouth is dry, but I force words out. "Being with you has taught me so much. Love is dangerous... wonderful... and scary... it carves its own path. Right now, it's taking me headfirst over the edge of a mountain, but I don't care, Izzy, as long as you're on the mountain with me."

I lower myself onto one knee, and when I lock eyes with Izzy, I have the light-headed sensation of floating. "Me marrying you might be one of Mum's wishes, but it's my only wish. My heart chose you. You are the best woman in the world." I open the ring box, my fingers trembling with hope. "Please marry me."

Izzy sinks to the ground next to me and stares at her left hand.

I grasp it tightly. "Say you'll be my wife. My world was bland without you in it. The sky is bluer, food tastes better—"

"Stop. It's a yes. I love you, Joe." She leans in to whisper, "I needed to be sure it was you doing the asking."

My head spins as I slip the ring on her finger. I smile and pick up a fig from the ground. Aim it straight at the knothole in the trunk. This time it's a bullseye.

An unexpected gust of wind rustles the branches, raining confetti leaves on our heads.

"That'll be Granny Blake chiming in," Izzy says with a laugh. "She's exhaling one of her ciggies and sending her seal of approval."

Izzy shivers and I wrap her in my arms—not that I needed an excuse. Strangely, I don't feel the cold. Must be because I'm no longer a Luke-Warm-Average-Joe. I kiss Izzy like the man on fire she's helped me become.

THE END

Acknowledgments

Thanks to the family, friends and writing partners who've taken turns either giving me a verbal slap, or offering a hand up after I've thrown myself into a crumpled heap and declared I cannot write another word.

Without your support, I would have given up writing to drink champagne and eat chocolate.

Hang on a minute...Why am I thanking you?

That's right, my thanks are for your persistence, for sticking with me and pushing me along that trickiest of roads; the one an author travels before typing THE END.

In a real world so full of troubles, there's a weighty satisfaction in writing characters who find themselves, and find that bit extra needed to help others (just like you guys have done for me).

A Note to Readers

Thank you for reading this book from beginning to end.

Can I please ask a favour?

A book review from you is a personal conversation between author and reader. So, if you get time, please leave your words. I read and treasure all of them.

You can find links to review sites at Miladouglas.com.au.

While you're there, please sign up for my newsletter and post any suggestions you have for a particular event in history you'd like me to include in book 3 of The Figs' Mysteries. If I use your idea, I'll name a character after you.

www.ingramcontent.com/pod-product-compliance
Lightning Source LLC
Chambersburg PA
CBHW030507120726
47904CB00005B/1370